"Scans show no sig...
The buoy appears to be in p...

As soon as they entered its communica... patched a simple encoded test message. Doing so while the ship was still at warp carried the risk of its signal or the buoy's response being detected by unwelcome eavesdroppers.

Hearing the turbolift doors opening behind him, Kirk turned to see Admiral Nogura stepping onto the bridge. Before the captain could call attention to his officers, the elder man held up a hand.

"As you were, ladies and gentlemen." Appearing satisfied that operations would not grind to a halt for the observance of protocol, Nogura made his way around the railing near Sulu's station and descended to the command well to join Kirk. His gaze shifted to the buoy on the main viewscreen.

"It seems to be none the worse for wear."

Kirk nodded. "We were just confirming that, sir." Looking to Uhura, he asked, "Lieutenant?"

The communications officer turned in her seat. "The message was received and processed, sir. I've just received its response with a summary of its operational status. There have been no other attempts at communication, or access to it. So far as I can tell, it's been undisturbed since its launch from the *Endeavour*."

"So far, so good," said Nogura. "Has it remained in this general vicinity since it was deployed?"

"After getting enough distance from the asteroid field to transmit its initial message to Starfleet Command, it executed a programmed instruction to return to within one hundred kilometers of the field's outer boundary. With occasional minor adjustments, it's been stationkeeping right here, relative to the asteroids. Its location is fairly well shielded from long-range sensors. Someone would have to be looking for it, but its programming also includes instructions to take evasive action and use the asteroids for cover if its own sensors detect the presence of scans from anything other than a Starfleet vessel."

STAR TREK®

THE ORIGINAL SERIES

AGENTS OF INFLUENCE

Dayton Ward

Based upon *Star Trek*
created by Gene Roddenberry

GALLERY BOOKS

New York   London   Toronto   Sydney   New Delhi   Qo'noS

Gallery Books
An Imprint of Simon & Schuster, Inc.
1230 Avenue of the Americas
New York, NY 10020

First Gallery Books trade paperback edition June 2020

GALLERY BOOKS and colophon are registered trademarks of Simon & Schuster, Inc.

For information about special discounts for bulk purchases, please contact Simon & Schuster Special Sales at 1-866-506-1949 or business@simonandschuster.com.

The Simon & Schuster Speakers Bureau can bring authors to your live event. For more information or to book an event, contact the Simon & Schuster Speakers Bureau at 1-866-248-3049 or visit our website at www.simonspeakers.com.

Manufactured in the United States of America

10 9 8 7 6 5 4 3 2

Library of Congress Cataloging-in-Publication Data

Names: Ward, Dayton, author.
Title: Agents of influence / Dayton Ward ; based upon Star Trek created by
    Gene Roddenberry.
Other titles: At head of title Star Trek the original series
Description: First Gallery Books trade paperback edition. | New York :
    Gallery Books, 2020. | Series: Star trek: the original series
Identifiers: LCCN 2019054670 (print) | LCCN 2019054671 (ebook) | ISBN
    9781982133689 (trade paperback) | ISBN 9781982133696 (ebook)
Subjects: LCSH: Star trek (Television program)—Fiction. | GSAFD: Science fiction.
Classification: LCC PS3623.A7317 A74 2020 (print) | LCC PS3623.A7317
    (ebook) | DDC 813/.6—dc23
LC record available at https://lccn.loc.gov/2019054670
LC ebook record available at https://lccn.loc.gov/2019054671

ISBN 978-1-9821-3368-9
ISBN 978-1-9821-3369-6 (ebook)

Dedicated to the memory of
Dorothy Catherine ("D.C.") Fontana,
one of the earliest and most influential shapers
and caretakers of the Final Frontier

March 25, 1939–December 2, 2019

Historian's Note

This story takes place in early 2270 during the final year of the *U.S.S. Enterprise*'s historic five-year mission of exploration under the command of Captain James T. Kirk, and approximately three months after the *U.S.S. Endeavour*'s encounter with the Lrondi derelict vessel in the Cantrel star system of the Taurus Reach (*Star Trek: Seekers #4—All That's Left*).

One

"We need to go, Morgan. Now."

The statement, tinged with anxiety and warning, was not what startled Morgan Binnix, but instead the simple fact that it was delivered in Federation Standard and not *tlhIngan Hol*. Speaking in anything other than the Klingon language was something to be avoided at all costs. That her companion, Phillip Watson, had done so was a clear indicator of his growing worry. It also served to emphasize the precarious nature of their present situation and that it likely was deteriorating by the second.

"Careful, *Kvaal*," she said, barking her reply in the native language and stressing the name serving as Watson's cover identity. "Remember your bearing."

Her junior officer, Watson offered a chastened nod. "You are right, *Liska*," he said, reverting to spoken Klingon and her own cover name. "But we cannot stay here. If you are correct and they have discovered us, it will not matter what language we use."

"Perhaps not," replied Binnix, "but until that happens, we do not break our cover."

It was one of the bedrock principles underlying the training inflicted upon her, Watson, and David Horst while preparing for their present mission, and it was one of the very few defenses against exposure. Every waking moment of the last three years had been spent talking, writing, and thinking like a Klingon, to the point that it now was ingrained into nearly every fiber of Binnix's being and every errant thought she carried in her head. The slightest lapse could prove costly not just for the three of them but also fellow operatives embedded in sensitive positions elsewhere in the Klingon Empire as well as other Federation adversaries such as the Romulan Star Empire and even the Orion Syndicate. Of course, Binnix knew—or at least was very confident—that the same could be said for enemy actors working within Starfleet and the Federation government. That the Klingons exploited such tactics was well known within the intelligence community if not the public at large, but there was only suspicion about similar activities on the part of the Romulans or anyone else. One could only speculate, but it was the job of Starfleet Intelligence to be on constant guard for such eventualities, and to Binnix it made perfect sense based on her own past knowledge and experience for the Romulans in particular to dispatch spies. After all, it would be difficult if not impossible to name even a single government entity that had not played the espionage game.

It's not a game, she thought. *Even if it had been, it's not anymore.*

That much was obvious just by looking at her reflection in the nearby window. The face staring back at her was not that of a human but instead a Klingon. Black hair instead of bright red, dark complexion instead of the fair skin she remembered from what seemed like a lifetime ago, and her blue eyes turned brown. Like Watson and Horst, she had been surgically altered to appear as a *QuchHa'*, a descendant of those who a century earlier fell victim to the Qu'Vat genetic mutation virus, which had affected, among other things, the cranial bone structure in many Klingons. Altering the agents in this manner was an easier proposition than the far more involved surgery required to make them resemble members of the *HemQuch* caste. The deception was enhanced by the addition of a collection of ten subcutaneous implants beneath the skin of their torso and limbs, which worked together to present a false reading to sensors, medical monitors, and other scanning techniques capable of revealing their human heritage. Additionally, the implant at the base of their necks also contained a transponder capable of sending an encrypted signal only the three of them could scan and decipher in order to locate one another anywhere within a radius of one hundred kilometers. Intended for emergencies like the one the agents currently faced, they could be used only once. After activation, the transponders emitted their signals for forty-eight hours. Binnix and her companions activated their respective implants less than an hour earlier, but she was unable to pick up Horst's signal. That meant he was outside scanning range, which she hoped was a good thing.

One way or the other, we're liable to find out.

Watson, formerly blond and tanned as one might expect from a native of California on Earth, ran a hand through his own dark hair as he paced the width of the small, unassuming apartment that was Binnix's residence. Located on the outskirts of the *wejDIch* Quarter of the First City, the capital not just of Qo'noS but the entire Klingon Empire, her dwelling offered what under normal circumstances would be a relaxing view of the Qam-Chee River, which served as the city's southern boundary. None of that appealed to Watson, who kept shooting anxious glances at her as he continued stalking back and forth across her main room's large bay windows.

"How much longer?" he asked.

"Another minute or so," Binnix replied without looking up from the computer interface she had positioned atop the apartment's small dining table. On the unit's compact, crimson-tinged display screen, a series of counters and status indicators flashed in rapid succession. Copying the most updated version of her protected data archive and transferring it to a pair of portable storage crystals was taking longer than she had anticipated. Despite planning for this day while at the same time anticipating and fearing the circumstances under which it might become necessary, she found herself growing more concerned with every extra second she perceived this process was taking.

The lag just by itself was enough to spark concern. Over the past three years, she had executed this type of data transfer more times than she could easily count. While there was always new information collected and added to the master repository maintained by Binnix and her companions, she had factored that into her planning in the event she needed to carry out a hurried move of data to the storage crystals. It was just one component of the team's larger emergency protocol to be carried out in the event they needed to flee, either because the nature of their mission and their true identities had been revealed, or they were facing imminent exposure.

Like right now, she thought, willing the computer to move her data faster. So far as she could tell, the computer gave no notice of her mental entreaties.

"It is taking too long," said Watson, his voice gruff as he continued speaking in *tlhIngan Hol*. "Something is wrong. Is it possible they have found your link to their central computer system?"

Binnix shook her head before replying in the Klingon language, "No. I have three different subroutines monitoring the connection even as it masks my activity. None of those have triggered any of the alerts I set up." Still, Watson's question gave her pause. "On the other hand, they may have enabled extra security software if they suspect illegal access. If that is true, then it is only a matter of time before they find my link, but I only need a few more seconds and then it will no longer matter."

At long last the counters and status icons provided the information she wanted to see, signaling the data transfer was complete. Retrieving the crystals from the computer's bank of access ports, Binnix dropped them into a leather satchel she had already slung over her left shoulder before pushing her chair away from the dining table and rising to her feet. From the satchel she extracted a small civilian disruptor pistol, a modest weapon possessing far less power than those used by Klingon soldiers, or even standard-issue Starfleet phasers. Adjusting its power setting, she aimed the disruptor at the computer terminal and fired. A single harsh red burst of energy erupted from the weapon's muzzle and enveloped the tabletop unit, reducing it to a puddle of liquefied metal and other composites.

"That's it," she said, returning the disruptor to the satchel. "Let's get out of here." Glancing at the chronometer on the wall of the apartment's small kitchen, she noted the time. "We need to get moving if we are to make the rendezvous with Horst."

If they were not already together when the decision was made to run, the team's evacuation plan called for them to meet at one of three designated rally points around the city. The primary location was an open-air bazaar near the Riverfront Enclave, one of several ancient monasteries scattered around the First City. The Enclave overlooked the Qam-Chee River, and from there it would be easy for Binnix and her companions to make their way to any of a dozen routes out of the city. While they each had personal communication devices that were encrypted, their signals could still be tracked by some savvy individual. Therefore, they would not be used unless absolutely necessary.

Their walking route to the Enclave would take them near the Federation Embassy. It would be so easy to just present themselves at the gate and—sticking with their Klingon cover identities—request asylum. Any regular citizen doing so would provoke all manner of protests from the Klingon government, but now? With the possibility of law enforcement and the military aware of spies who might be looking for a means of escape? Binnix suspected she and the team would be arrested the moment they tried to approach the embassy grounds, assuming they were not simply shot on sight.

Let's try to avoid that, shall we?

"Time to go," she said.

Watson nodded. "No argument from me."

Like her, he was traveling light, carrying only a thin, black leather bag slung across his back. While their mission and their very survival disallowed them from possessing any sort of personal keepsakes or other items that might provide clues to their real identities, Watson along with Binnix and Horst had still acquired a few items here on Qo'noS while working under cover. For her part, Binnix was taking with her a trio of books she had purchased over the course of the past three years, while Watson had taken a liking to bladed weapons of various design. Everything else he owned he had left in his apartment in the city's Old Quarter. Horst had collected a few knickknacks and other small items to decorate his own dwelling, and Binnix knew that he had left all of that behind once the team's evacuation protocols were activated. All he had to his name was a disruptor pistol like hers and a *d'k tagh* knife he wore on his belt. If they were stopped for some reason by law enforcement officers who had no clue of their real identities, carrying large travel bags or other bulky items might arouse suspicion. Better to present the part of two people just walking along the streets of the city.

Using a portable computer terminal, Binnix activated her connection to the apartment building's security system, giving her access to the internal network's camera feeds and computer interactions with other systems. No outside alerts or other message traffic out of the ordinary had been transmitted to the system. So far as she could tell, no one was monitoring the building with an eye toward watching her or Watson. It was just the usual sort of passive monitoring one might expect from a middle-income residential space where occupants paid slightly more in rent for additional safety and security measures. The system was easily exploitable, and Binnix saw nothing taking place to warrant concern.

Satisfied they weren't being set up for an ambush, she exited her apartment building with Watson following her. They both tried to affect the air that had become instinctive over the course of the past three years, acting as nothing more than a pair of citizens who had every right to be here. She had made similar walks through this, the proverbial pulsing heart of the Klingon Empire itself, uncounted times during this assignment. Like everything else, it was a routine she had developed as a survival mechanism, teaching herself to react to any sort of stimuli or distraction as a Klingon would. This meant breaking old habits like making unnecessary eye contact with or offering greetings to passersby, or striking up conversations with those she might encounter in a store or restaurant. The trick was not to avoid such things, but to react in Klingon fashion to those situations when they occurred. Her training had incorporated hours of classes and practical exercises on these subjects, drilling her to the point that when she arrived on Qo'noS, she along with her team could carry out their charade without thinking about it.

Of course, the real tests came when she assumed her duties as a midlevel employee on the administrative staff working for Maroq, a member of the Klingon High Council. Using that unassuming role as cover, Binnix spent most of her first year here working to identify for exploitation Maroq's list of contacts as well as take advantage of the classified information to which he was privy. Some of that was simplified by the fact that her work required her to have access to some of the same materials, while others required her to be more inventive. Another part of her training for this assignment involved learning how to operate and interact with Klingon computer systems. Despite holding an A6 computer specialist's rating in Starfleet, a holdover from her prior career as a science officer, she was still required to essentially learn how to write and reconfigure software in a manner not always compatible with her existing knowledge. Her experience working with Vulcan, Andorian, and Tellarite systems helped her in this regard, along with the fact that when it came down to it, there were only so many ways to tell a machine what to do or how to do it, and most of them were universal. One only had to account for the idiosyncrasies of the language being employed.

An additional, less pleasant aspect of her task called for her to tolerate Maroq's seemingly unending advances. A widower, the elder council member had never remarried and instead embraced a lifestyle of carousing with women on a frequent basis. It was Binnix's special hell that she maintained his schedule, including a calendar tracking his various rendezvous. Maroq's attempts to see her added to what she called "the rotation" were as annoying as they were frequent. Most of the time, she was able to keep his interests directed elsewhere, as there seemed to be no shortage of prospective partners waiting for an invitation to dinner or other activities on which she preferred not to dwell. Instead, she used the time he was away from his office to gain access to his protected files.

Improvise. Adapt. Overcome.

Binnix and Watson walked in silence for several moments, moving from the residential section of her neighborhood to an area populated more by commercial establishments. Without being obvious, she scanned the windows and doorways leading into shops, taverns, restaurants, and other businesses. It was early enough in the evening that many of them were still open, and the bars and eateries in particular were well trafficked. She checked faces, looked to see if eyes might be following her movements, but aside from the sort of brazen leers to which she long ago had become accustomed, no one seemed to take any undue notice of her or Watson.

Just because you're paranoid doesn't mean the entire Klingon Empire isn't out to get you.

Two

"Want to stop for a drink?"

It was the first time Watson had spoken since leaving her apartment. They had walked for nearly fifteen minutes in silence broken only by Binnix confirming their path through the city to the rendezvous point. She turned to look at him, noting he was not looking at her but instead at someone or something farther up the street. Her stomach tightened in sudden anxiety, and it required physical effort not to follow his gaze.

"This really isn't the best time for that sort of thing, Kvaal. Don't you think?"

"Liska, you look like you *could use a drink.*"

Nudging her arm, Watson directed her toward a tavern occupying the corner space of a building at the end of the block. Glancing through the establishment's lone window, she saw that perhaps a third of its tables and stools were claimed by patrons. It was still early, and she knew from experience places like these would become more active as the evening wore on. As they moved to the entrance, Binnix used the opportunity to glance up the street, but did not see whatever it was that had spooked her friend. At first, she considered Watson was just worried and therefore even more alert than she was, and might be overreacting to something that would prove innocuous. On the other hand, the junior agent had always displayed sound instincts. If something had his attention, it could not be ignored. Not now.

The tavern's doors parted, releasing a cloud of smoke and the sounds of numerous conversations, raucous laughter, and music from at least two different sources. The small crowd of male and female Klingons was making up for its lack of numbers with enthusiasm, and while Binnix and Watson earned a few cursory glances upon entering the room, their arrival provoked no reaction.

Binnix found a table near the back of the room that allowed them to sit together while keeping watch on the front entrance as well as the hallway leading to where she knew from previous visits the kitchen, storage, and lavatories were located. Another door on the room's far side led to stairs and, she guessed, either office or living space for the tavern's proprietor. The bar itself was dimly lit, with recessed lighting playing off the worn wood floor, stone walls, and the haphazard collection of tables, chairs, and stools scattered around the room. All manner of bladed weapons, family crests, and the skulls and hides of various game animals festooned the walls. A large stain discolored the floorboards near their table, and Binnix decided from its shape and size that it likely was caused by a patron meeting some form of unfortunate demise. A fight provoked by a perceived dishonoring of one's self or family? Perhaps a squabble over a mutual love interest.

Binnix slid into one of the chairs that provided her a good vantage point, glancing to the bar and seeing Watson waiting for the bartender to fill his order. She heard him ask for two tankards of bloodwine, and the burly, unkempt Klingon behind the bar with a metal disc over his left eye growled something in response. Binnix gave silent thanks for the medication they took that sheltered them from the worst effects of Klingon food and drink. One could not be an undercover agent among an alien people and be dainty about one's eating habits, after all. She also knew this was a momentary diversion; a test of sorts to see if they were truly being followed.

They were.

Two male Klingons, one taller than the other and dressed not in military or law enforcement uniforms but instead simple black leather pants and jackets, entered the tavern. Based on their wardrobe and mannerisms, Binnix guessed them to be with Imperial Intelligence, that branch of the Klingon government tasked with espionage and identifying external and internal threats to the Empire. Imperial Intelligence agents enjoyed tremendous latitude and autonomy while carrying out their duties, often operating above the law and even in defiance of cultural and social customs by which many Klingons defined their lives. They were the walking embodiment of "the ends justifying the means," earning them mixed measures of respect and disdain from the general populace.

If they were here, the situation as it pertained to her and Watson was even more dire than she had at first suspected.

While the taller Klingon made a pointed effort to look everywhere but in her direction, his companion was even less subtle as his gaze lingered on her for longer than the expected one or two seconds. They had to have seen her from outside, looking through the window into the bar just as she and Watson had done. The question now bugging Binnix was whether they were alone or if they might have friends waiting outside, or perhaps entering through a rear door in a bid to trap their quarry.

Damn.

With as much casualness as she could muster, Binnix opened her satchel and reached into it, her fingers sliding around the disruptor's handgrip. By touch alone, she verified the weapon's power level was set to stun. She did not want to kill anyone unless no other option remained, knowing full well any would-be captors were unlikely to give her similar consideration.

"You dare show yourself here?"

The sudden outburst almost made Binnix flinch, and it had the effect of causing nearly everyone else in the tavern to turn their attention to the source of the bellowed question: Phil

Watson. Standing at the bar, a tankard of bloodwine in his hand, he jabbed an accusatory finger at the new arrivals.

"After the dishonor you brought to my house," he barked in perfect *tlhIngan Hol*, "you have the audacity to stand before me now? Is this a challenge?" His stance seemed unsteady, as though he had already consumed far too much bloodwine, but Binnix knew it was part of whatever insane attempt at distraction this was supposed to be.

It seemed to be working, judging by the looks on the faces of the two Klingons, who exchanged glances with each other. Then they scowled at some of the other patrons who for their own reasons appeared to be taking Watson's side in this sudden, unexpected disagreement. Accusing a Klingon of bringing dishonor upon another individual or family was a bold action, and one that tended to engender automatic support for the person bringing such a challenge, and Watson now was using that to great effect. One Klingon male, obviously intoxicated, rose clumsily from his chair. His entire body swayed as he pointed to one of the new arrivals and uttered something Binnix could not understand or decipher. Whatever he said generated laughter from his companions, and only served to darken the expressions of the two suspicious Klingons. The taller of the two reached into his jacket, his hand emerging with a compact disruptor pistol. That was enough to set off several of the patrons, at least a dozen of whom stood to face the new challenge in their midst.

Oh, hell.

Pulling her own disruptor from her satchel, Binnix set the weapon in her lap, out of sight under the table. What the hell were they supposed to do now? Her first instinct was to head for the door at the back of the room, but that was an obvious move she was sure their pursuers were anticipating. They may not have expected the reception Watson had created with his gruff greeting, but if they had any training and experience at all, they would expect to face some kind of attempt to throw them off the chase. Indeed, the shorter Klingon looked to already be putting it together, grabbing his companion's arm and gesturing toward the back of the tavern.

At Binnix.

Wait, she thought. *They don't know about Phil?*

She realized they had not given Watson a second thought even after his brash posturing. Their attention was focused solely on her. Was it possible their information only detailed the actions of a single spy, and Watson and Horst had somehow escaped scrutiny?

Done bothering with the tavern crowd, the taller Klingon motioned to his companion to follow him. For Binnix, this only confirmed her suspicion that they had to be with Imperial Intelligence, who made a point to avoid identifying themselves in public. Both Klingons were now moving directly toward her, the eyes of the taller one locked on her. There could be no mistaking his intentions.

Time to go, Binnix decided. Her grip tightened around the disruptor resting in her lap.

Before she could raise the weapon, a flash of light and the shriek of unleashed energy filled the tavern. A bright crimson disruptor bolt slammed into the tall Klingon's chest with enough force to drive him into his companion. Both of them were still falling when a second shot struck the shorter Klingon in the head. Both dropped unmoving to the tavern floor.

Muscles tensing, Binnix turned toward the source of the disruptor fire and her eyes fell upon the barkeep. Still behind the high bar running the length of the room, he held what she recognized was an older model of disruptor once carried by soldiers in the Klingon Defense Force. His lack of a left eye seemed to have no bearing on his marksmanship.

"Draw a weapon in my bar at your peril," he snarled, his voice low and raspy.

Several of the patrons were moving to surround the bodies. Even with a now obstructed view, Binnix could tell the two
Klingons were dead. Minding the barkeep's warning, she returned her disruptor to the satchel. She looked up at the sound
of approaching footsteps and saw Watson maneuvering through
the gaggle of onlookers.

"Out the back."

Even as he spoke, he divided his attention between the scene
at the front of the room and the door offering them escape.
Without saying anything she followed him out of the bar and
down the short connecting corridor leading to the kitchen
and other rooms. The door at the end of the hallway was the
only one that mattered, and Watson dropped his shoulder and
slammed into it without breaking stride.

"Wait!"

Binnix's warning came an instant before the door swung
open to the left and a disruptor bolt punched into the wall just
in front of Watson's head. Only lightning reflexes saved him
from taking the shot straight in his face. He jerked himself back
through the doorway, fumbling for the disruptor he carried
beneath his jacket. Retrieving her own weapon, she shifted it
to her left hand and crouched low before angling herself so she
could lean close to the doorjamb. In the alley behind the tavern,
shadows danced along the wall of the building across the narrow passage, giving her an idea of the shooter's location somewhere to their right. Unless she was turned around from being
inside the bar, to the left should be the street on the tavern's west
side, and a chance at escape.

"We can't stay here," she whispered. "I'll try to draw their fire.
Ready?"

When a still visibly shaken Watson nodded, Binnix brought
up her disruptor and after drawing and releasing a deep breath,
she leaned through the doorway just enough to use her weapon.
Movement among the shadows at least a dozen meters down the

alley caught her eye and she angled the disruptor in that direction before firing four shots. She doubted she hit her intended target but she was rewarded with a string of Klingon curses followed by sounds of frantic movement as someone sought better cover.

That was Watson's cue, and he pivoted into the doorway and fired three shots of his own. One of them struck a lurking shadow and Binnix heard a grunt of surprise as a large shape fell against the wall of the adjacent building. She waited for signs of more movement. Was the Klingon alone out there?

Watson stepped into the alley, disruptor held up and aimed ahead of him. No one shot at him, but the sounds of anxious voices echoed off the walls around them.

"Someone's coming," she said. "Let's get the hell out of here."

Sounds of running footsteps were coming from the nearby street, leaving Binnix and Watson with the lone option of moving deeper into the alley. Jogging away from the tavern's rear door, they stepped over trash and other debris littering the ground here, including the unmoving form of a large, unconscious Klingon male. Even in the dim light filtering from the street, Binnix could make out their adversary's clothing.

"Same as the others. He must have been their backup."

"One of them, anyway," replied Watson.

They found an intersection leading to a smaller alley between two buildings. It was darker here, but Binnix was still able to see. So far as she could tell, this passage led to an adjacent street. She recalled what she could of this area, deciding that street could get them to the Riverfront Enclave and their rendezvous with Horst.

Two figures appeared at the alley's far end.

Binnix and Watson froze. Had they been seen? If not, that would last only a few more seconds, as the new arrivals were already heading in their direction. Faint voices from somewhere behind them told her they were about to be hemmed in. Their only choices were to try fighting their way out of this potential death trap, or take the drastic measure of ending their own lives before they could be captured. She was ready to try taking at least a couple of their pursuers with her before deciding on the more extreme course of action, and saw from Watson's expression that he felt the same way.

"Make it count?" he asked, as if verifying their unspoken decision.

"Yeah."

Before she could move to engage their newest adversaries, she felt her body seized by the calm, soothing sensation of a transporter beam. The shower of red-yellow energy enveloped her, blocking out her vision, then everything went dark for the briefest of moments. Then the crimson-and-gold curtain shone even brighter before fading altogether. The dark alley was gone, replaced by the dimly lit, and very close, bulkheads of a compact transporter platform.

"Welcome aboard, spies and saboteurs."

Standing before the room's small, utilitarian transporter console was David Horst. He was broad-shouldered and muscled, his physique barely contained by his leather pants and dark shirt. His smile was wide enough that Binnix thought it might actually break his reconstructed Klingon face.

"Holy hell, am I glad to see you," said Watson as he stepped from the platform, dropping both his use of the native Klingon language and any pretense that he was an actual Klingon.

Binnix echoed the sentiment, and the three of them pulled one another into a warm embrace.

"You used our transponders to find us?" she asked, also dropping the *tlhIngan Hol*.

"Seemed like a good idea. They were going to waste anyway."

Horst disengaged from the group hug before gesturing for them to follow him as he led the way from the transporter and down a short corridor until they arrived at a cramped cockpit.

It resembled the flight deck of the sort of Klingon civilian transports aboard which Binnix had occasionally found herself over the course of this assignment. Two seats were positioned before a large, curved control console, and when she looked closer she noted various instruments labeled in Klingon text. Beyond the cockpit's clear canopy, she saw the curve of Qo'noS.

"Do I want to know where or how you acquired this ship?"

Shaking his head as he slid into the cockpit's right seat, Horst said, "Probably not." Instead of elaborating, he tapped several controls on the console and Binnix noted that the ship immediately broke orbit. Within seconds, Horst brought the ship up to full impulse power.

"How in the world are you avoiding sensors?" asked Watson.

Horst shrugged. "I'm not. Instead, our ship's transponder identifies us as a diplomatic courier ship that's also in orbit. I simply forged their identity code and made sure planetary traffic sensors recorded us departing. The real ship's captain's going to be pissed when he gets boarded because his transponder code's the same as ours. Whoops."

Could it be that simple? Binnix knew if anyone could pull off that sort of insidious wizardry, it was Horst. The man had never met a computer system or other technology he could not bend to his will given sufficient time. His confidence was good enough for her.

For the first time in nearly a day, she allowed herself to relax and even laughed at Horst's report. No one said anything else until the transport made the jump to warp speed, and she only breathed easier when he confirmed there were no obvious signs of pursuit.

"Goodbye, Qo'noS," she said, to no one in particular.

Watson snorted as he collapsed into the copilot's chair. "Good riddance."

"We just have to make it to the border," said Horst. "Get to the border and the Ivratis asteroid field, and if all goes to plan a ship will be waiting for us. Then we're home free." He reached up to rub his jaw. "I'll be more than ready to get rid of all this. I miss my old face." Glancing to Watson, he smiled. "It looks good on you, though."

"Thanks."

As the weight of the past several hours seemed to fall from her shoulders, Binnix sagged against the bulkhead behind Watson. After more than three years undercover in the heart of one of the Federation's most formidable adversaries, it was almost impossible to believe she and her companions were finally going home. They would be debriefed, evaluated, and tested at length, of course, but after that? Surgery to restore them to their former selves and a lengthy vacation, for starters. Beyond that, she had no plans.

Before any of that could happen, she knew the days ahead would be filled with interviews, examinations, and a good dose of healthy skepticism. She and the others would expend a great deal of energy attempting to convince their masters they remained loyal agents of Starfleet and the Federation and had not been turned by the Empire into sympathizers or traitors.

Plenty of time for all of that later, she decided. For now, Binnix was just thankful to be heading home. The sooner she was aboard whatever Starfleet ship was being sent to retrieve them, the better she would feel.

Soon, she assured herself. *Home.*

Three

At first indistinguishable from any of the distant stars matted against the utter blackness of deep space displayed upon the *Enterprise* bridge's main viewscreen, Starbase 24 grew larger and more distinct as the starship continued its approach.

"Dropping to impulse," reported Hikaru Sulu from where he sat at the bridge's helm station. The lieutenant's hands moved with practiced ease over the console's array of controls. In response to his instructions, the ship offered a subtle reverberation as it made the transition from faster-than-light speed.

The effect was slight but James Kirk still noticed it, sensing the shift as the minute vibrations traveled up from the deck plates and into his boots. Seated in his command chair at the center of the bridge, he could not help a small sigh of satisfaction at seeing the deep-space station on the screen. He also took note of the looks of anticipation on the faces of various bridge officers. Everyone on the ship knew what this unscheduled yet still welcome stop meant.

"Continue on rendezvous course. One half impulse power," ordered Kirk before glancing over his right shoulder to the communications station. "Lieutenant Uhura, contact traffic control and request docking instructions."

"Aye, sir," replied Uhura. "Requesting instructions now."

Even from this distance the station struck an imposing image. It appeared as a smaller, trimmed-down version of far more formidable constructs such as Starfleet's primary Spacedock facility orbiting Earth. The station consisted of a large, saucer-shaped primary section sitting atop a long, slender secondary hull, which Kirk knew housed the facility's main power and life-support systems. It was the upper portion that served as home to more than one thousand Starfleet personnel and civilians, along with a varying number of transients who used the base as a way station between points of extended travel. Kirk himself, both as captain of the *Enterprise* and well before assuming his current assignment, had visited here more than once. Situated as it was near the border separating Federation and Klingon space, the facility also harbored an impressive complement of phaser banks, photon torpedo launchers, and defensive shield generators. Far more than most such bases receive, the enhanced armaments were a concession to harsh lessons learned from costly attacks on similar stations by hostile forces, reinforced by Starbase 24's relative isolation as well as its proximity to Klingon territory.

"Why can't Starfleet ever send us to a starbase that's constructed on an actual planet?" asked Leonard McCoy. The ship's chief medical officer, positioned to Kirk's left, leaned against the curved red railing separating the command well from the bridge's perimeter stations. As was his habit, the doctor affected his normal manner of looking as though he preferred any location to the one he presently occupied.

From where he sat at the science console along the bridge's starboard side, Commander Spock swiveled his chair to regard McCoy. "Starbase 24 is one of Starfleet's most advanced facilities, Doctor. It offers services and amenities lacking at other stations and ports of call. Despite its remote location, it remains one of the most requested assignments for personnel tasked with starbase duty."

"Does it have fresh air?" countered McCoy. "Green grass? Tall trees with thick branches and lots of shade you can use when you want a nap on a nice spring day?"

The first officer's initial response was to cock his right eyebrow, which he then followed with, "The station features an expansive arboretum and botanical garden."

"Sounds like my kind of place," replied Sulu.

Seated at the navigator's station to the helm officer's right, Ensign Pavel Chekov replied, "I've been reading the latest reports on planned upgrades for all Sierra-class stations. They're due for complete overhauls over the next three years." As was often the case, the young Russian's thick accent seemed to become more pronounced as he warmed to his chosen topic of discussion. "Among the listed upgrades are terrestrial enclosures similar to those found on Watchtower-class starbases."

"Engineered green spaces." McCoy shook his head, his mock frown almost making Kirk chuckle. "Still no substitute for the real thing."

"On that we can agree, Doctor." Spock rose from his chair, his Vulcan demeanor never wavering as he approached the bridge railing. He clasped his hands behind his back. "Studies have shown that the benefits of exposure to moderate amounts of genuine sunlight are far more beneficial than lamps or other artificial sources."

McCoy released a dramatic sigh. "Yes, Spock. That's exactly what I had in mind."

Whatever retort Spock may have offered was interrupted by Uhura, who turned in her seat. In her left ear she held a Feinberger receiver, which allowed her to rapidly filter the numerous requests channeled through the *Enterprise*'s communications system.

"Captain, we're receiving instructions from the dock master. We are cleared for entry."

"And not a moment too soon, Lieutenant." To his helmsman, Kirk said, "Mister Sulu, were you planning to let docking control bring us in, or do you prefer to do the honors yourself?" The lieutenant did not need to turn in his seat for his smile to be apparent.

"I was about to request permission to conduct a manual docking, sir. I don't get to practice that often."

"Just don't run into anything," offered McCoy in a mildly teasing tone. "I don't want to spend my shore leave tending to bumps and bruises because you forgot how to park."

Now Sulu did turn, his grin wide. "I'll do my best, Doctor."

The lieutenant had only just begun making the first of what Kirk knew would be several maneuvering adjustments needed to align the *Enterprise* for entry into the starbase's cavernous docking bay when Uhura once more swung her seat away from her console.

"Captain, we're being hailed by the station. It's on a priority channel for you, sir. Also? It's scrambled."

Frowning as he exchanged glances with Spock, Kirk asked, "Priority and scrambled? From the commodore?" The last message received from Starbase 24's commanding officer, Christina Peterman, was an invitation for Kirk and his senior officers to dine with the commodore after the *Enterprise* was secure in the docking bay. Nothing about that required the employment of scrambled, encoded communications traffic.

"I can confirm it's coming from the station, sir," replied Uhura, "but not whether it's coming from Commodore Peterman."

"Put it through, Lieutenant." There was a momentary lag as the communications officer accepted the incoming hail and applied the appropriate decryption protocols. That done, the image on the main viewscreen shifted from Starbase 24 to the withered visage of an elderly human male of Asian descent. Short black and gray hair framed a thin, wrinkled face dominated by a thin mouth, high cheekbones, and a pair of piercing blue eyes Kirk knew from experience missed absolutely nothing.

"Admiral Nogura?" Rising from his command chair, Kirk moved around Sulu to stand before the helm and navigation stations. He squared himself before the viewscreen as he nodded in greeting to his superior officer. "This is quite the surprise."

Heihachiro Nogura sat in a high-backed leather chair, his forearms resting atop a nondescript, standard Starfleet-issue gray desk. Behind him was an equally unimpressive, drab gray wall, which featured no accoutrements whatsoever. He seemed to have aged just since the last time Kirk had seen him months earlier, or perhaps he was simply tired. His gold uniform tunic appeared to be hanging from his already slight frame, and Kirk wondered how long it had been since the admiral last slept.

But why is he here?

"*Captain Kirk*," said Nogura, his voice low and all business. "*Under other circumstances, it'd be good to see you and the* Enterprise. *You know how I like to keep tabs on your activities.*"

While the admiral was known for his occasional flirtations with quiet, even deadpan humor, Kirk sensed none of that now. Choosing to ignore the remark, he asked, "I didn't realize you'd be waiting for us here, sir."

"*That was the idea. I don't like advertising my comings and goings, especially this close to Klingon space. So far as the Empire and everyone except a very small group of people are concerned, I'm on Earth, or maybe Deneva. I forget which of my cover itineraries they're using this week.*" Apparently deciding that too much time was being wasted on this discussion, Nogura waved a hand toward the screen. "*Your first officer and crew can handle the* Enterprise's *docking, Captain. Your communications officer should be receiving transporter coordinates. Have yourself beamed to that location immediately. Nogura out.*"

No sooner did the admiral's visage disappear from the screen, replaced with an image of the now much closer Starbase 24 as the *Enterprise* continued its docking approach, than Kirk heard a telltale beep from behind him.

"Coordinates received, Captain," reported Uhura, her features a mask of confusion. "They correspond to a personal transporter pad located on the station's command level."

Moving away from the bridge railing to stand next to Kirk's chair, McCoy said, "What in blazes was that all about?"

It was Spock who replied, "Admiral Nogura's presence indicates a matter of some importance and requiring prompt attention."

"There's only one way to find out," said Kirk. "Uhura, route those coordinates to the transporter room and notify them I'm on my way. Mister Spock, you have the conn." He waved to the viewscreen and the starbase depicted on it. "Continue docking maneuver, but no one goes ashore until I find out what's going on."

The first officer nodded. "Acknowledged."

Leaving his colleagues behind on the bridge, Kirk stepped into the turbolift and directed it to the transporter room. As the car descended, he could not help thinking that no matter the other reasons and consequences involving Nogura's presence, so far as his ship and crew were concerned, one thing was certain.

Shore leave was liable to be short. Very, *very* short.

Four

Just as he suspected based on the initial conversation with Nogura, the office in which Kirk now found himself was a drab, boring affair. The deck, bulkheads, and overhead were painted the same uniform shade of standard gray that was a hallmark of Starfleet facilities. Nothing was affixed to any of the walls, with only a single set of red doors and a large viewscreen set into the bulkhead to Kirk's right serving to break up the monotony. The only other items holding any interest were the desk and chair he had already seen, and the man to which they currently played host. Facing the desk sat two light blue, armless chairs with black leather backrests, which represented the rest of the room's meager furnishings. The only item on the desk was a standard computer interface monitor. It was obvious that Nogura had no intention of staying here any longer than absolutely necessary.

"Admiral," said Kirk, stepping down from the two-person transporter pad and crossing the office toward Nogura. "This is something of a surprise."

Without standing, the elder man replied, "The story of my life, Captain. Have a seat." He waited until Kirk settled into one of the chairs before adding, "You're aware Starfleet keeps me rather busy, overseeing a number of operations and other initiatives."

Kirk shifted in the chair in a vain attempt to get comfortable before resigning to himself that such an effort was futile. "From what I understand, sir, that's a bit of an understatement."

Based on his own previous interactions with the admiral along with a healthy dose of rumors and gossip, Kirk knew Nogura's portfolio as a senior admiral and one of the command hierarchy's foremost tacticians was among the most active and comprehensive in all of Starfleet. His duties included a number of mandates and tasks that kept him busy both on Earth and at various locations throughout Federation space. Many if not most of his assignments and even his movements were classified as closely guarded secrets. Given the often volatile relations between the Federation and the Klingon Empire over the past two decades, which had experienced no small number of flare-ups and brief brushes with open warfare, Nogura was designated by Starfleet as one of its most vital assets. Regulations prohibited him from even being in the same room with any of a short list of senior flag officers operating under similar mandates. He rarely remained in one place for any appreciable length of time, and only then in response to very atypical circumstances.

"It is an understatement," said Nogura. "I was being polite. The real version is that I'm busy. Damned busy, over a lot of things most people will never know about, starship captains included. That said, there are those occasions when I need to read someone in to a sensitive operation because I require their help, and I've decided they're the best person for the job. Congratulations, Kirk. This time, you're the lucky winner."

Unable to contain a small, knowing smile, Kirk replied, "I had a feeling, sir."

Relaxing into his chair, Nogura rested his hands in his lap and regarded the captain for a long moment before saying, "You've had some experience with Klingon agents working within Federation space, medically and cosmetically altered to appear human." It was a statement, not a question, which made perfect sense. Given his oversight of all matters pertaining to the Klingons, Nogura would know about even the smallest encounter between any Starfleet personnel and representatives of the Empire.

"A few times, sir. The most recent encounter—that I know of, anyway—was during that incident with the Klingons at Deep Space Station K-7. Arne Darvin, assistant to Nilz Baris, the Federation undersecretary of agriculture who was overseeing a pet project involving Sherman's Planet, the ownership of which was disputed by the Federation and the Klingons. Darvin was surgically altered to appear human and sent to sabotage the Federation's colonization efforts in a bid to seize control. He was unsuccessful."

Nogura nodded. "The grain. And the tribbles. The less said about that, the better."

"Agreed, sir."

His right hand having moved from his lap, Nogura began using his fingers to tap on the arm of his chair. "Here's the more important question, and one I'm sure you've pondered at least once: How long do you suppose Darvin was operating undercover?"

"So far as I know, that information is classified, sir. However, given the level of trust Baris placed in him, I'd have to say quite a while. Several months at least."

"Eighteen months."

Kirk felt his jaw slacken. "That long?"

"While you're thinking about that, think about this: We suspect there have been similar agents working undercover within Starfleet, the Federation government, and any number of other places for far longer. Years, Kirk. It's not a new idea, of course."

"I've read a few official reports, and heard a lot more stories." Rumors abounded, going back decades, of Klingon operatives disguised as humans or members of other Federation races, working in secret to gather information for their superiors or to influence events and actions within the borders of their sworn enemy. Some of the stories seemed far-fetched, but after the incident at the K-7 station, Kirk received an intelligence briefing that convinced him that there was more fact than fiction surrounding what he had previously heard. Espionage was not at all an original concept, and it made perfect sense that interstellar adversaries would carry out some of the same sorts of covert actions against the Federation as nation-states conducted against one another on Earth from the dawn of its civilization.

Nogura said, "Even though it's obviously not common knowledge, it probably won't come as a shock to you that we've been doing the same thing. Not nearly as long, mind you, but long enough to achieve tangible results."

Stories about such activities also were plentiful, Kirk knew, but far less circulated at least in anything approaching official circles. Indeed, Nogura's admission was the first time he had heard a confirmation of the practice.

"You're saying that humans are altered—"

The admiral raised a hand, cutting off the rest of Kirk's reply. "Most of the agents are human, but there are a couple of Vulcans, one native of Alpha Centauri B, and three Rigelians in the mix. It was determined that those three species present the least problems with the alteration procedure. Yes, they're subjected to surgery to reconfigure not just their appearance but there's also some rearranging of internal organs. Nothing too fancy, but enough to fool most Klingon scanners. Thankfully, their technology isn't as advanced as ours, but there's still an obvious risk of exposure. Each agent is also given a suite of subdermal implants that help disguise their bio readings on sensors. They show up as Klingon on routine scans. The cover won't survive intense or protracted scrutiny, but the idea is for such agents to avoid situations that might bring them that sort of unwanted attention."

"It still has to be pretty dangerous," said Kirk.

Nodding, the admiral replied, "Absolutely, but we and they

take every possible precaution to maintain their cover. Their missions generally involve inserting themselves as low-level personnel within the Klingon military and government. Primarily, they gather information, analyze it, and forward on anything relevant to their handlers, which in most cases is me. The communication is strictly one-way and conducted at their discretion, so it's not unusual to go months or longer without hearing from an asset on the ground."

"Months, or longer." Shifting in his seat, Kirk considered the implications. "How long has this been going on?"

Nogura leaned forward, resting his forearms atop the barren desk. "About six years since our first agents were sent in. One was extracted a year or so after that, and two were never heard from again. So far as we've been able to ascertain, they avoided exposure and capture. Other assets we had within the Empire's borders were able to confirm that much, so the most likely explanation is that they . . . took it upon themselves to make certain they weren't caught. It's not something we explicitly taught or ordered them to do, but every agent who went through the training program understood that the consequences of capture would be devastating, not just for them but for the entire Federation."

Nodding in sober agreement, Kirk cleared his throat. "Has any agent been exposed?"

"Not yet," replied Nogura. He rose from his chair and moved out from behind his desk, crossing to the large viewscreen set into the office's far wall. "And that's where you come in." Reaching for the keypad mounted next to the screen, the admiral tapped a control. The screen flared to life, depicting an image with which Kirk was familiar: a map of space highlighted by the border separating Federation and Klingon territory.

"Eight days ago, we received a coded emergency message from one of our teams working deep undercover within the Empire." Nogura turned from the screen. "And when I say deep, I mean as deep as it gets: Qo'noS."

The Klingon homeworld? The heart of the Empire?

Kirk was astounded by the sheer audacity of sending spies to the center of the Federation's fiercest enemy. While not in a state of war, the two powers had endured a strained relationship for more than a decade since the last major confrontation. What had threatened to explode into open conflict was stopped only by the machinations of the mysterious Organians, the highly advanced, extremely powerful race of noncorporeal life-forms who viewed humanoids with thinly veiled contempt. Using the staggering powers at their command, they brought both Starfleet and Klingon fleets to an utter standstill, stopping the threat of open hostilities and issuing an ultimatum that further actions in this vein would not be tolerated. This none too subtle threat left both adversaries with little more to do than stare at one another across the gulf of space separating their respective territories. Instead, each side plotted, maneuvered, and attempted to outthink the other, searching for any advantage or opportunity to exploit while at the same time avoiding rebuke from the Organians, who for their part remained frustratingly silent, but neither the Federation nor the Empire appeared willing to test the mysterious and otherwise reclusive race's resolve.

One wonders what they might think of this.

"How long have they been there?" asked Kirk.

Nogura tapped another control and the map zoomed in to focus on the star system that was home to Qo'noS. "Just over three years, working behind the scenes within the strategic-planning branches of both the central government and the military. Everything they do is meant to be subtle if not completely unnoticeable. They gradually augmented their intelligence-gathering mission over time by gaining trust and moving deeper into those organizations. We're talking about sowing disinformation about Starfleet movements and misdirecting the deployment of Klingon military assets in ways that end up benefiting us. They've even managed to interfere with certain areas of technological advancement so far as the weapons and defenses of the latest designs of Klingon warships."

Kirk shook his head in amazement. "Incredible."

"If there are any tangible gains from those specific efforts," said Nogura, "I don't know that we'll see them for a few years at the least. On the other hand, the agents have still brought us numerous gains about which the public knows little, while providing us with valuable information with which to base long-term strategic planning. If the Empire decides they want another war with us, we'll see it coming almost before they do." His expression fell. "At least, that was the idea until eight days ago when we got their emergency extraction message. For some reason we don't yet know, they felt they were in danger of being discovered and obtained transport off Qo'noS, carrying out their part of an extraction plan we'd put together even before they were inserted. The idea was simple: Travel to a predetermined location along the Neutral Zone for rendezvous with a starship that would bring them to me. Klingon observation outposts along the border are well aware of our patrol routes on our side of the zone, so this seemed like a decent enough cover for an extraction operation. With that in mind, I dispatched the *Endeavour* to handle the pickup."

"The *Endeavour*?" Kirk made no attempt to hide his confusion. "Last I heard, it was assigned to exploration and survey duty in the Taurus Reach."

Nogura replied, "Officially, that's what they're still doing, but I needed a ship and Captain Khatami's was the one available on such short notice. Besides, the Klingons and everyone else paying attention to our fleet movements knows *Constitution*-class ships are always reassigned at the admiralty's whim for all manner of reasons. So, this provided at least some cover for what we needed."

"If everything had gone to plan," said Kirk, "I wouldn't be sitting here."

Instead of replying, Nogura pressed more keys on the viewscreen's control pad, and the image changed to a stark white picture emblazoned with black text: U.S.S. ENDEAVOUR SHIP LOG. STARDATE 6045.8.

Two days ago, Kirk mused.

"As you've likely guessed," said the admiral as he touched the control to begin the log playback, "the entire operation's gone to hell."

Five

"Captain, cargo bay one reports all three passengers are safely on board."

Pacing the upper deck of the *U.S.S. Endeavour*'s bridge, Captain Atish Khatami stopped as she came abreast of the main viewscreen and nodded toward her communications officer, Lieutenant Hector Estrada. The older man sat at his station, a Feinberger receiver in his right ear and an expression of concern on his face. His gaze was not on her but instead appeared to be looking toward the overhead, and Khatami knew he was listening to some additional report coming over the active comm frequency.

"What's wrong, Estrada?" she asked.

"The . . . passengers, Captain. They're insisting we transport over some kind of small cargo container, but it's shielded from our scans and the transporter chief is worried."

Still studying the screen, Khatami nodded. She understood and appreciated such caution, as transporting any unknown item aboard the ship without proper screening and other safety protocols being observed was not only a violation of Starfleet regulations but also dangerous. Under normal circumstances, she would be the first to make the same sort of objection, and would support any subordinate voicing similar reservations.

The circumstances, however, along with everything else associated with this mission, were not normal, and Khatami knew the longer they stayed here, the more irregular the situation would become.

"Tell the chief to bring it aboard on my authority. Have the passengers open it for scanning, then the security detail is to place them and it into the quarantine facility immediately." She glanced at a chronometer on the environmental control near the front of the bridge. "And do it fast. I want to get out of here. We've already been here longer than I like."

She returned to studying the main screen and the image of the civilian transport displayed on it. Small and innocuous as it drifted among the asteroids, the vessel was nothing more than a dark metallic box with little in the way of aesthetic features. Everything about it was function over form and substance over style. It was not of Klingon design but neither did it look like any Federation ship she had ever seen. Khatami suspected it had come from one of the nonaligned systems in this region of space, but she was unable to place it. Not that it mattered. Her only concern was that the craft be untraceable to some point of origin that might implicate the agents who had used it to make their escape. Having been reassured on this point by Admiral Nogura, Khatami was content to forget about the ship as soon as their business here was concluded.

In accordance with the extraction plan as explained to her by Nogura, the *Endeavour* had only been in transporter range of the smaller vessel for less than ninety seconds after the starship's sensors registered its arrival at the outskirts of their present location, the Ivratis asteroid field. Located between the farthest boundary of the Omega Leonis system near the border between Federation and Klingon space, the region had fallen under Klingon control during the Empire's war with the Federation a decade earlier. With territorial lines redrawn following the cessation of hostilities, this area at present belonged to neither party. The asteroid field was marked as a hazardous area on most navigation maps and star charts due to the density of debris along with background radiation capable of hampering sensors. Both Starfleet and civilian ships tended to avoid the field itself, but Khatami knew from official reports and her own prior experience on border patrol duty that the region was not unknown to pirates and other parties who used it to mask their movements from the watchful eye of Starfleet and other law enforcement entities.

It also provided decent enough protection from casual observation for those seeking to make a covert rendezvous of the sort the *Endeavour* was now attempting.

"Captain," said Estrada. "The group's leader is asking to speak with you as soon as you're available."

Waving away the suggestion, Khatami moved from the main viewscreen. "Later. I want Doctor Leone and Lieutenant Brax to give them a good going over before they talk to anyone, including me. For now, we do everything by the book and according to Admiral Nogura's orders."

As part of the hasty briefing she and her senior staff received while en route from the Taurus Reach to Omega Leonis, Nogura had instructed them to follow all isolation protocols with respect to the retrieval of long-term covert intelligence agents. According to the information shared by the admiral, Morgan Binnix and her team had been under deep cover for several years, doing everything possible to blend into a hostile environment at great risk to themselves as well as Federation security. Then, there was the simple matter that the *Endeavour*'s three new passengers all looked like Klingons, and would continue to do so until they received the surgery necessary to restore their human features. Having them walk around the ship, even in Starfleet or Federation civilian clothing, would only cause disruption among the rest of the crew, most of whom were not yet aware of the true nature of their mission.

Until then, every precaution had to be observed during a retrieval operation, including quarantining the reclaimed agents until such time as they could be debriefed by authorized personnel. This took the form of confining the three new arrivals to a special containment facility hastily constructed for just this purpose in one of the *Endeavour*'s cargo bays located in the lower portion of the starship's primary hull. Part temporary housing, part medical bay, and part office space, there they would receive full medical physicals and their belongings would be searched for any illicit items. There was also the possibility that one or more of the operatives had been negatively influenced in some manner, and now worked as a converted asset for the Klingons. Such a development could prove dangerous if not disastrous should the rogue agent be allowed to slip undiscovered back into Federation society or some sensitive position within the government or Starfleet.

Not on my watch.

Khatami intended to follow every rule and regulation as well as each syllable of Nogura's instructions to the letter. There simply was too much at stake, the most immediate danger being to the *Endeavour* and its crew. To that end, only a small number of her people even knew the real reason for their current assignment and were sworn to secrecy. Only those with an absolute need to know would have access to the agents. The ship's doctor, Anthony Leone, and its chief of security, Lieutenant Brax, would conduct the first interviews. Leone would verify their overall good health and provide whatever treatments might be necessary, while Brax examined their belongings to ensure nothing dangerous had somehow been brought aboard and escaped initial scans. While Brax was barred from conducting full interviews or debriefings, he could still ask preliminary questions in an attempt to discover if any of the agents were being somehow duplicitous. At the very least, equipment aboard the *Endeavour* could ascertain whether the operatives were being truthful or spinning lies.

There were limits to what she could do without further authorization from Nogura, but that would not stop Khatami from leaving anything to chance. She knew the agents represented enormous value from an information standpoint to Starfleet Intelligence. Nogura had stressed the importance of protecting the assets until they could be handed off to him, but he was not here, and neither was anyone else who stood to benefit from whatever vital information the operatives carried in their heads. If she sensed for one moment that any of the retrieved agents posed a threat to the *Endeavour*, Khatami would take any and all actions necessary to protect her people.

Nogura and everyone else will just have to deal with it.

Stepping down into the command well, Khatami made her way around the helm console and to her chair at the center of the bridge. As she took her seat, she glanced to the science station along the bridge's starboard bulkhead. "Mister Klisiewicz, are we still alone out here?"

Hunched over the hooded sensor viewer that was his console's most prominent feature, Lieutenant Stephen Klisiewicz did not look up as he replied, "So far, so good, Captain. However, our sensors are still somewhat muddled thanks to the asteroid field. The picture will be clearer once we've got some distance from it."

"Let's get on with that, then," said Khatami. She had not liked the idea of bringing the *Endeavour* into the field, and the faster the ship was back in open space, the happier she would be. "Helm, take us out of here, nice and easy. Navigator, as soon as we're clear of the field, plot a warp-five course back to Starbase 24." Glancing again to Klisiewicz, she asked, "What about our friends' ship?"

The dark-haired science officer replied, "I've been monitoring all onboard systems since we arrived, Captain. No communications or other signals have been sent, beyond their contact with us."

"That doesn't mean they didn't get a call out to someone before we showed up," said Lieutenant Commander Katherine Stano, the ship's first officer. Making her own circuit of the bridge stations as she kept abreast of everything taking place around her, she paused near the engineering console and crossed her arms. "I know we didn't pick up any other signals on our way in, but with the asteroid field playing with our sensors, that's not saying much."

Klisiewicz gestured to his station. "I ran some reconfiguration protocols on the sensor array to mitigate the disruption. It helped some, but we're still dealing with some pretty heavy background interference."

"It's not going to matter in a couple of minutes," said Khatami. "Right?"

"Our passengers initiated their ship's self-destruct protocols prior to beaming over," replied Klisiewicz. "The warp engines are on a buildup to detonation and should go in about two minutes or so."

Wiping aside a lock of brown hair that had fallen across her forehead, Stano nodded. "Another fine reason to be somewhere other than here."

"Agreed," said Khatami. "Helm, can we handle full maneuvering thrusters in here?"

Seated before the captain at the left side of the combined helm and navigation console, Lieutenant Marielise McCormack replied, "I think so, Captain. This area of the field's not so dense as the way we entered."

Khatami watched as the compact, unimpressive transport receded on the main viewer. It took only a moment to disappear from view, blocked by asteroids drifting around it as the *Endeavour* continued its egress maneuvers. Once it was back in open space, the ship would have to skirt the edge of the field closest to Klingon territory in order to plot a clear course for Starbase 24. Only then would she allow herself to relax.

"Countdown to detonation in five seconds," reported Klisiewicz, stepping away from the science station to watch with the rest of the bridge crew as the transport's warp engines reached their programmed overload point.

The main viewscreen managed to catch one last view of the transport before the image automatically dimmed to counter the effects of the brilliant white sphere of energy erupting from the ship's hull, expanding outward until it consumed the entire vessel. It was over in seconds, with what little debris remained of the transport flung in all directions. While the *Endeavour* was already far enough away that the resulting shockwave would have little to no effect on the starship's shields, the impact on the closest asteroids was already noticeable. The invisible band of released energy struck more of the drifting and tumbling bodies than Khatami could count, pushing them ever farther into the field. Some would strike still more asteroids, she knew, perhaps creating a cascading action that might only be arrested by the presence of a large enough mass or another gravity field.

Could be a hell of a show. Too bad we won't be around to see it.

"How soon until we're clear of the field?" asked Stano, who by now had moved to sit on the curved red railing to Khatami's left.

Not looking up from her helm controls, McCormack replied, "About three minutes at our present speed, Commander."

"Course plotted for Starbase 24," added the *Endeavour*'s primary navigation officer, Lieutenant Neelakanta. Turning toward Khatami, the tall, lean Arcturian regarded her with deep, dark purple eyes staring out from the pronounced brow of his bald head. His soothing mauve complexion was at odds with his gold uniform tunic. "Estimated travel time at warp five is six hours, twenty-eight minutes."

Khatami nodded in approval. "Excellent. That should give Doctor Leone and Lieutenant Brax enough time to complete their evaluations of our guests."

An alarm tone from his console made Klisiewicz return to

the science station mere seconds before the red-alert klaxon erupted across the bridge. The indicator positioned between the helm and navigator stations began flashing as Khatami dropped her gaze to the astrogator separating McCormack and Neelakanta. Where only a moment ago it depicted the *Endeavour*'s course along the asteroid field's periphery, now it displayed an icon representing a second ship.

"Deflector shields just activated," reported McCormack.

Six

Once again peering into his sensor viewer, Klisiewicz said, "There's another ship in here with us. Sensors didn't pick it up earlier due to the background interference. They're on an intercept course." When he looked up from his station, his face was a mask of concern. "It's a Klingon cruiser."

"Weapons on standby," ordered Stano, pushing herself from the railing and stepping down into the command well. She moved to stand behind McCormack. "Be ready for evasive maneuvers. Let's see it."

On the main viewscreen, the image shifted to depict what Khatami recognized as a Klingon D7 battle cruiser maneuvering around a particularly large asteroid. One of the Empire's most advanced warships, it was more than capable of standing toe to toe with the *Endeavour*. The only saving grace was that the ship appeared to be alone, making this an even match, at least according to the technical specifications she had memorized and her own past experience along with that of her crew.

Feeling her muscles tensing in anticipation, she asked, "How long until we're clear?"

"Another minute or so," replied McCormack.

Klisiewicz added, "They're going to intercept us before then."

"Anybody want to bet against them *not* knowing why we're here?" asked Stano, glancing over her shoulder.

"They're across their border, lurking in the same asteroid

field where we just picked up three spies on the run from the Klingon homeworld." Khatami frowned. "No bet."

"They're already within range and powering up weapons," reported Klisiewicz.

"Mister Estrada," said Khatami. "Hail them. Ask them what they think they're doing and remind them they're not in their own yard anymore."

"Too late!" It was Klisiewicz, his voice rising in alarm. "Incoming fire!"

There was no time to warn the rest of the ship to brace for impact as seconds later the ship shuddered under the force of powerful weapons slamming into the *Endeavour*'s deflector shields. Lights and consoles around the bridge flickered as energy was automatically drawn from every available system to reinforce the shield generators. The impact was enough to pull Khatami off her seat but she clamped her hands on the arms of her chair to keep her place.

"Two hits to the rear deflectors," said Klisiewicz, holding on to his console while continuing to review sensor data. "They're already down to sixty-five percent."

This is the way it's going to be? Fine.

"Bring us about," snapped Khatami. "Return fire as soon as you've got a lock. Prepare for evasive, but I want to smack them across the mouth first." She hated the idea of a fight inside the asteroid field, but the Klingons were not giving her any choice.

Before McCormack could even respond to the order, she and the rest of the bridge crew were forced to hold on as another salvo of torpedoes struck the *Endeavour*'s shields. The effects were more pronounced this time as the compromised defenses absorbed the second attack, resulting in more deck shifting and additional alarms sounding off around the bridge.

"Another hit to the rear deflectors," said Klisiewicz. "They're at forty-two percent."

Stano, now holding on to the back of McCormack's seat, said, "We're coming around."

"Fire as soon as you have a shot." Khatami smacked her chair's intercom control. "Bridge to engineering. What's with our shields?"

Over the open channel, the *Endeavour*'s chief engineer, Lieutenant Commander Yataro, replied, "*There is an issue with the aft shield generators, Captain. The asteroid field appears to be having a disruptive effect not dissimilar to what is occurring with the ship's sensors. We are rerouting power to compensate.*" Despite the obvious tension enveloping the current situation, the Lirin maintained his normal composed, even detached demeanor. "*May I suggest presenting another profile to our adversary?*"

"Thanks for the tip, Mister Yataro. Just get those shields squared away. Bridge out."

Khatami closed the connection just as Neelakanta released a barrage of phaser fire toward the Klingon cruiser. On the main viewscreen, twin beams of bright blue energy lanced across space, striking the enemy vessel's shields.

"No significant impact," reported the navigator. As he fired a second time, the warship banked to its left, gliding past the viewscreen's right edge while releasing another pair of torpedoes. Then the screen itself flickered and static distorted the image in response to the latest impact against the *Endeavour*'s shields. To his credit, Neelakanta kept pouring it on, tracking the Klingon ship with the phasers even as the other ship moved away.

Klisiewicz said, "They hit the port shields this time. Moderate damage to the Klingon's defenses."

"Adjust your course, helm." To emphasize her point, Stano reached past McCormack and tapped one set of status indicators. "Put our aft shields facing this larger asteroid." Looking over her shoulder to Khatami, she added, "Trying to buy Yataro some time. We can route power from there forward."

Khatami nodded. "Do it." At least now the *Endeavour* was protecting its compromised rear defenses, but she did not like the idea of staying inside the asteroid field any longer than was absolutely necessary.

"They're coming around again," called Klisiewicz. "Looks like they're setting up for another strafing run."

"Fire phasers," ordered Khatami.

Neelakanta's aim was true and the viewscreen depicted multiple phaser strikes against the Klingon ship's forward shields. Then Khatami saw at least one hit on the cruiser's primary hull. The warship's immediate response was to alter course, banking upward and disappearing out of the screen's frame.

"Did we get through?" asked the captain.

"Looks like a hit near their forward disruptor bank." Klisiewicz looked up from his scanner. "They're not retreating, but they're giving themselves more maneuvering room than they had before."

Before Khatami could respond, every light and console around her flickered, and there was a pronounced droning sound indicating an abrupt interruption in power to the bridge. Everyone looked up from their stations, glancing to the overhead or to Khatami or each other with mirroring expressions of confusion and concern. The effect was fleeting, and when it faded it left a litany of new alert and status indicators flashing across the room.

"Did we get hit again?" Khatami asked, already knowing the answer.

It was Klisiewicz who confirmed her suspicions. Hovering over his sensor readouts, the science officer said, "Scans are registering a new energy reading. It's not like anything I've seen before, but it's having a disruptive effect on the shields as well as other onboard systems." After a moment, he added, "Captain, I'm picking up similar reactions from the Klingon ship. Whatever this is, it's affecting them as much as it is us."

"I think they might be worse off than we are," replied Stano, and Khatami turned to see her first officer pointing to the main viewscreen. The image there depicted the enemy cruiser appearing to deviate from its intended flight path and now on a course deeper into the asteroid field.

Klisiewicz called out, "All of their primary systems appear to be offline. I'm not picking up any activity in their engines. They're drifting on momentum alone, and . . . they're on a collision course!"

No one else on the bridge said anything, all of them instead watching as the Klingon warship drifted toward one of the larger asteroids.

"Tractor beam?" asked Khatami. She considered the disparity of offering assistance so soon after exchanging hostile fire with the other vessel, but Starfleet training and values demanded she look past the previous action. What was once an adversary now required aid if she was able to provide it.

As if in response to her question, every bridge station and monitor chose that moment to blink or shut down. Some of the screens at different consoles returned, their images indicating their internal systems were resetting, while others remained dormant. Even the lighting diminished, casting the bridge into partial darkness before emergency illumination activated.

"What the hell is going on?" asked Stano.

"Continued disruption to systems across the ship, Commander," replied Klisiewicz. "Whatever it is, it's definitely external but not the result of our fight with the Klingons." Looking up from his instruments, the science officer stared at the screen. "Dear god."

Khatami rose from her chair, moving around Neelakanta's navigation console in time to watch the Klingon warship drift ever farther from the *Endeavour*. From this angle it looked as though it was plummeting toward a planet, and it was almost out of sight before she saw the impact on the asteroid's surface.

With no atmosphere, the resulting explosion was over almost before it began. Then the viewscreen was forced to lower its lighting levels as the cruiser's impact site disappeared in a blinding flash Khatami recognized as resulting from the ship's warp core detonating. The explosion's effects faded, leaving only an immense crater scarring the asteroid's dull face.

"Any signs of escape pods, shuttles, or anything else that might indicate survivors?" she asked, unable to tear her gaze from the screen.

Consulting his sensor readings, Klisiewicz said, "Nothing, Captain."

Punctuating his report was another round of alerts as different stations around the bridge suffered the effects of whatever odd disruption was wreaking havoc on the *Endeavour*'s systems. Khatami turned from the viewscreen and eyed her helm officer.

"McCormack, get us out of here. Maybe this will clear up when we're out of the field." To Klisiewicz, she said, "What's causing this?"

The science officer shook his head. "I don't know. It's a localized effect, but the sensor readings are so muddled I can't even tell if it's a natural phenomenon or something artificial."

A new alarm sounded around the bridge, followed by the voice of Commander Yataro erupting from the intercom.

"*Engineering to bridge. We are suffering a number of system disruptions, including the antimatter containment systems. If we are unable to arrest the problem, the ship is in very real danger of an uncontrolled matter/antimatter collision explosion.*"

"In nonengineering jargon," said Stano, "we're in big trouble."

Khatami asked, "What about backup systems? They can't all be affected?"

The chief engineer replied, "*Under normal circumstances I would agree with you. Our current circumstances appear to defy normality.*"

A new string of alarms sounded on the bridge, this time

originating from the engineering console. With nothing else requiring her immediate attention, Stano moved to the station and consulted one of its small status screens. Even from this angle, Khatami saw the string of warning messages, all displayed as bright red text.

"According to internal scans," said the first officer, "the disruption is affecting the warp engines. Yataro's right. This is going to get very bad very fast."

The *Endeavour* shuddered around her. Across the bridge, everyone on duty looked up from their consoles, casting frowns and expressions of worry as the omnipresent hum of the starship's warp engines changed pitch as though struggling to maintain operating at their normal reliable efficiency.

"*Bridge,*" called Commander Yataro over the still open intraship channel. "*Antimatter containment systems are continuing to deteriorate. We cannot arrest the condition. I estimate four minutes until total failure.*"

Stepping away from the engineering console, Stano eyed Khatami. "Captain," she began, but said nothing else. Instead, the first officer simply shook her head.

Khatami drew a long, deep breath as though that might be enough to steel her for the next frantic moments she and her crew were about to face.

"Commander," she said, waving to Stano. "Initiate disaster-buoy prep procedures." Moving to her command chair, she tapped another control on its arm.

"This is the captain. All hands to evacuation stations. We're abandoning ship."

Seven

The image on the conference table's three-sided viewer faded and the lights in the briefing room came up. Sitting with his hands clasped together as they rested on the table, Kirk exchanged glances with Admiral Nogura, who had said nothing since the meeting began. He remained silent as Kirk regarded the faces of his senior officers. To his right and positioned next to the table's computer interface, Spock sat with his arms folded across his chest. As always, his composed Vulcan demeanor masked whatever emotional response he may have had to the *Endeavour*'s log recording. Across from Kirk, Leonard McCoy reclined in his chair and rested his right forearm on the table. He was tapping the table in absentminded fashion with his fingers as his gaze lingered on the now deactivated screens. To the doctor's right, Montgomery Scott shifted his attention from the viewer to Kirk.

"The *Endeavour*, gone?" The engineer shook his head. "That can't be right."

"Its loss will have marked impacts on Starfleet's ability to defend Federation security interests," said Spock. "I suspect this, along with the loss of the *Defiant* last year, will also complicate Starfleet's plans to modernize the *Enterprise* and other remaining *Constitution*-class starships."

Frowning, McCoy added, "Losing the *crews* of those ships has impacts as well, Mister Spock."

"You are quite correct, Doctor," replied the Vulcan, "and it was not my intention to imply otherwise. The loss is significant both to Starfleet as well as the families of both crews."

McCoy appeared mollified by the first officer's comments, if only for a moment. "Are we certain all hands were lost when the *Endeavour* was destroyed? This log came from the disaster buoy, which was launched before the ship exploded. Is there any chance any of the crew was able to avoid that after all?"

"According to the sensor readings taken by the buoy after its launch," replied Spock, "it recorded the overload of the *Endeavour*'s warp engines. This information was received by Starfleet Command via encrypted subspace message burst."

"So, you're sending us to look for survivors?" asked McCoy. His brow furrowed as he considered his own question. "You're obviously hoping one or more of these covert agents is still alive. Did the buoy record any launching of escape pods or shuttlecraft?"

"There's something else you gentlemen need to know," said Kirk. "The log you just watched along with the rest of the sensor data recorded by the buoy was transmitted with the expectation it would be intercepted and possibly decoded by the Klingons or someone else."

Scott replied, "Aye, that's to be expected, sir, especially given where the *Endeavour* was when all of this happened, and if anyone knew why she was there."

For the first time since entering the room to take his seat next to Kirk, and after having sat as still and silent as a statue, Nogura moved. Shifting in his chair, the admiral leaned forward, laying his hands atop the conference table.

"We're unable to confirm if anyone within the Klingon Empire was aware of the *Endeavour*'s retrieval mission. Further, we don't know for certain whether the agents' presence on Qo'noS was detected prior to their rather hasty departure. Given the nature of the message sent by Morgan Binnix, she believed she and her companions were about to be exposed. We certainly can't rule out their vessel being tracked to the border, particularly when considering how quickly Captain Khatami and her crew found themselves under fire. There's always the possibility that it was just a chance encounter by a vessel patrolling their side of the border, but the Klingon captain's willingness to cross into nonaligned territory suggests they at least suspected something untoward might be afoot." Nogura paused, then nodded to Kirk.

"Captain Khatami fully expected the *Endeavour*'s movements to be tracked by those parties," said Kirk, "including someone following up to verify whether the ship was actually destroyed as its log indicates. This makes the mission Admiral Nogura's given us that much more important, and to say time's of the essence would be a criminal understatement."

His expression and body language wavering not one iota, Spock said, "The *Endeavour* was not, in fact, destroyed."

Instead of being surprised, Kirk could only offer a small, wry grin. He had expected his first officer to see through the intricacies of the little mystery handed to him by Nogura. Indeed, Spock had figured it out in record time even for his incomparable deductive reasoning skills.

For his part, Nogura seemed unfazed by the Vulcan's blunt statement. "You are correct, Commander. The *Endeavour*'s log buoy contained an additional, highly encrypted message from Captain Khatami, which only I was able to decode using retinal identification after it was received by Starfleet Command. According to the good captain, the entire crew, along with the agents they retrieved, is alive. The crew was able to separate the ship's primary hull from the engineering section and maneuver to a safe distance before the warp engines failed. They used the resulting explosion as cover to maneuver the saucer section deeper into the Ivratis asteroid field. Their present position is unknown."

"Into the field?" asked Scott. "That's a mighty bold proposition with just the saucer section to provide power to deflector shields and maneuvering thrusters. What about the impulse engines?"

Nogura replied, "The damage the ship suffered during its

skirmish with the Klingon cruiser made it difficult if not impossible for it to exit the area in order to effect any sort of rendezvous, so Captain Khatami opted to use the asteroid field as cover while awaiting rescue. We've received no further reports, but the message sent to me contains a cipher for what I believe is a means to extract additional information from the *Endeavour*'s disaster buoy, which has not yet been retrieved."

"What about the crew?" asked McCoy, who was now leaning forward in his chair. "Do we know how they're doing?"

Shaking his head, Nogura said, "We only know that all hands were successfully evacuated to the saucer section before it separated from the rest of the ship. There was no information about casualties sustained during their fight with the Klingon cruiser, but I can't imagine Captain Khatami not mentioning it if they had any critical injuries. So, while we appear to have that going for us, it doesn't mean this isn't a time-sensitive operation."

"Given the circumstances of the agents' departure from Qo'noS," said Spock, "it is logical to presume some among the upper echelons of Klingon leadership at least suspect they were infiltrated. However, I would think it was a matter they would want kept confidential to the greatest extent possible."

"That's my thinking too," replied Nogura. "And I'm hoping that translates to them restraining themselves so far as what they do to investigate what may have happened. It would be most embarrassing for it to become public knowledge that Starfleet operatives were embedded within their government and military leadership for such an extended period."

Kirk added, "If these agents are captured and broken during what would surely be a protracted and very painful interrogation process, the entire operation could be exposed. It would give the Empire the reason it needs to declare war against the Federation."

Uncrossing his arms, Spock clasped his hands before his chest. "I am familiar with certain Klingon interrogation techniques. I was able to withstand the worst of their effects thanks to my Vulcan physiology and mental discipline. It is logical to assume a similar approach would be employed against subjects of such perceived value as these agents. Given that these agents are human, I do not believe they, even if they are able to draw upon whatever training they have received to endure interrogation and even torture, would fare well against the full onslaught of such a procedure."

"So that's something we'll want to avoid," said McCoy, making no effort to hide his displeasure at the thought of being subjected to such treatment.

Scott asked, "What about the ship? The buoy's message included something about the asteroid field's disruptive effect on the *Endeavour*'s deflector shields and other systems. I know they couldn't determine with any certainty whether it was a natural phenomenon or something else, but I have to say I'm leaning toward it being 'something else.' The only thing I'm going on is the science officer's report that the effect did not start until they'd already been in the asteroid field for some time."

"I am inclined to agree with Mister Scott," said Spock. "I have no knowledge of a recurring natural phenomenon consistent with Captain Khatami's descriptions of the interference. However, without more information, it remains a hypothesis."

"Hopefully, the buoy will have that information," said Kirk, eyeing his chief engineer. "Scotty, in addition to making sure the *Enterprise* is ready in the event we run into any Klingons out there, you and Mister Spock will work together to gain an understanding of the disruption effect, and come up with a countermeasure. I don't want what happened to the *Endeavour* to happen to us."

Scott nodded. "Aye, sir. If the two of us can't figure it out, then it canna be done."

"Investigating the *Endeavour*'s disappearance will provide cover for the *Enterprise* while it's operating in the asteroid field," said Nogura. "It has the virtue of being at least partially true.

I expect the Klingons will be searching for clues to what happened to their cruiser, as well, so you'll need to be ready for the possibility of your own unpleasant encounter. However, the primary mission here is retrieving the agents and the information they've acquired."

"And the *Endeavour*'s crew, of course," added McCoy.

Frowning at the doctor's barely masked challenge, Nogura replied, "Of course, but make no mistake: The agents are the priority here. All other concerns are secondary, if it comes down to having to make that kind of decision."

"I won't leave anyone behind," said Kirk. The very idea of sacrificing any of the *Endeavour*'s crew for the sake of this mission was appalling. So long as any option remained that did not call for such drastic action, he would refuse to even entertain the notion.

"I'm not asking you to do any such thing, Captain." The admiral turned in his seat so that he faced Kirk. "But don't believe for a second I'm not capable of issuing that order." Then, his features softened. "Let's just hope I don't have to."

Kirk relaxed. "Agreed, sir."

The ship's intercom whistled for attention, followed by the sound of Lieutenant Uhura's voice filtering through the briefing room speakers.

"Bridge to Captain Kirk. We're being hailed by a civilian transport. Sensors detected its departure from Starbase 24 ten minutes ago, and its pilot is now requesting permission to land the craft on the shuttlecraft hangar deck."

Scott was the first to voice concern. "A civilian ship?"

Offering a knowing smile as he exchanged glances with Nogura, Kirk replied, "Relax, Scotty. It's a little present from the admiral."

Unlike the clean, polished shuttlecraft and other smaller Starfleet space vehicles to which Kirk was accustomed, the transport now taking up space on the *Enterprise*'s hangar deck was as ungainly a contraption as he had ever seen.

"It's not going to explode or anything, is it?" asked Scott.

McCoy snorted, "Should I check to see if the pilot survived the flight?"

"I can say with complete confidence that I have never encountered a vessel as unique as this one," said Spock.

Though Kirk said nothing, he could not take issue with his officers' comments. To him, the transport appeared as nothing more than an assemblage of random parts and other bits of scrap taken or perhaps even stolen from other, worthier vessels. Twice the length and half again as wide as a standard Starfleet shuttlecraft, the ship's hull was comprised of hull plates of varying colors, which looked to have been welded together perhaps only moments before its arrival aboard the *Enterprise*.

"Don't let her outward appearance fool you, gentlemen," said Nogura as he led the way across the hangar deck to the waiting transport. "Underneath this admittedly unremarkable exterior is a top-notch propulsion and life-support system along with an enhanced sensor suite. The only thing we didn't do was add more powerful weapons. This is still supposed to be a civilian ship, after all."

Kirk added, "The cover story is that it's a courier vessel ferrying passengers who want to avoid detection by the regular Starfleet patrols and other law enforcement entities. According to our intelligence briefings about the region, most civilian ships tend to mind their own business. That said, there's an obvious risk to running into a Klingon ship or even a pirate or raider ship. We'll have to be careful."

"We?" McCoy scowled. "Please tell me you're not flying into the middle of an asteroid field in . . ." He paused, glancing toward the transport. "In *that*."

"Don't worry, Bones," replied Kirk. "I'm not dragging you along, this time."

The doctor grunted. "My lucky day, I guess. Does it have a name?"

"Its previous designation is classified, Doctor," Nogura replied. "For now, we're calling it the *Dreamline*."

"Seems like *Nightmare* would be more appropriate."

Ignoring McCoy's comments, Kirk gestured to the transport. "Sulu will be the pilot, and Lieutenant Uhura and I will be his passengers. We'll depart the *Enterprise* well before we reach the asteroid field, after which the transport will follow a prearranged course designed to mimic a typical trajectory for a civilian ship transiting the area. Mister Spock will be in command while I'm gone; between us, we can search the asteroid field a bit faster than either of us on our own. Whoever finds the *Endeavour* first contacts the other ship, and we set to work retrieving the crew before we all get the hell out of there."

As though anticipating Scott's next question, Nogura turned to the engineer. "Commander, I promise you I'll take no offense if you wish to go over every centimeter of that ship before you're comfortable allowing Captain Kirk and his team to board it."

"Aye, sir. That I do," replied Scott, his expression one of relief. "I appreciate that."

Nogura then shifted his attention to Kirk and Spock. "And if it's not too much of a burden, I'll be accompanying you on this mission." Despite the casual way in which the statement was delivered, Kirk harbored no misconceptions that the admiral was making a simple request to tag along.

"Admiral," he said. "Are you sure that's wise? Given the security protocols Starfleet has in place regarding your movements, this seems like an unnecessary risk." Kirk gestured to Spock. "We'll obviously keep you informed every step of the way."

"Of course you will," replied Nogura. "It'll be hard not to, as I'll likely be standing on your bridge throughout all of this." When Kirk opened his mouth to rebut, the older man held up a hand. "I'm simply overseeing the search and retrieval operation. You—and Mister Spock when you're off the ship—will retain command of the *Enterprise*. This isn't a reflection on you, Captain, or your crew, or my trust in your ability to carry out this assignment. Indeed, I think yours is the ideal ship and crew for such a difficult undertaking, and if I didn't believe you were up to the task, then I'd be standing on the hangar deck of some other ship and you'd be none the wiser to the current situation. My desire to come along is much simpler than that."

He paused, casting his eyes toward the deck, and Kirk noted the uncertainty that for the first time darkened the admiral's features. No, he decided. There was something more here. An almost paternal concern? Possible, if not likely. Was there some guilt there, as well?

"I recruited the agents," said Nogura after a few seconds spent composing himself. "All three of them, along with several others dispatched to various assignments over the years. A few of those operatives never came back. They either were killed in action or else took . . . whatever measures were required to ensure the security of their mission. Binnix and her team represent the most ambitious long-term covert operation I've overseen since this program began. There's a lot at stake here, not just to Starfleet and the Federation but also them personally. I just want to be there to see this thing through to the end." He fixed his gaze on Kirk. "That's not asking too much, is it?"

Kirk shook his head. "Not at all, sir. You're obviously welcome to accompany us."

"Excellent." Nogura offered a small smile. "And thank you. I know this is a dangerous mission, gentlemen, but I have full faith in your ability to accomplish it."

We'll have to. Otherwise, we're liable to start a war with the Klingons.

Eight

If she did not know better, Atish Khatami could almost believe the reduced lighting in this section of corridor was due to it being "ship's night" rather than a simple power-saving measure. Indeed, there were no outward signs from the crew members she passed that anything was amiss. No overcrowded hallways as she always imagined a situation like this might generate, no teeming masses hoping for some scrap of food or water before supplies were exhausted. As things currently stood, the *Endeavour*'s situation was far better than it had any right to be.

Let's not tempt fate, shall we?

As she rounded a bend in the corridor, Khatami saw Doctor Anthony Leone standing along with a pair of security officers in front of the entrance to one of the cargo bays located on this level. The guards, Ensigns Kerry Zane and Sotol. Zane, a muscled, imposing human with receding blond hair and a thick mustache, would be the first to admit his companion, a slender female Vulcan with short-cropped black hair, was by far the stronger and more formidable of the two. Sotol was the first to notice Khatami's approach and she offered a formal nod in greeting.

"Captain."

Acknowledging the security officers, Khatami turned her attention to Leone. The ship's chief medical officer appeared even more tired and disinterested than was his normal habit. Lanky and with dark hair thinning on top, Leone always seemed particularly ill at ease wearing the uniform of a Starfleet officer, and tended to eschew such formalities whenever possible. This was one of those occasions, as he wore the short-sleeved blue smock favored by members of the ship's medical staff. Khatami would not have been surprised to find him partnering the casual shirt with pajama bottoms and slippers, if in fact he even bothered opting for any kind of shoes. He almost always appeared as though he had not slept in years, with large bags forever hanging beneath his brown eyes.

"Captain." Leone nodded. "Fancy meeting you here."

His comment as well as the security entourage served to remind her this was her first visit to this part of the ship since bringing aboard the *Endeavour*'s distinguished guests. The hours that had passed since then had occupied her full attention, guiding what remained of the crippled ship to its current resting place, then conferring with department heads to gather a complete status report on the condition of all onboard systems as well as every single member of the crew. Khatami was still astounded and grateful that no one had died either during the fight with the Klingons or during the emergency hull separation and subsequent hunt for a hiding place. Only a handful of treatable injuries were sustained by members of the crew.

Small favors. I'll take them wherever I can find them.

"Tony," she said by way of greeting. "Everything all right?"

The doctor frowned. "So far as I know. You'll be happy to hear I've discharged the last of the injured from sickbay and sent them to their quarters for bed rest. I recommended twenty-four hours, but I understand if that needs to be cut short given the circumstances."

"I trust your judgment. Right now, rest is probably the best thing for as many of us as possible. It'll conserve resources, if nothing else."

While the *Endeavour*'s impulse engines could operate at full capabilities and generate power to support the primary hull and everyone in it for weeks, Khatami had opted for a conservation protocol just to be on the safe side. She gave silent thanks that the saucer section was already capable of sustaining the entire crew. The main requirements while the ship operated on impulse power were life-support and food, which meant reducing or even eliminating power to all but essential systems. Priority usage was reserved for the engineering and medical staffs, but even the latter's needs were minimal thanks to the small number of casualties suffered during the encounter with the Klingon warship. Lieutenant Commander Yataro and his team were operating out of the auxiliary engineering room located near the impulse deck at the rear of the ship, immersed in assessing damage not just from the fight but also their escape from the *Endeavour's* secondary hull before it exploded and the subsequent maneuvering and landing within the Ivratis asteroid field.

Finding a hiding place for what remained of the ship proved a tall order, with Lieutenant Marielise McCormack using every scrap of helm expertise at her command to guide the saucer section to a soft landing deep in the corner of a canyon on one of the larger asteroids. She had even found an area with a depression spacious enough to provide something of a cradle for the saucer, preventing significant damage to the underside of its outer hull. The result was that the primary section now rested with nearly its entire ventral hull below the canyon floor's surface. Having found a home, as makeshift as it might be, Khatami was counting on the same background interference that had so disrupted the ship's sensors and communications to now serve as a shield against anyone discovering their location. Of course, this would also complicate matters when Admiral Nogura sent someone to find them, but that was a problem that could be solved in due course. For that, she was leaning on Commander Yataro and Lieutenant Hector Estrada to come through with, respectively, their own engineering and communications miracles to see the crew through their current troubles.

Trust your people, Atish. They'll find a way.

"How are our guests?" she asked.

Leone replied, "It took me a bit to remove all the transponders they're fitted with so I could conduct proper physicals, but all three of them are healthy." He frowned. "They still look like Klingons, of course, but there's not much I can do about that. I mean, I could, but the time it'd take to carry out surgeries on all three of them and the power requirements for sickbay during all of that and post-operative care?" He shook his head. "They can wait until we're back home."

"You sound awfully confident we'll be getting back home." Khatami punctuated her comment with a wry smile. "Who are you and what've you done with the real Anthony Leone?"

The doctor grimaced. "A moment of optimistic weakness. I'll be back to my doom-and-gloomy self after I've had dinner." He gestured toward the door. "Anyway, since this is your first time meeting them, I wanted you to be ready."

"I've seen Klingons before, Tony. Even ones who didn't want to kill me."

"And thank you for making my point." Leone gestured to the cargo bay entrance. "They're *not* Klingons. They never were. They're humans, surgically altered and highly trained to pass themselves off as Klingons. At great personal risk to themselves, I might add. They've just left an environment where even the simplest slipup could have been fatal, so they trained to talk, write, and even think like a Klingon. Even if I was able to undo what was done to their bodies, that kind of intense training and immersive, dangerous assignment they just completed won't simply go away."

Khatami frowned, realizing she had fallen into some kind of subconscious trap about Morgan Binnix and her fellow agents. How had she let that happen? She had yet to even meet the operatives, and yet she had allowed herself to somehow view them as something other than what they were. What of other members of her crew who had actually interacted with Binnix and the others? Had they made the same mistake?

"You're saying it's going to take time for them to adjust, and they'll need plenty of help and support to do that."

"Exactly." Leone rubbed his jaw. "If everything had gone to plan, they'd be on their way to a Starfleet medical facility set up to take care of everything. Now they're stuck here with an entire starship crew that doesn't even know why they were diverted to an asteroid field in the first place, let alone why we ended up fighting Klingons and crashing our ship into a ditch."

"You're right. How the hell did I not see that sooner?" This was something Khatami would need to address quickly, particularly given the current situation. Her crew deserved to know the full truth about the predicament in which they now found themselves. Further, it was unreasonable to keep the agents confined to the quarantine facility now that the retrieval operation had become so complicated. There was no way to know how long they would have to wait for rescue, and Binnix and her companions might well be able to contribute in some fashion toward keeping the ship and crew safe until help arrived.

Sighing, Leone reached out and patted her arm. "Don't be too hard on yourself, Captain. You've kind of had your hands full these last couple of hours."

"That's no excuse," countered Khatami.

The doctor eyed her with skepticism. "Show me the chapter in the manual that covers this situation and all the variables tossed your way, and I'll back off. Until then? As your friend and chief medical officer, I'm prescribing you one piece of slack. Use as directed."

Until this point, Ensign Zane had said nothing, but Khatami caught the small smile teasing the corners of his mouth before he brought his features back under control. It was enough to make the captain realize she had perhaps been a bit unforgiving of herself these past hours.

"Very well, Doctor. Consider your prescription filled." She gestured to the cargo bay entrance. "Care to introduce me to our guests?"

Sotol entered a code on a keypad set into the bulkhead next to the entry, and the heavy, reinforced double hatch parted to reveal the makeshift quarantine facility assembled by Leone and a team of engineers and members of his medical staff. The cargo bay had been outfitted with a trio of field shelters of the sort used by colonists or survey parties tasked with spending extended periods on a planet's surface. A common area linked the three shelters and included a pair of sofas along with two recliners and a small table with its own tri-sided viewer. Another area to the side harbored a dining table. Beyond that was a small field medical setup where Leone and his team conducted their evaluations of the three agents.

Three individuals, a woman and two men—dressed in the standard red Starfleet jumpsuits worn in lieu of duty uniforms when work demanded more practical attire—rose to their feet upon seeing Khatami enter the bay. Their uniforms only served to make their alien visages that much more prominent. Their dark olive complexions along with black hair as well as the men's beards and mustaches were impressive. Lacking sufficient information, Khatami had every reason to believe she was standing before three Klingons.

"Captain Khatami," said the woman, who stepped forward and extended her hand. "I'm Morgan Binnix. It's nice to finally meet you. I can't thank you enough for coming to get us." Her expression faltered. "I'm also very sorry things took the turn they did."

Accepting the proffered handshake, Khatami replied, "Things taking odd turns are a way of life aboard the *Endeavour*, Ms. Binnix." She paused, then added, "I'm sorry. I don't even know your rank."

Binnix smiled. "That's because such information is classified." She leaned closer and when she spoke again it was with a conspiratorial whisper. "It's commander, though."

She introduced her companions, Phillip Watson and David Horst, after which Leone excused himself and headed toward the facility's medical bay. This left the agents alone with Khatami, who gestured toward the seating area.

"Admiral Nogura only gave me the high points about your assignment," she said after everyone found places among the sofas and chairs. "From what I gather, your role was mostly information gathering."

It was Watson who replied, "Mostly, though there were a few occasions when we were able to be a bit more proactive. Every so often, the opportunity to plant disinformation presented itself." He nodded to Binnix. "That was more her purview, given her position working for Councilor Maroq, but Horst and I were able to get in on the act, every once in a while."

"My role was on a design team," said Horst. "Computer, communications, and power distribution networks, that sort of thing. My former role in Starfleet was as a software design specialist, so I made myself familiar with Klingon design methodologies. I spent a lot of my time identifying ways for these systems to be exploited. Trying to sabotage anything at the design or construction stage carried too much risk, but there's not a lot about the internal workings of the newest class of battle cruiser that I don't know. I kept very detailed records of everything I worked on for our protected archive."

Binnix said, "I used my position to gather information related to government policy and strategic military planning. I can tell you everything about the Empire's plans for increasing access to much-needed natural resources, and how they intend to engage various enemies. Obviously the Federation is high on that list, but they've got scenarios for taking on everyone from the Romulans to the Tholians to the Gorn and even a handful of nonaligned regions in a bid to expand their borders. Some of those aren't of much consequence from a Federation perspective, while others are more concerning from a long-term view. For example, if the Klingons extend their territory in certain directions, then in a few years they might be in a position to launch multipronged attacks into Federation space that we'd be hard-pressed to defend against."

"There's nothing in any of the latest intelligence reports to suggest this," said Khatami.

Watson replied, "There wouldn't be. This is very protected information. We're talking compartmented to such a degree that fewer than ten people even know about it." He indicated Binnix and Horst with a wave. "Not counting us, of course. If any of this made it to a Starfleet intelligence brief, the Klingons would know they had spies deep in their inner circle. To that end, all we could do is collect the information and hope to dispatch it back to Nogura or whoever when we could."

Khatami eyed the man. "And what did you do?"

"Infrastructure." Watson shifted on the sofa so that he leaned forward with his elbows resting on his knees as he faced her. "Domestic energy production, primarily for military use but also the civilian populace, as well. The Klingons have always been hampered by limited natural resources, both on Qo'noS and a large number of planets within the Empire. It's been a key driver for expanding their sphere of influence, but their military machine is a perpetuating cycle of need and exploitation. Their avenues of expansion are curtailed by the borders of neighboring interstellar powers, and the directions open to them don't offer much in the way of resource-rich star systems."

"So, all of this will come to a head sooner rather than later," said Horst. "If they can't find what they need elsewhere, they'll start looking to take it from someone else. That will only get more serious as they continue to deplete their own native resources."

Rubbing his hands together, Watson said, "Speaking of which, you know about Praxis, the moon orbiting Qo'noS? At the rate they're ripping minerals out of there without regard for safety or environmental impact, they're about twenty, maybe thirty years at the outside from an irreversible catastrophe." When Khatami asked him to elaborate, the engineer used his hands to indicate a rapidly expanding explosion.

"Do they know?" asked the captain.

"I don't think they believe it," replied Binnix. "Or, they think they have a handle on it, or they'll somehow get a handle on it. The public certainly doesn't know, and it's another of those things we didn't dare leak back to Admiral Nogura, but I've seen Phil's projections." Instead of saying anything further, she simply shook her head.

Despite the fact the Klingons had been a mortal enemy of the Federation for more than a century, Khatami could not help feeling a pang of concern upon hearing this news. If what the agents described came to pass, it might mean annihilation for everyone living on Qo'noS. The Empire would be crippled. The seemingly endless state of hostilities that existed between it and the Federation would become moot. While the idea of no longer having to worry about war with the Klingons was an attractive prospect, this was not the way to achieve that goal.

"And Nogura doesn't know about this?" she asked.

Binnix replied, "Not yet." She nodded her head in the direction of an equipment locker situated near the entrance to Leone's medical area. "The details of that and so many other things are locked in those encrypted storage crystals. Your chief engineer, Mister Yataro, has already scanned them as part of our initial debrief and examinations, and determined they're completely safe and totally uncooperative so far as trying to open them. Only Nogura can access the information they hold, once they're in his possession."

"Until then, they're just really nice paperweights," added

Horst, "but after that? There's enough material on those things to make Starfleet Intelligence lose sleep every night for a decade."

Before Khatami could respond to that, the doors to the cargo bay opened, this time to admit Lieutenant Commander Yataro. A Lirin, the *Endeavour*'s chief engineer was slight of build, with a bulbous head sitting atop a long, thin neck. Hairless, his lavender skin looked oily beneath the bay's stark lighting. Large, dark blue eyes regarded Khatami as she rose from her chair to greet him.

"Captain," he said as he approached before indicating Binnix and her companions with a nod. "I apologize for the interruption, but you wanted me to keep you informed of our damage-control efforts."

"Indeed I did, Mister Yataro. I take it you have something new to report?"

The engineer replied, "We have completed a survey of the entire hull and found no significant damage, either from our encounter with the Klingon ship or from our emergency landing maneuver. Lieutenant McCormack is to be commended for her skill in accomplishing a most impressive feat."

"We can save the commendation write-ups for a later time, Commander," said Khatami. "What else have you got?"

Unfazed by the captain's statement, Yataro continued, "As I indicated when we first landed, the asteroid field's background radiation continues to disrupt our sensors and communications. Without the warp engines to increase power to these systems, our ability to detect approaching vessels is severely compromised."

"I'm guessing the same disruptions affecting our equipment will do the same for anyone looking for us?" asked Khatami.

"That is correct, Captain. However, the same thing keeping us hidden from potential adversaries also camouflages us from detection by anyone hoping to effect our rescue. As things currently stand, we may miss contact with any search vessels. With that in mind, Lieutenant Estrada and my team have formulated a plan to address the issue. We propose deploying a small number of sensor buoys along the outer edges of the canyon in which the ship now rests, which could act as boosters for our sensors and communications array. If properly configured, they may also help to counteract the background interference, at least to a partial extent. To accomplish this, the buoys will have to be positioned at a specific distance from the *Endeavour* as well as one another."

From where she stood a few paces behind Khatami, Binnix said, "That sounds like an EVA job."

"I estimate that a team of twelve personnel can successfully deploy four buoys in the required manner and in the least amount of time," replied Yataro.

Although she was not enamored with the idea of sending any of her people onto the surface of an asteroid about which they knew little thanks to their compromised sensors, Khatami understood the only way to improve things on that front was to embrace unwelcome ideas. There might also be other benefits to Yataro's proposed course of action.

"Do you think you can boost power to the comm system enough for us to make contact with the disaster buoy?" she asked. "Maybe find out if the message we sent was received?"

Yataro cocked his head as though considering that notion for the first time. "Based on the data provided by Lieutenant Tomkins, I believe that may be possible, Captain."

"Tomkins?" Khatami recalled what she knew of Lieutenant Ivan Tomkins; one of the newer members of Yataro's team, the young engineer had distinguished himself early on during the *Endeavour*'s mission to Cantrel V to assist a Federation research colony. The personnel reports submitted by Yataro since the lieutenant's arrival portrayed him as a capable young officer with unlimited growth potential. "This was his idea?"

The Lirin nodded. "Indeed it was, Captain. I was skeptical at first, but Mister Tomkins proved quite persuasive. I believe this task is well within our capabilities."

That was enough to convince her. "Your plan's approved, Commander. Prepare your team and head out whenever you're ready."

"I might be able to help, Captain," said Horst, who had moved to stand next to Binnix. "I've got some experience with field communications systems similar to those used in the buoys."

Watson added, "I'd like to pitch in, too, if you can use another set of hands."

"Your assistance would be most welcome, gentlemen," replied the engineer before looking to Khatami. "Provided there are no objections."

"I know we're supposed to be in quarantine, Captain," said Binnix, "but that doesn't really seem to make much sense now. We're three able bodies. Let us help."

Khatami replied, "I'm not about to turn away any help I can get. I accept and appreciate your offer. The rest of the crew will need to be briefed on you, of course. Seeing you wandering about the ship is liable to turn some heads."

Binnix offered a wry smile. "For the first time in a very long time, Captain, I'm actually okay with the extra attention."

Nine

The small civilian freighter dominated the image on the command deck's forward viewscreen. It drifted, not quite tumbling, but in danger of doing so if left unchecked. D'zinn had no intention of letting that happen, of course. While the ship itself looked to be of little value, its cargo would more than make up for the effort expended by D'zinn and her crew to capture it.

"Verify life signs," she snapped without taking her eyes off the screen. Hands folded across her chest, she continued to study the inert vessel, which showed no signs of functionality.

"Scans detect three life readings," reported Melac from the cramped sensor station to her left. The muscled Orion male looked as though he might spill out of the chair that was almost too small for his physique. Bare arms extended from the sleeveless tunic he wore stretched across his broad chest, ending with large hands that played across the comparatively fragile-looking sensor control console. "Two Andorians and a Rigelian. The ship itself has no weapons, but I cannot believe they are completely unarmed."

D'zinn shrugged. "It will not matter." Preliminary scans showed the freighter was largely automated, with the minimal crew likely present only for launches, landings, and the occasional maintenance task while in flight. She guessed they spent the rest of their time sleeping, getting fat on whatever foodstuffs sustained them during their voyages, or drinking. If they did anything else to pass the hours, she did not want to know about it. The important thing was that they posed little if any threat. Indeed, D'zinn suspected they were at this moment formulating a plan for peaceful surrender and perhaps even assisting in the transfer of their cargo from the freighter to her ship, the *Vekal Piltari*.

"Netal," she said, turning from the viewscreen to face her second-in-command. "Prepare a boarding party. I want the cargo moved as quickly as possible."

Another exquisite specimen of the best the males of her species had to offer, Netal regarded her with dark green eyes looking out from beneath a heavy brow. The green skin of his hairless scalp reflected the command deck's subdued lighting, as did his chest, which was bare save for the pair of bandoliers he wore in crisscross fashion around his torso. An effective overseer on her behalf of the *Vekal Piltari*'s crew, he was obedient and loyal to her almost to a fault, always conducting himself in a professional manner, particularly in front of subordinates. In private, D'zinn allowed him to demonstrate his fealty in a number of other ways, most of them to her continuing satisfaction. While others in his position might use their station to undermine their captain for their own personal gain, Netal had never shown such inclinations. Like almost every other member of her crew, he had earned her trust.

Nodding in response to her instructions, he said, "It will be done, D'zinn. And what of the crew?"

"If they do not resist, make sure no harm comes to them." Then, she frowned. "If any of them *do* resist, kill them all. Make sure they understand that from the start, but also ensure they comprehend the good fortune we are extending to them." Unlike others who made their living as pirates and privateers working for the Orion Syndicate, D'zinn had never seen the need to inflict harm so long as other options remained. Her current employer had scoffed at this notion, but she was immovable on the subject. On the other hand, the safety of her crew was of paramount importance. To her, an attack on any of them was an attack on all of them and required answering in the strongest possible terms. She knew her reputation on this front was well known among other Syndicate ship masters, earning her no small amount of derision, but she did not care. It was this attitude that engendered her crew to follow her wherever she might lead, and to her that was of more value than any percentage of profit she might lose due to her leniency.

Netal moved to the rear of the command deck, the doors ahead of him parting to grant him access to the corridor beyond. As he left, he was passed by another member of the ship's crew entering the control center. An older male and more slender than many of his shipmates, he nevertheless remained in excellent physical condition for one of his greater years. A single strip of gray hair adorned his otherwise bald head, and unlike his younger counterparts he preferred not taut shirts or flaunting bare muscles but instead wrapping his body in a rich blue tunic tucked into tailored black pants. A wide leather belt circled his waist, and his polished black boots rose to a point just below his knees. His right earlobe was adorned with a gold hoop that matched the one piercing his left nostril. Normally a person of good cheer, on this occasion his expression was almost unreadable.

"Tath," said D'zinn, smiling at her friend's arrival. "You seem particularly troubled today." She gestured to the viewscreen and its image of the freighter. "You should be happy."

"Oh, I am," replied her engineer. "The new configurations for our sensors worked flawlessly. The other ship's crew had no idea we were closing on them until it was too late, and by then the disruption field had wreaked havoc on their own onboard systems. All in all, it made for a very easy seizure of the freighter."

Gesturing for Tath to walk with her, D'zinn exited the command deck and entered the corridor on her way to her quarters. "And yet I sense something still concerns you."

Tath glanced behind and ahead of them, as though ensuring no one else might overhear them. "This new technology the Klingons are developing is quite interesting, but I worry about the role we are playing in its testing. For now, our participation is convenient, as it allows the Klingons to remain anonymous while putting forth the fiction that what they have developed is in fact a mysterious effect of the asteroid field."

"This area is largely avoided except for those in our chosen profession," said D'zinn. "It is also mostly uncharted, so there is no way to thoroughly discount the possibility of the field possessing the very characteristics this technology is attempting to mimic. By the time anyone suspects anything untoward occurring here, the Klingons will have finished their research efforts and gone back to their Empire."

"And what of us?" asked Tath. "When our usefulness is at an end, will the Klingons allow us to return to our normal ventures? It seems to me it is in their best interests to ensure we are unable to reveal the truth about their technology."

D'zinn said nothing as they turned at an intersection in the corridor. She had considered the potential for something like her friend described, but discounted it as unlikely. "This is not the first time the Klingon Empire has engaged in clandestine business with the Syndicate. For all their posturing, they are eager to avoid their activities becoming known to the Federation until the appropriate time. This is one of those occasions. By the time Starfleet is aware of this new technology and the challenge it presents, it will be deployed aboard far more Klingon warships and forward operating outposts than can easily be countered."

After being approached by her contact within the Syndicate about this proposal of working with a group of Klingon scientists wanting to test a new form of technology designed to disrupt the onboard systems of enemy vessels, D'zinn was intrigued. The idea, as presented to her, offered substantial opportunities to increase her personal wealth and the financial status of her crew, to say nothing of her standing within the Syndicate. It was a simple plan, with the Klingons providing her the necessary safeguards to protect the *Vekal Piltari* from the disruption-field generator's harmful effects while it was aimed at other vessels traversing the region.

The Ivratis asteroid field was a popular route for smugglers, privateers, and others who preferred to travel while avoiding scrutiny. This meant the watchful eye of Starfleet or Klingon border patrols, who tended to avoid the region due to its existing background radiation, which had an actual effect on sensors and other delicate systems. The field was therefore an ideal testing ground for the Klingon scientists eager to put their new invention through its paces, and allowing the *Vekal Piltari* and a few other Orion vessels to operate in the area—reporting on the disruption technology's effects on other ships as well as the effectiveness of her ship's system upgrades—was a simple task. D'zinn and her crew, along with the crews of the other pirate vessels, were rewarded for their efforts by being free to plunder any ships unfortunate enough to find themselves in the asteroid field and subjected to the Klingons' experiments.

A cozy arrangement, D'zinn admitted. *We should enjoy it while we can.*

They arrived at her quarters and she entered a code into the door's keypad, granting her access. Tath followed her into the opulent suite of oversized rooms that was her private sanctuary aboard the *Vekal Piltari*. Ornate, multicolored tapestries lined the walls, which along with a thick beige carpet and silk veils suspended from the ceiling worked to disguise the fact that this was not a luxury apartment on the homeworld but instead a pair of the ship's retrofitted storage bays. A plush, dark-maroon sofa arranged in a near complete circle was the front room's dominant furnishing, surrounding a round low table forged from obsidian glass. Behind the sofa was a small yet well-appointed kitchen featuring both cooking appliances as well as a food slot. D'zinn preferred to cook her meals whenever time allowed. Better still, she liked it when opportunity afforded her a companion to cook for her.

Following her motion toward the sofa, Tath settled himself there while she retrieved a bottle of her favorite wine and two glasses from the kitchen. The engineer fancied the same brand, and was the only person aboard the ship with whom she shared her personal stock.

"I am not concerned about the Klingons reneging on us," she said as she poured for them both before setting the bottle on the table. Settling onto the sofa, she tucked her legs under herself. "Even if they decided to take action against us, others within the Syndicate are aware of their activities, and would not allow such a betrayal to stand unchallenged. That is our insurance policy. If we reveal their presence here, so close to Federation territory, it would set off a firestorm within the Federation Council, with the Klingons' actions being viewed as espionage if not an outright act of war."

"We may already be past such a declaration," countered Tath. He drank from his wineglass, closing his eyes in obvious satisfaction. "We know the scientists working here are operating from within the Empire's intelligence apparatus, and their efforts are classified even from most members of the High Council. The chancellor will be able to convincingly disavow all knowledge of these experiments and their associated border violations, but that does not alleviate the problem with what happened to the Federation starship and the Klingon cruiser. The loss of these vessels will undoubtedly compel both sides to send additional ships to investigate. While I have my doubts about the ability of the average Klingon warship's captain and crew to discover what is happening here, Starfleet is more than capable of investigating and learning the truth."

D'zinn finished her wine before reaching for the bottle and

replenishing her glass. "At which time, the good fortune we have been enjoying to this point will be over." She paused, studying the glass in her hand as she swirled its contents. "After that? It is entirely possible the Federation and Klingon Empire may go to war with each other, and we will be in the best position to watch it all unfold before our very eyes."

Ten

The tankard sailed across the room, slamming into the stone wall and shattering into uncounted pieces. Its contents splattered everywhere, staining the wall and running downward in rivulets as the cup's shrapnel fell to the floor.

It was not nearly enough to assuage Kesh's mounting fury. He stalked around the room and felt his anger rising with every passing moment. The low-level, crimson-hued lighting from recessed panels and augmented by the flames from torches positioned at regular intervals along the chamber's walls only served to heighten his aggravation.

"Spies, walking among us. Working and living among us. Trusted to keep our most guarded secrets, and no one ever suspected a thing. How was this allowed to happen?"

The other members of the Klingon High Council stood in silence, watching their chancellor storm about the storied hall, which had served as the center of the Empire since the dawn of what now was known as modern Klingon civilization. It was the greatest honor of Kesh's life that he had been called to serve in this capacity, and not so much as a single day had passed where he did not feel pride swell within him upon entering this most hallowed of chambers.

Until today.

"How have we so utterly failed the Empire? What has brought us to this? Incompetence? Laziness? Perhaps there are those among us who are as corrupt as those we allowed into our midst." He paused his pacing of the room's perimeter, turning to face the other council members. All of them stared back at him, their faces offering to him expressions of confusion, shock, and fear. These were supposed to be the foremost Klingons in all the Empire, chosen for their proven abilities to lead and their demonstrated desire to guide all Klingons ever forward on a path of prosperity and conquest. Some of them Kesh had known from childhood. A few he had served with as a young soldier in the Klingon Defense Force.

One, Novek, was his oldest and closest friend, and a warrior to whom Kesh had entrusted his very life, and he would do so again without hesitation. Indeed, Novek had nearly given his own life in defense of Kesh's more than once over the course of careers that seemed inextricably linked. Kesh had come to know him while serving as a junior officer aboard the *I.K.S. Sorvilan*, where Novek was posted as a tactical officer. The older Klingon became a mentor, guiding Kesh through the tumultuous learning curve that every young soldier faced after graduating from the military academy. Never one to seek glory or a command of his own, Novek carried out his duties while Kesh and others gained promotions and ever more demanding assignments. Upon receiving orders for his first command, Kesh selected Novek as his second, a position from which the older Klingon never strayed even after his friend left the military and sought political office. With his wife having died years earlier, Kesh looked to Novek for counsel more than anyone else alive. Despite his age and the gray that had replaced his once long, black hair, time had dulled neither Novek's fierce warrior spirit nor his loyalty to the Empire.

Their eyes met, and Novek nodded to him in that subtle way Kesh knew meant his friend once again supported him and would do anything to carry out whatever orders he received from the chancellor who also was his lifelong friend.

"Well?" Kesh barked the single word. To their credit, none of the other council members flinched or otherwise reacted defensively to the unspoken accusation. If they had, he might well have drawn his *d'k tagh* from the sheath along his left hip and killed each of them. Removing a member of the High Council in such blunt fashion was not a regular occurrence, but neither was it without precedent. So raw was his fury that Kesh cared not at all for whatever conventions governed acceptable behavior even within these walls.

"Chancellor," said Shuuq, another of the councilors. "We are still attempting to discern what happened, as well as the extent of their activities. From what I was told this morning, the spies were here for quite some time. They would have had ample opportunity to insert themselves into any number of sensitive areas, both within the government and the military. Indeed, based on what I have gathered, there may well be other such agents operating on Qo'noS as we speak. This is something we will have to devote tremendous resources to investigate, so that we can find and contain this infection before it is allowed to spread any further."

"You have spent too much time sitting across a table from Earther diplomats," said Kesh, not bothering to subdue his contempt. "You talk as they do. Perhaps your thoughts have become polluted by too much exposure to those who speak for our enemies."

As one might expect, Shuuq bristled at the remark as well as its deeper implications. One of the council's younger members, he was nevertheless a proud Klingon, dressed impeccably in the robes and sash denoting his position. His black hair fell beneath his shoulder blades, secured at the base of his neck with a leather band. What his ensemble lacked were the decorations and awards and even weapons of a warrior who had seen battle. Unlike several of his contemporaries here, Shuuq had never served in the Defense Force, owing to some heart defect that in another, less enlightened time would have been a death sentence before he even reached adolescence. Despite this setback, he had devoted his entire adult life to serving the Empire in other ways. Kesh's predecessor, Sturka, had seen Shuuq's value early on, assigning him the sort of diplomatic and oversight duties many warriors tended to disdain. His record in this regard was exemplary and was the primary reason Kesh, after assuming the role of chancellor only months earlier, requested he remain on the council. His insights, forged not in the heat of battle but elsewhere and against many of the same adversaries Kesh had faced, were different enough from those of his counterparts that he had proven to be a valuable asset.

None of this meant Shuuq was a coward, and when he spoke again Kesh heard the barely controlled contempt lacing the other Klingon's words.

"Are we to spend the day trading insults, Chancellor, or devoting our energies to seeking solutions to the problems we now face?"

Instead of responding in kind, Kesh offered a small, knowing grin. "You speak the truth, Shuuq." He had never truly liked the councilor, owing to his penchant for spending inordinate amounts of time conferring with counterparts within the governments of the Federation and other interstellar powers. Still, that predilection had proven useful on occasion, which was why Kesh had not yet opted to remove Shuuq from the council. Indeed, he was pleased to see the other Klingon refusing to accept the harsh and possibly unfair words thrown his way. It was a rare display of fortitude toward a superior, and one Kesh welcomed.

There may well be hope for you after all.

"These spies," Kesh said as he resumed pacing around the chamber's perimeter. "Kvaal, Liska, and Toraq. What do we know about them?" He was now abreast of the throne that was his to occupy, but he paid it no heed. He was in no mood to sit idle, preferring to move around while trying to harness his thoughts. The activity also helped to subdue his emotions.

Focus, Chancellor, he told himself.

Shuuq replied, "Kvaal was assigned to one of our main energy-production facilities. Not just for the First City but across the planet. His role saw to it he had knowledge of all the energy requirements for military bases as well as civilian population centers." The Klingon frowned. "By itself, this seems innocuous, but then one realizes he likely was aware of the energy demands for our orbital dock and ship-construction facilities, including the ships currently being built there. He would have known about power requirements for vessels undergoing tests in preparation for launch, which means access to technical schematics and other sensitive information."

One of the other council members, Di'natri, stepped forward. Like the majority of those in the room, he was also a former soldier elevated to his current position after a long career in the Defense Force. Unlike Kesh, Novek, and a few others, he had never served aboard a warship but instead was posted as an infantry officer to the imperial ground forces. The experience shaped a perspective different from Kesh's, making Di'natri a valuable source of alternative insight. However, he could also be an insufferable boor, and on more than one occasion Kesh had imagined various unpleasant demises for him.

"Toraq presents a different kind of concern," said Di'natri. "Like Kvaal, he was not a soldier but instead a computer and communications engineer. He was heavily involved in the design of the systems to be installed aboard the *K'tinga*-class warships. According to what his superiors have forwarded for our review, there is very little about these systems that Toraq did not know. Indeed, he was one of their leading architects."

This took Kesh by surprise. "Do you mean to tell me that this spy—this *traitor*—so insinuated himself into that effort that he actually contributed to the creation of the very systems we will one day use against our enemies?" The very idea was maddening. What kind of vulnerabilities had this *petaQ* sown into the Empire's newest class of battle cruiser, which was being developed as a means of countering the Federation's most powerful vessels?

"Supervisors have ordered a complete review of the system design," said Di'natri. "So far, they have found no evidence of any deliberate undermining of the software responsible for controlling these systems. However, an engineer of Toraq's apparent skill would have knowledge of any design strengths and weaknesses."

"Which he could then convey to those overseeing his espionage activities," replied Kesh. He could feel his anger once more beginning to rise. One did not have to sabotage an enemy vessel if one already knew its vulnerabilities. "This means our most powerful warships could be compromised before they ever leave their construction docks."

Di'natri nodded. "That is unfortunately true. However, supervisors overseeing the effort assure me that any points for exploitation can eventually be identified and remedied." His expression fell. "Unfortunately, that is likely to be a time-consuming process."

"There is one small bit of encouraging news," said Novek. "The agent's duties were limited to work on systems being incorporated into the *K'tinga* warships. While there is no denying his presence on the project is cause for alarm, we can take some comfort in the knowledge he apparently was unable to secure any damaging information about our existing ships or our other space- or planet-based installations." He moved toward Kesh. "I have instructed his supervisors to conduct a thorough examination of any files or records to which Toraq may have had access during his tenure. It is another task that will take some time to complete."

Shuuq said, "While those efforts may show that Toraq's

activities, however costly to the Empire they may be, pale in comparison to those of the third agent, Liska."

At the mention of the Klingon woman's name, all eyes in the room turned to focus on Maroq. The oldest member of the High Council, he was like several of his companions a politician whose career began as a brash young military officer. Having lost his own wife to illness some years earlier, the elder Klingon's grief over time turned into a predilection for drinking and cavorting with younger women. It was a well-known facet of his personality, and for the most part, Maroq was disciplined enough to conduct such frivolities out of the public eye. So far as Kesh knew, he had never allowed this behavior to interfere with his duties. Indeed, many tended to dismiss the activities, but now Kesh wondered if this may have been his weakness.

"This female," said Kesh, moving closer to the elder Klingon. "Was she but another of your distractions? Perhaps she used your susceptibility and lack of awareness and discretion to burrow ever deeper into our affairs."

Shaking his head, Maroq replied, "No, Chancellor. She was an assistant, nothing more." He paused, casting his gaze to the chamber's stone floor. "I admit I attempted to entice her, on many occasions, but it never went beyond that."

"I commend her on her selective nature," snapped Novek. "Or, I suspect she fended off your clumsy advances. What better way to take advantage of the opportunities your activities provided her while you were off satisfying your personal needs rather than protecting the security of the Empire."

Maroq glared at him. "You dare question my loyalty?"

"To your glands? Never." Novek pointed an accusatory finger at him. "But what exactly was this spy doing while you were away debasing yourself? To what vital information did she have access?" When Maroq started to protest, Novek cut him off. "Your response is not required. I already have my answer. A review of the data logs shows numerous entries to protected files regarding military planning and council policy directives. Our plans for border expansion. Strategic outlines for how to deal with the Federation, the Romulans, and numerous other threats to the Empire. If she acquired copies of that data, her handlers will have knowledge of everything we have been developing. The damage may well be insurmountable."

Without warning, Novek's other hand, which until now Maroq thought was simply tucked into the sash he wore across his chest, emerged from the garment along with his *d'k tagh*. The knife's blade gleamed even in the council chamber's muted lighting. Before Kesh or anyone else could voice a protest, Novek slung the weapon across the space separating him from Maroq.

The knife sank to its hilt in the Klingon's throat, and Kesh even saw the point of the blade emerge from the back of the elder councilor's neck. Maroq's eyes bulged in surprise and he reached with both hands for the knife's handle as blood poured from the wound and down across his chest. Distressed gurgling sounds escaped his mouth and throat, and he sagged to his knees, falling forward and slumping in an unmoving heap onto the chamber floor.

Silence gripped the remaining council members, and Kesh waited for someone—anyone—to step toward Maroq's body. Instead, everyone watched the pool of blood expanding from beneath the fallen Klingon as it discolored the stone on which he lay. After several moments, it became obvious no one would be taking the lead in any sort of traditional death ritual. None of the council members, Kesh included, felt compelled to take charge of Maroq's spirit or turn to the sky and announce the imminent arrival of another warrior at the gates of Sto-Vo-Kor. Maroq had proven himself unworthy of such an honor, and therefore would have to navigate the afterlife on his own. Even Novek made no such attempt, instead bending over the fallen Klingon long enough to remove his *d'k tagh*. A single tug was enough to extract the knife with a slick sucking sound, after which Novek wiped the blood from its blade across Maroq's tunic and returned the weapon to its place beneath his own sash.

"He was a fool," said Novek. "Let his idiocy bring no further shame to the Empire."

Though he agreed with his friend's sentiment, Kesh could not bring himself to celebrate Maroq's demise. For all his faults, he had been a loyal member of the council, offering unwavering support both for his chancellorship and an agenda designed to advance the prosperity of the Klingon people. None of that excused his personal lapses and neither did it mitigate whatever damage his inattention may have allowed to occur, but it was not as though Maroq had been a proponent of evil or corruption. There were more than enough Klingons who personified such failings, whereas his ultimately fatal flaw was one of simple incompetence.

Di'natri notified a pair of guards stationed outside the chamber to remove Maroq's body for disposal while the rest of the council members began murmuring amongst themselves. Only Novek moved toward Kesh, always alert for any sign his friend might require advice or guidance. Before he could voice any question, Kesh's attention was caught by the appearance of one of his aides entering the room. The young Klingon was carrying a data tablet and crossed the chamber in long, urgent strides. His expression was one of worry.

"My apologies for the interruption, Chancellor, but this message was just transmitted from orbital traffic control. They insisted you be made aware of it immediately."

Taking the proffered tablet, Kesh scanned the contents of the message meant for his direct attention. While he had been imagining all manner of scenarios involving the three spies, he had dared to hope the truth of their activities might be limited to something easily countered, either through trade, coercion, or the simple application of military force.

Instead, the situation was much, much worse.

"Kesh," said Novek, his tone laced with concern. "What is it?"

"What we most feared." Passing the data tablet to his friend, Kesh drew a long, deep breath as he clenched his fists hard enough to feel his fingers beginning to cramp. "The spies have fled, apparently bound for Federation space."

Scowling as he read the report, Novek said, "They commandeered a transport. Long-range sensors from observation outposts along the Neutral Zone detected its passage and crossing into unaligned space."

"Those same sensors registered the presence of a Starfleet cruiser in that area before contact was lost. One of our own vessels was also reported in the vicinity, and its captain is now overdue for reporting to his superiors." Kesh struggled to maintain control of his emotions, but the task became more difficult the more he pondered this new development. "If they were traitors working on behalf of Starfleet, then it is possible our warship was lost to some confrontation. The damage they have inflicted upon us may well be incalculable."

Novek said, "According to the observation outposts in closest proximity to that area, no sign of the transport or the Starfleet vessel has been detected since that initial sighting." He frowned. "The asteroid field in that area has a disruptive effect on sensors. Might they be using that as camouflage?"

"The thought occurred to me as well," replied Kesh. "Perhaps it sustained damage in an altercation with our warship. If that is the case, then Starfleet will want to send another ship to investigate."

Moving closer, Di'natri said, "Then should we not do the same? There may still be time to prevent the worst aspects of the spies' activities from being used against us."

Kesh nodded. "We must be cautious to avoid attracting

undue attention from our Federation adversaries." He would need to speak with his director of intelligence. Perhaps an undercover operative working within Starfleet might be able to offer helpful insight into this new information. Unfortunately, due to the nature of such clandestine agents working so far behind enemy lines, any response to his queries might take more time than he had at his disposal. This was a situation that called for immediate—if calculated—action.

Doing nothing might well put the very future of the Klingon Empire at stake.

Eleven

"Sensors detecting an object at the edge of the asteroid field. It should be within visual range within one minute, twenty-seven seconds."

Nodding at Spock's report from the science station before asking Lieutenant Uhura to call Admiral Nogura to the bridge, Kirk pushed himself from his chair and stepped around Chekov's navigator station. He leaned against the console, centering himself between the ensign and Lieutenant Sulu before crossing his arms. On the bridge's main viewscreen, more asteroids than he could easily count dominated the image. Some were almost too tiny to see, while others rivaled small moons. Many tumbled while others just drifted, and though Kirk knew the entire field, like everything else in space, was moving, that motion was all but undetectable to the naked eye.

"I haven't been out here since before I was posted to the *Enterprise*," said Sulu from the helm station. "I'd forgotten how big this field was."

Chekov said, "The nearest star system is days away even at low warp speed. Is this all that remains of a rogue planet?"

"No one knows," replied Sulu. "Starfleet did its initial mapping of this region more than a century ago, using automated survey probes. Scans of various asteroids weren't able to tie it to the mineral composition of any planet in the three closest star systems. A rogue planet is just as good a theory as any, but it would have to have been an *awfully* big planet."

The Ivratis asteroid field had been a component of star charts at least as far back as Starfleet records were kept, either through its own information-collecting efforts or as part of data exchanges between Federation member worlds or with other friendly interstellar neighbors and even the occasional enemy. Kirk himself had never visited this region, and his knowledge came only from studying navigational charts and a recent review of the information contained in the *Enterprise*'s library computer. Most of the data contained in that file was a combination of official reports as created following studies of automated probes and those starships that had surveyed the field in the decades since its initial discovery. The background radiation permeating the area was its most prominent characteristic, and anecdotes from the logs of ships assigned to border patrol duty often contained reports about the disruption encountered by sensors and other delicate systems. Other reports detailed encounters with civilian ships, be they legitimate merchant vessels or those piloted by less savory individuals. Even those pilots tended to avoid the region whenever possible, but Kirk was not so naive to believe they were being entirely truthful.

"Captain," said Chekov. "We have a visual on the buoy."

Glancing over his shoulder at the young navigator, Kirk replied, "Let's see it."

The viewscreen's image changed to offer a closer look at the Ivratis field, only now another object was centered on the large display. Kirk instantly recognized the familiar shape of a starship's disaster buoy. It was a compact cylinder with a duranium hull, the same plating used to construct vessels like the *Enterprise*, which protected the unit's sensitive interior components. While it was small and almost inconsequential compared to the asteroids around it, he knew that the device was nearly two meters in diameter and half again as tall. A navigational deflector dish was just visible, partially recessed within its top hull area, which allowed the buoy to detect and avoid hazards in space while traveling at impulse power. It possessed no warp drive, with the bulk of its internal space devoted to its onboard computer and accompanying data storage, communications, a single impulse engine, and a deflector-shield generator. The unit also housed a battery backup power system, which could be replenished by deployable solar energy collectors. Though not visible in its current configuration, the buoy also contained a trio of short landing legs in the event its course allowed it to make a powered descent to the surface of a planet or other spatial body. Otherwise, its primary mission once launched from its parent vessel was to transmit distress messages and await recovery while protecting the recorded information entrusted to it. Automatically updated as part of a ship's regular, autonomous computer activity, the buoy was designed to be launched with little or no warning or preparation time, acting as a failsafe repository for a ship's main computer in the event of catastrophe. In most circumstances, finding such a device adrift in space meant the ship to which it belonged had suffered a rather unpleasant fate.

Let's hope that's not the case here.

"Mister Spock?" he prompted.

Without looking up from the information being relayed to him via the hooded viewer at the science console, the *Enterprise*'s first officer replied, "Scans show no signs of damage. The buoy appears to be in perfect operating order."

As soon as they dropped to impulse power and entered communication range, Uhura dispatched a simple encoded test message. Doing so while the ship was still at warp carried the risk of its signal or the buoy's response being detected by unwelcome eavesdroppers.

Hearing the turbolift doors opening behind him, Kirk turned to see Admiral Nogura stepping onto the bridge. Before the captain could call attention to his officers, the elder man held up a hand.

"As you were, ladies and gentlemen." Appearing satisfied that operations would not grind to a halt for the observance of protocol, Nogura made his way around the railing near Sulu's station and descended to the command well to join Kirk. His gaze shifted to the buoy on the main viewscreen.

"It seems to be none the worse for wear."

Kirk nodded. "We were just confirming that, sir." Looking to Uhura, he asked, "Lieutenant?"

The communications officer turned in her seat. "The message was received and processed, sir. I've just received its response with a summary of its operational status. There have been no other attempts at communication, or access to it. So far as I can tell, it's been undisturbed since its launch from the *Endeavour*."

"So far, so good," said Nogura. "Has it remained in this general vicinity since it was deployed?"

"After getting enough distance from the asteroid field to transmit its initial message to Starfleet Command, it executed a programmed instruction to return to within one hundred kilometers of the field's outer boundary. With occasional minor adjustments, it's been stationkeeping right here, relative to the asteroids. Its location is fairly well shielded from long-range sensors. Someone would have to be looking for it, but its programming also includes instructions to take evasive action and use the asteroids for cover if its own sensors detect the presence of scans from anything other than a Starfleet vessel." Uhura gestured toward the screen. "The *Endeavour*'s crew was pretty ingenious, adding that little touch."

Nogura smiled. "It's not Captain Khatami's first rodeo."

"Spock," said Kirk as he turned to regard his science officer. "Have you found anything that makes you think the buoy is unsafe to bring aboard?"

The Vulcan shook his head. "No, sir. All of my scans indicate the buoy is functioning within expected parameters, and contains no dangerous or illicit materials."

Satisfied with Spock's assessment, Kirk moved to his command chair and pressed the intercom control set into its right armrest. "Bridge to cargo bay one. Scotty, are you ready down there?"

Montgomery Scott replied, *"Aye, sir. Just say the word, and we can bring that beastie aboard. I'm transmitting a signal for it to deploy its landing struts in preparation for the transfer."*

"Beam it over, Mister Scott." Closing the connection, Kirk stepped away from his chair and onto the bridge's upper deck to join Spock at the science station. "Let's have a look, Spock."

Without replying, the first officer keyed a control on his console and one of the larger monitors above his station shifted from its display of a star map to an image of the *Enterprise*'s main cargo bay. In the chamber's far corner was an oversized transporter pad. Though capable of accommodating living beings, this platform's main purpose was transferring to and from the ship bulk cargo that was too large for delivery by shuttlecraft or one of the regular transporter rooms. Once aboard, cargo could be maneuvered from the pad to a designated storage area within the bay by crew members using antigravity assistance units. In the event the cargo was too sensitive for transporters, it could still be brought aboard through the massive airlock hatch at the room's far end.

Positioned to the left of the pad was a transporter console, behind which stood Scott and a female crew member dressed in a standard engineering jumpsuit. The *Enterprise*'s chief engineer was manipulating the console's array of controls and within seconds a beam of golden energy appeared on the pad. It quickly coalesced into the now familiar cylindrical shape of the disaster buoy. In accordance with instructions received from Scott, the buoy's trio of landing struts had been extended from its base, allowing it to settle onto the pad as it materialized. Despite knowing better, Kirk could not help glancing over his shoulder to the main viewscreen to see that the buoy had in fact disappeared from where it drifted in space mere moments earlier. He caught Nogura doing the same thing, and both men exchanged knowing smiles.

"I won't tell anyone if you don't," said the admiral.

"Deal."

That matter apparently settled, Nogura returned his attention to the smaller screen. "All right, at least now we can access that thing's innards without having to worry about somebody intercepting its signals."

Spock tapped several controls on the science station's console before turning to regard the admiral and Kirk. "I have initiated a complete transfer of the buoy's memory banks. The data is being stored in a quarantined section of our library computer, so that the admiral may review it for classified information or other sensitive material."

"Thank you, Mister Spock," replied Nogura. "I suspect anything the agents brought with them from Qo'noS won't be in those memory banks. They wouldn't risk it falling into the wrong hands or, worse, the Klingons discovering Starfleet's involvement in espionage." He paused, studying the buoy on the screen for a few additional seconds before clearing his throat.

"Computer, this is Admiral Heihachiro Nogura. Starfleet Command voice authorization one eight zero two eight six, enable."

"*Working,*" replied the feminine voice of the *Enterprise*'s main computer. "*Recognize Admiral Heihachiro Nogura. Standing by for command-level query.*"

"Transmit the following code to the *Endeavour*'s distress buoy in cargo bay one." Nogura then proceeded to recite a seemingly random string of letters and numbers in rapid-fire fashion, faster than Kirk could follow. The admiral then punctuated the entire thing with, "Command authorization Nogura, zero five three three eight. Execute."

The response was immediate, in the form of several of the science station's computer-activity monitors flaring to life. Flashes and streaks of multicolored light danced on the compact screens, indicating the *Enterprise*'s computers were processing Nogura's directives and dealing with whatever transfer of information it had triggered.

Spock, his attention fixed on the computer's activity, said, "The buoy has transmitted a new encrypted message directly to my station."

He entered more commands to the console, and its other overhead monitor activated to reveal an image of Captain Atish Khatami. Kirk noted the strain in her face as she earnestly looked into what he guessed was the visual pickup of the desktop computer terminal in her quarters. The room's lighting was subdued, likely a concession to conserving whatever remained of the *Endeavour*'s power reserves. When she spoke, the fatigue was evident in her voice.

"*Admiral Nogura*," she said, then paused as though pondering something amusing. "*I mean, I guess I'm talking to Admiral Nogura. This file is supposed to be locked with a decryption cipher under your voice-print access. I suppose this is a test of Starfleet's programming and communications expertise, so if you're watching this and you're not Admiral Nogura, I applaud your ingenuity.*" Whatever humor she may have found in the momentary diversion vanished, and her expression turned serious. "*Hopefully, you're watching this because you found the encoded message we hid in the buoy's original transmission to Starfleet, and you know my crew and I are alive, along with our* cargo." Her emphasis on the last word was enough to make Nogura utter a low grunt of approval.

"*We separated the* Endeavour's *saucer section from the rest of the ship and were able to move far enough away from the secondary hull before the warp engines went. According to my science officer, the resulting explosion combined with the asteroid field's background radiation provided sufficient cover for us to maneuver deeper into the field. The Klingon vessel we encountered was destroyed during our skirmish, but not through our direct action. Whatever disruptive effect impacted us hit them as well, and combined with the damage we inflicted during the fight to render them helpless. All of this is in the official log stored in the buoy's memory banks. Not that any of this matters. You can be sure the Klingons will send someone to investigate. Here's hoping you find us first."*

"Working on it," said Kirk, more to himself than anyone else.

Khatami continued, *"For that reason, this will be my last update to the buoy's memory banks. As I record this, my helm officer is plotting a maneuver that will afford us some concealment from anyone who might be looking for us. We can't stay out here in the middle of the asteroid field. Without the warp engines to provide primary power, we're relying on impulse for everything. Deflector shields would cost us too much in energy."* She paused, looking into the pickup as though waiting for Nogura or whoever else might view this file to respond in some fashion. After a moment, she added, *"Yeah, you know what I mean. I'm not able to give you a precise fix on our position, because, to be honest, we're not exactly certain where we're going to end up. However, if you found the buoy, you should be able to cut through the worst of things and find us, sooner or later."* She smiled. *"Here's hoping you're as smart as I'd like you to be. Looking forward to seeing you, sir. Khatami out."* The message ended and the captain's image faded from the screen.

Nogura frowned. "That's not much to go on, is it?"

"It is logical to presume they have soft landed the *Endeavour's* primary hull," said Spock, turning to face Kirk and Nogura. "Such a maneuver would offer the ship greater protection against random asteroid collisions than simply remaining adrift within the field."

Kirk was not convinced. "Simply landing on the surface of an asteroid doesn't get them completely out of the woods. Asteroids slam into each other all the time. Besides, even if we rule out those asteroids that are too small to support landing something the size of the *Endeavour*'s saucer section, that still leaves a rather large field to search."

"Maybe not, sir."

It was Uhura, moving from her station toward the group, with Spock stepping aside to allow her to join them.

"You have something, Lieutenant?" asked Kirk.

She nodded. "Yes, sir. Remember when I mentioned how the buoy's been maintaining a largely static position at the asteroid field's outer boundary? At first I thought it was just a way to make it simpler for us to find it, but now I'm wondering if there's not more to it."

Without waiting, she leaned toward the science console and tapped several controls. Once more, the monitor above the workstation came to life, this time showing what Kirk recognized as a computer-generated representation of the Ivratis asteroid field. Icons appeared on the screen, including one marking the *Enterprise*'s present location and where the *Endeavour*'s buoy was found. Uhura pressed another control and a bright blue line began tracing a direct path through the field, beginning at the icon representing the buoy. It did not stop until it sliced through the entire field, at which point it cut across the screen in a line parallel to the field's far boundary before changing direction and returning to the buoy's position. The resulting triangular section then highlighted itself in light blue.

"I'm betting the buoy is acting as a literal flag, marking a starting point to search for the *Endeavour*," she said. "Assuming that's the case, I created a model to account for the drift of the asteroids as they move in relation to one another within the field, giving us a possible search area. It's still a decent-sized piece of the pie, but it has to be better than nothing."

Kirk grinned. "What did Khatami say? If we found the buoy,

we should be able to cut through the worst of things and find them?" He offered Uhura an approving nod. "Nicely done, Lieutenant." He studied the map's highlighted region. "Compared to other parts of the field, this section really isn't too dense." Gesturing to an area just outside the blue triangle, he added, "If I were a civilian pilot looking to escape Starfleet or Klingon scrutiny, this would be the sort of route I might pick through an asteroid field to avoid detection."

"I was thinking the same thing, Captain," said Nogura. "This lends itself rather well to our cover story." He turned to Uhura. "My compliments, Lieutenant. You may well have saved us a great deal of time we can't afford to waste."

The communications officer nodded. "My pleasure, Admiral."

"Spock," said Kirk, "how long until Scotty's finished upgrading the sensors on our civilian transport?"

"Mister Scott estimated less than two hours remaining to complete that task."

Though not excited or comfortable with the current situation, Kirk still could take some satisfaction from knowing he and his people now had an actionable plan in place. "All right, then. Let's figure out how to divide up a search grid that doesn't make it look like we're dividing a search grid. Whatever we do, we have to be ready to be confronted, whether by Klingons or anyone else who might be prowling around out here. Mister Spock, your primary task is to determine the nature of the odd interference that started this whole mess. Now that you've got the *Endeavour*'s sensor logs, hopefully you can find a clue in there to point you in the right direction."

Spock replied, "Understood."

His gaze still fixed on the map of the asteroid field, Kirk tried not to dwell too much on the sheer number of uncertainties and complications that might be waiting for him the moment he, Sulu, and Uhura departed aboard the *Dreamline* to carry out their part of this scheme.

"Hopefully, we'll avoid any unwelcome surprises," he said.

"Is that usually what happens with you and your crew, Captain?" asked Nogura.

Suppressing the urge to chuckle, Kirk shook his head. "Almost never, Admiral. Then again, where's the fun in that?"

Twelve

Atish Khatami entered the engineering space devoted to overseeing the *Endeavour*'s impulse engines to find it a hub of activity, if not a gathering spot for members of her crew. Containing six control consoles and their associated status monitors and display screens set into three of the room's four walls, this area also served as an auxiliary means of monitoring main engineering should circumstances warrant such actions. Under normal conditions, this area was a redundancy, often used for training or conducting noncritical engineering tasks that did not warrant the resources of the primary engineering deck. Given the starship no longer had a main engineering section or an auxiliary control room to substitute for the bridge, this secondary space had received a promotion and increase in its usefulness. While the lighting here was subdued as a power-saving measure, all of the consoles were up and running.

"Captain," said Lieutenant Hector Estrada as he took notice of her entering the room. He offered a knowing smile, gesturing around him. "Be it ever so humble."

Khatami surveyed the makeshift control center. "Not exactly what was advertised when you made your reservations?"

"The accommodations aren't so bad," said Estrada, "but when I booked rooms, they didn't warn me the pool was closed."

"Remind me to leave a bad review with management after we check out, Lieutenant."

As part of the overall plan to reduce the *Endeavour*'s power expenditures, Khatami had ordered the main bridge deactivated and the use of turbolifts restricted to emergencies only. To that end, she had appointed this space as a "temporary bridge," where she could gather her communications, science, tactical, and engineering heads without having to use ladders to make the climb up to the saucer's topmost deck. With piloting the ship no longer a priority, that left Lieutenant Marielise McCormack to help with overseeing what remained of the ship's weapons and defenses, while Lieutenant Neelakanta set aside his navigator's duties in favor of assisting Chief Engineer Yataro and his staff with repairs and related tasks. Other bridge officers with nothing to do so far as their primary responsibilities were lending themselves out in similar fashion across the ship. Not for the first time, Khatami applauded Starfleet's policies of cross-training every member of a starship's crew. It was a mindset championed by her predecessor, the late Captain Zhao Sheng, and was just one of many traditions and expectations she carried on in his stead.

Aside from Estrada and McCormack, the room was deserted despite all of the consoles being active and displaying information pertaining to systems across what remained of the ship. Katherine Stano had overseen the transfer of functions from the main bridge, making sure she and Khatami had instant access to the most current status updates. The *Endeavour*'s first officer and the team she assembled for the purpose made quick work of the task, getting this makeshift control center into working order within an hour of the ship's soft landing.

"Anything new to report?" asked Khatami.

Estrada replied, "Lieutenant Brax and his team have just finished setting up the phaser cannons he wanted along the upper hull. They're making their way back inside right now."

"And no problems getting them placed?"

"No problems." Estrada tapped a control on his console and

one of the station's small inset monitors activated. On the screen was a computer-generated image of the top portion of the *Endeavour*'s primary hull. Four blue dots, arrayed around the edge of the saucer section at the forward, aft, starboard, and port positions but all facing to the ship's rear, signified the quartet of phaser cannons now deployed in a defensive perimeter. Lieutenant Brax, the ship's Edoan chief of security, had offered the suggestion, after informing Khatami the large weapons were among the equipment that escaped damage both from the fight with the Klingons and the *Endeavour*'s landing. He submitted that along with the natural cover of the steep canyon walls surrounding the ship on three sides, the cannons could provide at least some means of warding off unwanted visitors should the need arise. Designed to be operated either remotely or by a two-person crew, they did not require constant oversight once placed. With the ship grounded and its primary weapons unusable, this was the best solution Brax and his security team could provide.

Let's just hope we don't need them, Khatami thought.

She asked, "How about our buoys?"

"Nothing exciting." Estrada gestured to the console that he had appropriated for his communications duties. "We're getting solid signals back from all four of them. They're transmitting on an extremely low frequency, well below the band you'd normally expect other ships to be monitoring, so they should escape detection unless another ship just happens to wander past our asteroid."

"As long as it's the right ship, I'm good with that." She nodded toward the console he had commandeered. "Since we're on that subject, have you detected anything with your new setup?"

"Not yet, but it's early. The buoys have only been online for less than an hour."

The mission undertaken by Lieutenant Commander Yataro, Lieutenant Tomkins, and other members of the engineering staff to deploy the quartet of sensor buoys had thankfully gone off without a hitch. Using two of the six work pods stored in the primary hull's cargo bays, Yataro and his team had maneuvered the buoys to equidistant points around the lip of the canyon in which the *Endeavour* rested. Less than two hours after the engineers ventured from the relative safety of the ship onto the asteroid's unwelcoming surface, Estrada along with Lieutenant Klisiewicz were interfacing the ship's communications and sensor arrays into those of the buoys.

"We've set up a process that allows the buoys to remain in a passive mode so far as their onboard sensors," said Estrada. "Their power output is very low; hopefully low enough that someone else's scans won't pick them up." The lieutenant shrugged. "It's a gamble, but I figure only a military ship would even bother to reconfigure their systems this way, and only then if they had a specific reason to do so. If somebody finds one of the buoys, they'll figure out what's going on and adjust their scans accordingly. Until then, I think this plus the asteroid field's normal background interference will give us pretty good cover."

Khatami nodded. "Good work."

A tone from the console made Estrada turn from her, frowning as he studied the information being relayed to the station's various monitors. Khatami watched as the communications officer pressed several controls, leaning closer to review data streaming across one screen.

"I'll be damned."

Khatami asked, "What is it?"

"Our distress buoy." He stood up, turning from the console. "It's gone."

Feeling her eyes narrow as she pondered this news, Khatami looked to the workstation, reviewing the various readings and other updates. "Gone? Destroyed?" A knot of dread formed in her stomach as she considered the possibility of an enemy vessel finding them all but defenseless down in this canyon.

Estrada moved to the adjacent console, which she knew was

now configured to act as Lieutenant Klisiewicz's interface to the ship's sensors and main computer. "We weren't even able to get a lock on its position until the buoys came online and we tied in our sensors. It was there an hour ago." After a moment spent reviewing the data being fed to that station, he shook his head. "I don't think it was destroyed. So far as I can tell thanks to the other buoys enhancing our sensors, there's no sign of any weapons discharges or debris. It's just . . . gone."

"Could someone have picked it up?" Khatami grimaced at the potentially unhappy possibilities that conjured.

Estrada replied, "Maybe." He tapped a few controls. "We're too far from its last position to get a clear look with sensors. Not without increasing the buoys' power levels and possibly giving away their location." He frowned. "And ours."

Khatami did not like this. Somewhere out there, beyond the hull of what remained of her ship, things were happening that she could not see. It was possible Starfleet had received and decoded her messages and dispatched someone to find her ship. They could very well be searching for them right now, using the purposely vague clues she had left hidden within the distress buoy's memory banks. Every fiber of her being wanted to activate every means of attracting attention the *Endeavour* had to offer, even as she knew that was a foolhardy course of action. No matter how frustrating it might be for her, the best thing she could do for the sake of everyone involved, rescuers and her crew alike, was sit tight and await the right opportunity to make contact with their saviors.

Patience, Captain, she reminded herself.

Another alert tone from Estrada's console made the lieutenant return to the workstation. He turned from reviewing the litany of information displayed on various monitors to face Khatami.

"We've got a problem. One of the buoys has increased power to its sensor array. It's not much, but it's out of sync with the others. I only noticed it because I was running a diagnostic on our connection with them." He pressed several controls, and one of the status monitors changed its output to display long strings of computer code. "I'm not doing anything that might have triggered such a change, and so far as I can tell it's not a malfunction, but it's the only thing that makes sense. I'm taking them all offline until we can figure this out."

Summoning Yataro to join them, Khatami spent the ensuing minutes working with Estrada to review the sensor data now being relayed from the quartet of deployed buoys. So far, their attempts to scan for the presence of other vessels had turned up nothing, and now that Estrada had deactivated them until this new problem could be addressed, the *Endeavour* was back to being in the dark.

The entrance doors slid apart to admit Yataro and Lieutenant Ivan Tomkins. Both engineers wore utility jumpsuits in lieu of their standard duty uniforms, and each appeared as if it had been some time since they last slept. Khatami knew that much was true for the bulk of the crew, to say nothing of herself, but for now sleep remained a luxury.

"Commander," she said, greeting the new arrivals. "We've got a problem." She allowed Estrada to provide the details of the current situation. Once Yataro and Tomkins had time to process this news, she asked, "What can we do?"

Yataro replied, "Implementing a full diagnostic of the buoys by remote would impact their power utilization, Captain, and perhaps draw unwanted attention. Alternatively, conducting such a test on site while interfacing directly with the onboard systems would pose a far lesser risk with respect to discovery."

"Another EVA?" Khatami frowned at the thought. Extravehicular activities, while routine aspects of life aboard a starship, especially for those members of a crew's engineering contingent, still came with unavoidable risks under the most benign of circumstances. The current situation was anything but benign and she did not relish the thought of sending any of her people out a second time even to conduct what should be a fairly simple test and possible repair.

Stepping forward, Tomkins said, "I can do it, Captain." He looked to Yataro. "Commander. It's an easy check and fix. Maybe a circuit's acting up. I can take spares and swap out anything that looks questionable."

"You may be correct," said the chief engineer, "but I propose a simpler alternative. We can simply recall the buoy, carry out whatever tests and repairs are required, then program it to return to its previous position. Indeed, we could easily reconfigure another buoy and send it out to replace the one we are bringing back."

"I like that idea a lot better," said Khatami.

Tomkins seemed to consider that before replying, "With all due respect, we had to place those buoys in specific locations in order to best take advantage of their enhancement to our communications and sensors. That required teams to be hands-on with the buoys on the surface. If we send one back remotely, there's a chance we might position it incorrectly."

"Then we can adjust it accordingly," offered Estrada. "Now that we've got the enhanced readings from the other buoys, we can use our boosted power to make a better calculation for the one giving us problems." He glanced to Khatami. "It's still a lot less risky than another EVA."

Khatami nodded. "Agreed. Mister Yataro, proceed with your plan. It's up to you so far as repairing or replacing the buoy; whichever you think is the best way to go. Keep me informed."

"Understood, Captain." Taking his leave of Khatami and Estrada, Yataro exited the room with Tomkins following close behind. When the doors closed, the lieutenant turned to Khatami.

"Something's still bugging me about all of this, Captain."

Eyeing her communications officer, Khatami asked, "What's eating you?"

He waved toward his console. "That malfunction. It was small enough it didn't impede the buoy's systems or affect our ability to use the boost all four of them are giving our systems, but still sufficient to attract attention if someone knew to be looking for it." He grimaced. "Hell, I might have completely missed it if I hadn't decided to run some checks. Otherwise? There's no telling how long it might have gone unnoticed."

"You're not getting paranoid on me in your old age, are you, Hector?" She punctuated the question with a gentle smile.

Estrada said, "First, I prefer the term 'advanced middle age,' if it's all the same to you, Captain." After they both chuckled at that, he added, "I know it doesn't make sense to look at this in that way, but at the same time, we *are* involved in a whole bunch of crazy cloak-and-dagger spy games here." He paused, then rolled his eyes. "Okay, when I say it out loud like that it just sounds crazy." Waving his hands in the air, he turned back to his console. "I'm sorry, Captain. Forget I said anything."

Patting him on the shoulder, Khatami said, "No, I don't think I will." When he looked over his shoulder at her, she pointed to his workstation. "Do me a favor. Review everything you have from the buoy's system logs since it was brought online. Even before Yataro and his team took it outside."

"What are you thinking?"

She reached up to rub her chin. "I'm not sure, other than there's no sense in not ruling out causes for the buoy's acting up on us. If nothing else, it'll help Yataro with his diagnostics. I mean it, Hector. Check everything."

Estrada patted his console. "Aye, Captain. However, I should warn you it could take a while."

Making a show of looking around the dimly lit, repurposed room that was now the hub of activity for her and her senior staff, Khatami stifled an urge to laugh.

We're not going anywhere. May as well use our time wisely.

Thirteen

Shaking off the last vestiges of sleep following what had been an entertaining if not life-altering evening's worth of recreational activities, D'zinn stepped through the doors leading to the *Vekal Piltari*'s command deck. It was the middle of the night, at least so far as the ship's onboard schedule was concerned, and the control center was only sparsely occupied with members of the crew serving as relief for her primary staff. Thankfully, the ship's complement was small enough that she still knew each of their names. Vodat, one of her engineers, was tasked with overseeing the command deck's overnight operations. He did so while struggling to avoid the obvious lure of Avron, who operated the helm console while tossing furtive glances over her shoulder at him.

"What is the problem, Vodat?" D'zinn asked, not quite succeeding in her attempt to mask her irritation at being awakened at this early hour.

Clearly uncomfortable with having summoned her, Vodat nevertheless maintained his composure as he directed her attention where another younger male Orion stood at the sensor station.

"Ralanna has been monitoring scan readings and found something I thought you would find . . . interesting." He gestured to the other Orion, and D'zinn almost laughed as the younger man—barely out of adolescence, really—cleared his throat in obvious nervousness while regarding her with wide, anxious eyes.

Is he worried I might kill him, or take him back to my bed? He had given her no reason to do the former—at least not yet—and if the rumors circulating around the *Vekal Piltari* were any indication, then he was far too inexperienced for the latter. On another occasion she may well have accepted the challenge for simple amusement, but she was in no mood for such things just now.

"Ralanna," she said, keeping her voice level. "What have you found?"

The younger man replied, "Our scans detected another vessel. It seems to be taking great care to avoid the Federation starship we registered earlier."

Another ship? This was surprising news. "What kind of vessel?"

"Recognition database shows it is a personnel transport craft. The design is consistent with similar ships manufactured in the Alpha Centauri system and used by civilian merchants throughout the quadrant." He tapped a trio of controls and the image on one of his console displays changed to what D'zinn recognized as a technical schematic. The computer-generated diagram zoomed in to highlight its aft section.

"This particular craft has undergone a variety of modifications and enhancements," added Ralanna. "A more powerful propulsion system and defensive shield array, and its weapons are stronger than those typically found on civilian vessels. There is also a pair of shielded areas corresponding to its cargo holds that I am unable to penetrate with sensors."

"Shielded?" Now D'zinn was intrigued. "Even with our enhancements?"

The younger Orion nodded. "The enhancements are what allowed us to register the shielded compartments in the first place. Without the configuration given to us by the Klingons, our scans would likely have registered nothing out of the ordinary, assuming we even detected the vessel at all."

"Were you able to tell whether their sensors scanned our vessel?" asked Vodat.

"No. So far, there is no such indication."

D'zinn asked, "And you think they are deliberately trying to avoid the *Enterprise*?"

"The course takes them through one of the asteroid field's most dense and dangerous areas." Ralanna punctuated his reply by gesturing to another of his station's monitors, which depicted a map of the Ivratis field. "It would be a challenge even for a highly skilled pilot, who likely would find a way to avoid such a hazard in the first place unless there was no other alternative."

Stepping closer, Vodat examined the sensor readings that continued to stream across the console's status monitors. "Where did they even come from?"

"That is a question I tried to answer myself," said Ralanna. Another series of commands entered into the station's interface resulted in more data that began streaming down an adjacent display. "I attempted to track their course to the point they entered the region, but so far I have been unsuccessful. It is as though they simply appeared within the asteroid field, but that is obviously incorrect. Perhaps the ship's pilot is more skilled than I first believed." He gestured to the screen. "We know that those wishing to avoid detection have charted their own courses through the field, but such paths are not constant owing to the nature of the asteroids drifting through the area. However, an accomplished pilot or even a lesser-skilled person who still possessed experience traversing the region would be able to pursue such a course and adapt accordingly."

D'zinn was not convinced. "Or, there is another explanation. This may be a ruse perpetrated by the crew of the Starfleet vessel."

"You think that ship's pilot is working with Starfleet?" asked Vodat.

"Or, they *are* Starfleet." Though she admitted the idea seemed unlikely as she first voiced it, upon further consideration she began to see the possibilities this new situation represented. "They may be using the transport to assist in the search for whatever remains of their missing starship."

At last report from her superiors, the *U.S.S. Endeavour* was destroyed as a consequence of its encounter with the Klingon warship that suffered a similar fate. It made perfect sense for Starfleet to dispatch another vessel to investigate, which explained the presence of the *U.S.S. Enterprise* in the area. D'zinn did not relish the idea of such a powerful ship lurking on the asteroid field's outer boundary, but so far it had maintained a course one might expect to see from a ship carrying out a search for wreckage or any signs of survivors. The *Vekal Piltari*'s sensors had picked up evidence of the *Endeavour*'s destruction, apparently caused by a breakdown of its faster-than-light propulsion system resulting from damage inflicted by the Klingon cruiser. So powerful was the explosion that precious little remained of the starship, and D'zinn had ordered the collection of some remnants they happened across. So far as she could ascertain, the vessel was obliterated, and there had been no signs of escape pods, shuttlecraft, or anything else that might be providing temporary refuge to survivors.

"A simple search operation would not require such elaborate coordination," she said. "The only reason to engage a civilian vessel in what is clearly a military operation is if there remains a strategic objective."

Ralanna, displaying his youth and inexperience, asked, "What sort of objective might that be?"

Smiling, D'zinn appreciated that such a simple, innocent question nevertheless harbored any number of potentially interesting answers.

"Perhaps the *Endeavour* was carrying some kind of valuable cargo," she said. "Or they were testing their own form of newly developed technology they hope to one day employ against an enemy. They may even have planned some sort of covert rendezvous. Despite its vaunted reputation as the defender of high ideals and progressive, inclusive civilization, Starfleet still conducts itself as a military organization, with everything that implies."

While she knew nothing about the *Endeavour* or its captain and crew, the *Enterprise* was another matter. That ship was fodder for all manner of stories, only some of which D'zinn actually believed to be true. By many accounts, its captain, a human named James Kirk, had a propensity for finding trouble in the most unlikely of places. Intelligence reports filtered down to her included information on Starfleet vessels, as well as others representing various Federation worlds, the Klingon Empire, and even the Romulans. Kirk's name was a familiar one to her. According to those reports, he along with his ship and crew had survived multiple encounters with both the Klingons and the Romulans. There were unconfirmed rumors that Kirk himself, disguised as a Romulan, had successfully stolen aboard a Romulan vessel and obtained its cloaking device while managing to capture its commander in the process.

D'zinn was not quite ready to believe such an improbable tale, but as a general rule she tended to err toward the notion that even the most outlandish of stories had at least some basis in truth. If the stories about Kirk were even partially accurate, they described a person who was formidable, comfortable with taking risks, and quite capable of carrying out acts of subterfuge. Bearing this in mind while considering the fact the *Enterprise* was here, now, made D'zinn wary.

Interesting. Very interesting.

Moving away from the station, D'zinn began pacing a circuit around the command deck. Was it possible she had stumbled across a clandestine Starfleet operation? If so, what were its goals? Who was involved? She knew all of this was just theorizing on her part; there was no evidence to support the notions she currently entertained. However, the unexpected appearance of the civilian transport in such proximity to the Federation starship now lurking at the edge of the asteroid field was curious.

There was, she decided, a simple way to gauge the situation for herself.

"Ralanna, transmit the location of that transport to the helm." Halting her pacing, she turned to Avron. "Plot an intercept course, and call Melac and the others to their stations."

If there was nothing untoward about this mysterious ship, the *Vekal Piltari* and its crew would benefit from an extra opportunity so far as taking advantage of wayward vessels traversing the region. On the other hand, if it turned out to be something more, then she would alert her Klingon suitors and let them deal with it. She suspected they would be most appreciative upon learning of this new concern.

Either way, D'zinn would be paid, and that was sufficient for her.

Fourteen

There was, Kirk decided, just no way to get comfortable.

"Considering what I'm paying for this charter," he said, shifting his position on one of the couches lining the bulkheads of the *Dreamline's* passenger cabin, "I expected a little more value for my money."

Truth be told, he had to admit this section of the civilian craft was well appointed. The couches and accompanying recliners were overstuffed to such a degree that they seemed bound and determined to swallow him every time he attempted sitting on them. In contrast to the furnishings he was used to aboard the *Enterprise*, which were not spartan but hardly luxurious, the *Dreamline* appointments bordered on opulent. Tapestries featuring embroidered artwork that he recognized as representing at least a half-dozen Federation worlds adorned the bulkheads, hiding from view their utilitarian and comparatively unsightly metal finish. A thick red carpet of some material Kirk could not place covered the floor. The compartment was divided into this sitting area and a berthing space containing a bed and a lavatory. Traveling via this vessel was a fair step up from the shuttlecraft and other Starfleet transports to which he had long ago grown accustomed.

Lounging on the couch set molded into the cabin's opposite bulkhead, Lieutenant Uhura did not even bother trying to suppress a smile. "You should probably take that up with our travel agent when we get back, sir."

"Something tells me I won't get much sympathy in that regard," replied Kirk. "Our agent doesn't seem to care much for creature comforts or other distractions."

He recalled those few occasions when he had spent any time with Nogura. Fewer than could be counted on one hand, and always in a professional setting such as the admiral's office or briefing room. From what Kirk could remember, the admiral had little use for keepsakes, photographs, or other mementos. Indeed, it appeared he eschewed any flavor of the usual assortment of personal items one might reasonably expect to find littering the desk and shelves of a workspace in which its occupant spent considerable time. Further, Kirk realized he knew nothing about Nogura's personal life. Was he married? Did he have kids? As hard as he tried, Kirk could not even conjure an image of the man in civilian attire. From all available evidence, it seemed the admiral's life was his work. There was no arguing he played a vital role in the Starfleet Command hierarchy and was a prime mover in the realm of Federation security, but was that really all there was to Heihachiro Nogura?

Maybe so.

Giving up on the sofa, Kirk pushed himself to his feet and moved to the food slot set into the cabin's forward bulkhead. Perhaps coffee might help, and he decided he might as well go forward and assist Sulu with monitoring the sensors. Though they were programmed to carry out their tasks without the need for operator intervention, Kirk preferred a pair of eyes watching over the machines working on their behalf. Besides, Sulu would welcome the company, as he had been alone in the *Dreamline*'s cockpit for nearly an hour after Uhura wandered into the cabin.

"Is it possible that you're just having an allergic reaction to civilian clothing?" Uhura could not help laughing at her own joke.

Studying the food slot's control pad as he prepared to order coffee for himself and Sulu, Kirk grinned. "As good an explanation as any. Now that I think about it, I can't remember the last time I wasn't wearing a uniform or some kind of Starfleet-issue clothing."

He took note of the jade-green sweater Uhura wore, the bottom of which fell to her thighs and partially covered a pair of black leggings. She also had styled her hair so that it did not reflect anything a female Starfleet officer might choose. Like hers, his own ensemble of dark trousers and shirt along with a leather jacket came courtesy of the *Enterprise*'s stores and clothing manufacturing system, which normally was used to provide the crew with replacement uniforms as well as appropriate attire if required when interacting with the indigenous population of whichever world the ship might visit during the course of its mission.

Though he possessed a small civilian wardrobe stored in his cabin aboard the *Enterprise*, occasions to wear it were rare. Even the brief respite at Starbase 24 enjoyed by him and his crew before Nogura cut short their leave had not afforded him the opportunity to shed his command-officer persona. In truth, it had been years since he felt comfortable wearing anything but a uniform. Nothing else seemed natural or appropriate anymore. Was he so far gone, ensconced in a career that demanded so much of himself, that there was little to nothing left with which he could simply enjoy life?

Well, that's not depressing at all.

His odd thoughts were interrupted by the sound of the intercom system filtering into the passenger cabin, followed by the voice of Hikaru Sulu.

"Captain, you need to come up here. We've got company."

Exchanging glances with Uhura as she rose from her couch, Kirk tapped the intercom's keypad. "On our way."

A door set into the cabin's forward bulkhead slid aside at his approach, revealing a short service corridor lined with storage compartments. The passageway could be crossed in two or three steps and ended at another door, which was already opening as Kirk moved toward it. Beyond that hatch was the transport's cockpit. The compact space was crammed to overflowing with consoles and controls lining every available surface, with just enough room remaining to accommodate chairs for two pilots. Sulu occupied the leftmost chair, dressed in a simple yet stylish pair of gray trousers and a bright blue tunic worn snugly across his lean physique. Before him and his console was the cockpit's forward canopy, which at present offered an unfettered view of the Ivratis asteroid field. The view was something of a trick, with the canopy equipped with imaging sensors that compensated for the near total lack of ambient light in the field. Thanks to this effect, Kirk could see numerous asteroids drifting in the void around them. Some could have passed for small moons, surrounded by smaller bodies of varying shapes and sizes.

Deferring to Uhura, Kirk stepped aside and allowed her to slip past him and take the empty seat to Sulu's right. Standing in the cockpit's open doorway, Kirk regarded his helm officer.

"What have we got, Mister Sulu?"

Without looking away from his console, the lieutenant replied, "Sensors just picked it up, sir. It's an Orion vessel, heading directly for us."

"Orion?" repeated Uhura. "There have been scattered reports of their pirate vessels operating in this region, but nothing substantiated."

"We already know this is the kind of place pirates love," said Kirk. "That said, I have to wonder how any ship, Orion or otherwise, managed to find us." He grimaced. "Damn." It had only been three hours since the *Dreamline*'s departure from the *Enterprise*.

Using the search grid devised by Uhura after her hypothesis based on Captain Khatami's message, Sulu had been following a course through the asteroid field that—in theory—made it appear the transport was in a hurry to be somewhere rather than searching for the *Endeavour*. It obviously had been too much to hope they might find the disabled starship before encountering some sort of obstacle.

In other words, Kirk thought, *just another day.*

Sulu replied, "They had to have seen us before I saw them. If I didn't know any better, I'd think their sensors have to be much better than ours, even with our modifications to counteract the fits the asteroid field's background interference is giving us."

"Anyone using this area for whatever reason might have found a way to tune their sensors to account for that disruption," said Uhura. "They may have a few other tricks up their sleeve as well." A tone sounded from the console and she leaned forward to inspect it. "They're hailing us, Captain."

Kirk said, "What kind of weapons do they have, Mister Sulu?"

The lieutenant reviewed several of the console's status indicators before answering, "Disruptor cannons only, sir, but still enough to hurt us if this turns into a fight."

"Let's hope it doesn't. Uhura, let's hear what they have to say."

She pressed controls on the console before her and the cockpit's confined space was filled with a low, intimidating voice.

"Unidentified vessel. You are trespassing in this region. Power down your engines, deactivate your deflector shields, and prepare to be boarded."

"I don't like the idea of dropping our shields in here," said Sulu.

"Neither do I." Kirk examined the cockpit console's status board for himself. "I'm betting if this were the *Enterprise*, we'd be getting a different kind of welcome."

"Shall I signal them, sir?" asked Uhura.

Kirk shook his head. "Not yet. Right now, this may be nothing more than pirates looking to take advantage of a wayward ship a long way from home." He had no desire to blow their cover so early into their mission. For the moment, he was willing to play his part in their covert scheme. "Activate ship-to-ship communication, but let's put that scrambling protocol of yours to work."

At Admiral Nogura's suggestion, Uhura had devised a software routine for the *Dreamline*'s communications systems that, when activated, allowed it to simulate static and other interference with any transmission. In theory, this would present to the contacted party the appearance of a compromised signal impacting its visual feed, effectively providing a disguise for Kirk and the others. He had no idea whether the captain of a random Orion vessel might recognize him on sight, but neither did he desire to take unnecessary chances.

"You're up, Sulu," he said.

The lieutenant keyed the communications link and activated the compact viewscreen set into the cockpit's helm console. Static on the screen cleared to reveal a bald, imposingly muscled Orion male wearing a sleeveless shirt taut across his broad chest. His bright green arms featured an assortment of tattoos and piercings.

"This is Masamune Shirow, captain of the transport vessel *Dreamline*," said Sulu, employing the name that was part of the cover identity he had created with the help of Admiral Nogura. "I am ferrying two passengers to the Rigel system. I was unaware this area is claimed by any interstellar power. Please identify yourselves."

"That sounded pretty convincing," said Uhura, after waiting for him to mute the connection.

Keeping his expression impassive, Sulu replied in a soft voice, "Let's just hope they're not familiar with sequential-art storytelling from twentieth-century Earth."

Over the open communications link, the Orion scowled. "*We claim this region, and you are here without our permission. Power down your engines and prepare for boarding. Any other action will be interpreted as hostile and we will take all appropriate measures.*"

"They seem nice," observed Kirk. "Let me try." He gestured for Sulu to unmute the connection, and remembered to employ his alias, before saying, "Um, hello? My name is Charles Finley, and I'm on my way to an important meeting on Rigel XII. We certainly didn't intend to trespass through anyone's territory, and we apologize for our error. If you're willing, we would appreciate a guide out of the asteroid field so that we might be on our way."

On the screen, the Orion paused and directed his attention to something Kirk could not see. Then another Orion, this time a woman, appeared in the image, and when she directed her gaze to him, her expression was hard and suspicious.

"Your communications link is weak. Boost power to your array so that your signal clears. I do not trust anyone whose face I cannot see."

Engaging the mute control again, Uhura said, "I guess my trick worked."

"Looks that way." Kirk leaned forward, reactivating the connection. "I'm sorry. I'm afraid our comm system is at maximum output. Apparently something to do with the radiation or whatever else is permeating this asteroid field. We apologize for the inconvenience. Now, surely we can come to some form of arrangement here?"

The female Orion's eyes narrowed. *"Yes. The arrangement is prepare to be boarded, or I will destroy your ship."*

Fifteen

Kirk had heard enough.

"Sorry you feel that way," he said, before cutting the link and stepping away from the console. "Get us out of here, Mister Sulu."

Part of their planning for this covert reconnaissance mission included the possible need to evade other spacecraft. Though both Kirk and Nogura anticipated complications raised by Klingons also seeking answers for what happened here to their own warship as well as the *Endeavour*, both men also knew there was a better than even chance of encountering some kind of rogue ship such as one crewed by pirates. It was a gamble, Kirk conceded at the time, but one worth taking if it meant finding Captain Khatami and her crew.

Time to up the ante, he thought.

The Orion woman and her male companion, each sporting matching looks of surprise and contempt in response to Kirk's abrupt dismissal, vanished from the console's viewscreen just as Sulu set to work on the *Dreamline*'s helm controls. Despite the transport's artificial gravity and inertial damping systems, Kirk still felt a twinge in his gut as Sulu guided the ship into an abrupt starboard bank and accelerated, altering his view of the asteroid field beyond the cockpit canopy. In the distance, larger bodies shifted to the left and up and out of his field of vision as the transport arced its way deeper into the field.

"You may want to hang on, sir," said Sulu, not taking his eyes from his controls.

Bracing himself in the doorway, Kirk grunted. "Now he tells me."

"They're increasing speed and continuing on their intercept course," reported Uhura.

Sulu replied, "They're bigger than we are. I may be able to use that."

Almost afraid to ask what that meant, Kirk instead leaned against the door's frame as the helm officer guided the *Dreamline* in a twisting dive toward what at first looked to be a collision course with one of the larger asteroids. The enormous, space station–sized chunk of rock seemed to fill the cockpit canopy before Sulu adjusted the ship's trajectory, and the transport curved just to port. They passed the asteroid at such close distance that Kirk was able to make out terrain features.

"Mister Sulu," he began, but he was cut off by Uhura.

"The Orion ship has cut its speed." She frowned, looking up from her console. "Not by much, but it's something, and I think their shields just took a hit from one of the smaller asteroids. So far as I can tell, it was no bigger than a communications buoy, but in here it won't take much."

Sulu smiled. "Their pilot isn't as good as I am."

"Or humble," countered Uhura. "Or crazy."

"That too."

Reviewing her sensor readings, Uhura said, "They're definitely slowing their speed but still maneuvering to intercept us. They're altering their course through the field. Looks like they're trying to get abreast or ahead of us."

"I see it." Sulu's voice was calm and confident, his hands moving across the transport's helm console as if he had been piloting the ship for years rather than hours. Kirk divided his attention between the lieutenant's work and its effects as depicted outside, with the asteroids appearing to twist and arc first right, then left as Sulu's deft maneuvering took them deeper into the field.

"Is it just me," Kirk said, "or is the field getting more dense?" As he posed the question, Kirk watched two asteroids, one much smaller than the other, collide with each other as though wanting to help him make his point. The impact was subtle, almost a passing glance, but it was enough to alter the smaller rock's trajectory and send it drifting off its original course, requiring Sulu to navigate around it.

Sulu replied, "I'm taking us into a more crowded area." He reached to a different set of controls and tapped several keys in rapid succession. "I'm reducing power to our deflector shields and narrowing their envelope around us. This far into the field, the shields are actually more of a hindrance." Sparing a glance to his companions, he added, "When I was a cadet at the Academy, we used to make runs like this through the asteroid belt between Mars and Jupiter. Compared to this, that one's practically empty, but at impulse speeds you can get a similar effect." He smiled. "It was fun."

"Mister Sulu," Kirk said, "assuming we make it out of this, we need to discuss your ideas about fun."

Instead of answering, the lieutenant made another adjustment to the *Dreamline*'s course, lining up the craft on a direct course for yet another very large asteroid. Kirk noted that there seemed to be no other pieces of debris in this part of the field, though more asteroids were visible in the distance beyond their current target. For a moment he worried about the lack of cover and concealment as the transport made its latest dash under Sulu's expert if unorthodox guidance.

"Orion ship bearing two one five mark seven," said Uhura. "They're maneuvering in behind us. Sensors show they've powered up their weapons."

Sulu said, "Transferring shield power to rear deflectors."

The move came just in time, as seconds later Kirk felt the entire *Dreamline* shudder under the impact of something slamming into the ship's aft shields. The cockpit's interior flickered, accompanied by several rows of the helm console's status indicators flashing for attention. For his part, Sulu appeared to ignore the various warnings, focusing his attention on his instruments. Looking over his shoulder, Kirk noted the astrogator scanner showing the transport's position relative to nearby asteroids including the massive one in front of them, and watched as a new icon appeared on the small screen.

"They're closing fast," he said, unable to resist looking through the canopy at the looming asteroid.

Sulu nodded. "That'll change once we get around this one."

"We're being hailed," reported Uhura. "The Orions sound pretty insistent this time."

Kirk said, "I'll bet. Ignore it. Mister Sulu, how are we doing?"

Instead of replying, the helm officer executed another maneuver and applied even more acceleration to the *Dreamline*'s engines. Kirk could not help noting their course did not seem to be changing, as the massive asteroid grew larger with each passing moment.

"Mister Sulu?" he repeated.

Uhura reported, "The Orions are moving in behind us. Sensors show another buildup in their forward disruptors."

As though anticipating the next volley of weapons fire, Sulu tapped another of his helm controls and the transport banked to port, executing a steep dive toward the asteroid's surface. Kirk watched twin beams of bright green energy streak past the forward window, slicing through the space the *Dreamline* had occupied mere heartbeats earlier. Then he saw nothing but kilometers of jagged, scarred rock filling the cockpit's window. Even with the internal systems masking the effects of gravity and inertia, he could not keep from gripping on to the door frame.

"Hang on," said Sulu, his voice for the first time betraying a hint of tension. He shifted his gaze between his controls, the canopy, and the astrogator screen, and Kirk observed the Orion ship's position in relation to their own. The distance between the two vessels had shrunk to an alarming degree.

Uhura said, "They're getting ready to fire again."

Though he did not respond to the update, Sulu acknowledged it by forcing the transport into another hasty maneuver. This time Kirk did feel his stomach lurch as the lieutenant applied more thrust in concert with pulling up the ship's nose. The asteroid ahead of them—now much too close for Kirk's comfort—disappeared beneath his field of vision as the *Dreamline* climbed away from its surface. His gut and the cockpit instruments told him Sulu had put the ship into a tight loop back the way it had come.

"Please tell me you practiced this when you were a cadet at the Academy," said Uhura, who was leaning back in her seat and bracing herself against her console.

"Not really, no."

Still propping himself in the doorway behind his officers, Kirk said, "We also need to talk about your deadpan sense of humor, Lieutenant."

The transport's maneuver continued, banking up and away from the asteroid until it began to resume its original course. Only this time, the Orion vessel was centered in the canopy window before them. Its own helm officer had obviously realized what was happening and had taken steps to mitigate the surprise tactic, but by then Sulu had seized control of the situation. Having proved the *Dreamline*'s greater maneuverability, he now was pushing that demonstration to maximum effect, thwarting the Orion ship pilot's every attempt to shake his new pursuer. As he completed the looping maneuver, Sulu tapped another set of controls, and Kirk saw a pair of status indicators flash from red to green.

"Forward phasers on standby," he said. "And thank you for the modifications, Mister Scott." The *Enterprise*'s chief engineer had ensured the meager phaser banks already installed aboard the transport were properly augmented, installing power converters and additional relays that allowed the components to operate at a level well above the normal capacity for civilian versions of such weapons.

"Always looking out for us, our Scotty," said Kirk.

Uhura called out, "Sensors show they're diverting power to their aft disruptors."

Pointing to the canopy, Kirk snapped, "Sulu, target those weapons ports and fire to disable."

Sulu responded by pressing the console's firing controls, and a pair of orange beams spat forth from either side of the cockpit's canopy, crossing the distance separating the *Dreamline* from the Orion ship and striking the other vessel's aft shields. Energy collided, flaring up to briefly obscure the other ship even as Sulu fired again. This time he continued the assault, following each salvo with another right on its heels. The Orion ship did its best to evade the attack but Sulu was locked in, holding pace and course with the other craft even as they both careened through the field.

"You punched through their shields," said Uhura. "Their aft disruptors are down! There's some hull damage and I'm picking up some fluctuations in their main engines. It's not critical but it will impact their maneuvering and ability to navigate the field." After another moment spent reviewing her readings, she added, "No hull breaches or other signs of major damage."

"Good," replied Kirk. "Let's hope there are no casualties." He had no desire to let this encounter devolve into a situation that cost lives. Hopefully the Orion ship's commander harbored similar feelings. Ahead of them, the other vessel was banking away from the asteroid but making no obvious move to resume the confrontation. A glance at the astrogator near Sulu's left elbow confirmed this for Kirk. "Set a course deeper into the asteroid field. I want to demonstrate we're not looking to press anything. Hopefully, with the damage to their ship, they'll take the hint."

Uhura said, "They're continuing to move away, sir."

Allowing himself a small sigh of relief, Kirk kept his focus on the console readings and the space ahead of them. While he wanted to think the Orions would accept the figurative smack they had just received across their proverbial nose, experience told him a different story.

They would be back. They might even bring friends.

Meanwhile, the *Endeavour* was still out there, waiting.

At least all of D'zinn's most experienced people now occupied their respective stations on the *Vekal Piltari's* command deck. She knew they would respond to the sudden and unexpected turn of events confronting them with practiced confidence. However, despite her attempt to reassure herself, she was unable to quell either her concern or her anger at how quickly the situation had shifted against them.

"Damage report!"

Moving between stations around the command deck, Netal replied, "Both rear weapons ports are offline. Their phasers penetrated our rear shields and struck one of the primary engine manifolds. We still have partial power, but our maneuvering ability has been impacted. We need to transfer additional power to the shields if we are to remain in the asteroid field."

D'zinn seethed at the report. Whoever the pilot of that transport was, he had obviously upgraded his vessel's systems beyond even what her own ship's sensors had been able to detect. That meant he either was someone with much to hide from the likes of Starfleet or other law-enforcement entities, or else he *was* Starfleet, as she had earlier suspected. At the moment, she had insufficient evidence to bolster her theory, but there was no denying the transport pilot possessed exceptional skill. His maneuvering within the asteroid field far outmatched that of her own pilot, suggesting someone with specialized training or else raised in an environment where such talents were cultivated as a means of surviving in, for example, the unforgiving realm of independent merchants, privateers, and even pirates such as herself and her crew.

"Where is the other ship?" she snapped, stalking around the command deck's perimeter and studying the various station monitors and status displays for herself.

Netal said, "They are moving away." He stopped near the sensor station where Melac once more hovered over the controls. "Their course indicates an escape route deeper into the asteroid field; likely an attempt to evade our sensors."

While it was possible the pilot was simply acting out of self-preservation and taking advantage of the *Vekal Piltari*'s current predicament to make a dash for possible safety, D'zinn remained unconvinced.

"A pirate or someone looking to save their skins would have seized the initiative and finished us," she said. "But someone trained to apply moral standards even in a combat situation, such as a Starfleet officer, would not do such a thing."

Netal frowned. "Would Starfleet officers not also offer to render assistance?"

"In many circumstances, yes." She had heard about such things regarding encounters between Starfleet vessels facing off against enemy ships. In addition to showing mercy after winning a battle instead of destroying their adversaries, many Starfleet captains were notorious for extending offers of aid; everything from medical treatment of casualties to repairs so a crippled ship's crew did not die from lack of power or atmosphere. It was, D'zinn supposed, a noble attitude and well in keeping with vaunted Federation morals, but it also made their people naive and subject to exploitation. Better to finish off an enemy and be done with them, rather than help them regain their footing and provide an opening to betray you.

"You still believe they are Starfleet," asked Netal. "Working with the *Enterprise* in some manner?"

"I do not know." D'zinn paused before the command deck's central viewscreen, taking a moment to study the asteroid field displayed there. Something about this entire affair felt wrong to her. She had hoped to get a look at the *Dreamline*'s pilot and passengers and perhaps compare their likenesses to her ship's database of known, prominent figures within Starfleet and the Federation government. Someone like James Kirk, for example, would be in the computer files. The transport's odd communications issues prevented her from doing that, which only deepened her suspicions. Such a tactic, employed deliberately, was the perfect means of obscuring one's true identity.

"What I do know is that I am no longer comfortable keeping this information to ourselves." It was not that she feared her Klingon benefactors, but there was no denying their ability to make life difficult not just for her but the entire Orion Syndicate and its efforts to exploit this region. The better course, she knew, was to make every attempt to further the odd partnership struck between her superiors and the Klingon scientists.

She turned from the viewscreen to face her second-in-command. "Netal, I think we need to break communications silence and alert our Klingon friends. It is well past time they were informed about this."

Sixteen

On those occasions when Captain Kirk was off the ship and he was left in command, Spock tended to avoid sitting in the bridge's command chair unless circumstances warranted it. For emergency or combat situations, logic dictated he occupy the one position that served as a focal point for the other officers manning stations around him. Simply seeing the person in command at the hub of activity, beyond the human requirement for emotional stability during such times, also was vital for the effective communication of status updates and other important information. This more than anything else guided the design of a starship's bridge with its captain at the center. More than once during times of distress, and while he would never give Doctor McCoy the satisfaction of knowing such a thing, Spock himself had taken a measure of comfort from the presence of James Kirk in that chair.

This did not mean he experienced anxiety when the captain was absent, as was now the case. With Kirk as well as Lieutenants Uhura and Sulu engaged in their covert reconnaissance of the asteroid field, and despite his own disciplined control of his emotional reactions, Spock still harbored reasonable concern for his shipmates' safety. That was mitigated by knowing the *Enterprise* and its crew stood ready to assist them at a moment's notice. The captain chose to undertake risks such as this precisely because he held confidence in Spock and his crew to provide that support.

Bolstered by that knowledge, Spock felt free leaving the command chair vacant for the time being while concentrating on his various duties. Walking a slow circuit around the bridge's upper deck stations, he entered instructions into a logcomp, a handheld computational device that allowed him to remotely access the *Enterprise*'s computer banks. While he could and did often spend hours at the science station immersed in his work, he found that infrequent intervals spent away from the console allowed his mind to consider calculations and other matters requiring extensive thought. Spock had observed this behavior in colleagues throughout his tenure in Starfleet, and after experimentation came to realize the exercise did have its benefits.

Something else I would prefer Doctor McCoy not know, he thought with a hint of amusement he dared not reveal.

As if summoned, the *Enterprise*'s chief medical officer arrived via the turbolift, exiting the car at the back of the bridge. As was his habit, McCoy took a moment to quickly assess the officers at their stations. Once he seemed satisfied with what he saw, the doctor made his way to where Spock stood near the main viewscreen.

"Hello, Spock."

His pacing having brought him to the front of the bridge, Spock paused his work with the logcomp and regarded McCoy. "Doctor, do you require assistance?"

Shaking his head, McCoy replied, "No. I was just making my rounds."

Spock knew the doctor preferred to spend as much time outside of the ship's sickbay as was practical given his duties. Instead, he opted for what he called "a hands-on approach" to interacting with the rest of the crew, seeking them out at their assigned duty stations or the messes, lounges, and recreation spaces. For him, medical files and scheduled visits merely supplemented these more personal interactions as a means of knowing and being more aware of the crew's general physical and mental health. His wanderings about the ship inevitably brought him to the bridge, where Spock knew he took the opportunity to check on the well-being of the ship's captain and first officer without being obvious about his motives. While Spock initially had little use for the doctor's method of staying abreast of the crew's condition, he soon realized McCoy found the practice efficient. It was therefore logical to avoid impeding that process and support it whenever possible.

"Any news from Jim and the others?" asked the doctor.

Spock replied, "In keeping with the mission profile, we have received no communications from the *Dreamline* since its departure. If all remains as scheduled, I expect a short, encrypted burst transmission relayed to us in one hour and nineteen minutes."

"I've never been comfortable with sneaking around," said McCoy, making no effort to hide his evident irritation. "Jim's no spy, and neither are Uhura and Sulu. Starfleet should've sent someone who knows how to do this kind of thing. Or, at least let us bring along someone like that."

Though the doctor raised a valid point, Spock knew other factors were in play. "The secrecy surrounding the agents embedded on the Klingon homeworld is such that only a very limited number of people are even aware of their activities. Admiral Nogura has elected to keep that group very small, doubtless to protect not only the agents' identities but also the program's very existence."

McCoy nodded as he crossed his arms. "That makes sense, I suppose. We already know they can plant their own spies within the Federation, and maybe even aboard Starfleet ships and starbases." He blew out his breath. "I don't even like thinking about that."

"It is a most unpleasant prospect, but it is for that reason among others that the admiral has taken this course of action. It therefore falls to us to see this mission through to a successful completion."

Turning, Spock regarded the main viewscreen. Dozens of

asteroids were visible, many of them appearing large and imposing despite the distance separating them from the *Enterprise*. The starship's current course kept it at the Ivratis field's outer boundary while it conducted its search and survey mission.

"I take it our sensors haven't had any luck finding anything yet, either," said McCoy.

Spock replied, "Neither sensors nor communications have turned up anything out of the ordinary. Even with the search grid devised by Lieutenant Uhura to reduce the area we believe needs to be examined, a sizable portion of the asteroid field remains. This also assumes that the lieutenant's calculations are correct." He held up the logcomp. "However, using the same information provided by Captain Khatami, I performed my own computations and produced similar results. Indeed, Lieutenant Uhura's findings may well prove more accurate than mine."

That was enough to evoke a grin from the doctor. "I'll bet that hurt to say."

"Not at all. The lieutenant is a skilled officer and her expertise in this regard is superior to my own. It is logical to presume her knowledge would provide her a distinct advantage."

"Spock," said McCoy, "you never cease to amaze me."

Now sensing his colleague had launched yet another in their ongoing series of gentle verbal sparring matches, Spock replied, "As I have never set out to amaze you in any fashion, I am content to view this as a fortunate byproduct of my efforts."

The doctor's chuckle was interrupted by the sound of an alert klaxon wailing across the bridge. The alarm indicator mounted along the forward edge of the bridge's helm and navigation console began flashing.

"Report," said Spock, moving from the viewscreen and stepping down into the bridge's command well. Making his way around the navigator's station, he took his place in the center seat and placed the logcomp on the chair's left armrest.

Ensign Chekov, who now monitored the science station

while Spock was in command, turned from the console to regard the first officer.

"Sensors have detected the approach of another ship, Mister Spock," said the young officer, his thick Russian accent wrapping around every word. "It is a Klingon scout-class vessel, sir. Their shields are up and their weapons are active, but in a standby mode."

"Where in blazes did they come from?" asked McCoy, who was walking around the bridge's upper deck until he could stand behind and just to the left of the command chair.

"Our shields activated the moment sensors detected them, sir," added Lieutenant Naomi Rahda, a young, dark-haired woman of Indian descent and another of the *Enterprise*'s helm officers. Normally assigned to gamma shift, she also was one of the first called upon to substitute for Lieutenant Sulu when he was away from the ship. "Shall I activate our weapons?"

Spock pondered the notion before asking, "Mister Chekov, is the Klingon ship on an intercept course?"

"Yes, but they do not appear to be aggressive." The ensign was now bent over the science station's hooded sensor viewer. "Their course change and current speed do not indicate an attack posture."

"Hold on activating weapons, Lieutenant Rahda," said Spock.

Behind him, the turbolift doors opened to reveal Admiral Nogura. As with his previous visits, he directed the officers on duty to maintain their posts. Rather than descending into the command well to join Spock, the admiral instead took up a position next to the communications station.

"I take it we have company?" he asked.

Spock nodded. "Affirmative, sir. A Klingon scout ship has taken an interest in our activities."

"Well, we knew to expect that," said Nogura.

At the communications station and acting in Lieutenant Uhura's stead, Lieutenant Elizabeth Palmer called out, "Mister

Spock, we're being hailed by the Klingon ship." Spock turned to face her, noting that she had shifted in her chair toward him.

"Patch them through, Lieutenant."

The asteroid field as depicted on the main viewscreen dissolved into the image of a swarthy-looking Klingon male sitting in a high-backed chair at the center of a cramped, dimly lit bridge. Spock noted only two other Klingons standing at background stations, but the image quality was such that making out any details was next to impossible. This, he knew, was almost certainly by design. As for the Klingon dominating the screen, his skin was dark, almost olive in appearance, and his face and head were framed by short black hair cut in such a way that it formed a point at the center of his forehead. His features were complemented by a thin mustache and goatee. The gold sash he wore slung from his left shoulder and across his chest bore what Spock recognized as the rank insignia of a ship's commander, along with a pair of other decorations denoting awards. Interestingly, he smiled as he stared out from the viewscreen.

"Federation vessel, identify yourselves and state your reasons for being in this area."

Glancing to Nogura, who nodded for him to proceed, Spock returned his gaze to the screen. "I am Spock, commanding the Federation *Starship Enterprise*. Commander, this region is known to both our governments as free space open to all traffic. Our presence here defies no treaty or other agreement between our peoples. However, in the interests of avoiding confrontation, I can inform you we are currently engaged in a search operation to locate another Starfleet vessel that has gone missing. I assure you our intentions here do not extend beyond that effort."

"I do not need to be lectured by a Vulcan about the intricacies of treaty agreements and border understandings." Still, the Klingon seemed to consider this for several seconds before adding, *"A rescue mission, you say?"*

Not convinced the Klingon's use of the term *rescue* rather

than *search* was an innocent slip, Spock replied, "According to the ship's disaster recorder buoy, it suffered a catastrophic failure in its warp engines and exploded. We are here to ascertain whether there might be any wreckage worth salvaging." Then, after waiting a deliberate moment, he said, "The buoy also contained a record of an encounter with a Klingon warship. The exact circumstances of that encounter or the reasons behind it are also a matter of concern, but if there is a Klingon vessel in need of assistance, I offer that aid, in the hopes of avoiding any further unfortunate incidents." Though no one else on the bridge likely heard it, Spock's Vulcan hearing detected the almost inaudible grunt of satisfaction escaping Nogura's lips.

As Spock expected, the commander bristled, both at the implication of something untoward involving another Klingon ship, and being caught off guard at having it mentioned. There could be no denying the fact of the other vessel operating in the region. His expression had already given away his knowledge of that matter.

"*I am aware of the warship that went missing in this area,*" he said with obvious irritation. "*We have been tasked to search for it or anything or anyone that remains of it. Your assistance is not required.*" He placed his right hand against his chair's armrest, propping himself as he leaned closer to the screen. "*And you would be advised to keep your distance, Vulcan, so we might avoid any of those incidents that worry you so.*"

Spock regarded him in silence for precisely five seconds before replying, "Understood, Commander, just as I presume you will not disturb any wreckage or other remains of our vessel. I would regret an interstellar diplomatic incident resulting from our inability to work or even communicate with each other." The comment earned him another nearly silent murmur of approval from Admiral Nogura.

The Klingon commander harbored no such feelings. "*Keep your distance, Vulcan. You have been warned.*" He did not wait for a response but instead severed the connection and his image disappeared, replaced by the view of the Ivratis asteroid field.

"Charming fellow," said McCoy from where he still stood just to Spock's left. "We should invite him to dinner."

From the science station, Chekov said, "They're moving off, Mister Spock. Sensors show them backtracking along their original approach vector."

"Maintain scans, Mister Chekov, for as long as you're able."

Behind him, Nogura said, "Nicely played, Commander." He stepped closer to the red railing separating him from the command chair. "We can be sure they know about the *Endeavour*. What we don't know is if they know why the *Endeavour* was here in the first place."

"Mister Spock," said Chekov, who had pushed away from his station and now also stood at the railing. "Our scans of the Klingon ship noted something I find odd. According to our readings, that vessel's warp drive has not been used recently. Further, its hull shows signs that it has experienced long-term exposure to the radiation permeating the asteroid field. We're talking weeks at least, sir."

"Weeks?" McCoy frowned. "That would mean the Klingons have been up to something out here for a while, since long before the *Endeavour* happened along."

Spock replied, "That is a logical assumption, Doctor. It also would explain the Klingon commander's reluctance to share information or accept our offer of assistance."

"You may be right," said Nogura. "Klingon pride might also explain that, but only to a point. If there's a Klingon presence in this region, then it's something we know nothing about. That makes a suspicious old man like me very curious. They'd definitely want to avoid us learning whatever it is they're doing here, so our presence is likely quite an irritant."

Snorting in disapproval, McCoy replied, "Meaning we haven't seen the last of them."

"I wouldn't bet against it," said the admiral.

"Of greater concern is how this new development impacts Captain Kirk and his team." Spock turned the command chair to face Nogura. "Under normal circumstances, Admiral, I would attempt to make contact with the captain."

Nogura nodded. "Unfortunately, the circumstances are very much *not* normal, Mister Spock." He sighed. "For now, I'm afraid we have no choice but to continue observing the communications protocols for this mission. We need to wait until Captain Kirk or the *Endeavour* makes contact with us."

"But what if the Klingons have already found Jim and the others?" asked McCoy. "While we're sneaking around out here with all of this cloak-and-dagger business, they could be in real trouble." His disdain for the necessities of various Starfleet rules and regulations was evident on frequent occasion, though most of the time he at least attempted to observe decorum. In situations like these, however, the doctor could be counted upon to give voice to his thoughts and feelings with little regard for the chain of command.

Nogura eyed McCoy. "I sympathize with your frustrations, Doctor, but for the security of the mission and *everyone* involved, this is the way it has to be. At least for now."

Though he said nothing, Spock also understood McCoy's anxiety about the present situation, even if he might disagree with his friend's methods of expressing himself. He shared the doctor's worry. His captain and friend along with Lieutenants Uhura and Sulu were out there, somewhere, doing their best to play a role while undertaking an already risky mission. They were now in even greater danger than they might know.

There was absolutely nothing Spock could do to help them.

Seventeen

Many Klingons aspired to be warriors. Le'tal was not among them.

There were of course many females serving in the Klingon Defense Force, but it had never been her calling. As a child, she endured her three brothers and their tireless daydreaming and fantasizing about one day becoming soldiers of the Empire. She never blamed them for such things, as they were understandable outgrowths of wishing to hew to the tradition of service observed by her family for generations. In her youth, her father was the embodiment of that call to duty, so it made sense his sons would want to follow his example.

Le'tal recalled the fear she felt at the prospect of informing her father about her desires and intentions, along with his initial disappointment when she voiced her decision to enter the engineering field. Joy quickly replaced that uncertainty as he told her service to the Empire came in many forms. The talents and aptitude she displayed during her formative schooling period would afford her options not available to her brothers, each of them capable young Klingons with the potential to distinguish themselves as warriors.

"Perhaps your destiny lies along a different path," he had said to her. Always far wiser than he tended to reveal to others, he confessed to knowing she might one day make such a choice. Rather than disapproving, he commended her not just for her choices but the conviction with which she made and held to them. "We must each feed the fire that burns first within our own hearts. Do that, and you will honor your family and the Empire."

I wonder what Father would think of where feeding that fire has brought me.

As a youth applying herself to her studies, Le'tal had no way to know someone from the military or intelligence apparatus would find her. Indeed, it was not until her formal education neared its completion that a Klingon female approached her, telling her about all the ways she, a young scientist, could contribute to the Empire's security and its ability to push back against its enemies. While Le'tal had no interest in developing weapons, she soon realized there were other ways her training and natural talents could be brought to bear.

Her reverie was broken by the sound of the chime announcing that someone now stood outside the door to her quarters. Sitting at her desk, she glanced at the chronometer displayed in the corner of one of the three computer terminals dominating her cluttered workspace. It was well after the conclusion of her normal duty shift. Momentary concern was alleviated when she checked another of the computer interfaces and saw no alerts or other urgent advisories waited for her attention. The disruption-field generators were continuing to operate within expected parameters, as Le'tal was detailing in her latest status report.

So, what is this about?

Swiveling her chair so she faced the door, she called out, "Enter." In response, the heavy, reinforced pressure hatch slid aside to reveal No'Khal, her longtime colleague and perhaps her closest friend, standing in the entryway. Short and burly, he nevertheless could be very intimidating when he wanted to make that impression. That was something Le'tal had learned when he was her teacher. Despite being relieved from his work shift, he had not yet changed from the loose-fitting jumpsuit worn by each of the team's twenty members. She knew that in short order, her friend would revert to his preferred ensemble of a heavy woven robe and sandals for his feet. Whatever else he wore—or chose not to wear—beneath the robe was a topic of much spirited conversation among their colleagues.

"Good evening, Le'tal," he said, waiting until she gestured for him to step into the room. "I hope I am not disturbing you."

Le'tal smiled. "You? Never."

Though the nature of their work saw to it that she and the other members of her team became a small, tight-knit community, the friendship she shared with No'Khal long preceded their current assignment. Older than her—perhaps the same age as her father when she was an adolescent—No'Khal and she first met while she was still a systems engineer student and he a teacher at the technical school where she studied. He was an accomplished computer systems expert before transferring to academia, and may have been content to remain in that scholarly role until Le'tal came calling with an opportunity to work with her on a new project.

How long ago was that, now? She almost laughed at the question to herself. *It seems like a lifetime.*

Entering her quarters and allowing the door to close behind him, No'Khal made a show of inspecting the room. "I see your housekeeping prowess has progressed not at all since your days as my pupil." He smiled, dulling the sting out of the gentle verbal jab.

As was the case with the rest of the outpost, which in reality was little more than a collection of a dozen prefabricated modules of varying sizes sitting atop a larger structure built into the body of an asteroid, her quarters were stark and utilitarian. The cramped room was filled to overflowing with all manner of personal belongings as well as items she used in her work. Clothes hung on the backs of chairs or were piled on a corner table, or were simply discarded where she dropped them on the floor.

The small kitchen nook near the door might as well be labeled a quarantine zone. Computer equipment was scattered on shelves along the far wall as well as a cabinet near the door leading to her sleeping area. Strewn about were components in various stages of assembly, along with parts that might well be orphaned forever from whatever piece of machinery they had originated within. Data cartridges containing everything from status reports to journal entries to technical specifications and computer software code were stacked wherever there was a place for them atop most of the compartment's horizontal surfaces. Though the outpost's main computer was more than capable of generating whatever schematics or other data she required to further her work, Le'tal preferred physical copies of such products. The better for scratching and scribbling notes, thoughts, and ideas as they came to her during those frenzied moments late at night when she found herself unable to sleep.

"I once read something written by a human," she said, quick to defend her living habits, "that disorganized people tend to be among the most intelligent. A famous human scientist who lived centuries ago on Earth once said, 'If a cluttered desk is a sign of a cluttered mind, of what, then, is an empty desk a sign?' I have always found it amusing to contemplate this question."

Now No'Khal laughed. "If you are any indication, those Earthers were quite correct indeed."

Pushing herself away from her desk, Le'tal rose from her chair. "Are you really here to remind me how slovenly I am?"

"I learned long ago that is a lost cause." He gestured toward the door. "I seek sustenance, and decided to come draw you out of your cave so you might dine like a proper Klingon, rather than subsist on the dreck that is those ration packs you seem to enjoy beyond all reason." He paused, then added, "All right, even the best this facility has to offer does not approach a civilized Klingon feast, but it is the best we can do under the circumstances. Join me. A meal is better when shared with friends." He always talked this way, like a character out of literature, when he labored to make any kind of point, and Le'tal could not help grinning in response.

"I was going to eat later," she replied, nodding toward her desk. "I have work." While she confessed to relying upon the prepackaged meals rather than the outpost's admittedly versatile food synthesizer units, it was less a function of taste than of simple convenience. She preferred to work late into the evening and therefore always kept a selection of the rations in her quarters. In truth, the menu options they afforded were limited, but they served their primary purpose.

No'Khal snorted. "You work too much, my former student. The grand plans of the Klingon Empire can wait until your belly is full and you have benefited from actual rest." His smile broadened. "I am told we are opening one of our precious kegs of bloodwine tonight."

"Now that is a convincing argument. Lead the way." With a final look at her trio of computer monitors, Le'tal decided that, yes, her work could wait a little longer on this evening. Perhaps she might eschew it entirely and instead spend that time attempting to correct what No'Khal called her "sleep deficit." A meal with her friend and perhaps a single portion of bloodwine before falling into deep slumber was sounding better with each passing moment.

She was just following No'Khal out of her quarters when one of her computers emitted an annoying tone she immediately recognized: an alert of an incoming communication. Shaking her head, Le'tal released a small sigh of resignation.

"Unless it is Kahless himself," said No'Khal, "returning as foretold, ignore it."

Le'tal grunted. "If only that were an option." Part of her duties as project leader at this remote, hidden facility was to monitor and respond to any communication. Given the security under which she and her team worked, transmissions of any sort to or from the outpost were rare and normally occurred only when they fell within a very strict set of parameters. Messages to family or loved ones were forbidden, and even the status reports for her superiors at Imperial Intelligence were sent via encrypted burst transmission at irregular intervals. She was the sole keeper of the schedule for dispatching and receiving of such missives.

A status update from the communications system told her the message was encrypted in such a manner that Le'tal knew the point of origin. "The Orion," she said, glancing over her shoulder at No'Khal before keying commands to her computer terminal. A moment later, the strings of data streaming across one screen were replaced by an image of D'zinn, the alluring female who was her point of contact for the Orions with whom the outpost had a "business arrangement." Tall and lithe, she wore her dark hair piled atop her head, and she was dressed in a form-fitting black jumpsuit rather than some of the more exotic clothing choices for which her people were known.

"D'zinn, this is an unscheduled communication," she said, her tone one of warning.

For her part, the Orion had never seemed intimidated, either by Le'tal or the commander of the outpost's small military contingent. Such was the case now as she replied, "I would not contact you without good reason, Le'tal. Rest assured, I have information you may find useful, if not concerning."

Le'tal listened as D'zinn detailed her encounter with the civilian transport, and her suspicions about the small, innocuous-looking craft. The presence of the Federation starship at the asteroid field's outer boundary was an expected development, as was their search for an explanation into the loss of the other Starfleet ship. Klingon Intelligence had likewise demanded information about the destroyed battle cruiser. The outpost's military garrison commander, Karamaq, was in the midst of conducting his investigation, and Le'tal was content to let him obsess over such things. The Federation ship, on the other hand, demanded her attention.

"This transport," she said. "You believe it is working with the *Enterprise*?"

D'zinn scowled. *"I have no evidence of this, but the timing of the transport's presence with the* Enterprise *in such proximity seems rather convenient. Further, its pilot seemed far more skilled than a simple civilian."* She recounted how the *Dreamline* had bested her own vessel during their previous engagement. *"I would wager he possessed some kind of Starfleet or other military training."*

"But why would they do this?" asked No'Khal, stepping closer to the computer terminal. "Why such subterfuge for what should be a straightforward search? Even if they hope to find survivors, that would not be cause for acting in this way."

"Perhaps they suspect something." It was obvious, the more Le'tal considered it. Was it possible the crew of the lost starship had somehow communicated information regarding what caused their vessel's mishap? Had the ship's sensors detected something about the disruption-field technology?

No'Khal said, "Unless Imperial Intelligence has seen fit to brief them, even the High Council is unaware of our presence here. If Starfleet has discovered us, the repercussions could be quite severe. All our work, everything we have accomplished, will be for nothing."

Of this, Le'tal was well aware. From the moment she first learned of this new initiative sponsored by the Empire's intelligence bureau, she was intrigued by the possibilities. Disabling a vessel rather than damaging or destroying it allowed for numerous opportunities to study and exploit an enemy's technology. Learning Starfleet's protected techniques for combating and defeating Klingon weapons and defenses was also of great value.

As explained to her, the disruption-field generator she was to design and create was not without precedent. A more limited, even primitive version of this concept had been field tested by imperial warships not long ago. While results varied, it was decided that iteration of the device was too costly in terms of ship's power requirements at the expense of other vital systems. She found it amusing to learn the *Enterprise* was actually one of the vessels targeted with that version of the technology, and here it was now. Le'tal had to wonder if fate or some form of supernatural influence saw to it this particular vessel continued finding its way into such situations.

By comparison, the disruption generators developed by her and her team were far more efficient. Though deployed here within the asteroid field, the ultimate goal was to make the emitters practical enough that they could be installed aboard any class of ship in the Klingon Defense Force. The results recorded to this point were favorable, but Le'tal knew more testing was required, both in the emitters' current configuration as placed on various asteroids within the Ivratis field and, eventually, aboard the small squadron of military vessels assigned to the outpost. While he largely observed the present phase of experiments, Karamaq was anxious to see the system tested in ship-based scenarios.

All in good time, Commander.

To date, her team's work with the new technology had proceeded with much success and little in the way of problems. The only true issue encountered so far was the unexpected presence of the Federation starship and the Klingon battle cruiser and the field's unfortunate impact on both vessels. Le'tal remained convinced neither she nor her people were at fault, and she was including that along with the official logs in her report. She would not allow her work or that of her colleagues to be blamed for circumstances beyond their control.

"D'zinn," she said, "where is this transport?"

The Orion seemed to hesitate, as though she preferred not to answer. Drawing herself up, she replied, *"If it is what its pilot claims and held to its original course, it would likely be clear of the asteroid field by now, on its way to whatever destination awaits it."*

"And if it is a ruse," said No'Khal, "then it is certainly still somewhere in the field."

Le'tal nodded. "Exactly." To D'zinn, she said, "Alert your other ships. Your new priority is a thorough search for this transport. If it is out there, I want it captured."

"That will take some time," said the Orion.

"Not too much. Remember, if the Federation discovers what we are doing here, your involvement will not go overlooked." In truth, Le'tal did not care about the Orions. Let D'zinn and her people flail about searching for this other ship. Their activities would continue to conceal the outpost's presence, but if this mysterious ship was part of some larger Starfleet operation, life for Le'tal and her people here might soon get very complicated.

"Find that ship, D'zinn," she warned. "Quickly."

Eighteen

Khatami loved the warmth of the sun on her face. Lying back on the blanket in the open meadow, she looked up toward the brilliant blue Deneva sky. It was a perfect day. How long had it been since she had enjoyed a slice of peace and quiet like this? Too long, which was almost always the answer. She could stay here forever. All she needed were her husband, Kenji, and their daughter, Parveen.

Where are they?

No sooner did she consider the question than something made her rise from the blanket spread on the ground beneath her. Using her elbows to prop her upper body, Khatami looked across the meadow's green grass and saw Kenji and Parveen walking toward her. The girl waved in her direction, and even from this distance there was no mistaking Parveen's beaming smile. Upon seeing her, her husband and daughter began jogging across the meadow. Khatami watched them run toward her, but they did not come closer. The open field separating them widened, with more grass appearing as if from nowhere to block their path. She held out a hand and shouted their names, but she heard nothing. All was silent around her, while Kenji and Parveen now seemed to grow smaller. Khatami shouted again with as much force as she could muster but still heard nothing. Until . . .

"Captain Khatami?"

Her eyes snapped open. The blue sky, lush meadow, and her family were gone, replaced by the bland gray ceiling of her quarters on the *Endeavour*.

The ship, her sleep-fogged thoughts reminded her. *Asteroid. Crashed. Still here. Damn.*

"Yes." It was an effort to force even the single word. Casting aside her sheets, Khatami sat up in the bed. She swung her legs over the side until her bare feet touched the maroon area rug situated between her bed and the divider separating the two halves of her quarters. While she thought of her family every day she could not remember the last time she dreamed of them. Was that a sign? She was not prone to superstition, but something about the vivid nature of the dream lingered. It was an odd, not entirely welcome sensation.

Shaking off the last remnants of sleep, Khatami looked across her quarters to the small foyer before the entrance to her suite's seating area to see Katherine Stano standing there. It was no wonder she had not heard the first officer's entrance, as the door in that half of the room was locked open. Like numerous other doors leading to all of the ship's remaining noncritical interior sections, hers had been left in this state, reducing the power requirements needed for the computer's automated entry and exit system. It was one of several ideas put forth by Commander Yataro and his engineering team as a means of conserving the *Endeavour*'s limited energy reserves. For the moment, privacy in this situation was a luxury.

Khatami cleared her throat and waved toward Stano. "I was that far gone, wasn't I?"

"I really hated disturbing you, Captain," replied Stano, her expression emphasizing her regret. "I know you've only been in the rack an hour or so, but something's come up. Klisiewicz thinks there's a ship out there. Somewhere close."

Khatami felt any possible chance of her returning to sleep vanish in the face of this news. "He's sure?" Rising to her feet, she retrieved the black trousers she had flung across the chair next to her bed and pulled them on.

"He's Klisiewicz." Stano shrugged. "Good enough for me."

"Fair enough." After donning her gold tunic, Khatami reached for her boots and socks. "Any idea who it might be?"

Stano shook her head. "Sensor returns are still being affected by the background noise around here. Even with our buoys and their little booster trick, it's still too far away for him to get a lock on it."

Moving to the small bureau set into the wall opposite her bed, Khatami examined herself in the mirror. She ran her fingers through her black hair, which she kept styled in a simple bob cut. The feeble gesture was enough to get it to lay in something resembling a normal fashion and perhaps hide the fact she was just roused from sleep, and she declared victory.

"Let's pay a visit to Mister Klisiewicz."

The transit to the *Endeavour*'s makeshift auxiliary control center was easy enough, with Khatami and Stano making use of the engineering ladders connecting decks in lieu of turbolifts taken offline to conserve power. They arrived to find the science officer along with Lieutenant Estrada as the room's only occupants. Both men were hunched over the console Klisiewicz had reconfigured to act as an interface to the main computer as well as what remained of the ship's sensor array. They turned from the station upon hearing the sound of new arrivals.

"Gentlemen," said Khatami, forcing herself not to groan in protest as she caught sight of the console's chronometer and the unholy hour displayed upon it. "We've got company?"

Klisiewicz grimaced. "Looks that way, Captain. It entered our sensor range about ten minutes ago, and has been making a slow circuit through the area. Whoever they are, they're definitely looking for something."

"Still not able to identify them?" asked Stano. The first officer had made her way to the console and was already studying the sensor returns.

"Not yet, Commander," said Estrada. "Whatever it is, it's not very big. Maybe a scout-class vessel, but I can't tell you who it belongs to. Its power signature isn't consistent with a Klingon or Starfleet ship, but that's as much as I can get with our current setup." He gestured to the workstation. "If we boosted power to the buoys, that'd likely help, but it'd also be like ringing a bell."

Blowing out her breath, Khatami shook her head. "Right."

The new development only served to hammer home the harsh truth about their current plight. Lying on the bottom of a canyon on a desolate asteroid, damaged to the point that any kind of lift-off was impossible while her crew survived on the limited resources left to them until help arrived. They were completely helpless prey for anyone who might happen by and realize the opportunity for plunder the wounded *Endeavour* represented.

Well, maybe not completely helpless, Khatami thought.

Stano had ordered the security detail to prepare for the possibility of boarding by unfriendly operators such as pirates or others looking to take advantage of the crippled starship's situation. Security details were posted to each of the ship's access points, and the intruder control system would alert the crew if anyone or anything attempted to breach the hull. Khatami knew it might all prove futile in the face of a determined adversary like a Klingon boarding force or even a band of determined Orion privateers. Still, anyone taking up such a challenge would have to earn their spoils. Given the current circumstances, she almost welcomed such a fight. If nothing else, it would at least confirm *someone* knew they were here. The thought was enough to make her smile to herself.

Come one, come all.

"Captain, I think we've got something."

Sulu's comment, delivered with the first thing resembling anticipation since their mission began, was enough to bring

Kirk running from the *Dreamline*'s passenger compartment. He crowded the cockpit's entryway to find his helm officer leaning forward in his seat, reaching for controls positioned near his console's forward edge just under the canopy. Outside the ship, a monstrous asteroid loomed ahead of them, cloaked largely in shadow as it filled Kirk's field of view. Other than the color—deep browns instead of shades of gray—it reminded Kirk of Earth's moon instead of a rogue piece of discarded interstellar flotsam. To Sulu's left, Uhura once more occupied the copilot's position, immersed in whatever scanning tasks with which she was assisting her companion.

"What've you got?" asked Kirk.

Uhura indicated the controls before her. "Sensors hit on something as we were flying past this asteroid, sir. The field's background radiation along with interference from mineral concentrations inside the asteroid itself are continuing to hamper our scans, but we still picked it up."

"It happened pretty fast," added Sulu, "so I brought us around to take another look."

His gaze shifting between his officers and the asteroid, which looked too close for comfort, Kirk asked, "Any signs of other ship activity out here?"

"Not so far as we can tell, sir," replied Uhura.

"What about that Orion ship?"

Sulu said, "Wherever they went after our last run-in, they don't seem to be anywhere nearby."

"Let's hope it stays that way." Kirk knew their ruse likely would not survive another encounter with the Orion ship commander. Their cover story of being a civilian transport would evaporate if they were found still wandering around within the Ivratis field rather than having departed the area for their supposed destination. The longer Kirk and his people stayed out here with nothing to show for their efforts, the more dangerous their situation became.

"Hang on," said Uhura after a moment. Hunching over her console, she adjusted several controls and Kirk watched as the display screen she had configured to serve as a readout for the transport's sensor data began scrolling in rapid fashion. "Wait." She looked to Sulu. "Can you take us in closer?"

The helm officer nodded. "How close do you want to go?"

"I'll let you know."

His fingers moved masterfully across the pilot console as Sulu guided the ship toward the asteroid's surface. Despite his confidence in the lieutenant, Kirk could not help the slight churning in his stomach as unforgiving rock drew closer, then began to shift beneath them as Sulu leveled out the transport and slowed its speed. Now the surrounding landscape looked no different than traversing the surface of a barren planet or a moon at night. Only the presence of other asteroids in the space above them disturbed the illusion. Jagged mountain peaks flanked the ship as Sulu guided it along the surface, and the terrain ahead of them offered nothing but the same grim view of utter desolation.

"Something ahead of us," reported Uhura. "It's an energy signature. Very weak, but it's there." She tapped another set of controls before glancing over her shoulder to Kirk. "It's a Starfleet sensor buoy, sir. Operating in a low-power mode, but definitely one of ours."

Sulu added, "There's more than one." He paused, checking his instruments. "There are three of them, sir. No, wait. Four. Readings show four buoys. They're positioned at equidistant intervals from one another. No chance that's an accident." He tapped one of the sensor controls. "Scans show there's a valley or canyon of some sort in that vicinity."

"A canyon?" Kirk stepped into the cockpit, leaning close to the console between Sulu and Uhura. "Big enough to hide a starship?"

"Or what's left of one?" prompted Uhura.

Smiling, Sulu returned his attention to the pilot's console. "Exactly what I was thinking." Under his guidance, the transport's course shifted to port as the lieutenant nudged the ship's nose downward, reducing their altitude above the asteroid's surface.

Kirk stepped back from the console, giving his officers more room to work. "Any ideas about the sensor buoys? Maybe a way to increase communications? Sensors?"

"That's my guess, sir," replied Uhura. "Buoys like this can be reconfigured to interface with a ship's systems and act like boosters for weak signals. I don't know how well they'd do combating the interference we're dealing with, but maybe they figured they had nothing to lose by trying."

"And the low power signature would likely only attract attention if someone was looking for it," said Sulu.

"Someone like us," replied Kirk. "Let's hope no one else is as smart as you two."

The area ahead of the *Dreamline* was flatter now, though hills and peaks were still visible far ahead of them and to either side. Not so distant was a dark patch that had appeared from the gloom. As they drew closer, Kirk saw the gap extended for kilometers to either side of the transport, and was at least a kilometer wide.

"That's our canyon," said Sulu. He pointed toward the canopy. "Look."

Ahead of them, Kirk recognized the shape of a Starfleet sensor buoy resting on the asteroid's surface near the canyon's edge. It had not crashed there; that much was obvious. No, he decided. It had been deliberately placed there, along with three others he could not see.

"According to its encrypted transponder," said Uhura, "it's from the *Endeavour*."

Kirk felt excitement welling up within him. "Now we're talking."

He resisted the urge to grab on to something as Sulu guided the transport into the expansive maw. The canopy's imaging processors translated data from the sensors and provided depth and detail to the canyon walls rising past the descending ship.

"Something's definitely down here." Uhura was making frequent adjustments to her sensor controls. A quick glance told Kirk she was refining the scan data that was now being fed to her in a torrent, filtering through whatever information failed to serve her more immediate needs. "Something big." A telltale beep from her console made her look up, offering a triumphant smile. "I'm registering duranium, sir."

"Like a starship's hull." Kirk gestured to her console. "Uhura, open a channel. Low frequency and scrambled, just in case somebody else is out here. If those buoys did their job, then the *Endeavour* already knows we're here." He waited until Uhura established the frequency, then said, "*Starship Endeavour*, this is Captain James Kirk of the *U.S.S. Enterprise*. Captain Khatami, if you can hear me, Admiral Nogura sends his regards."

Static was the initial response through the open connection, but a few seconds later a female voice replaced it. "*Jim? You won't believe how happy I am to hear your voice.*"

"Same here, Atish."

"*What the hell are you flying? We were sure you might be Orion pirates or some other lowlife looking for a quick score.*"

Kirk suppressed the urge to chuckle. "It's a long story, and one of the admiral's ideas. We found your buoys, and if my helm and communications officers' instincts are right, we're on our way down to you."

"*We've got you on what's left of our sensors. Just keep descending. You won't be able to miss us.*"

"She's right, sir," said Uhura. "The duranium signature is growing stronger by the second."

Without saying anything, Sulu maneuvered the *Dreamline* so its nose angled downward. Even with the cockpit canopy's enhancements, Kirk could see nothing but the walls around them. Then, more detail formed ahead of them and he realized it had to be the canyon floor. Near a point where the canyon narrowed, with rock walls stretching hundreds of meters above it, was an obviously artificial, circular shape.

"Bingo," said Sulu, his attention locked on his instruments.

There could be no mistaking a starship's saucer section, and Kirk's pulse began to race as the transport's descent brought them ever closer to their prize. Details were coming into view, and he recognized the raised section at the center of the hull cradling the ship's bridge. That area was dark, and only a few light sources betrayed the vessel's location. With the aid of the transport's imaging processors, it was now easy to make out the lettering sprawling across the hull, which still proudly identified the ship as the *U.S.S. Endeavour* NCC-1895.

"Well done, you two," he said, reaching out to pat both Uhura and Sulu on their shoulders. "Very well done." Then, for the benefit of the still-open communications frequency, he added, "All right, *Endeavour*. We've got you."

Over the connection, Khatami replied, *"You'll have to pardon our dust. We're remodeling. You're more than welcome to join us, but our transporters are offline. Feel like taking a walk?"*

"We'll be right over," said Kirk. "Uhura, break out some environmental suits." As she maneuvered her way out of the cockpit, he looked to Sulu. "What do you think? Should we avoid landing on the hull?"

The helm officer nodded. "I would. She looks to be in rough shape, but I can set her down pretty close. We won't be outside for more than a couple of minutes, sir."

"Do it."

Noting some buckling along the saucer's edges, Kirk could only agree with Sulu's informal assessment of the ship's condition. The damage was mute evidence of the stress put on the ship during its own descent and landing. Kirk wondered how sound the *Endeavour* might still truly be, and if it would hold up long enough to get Khatami, her crew, and her precious cargo to safety.

One thing at a time, Captain, he mused. *One thing at a time.*

"All right, Mr. Sulu," he told his companion. "Now the real work can begin."

Nineteen

A full welcoming committee greeted Kirk, Uhura, and Sulu as they stepped through the airlock's inner hatch and into the service corridor. There was no applause or cheering, but also no small shortage of relieved smiles as their hosts got their first look at their would-be saviors.

"Permission to come aboard?" asked Kirk as he removed his helmet, and both he and Khatami could not help chuckling at the absurdity of observing protocol in such circumstances.

She replied, "Permission granted. Welcome to what's left of the *U.S.S. Endeavour.*" One of her officers, a young human male with lieutenant's stripes on his blue uniform tunic, gestured to the helmet, and Kirk handed it off to him.

"Lieutenant Klisiewicz," he said, recalling the name from his review of the *Endeavour*'s crew roster. "Isn't it?"

The younger man nodded. "That's right, sir. Good to see you."

"Likewise." Turning his attention to Khatami, Kirk said, "I'm going to hazard a guess you and your crew aren't exactly ready for a formal inspection." He punctuated his statement with a small, knowing grin.

Khatami replied, "I never liked inspections."

"Same here." Kirk quickly introduced Uhura and Sulu, after which Khatami returned the favor with her own senior staff.

"With your permission, Captains," said Commander Stano, the *Endeavour*'s first officer, "we can get you something more comfortable to wear, and then I can brief Lieutenants Uhura and Sulu about our current situation and maybe get started on an evacuation plan."

"Sounds good," replied Khatami. She gestured to Klisiewicz and her engineer. "Take Klisiewicz and Yataro with you. May as well get the straight scoop from the horse's mouth." Turning back to Kirk, she added, "And you and I should probably have a conversation as well."

Kirk said, "Admiral Nogura would appreciate that."

Once everyone had their orders, Kirk and his group availed themselves of the standard-issue olive-green jumpsuits provided by Stano. Kirk was happy for the switch, as the EV suits taken from the *Dreamline's* supply locker lacked the comfort and better fit of their Starfleet counterparts. Designed for use in emergencies, the simpler models were intended as a last resort option in the event of a hull breach or crash landing from which the passengers and crew might be forced to abandon ship. Not a fan of any sort of extravehicular activity if it could be avoided, Kirk preferred the Starfleet versions with which he was far more familiar.

"Sorry for the jumpsuits," said Khatami as she and Kirk traversed one of the corridors on deck nine on their way to the cargo hold on this level. "Best we could do on short notice. Making do with what we've got has become the name of the game around here."

Kirk waved away the apology. "From what I can tell, you and your crew have done a fantastic job holding things together."

"It all starts with my helm officer, Lieutenant McCormack," Khatami replied. "I swear that woman could fly a cotton ball through an ion storm if she had to. If not for her skill, we would've been in a lot worse shape when we set down on this rock. I know saucer separation is supposed to be something all pilots learn and train for, but doing it for real with four hundred people counting on you not to screw it up is a different game altogether."

"Sounds like Lieutenant McCormack and Mister Sulu should get together and compare notes," said Kirk, taking a moment to brag on his own helm officer and how he had pulled the *Enterprise* out of danger more times than the captain could count.

"Since then," said Khatami, "it's all been about conservation while we hunker down, keep quiet, and wait for the cavalry to arrive."

Kirk replied, "Sorry it took so long." The lighting in the corridor was subdued, as he suspected was true for the rest of the ship as a power-saving measure. Though Khatami had not said so, it likely was the reason he had also followed her two decks down a service ladder from the airlock's location rather than use a turbolift. As they walked, he brushed his hand across the empty spot over the left breast pocket, where a patch with the wearer's name and rank would normally be placed. "Besides, it's better if the crew only sees one person running around here with captain's stripes. Not that anyone should be confused by who's in charge, but this keeps it simple. It's your ship, and we're here to help."

"But you're in charge of our guests, right? I mean, all this top-secret, cloak-and-dagger sneaking about really isn't my specialty."

"Hard to believe, given how well you did with what Nogura threw at you in the Taurus Reach."

"My ship and I were assigned to exploration duty in the Taurus Reach, Captain," she said. Then, she cast a wry grin in his direction. "I can only assume you read all of the *official* reports, of course."

"Of course."

Thanks to his own experiences with Nogura and the region in question, Kirk was well aware of Khatami's and the *Endeavour*'s role in a still-classified assignment involving Starfleet operations in the Taurus Reach. A wedge of unclaimed and largely unexplored space sandwiched between the borders of the Federation, Klingon Empire, and the Tholian Assembly, the region had become a flashpoint for all three parties following the discovery of artifacts and other remnants of an ancient, incredibly powerful, and supposedly extinct alien race known as the Shedai. When Starfleet realized both the potential and the danger to be found from studying the technology, it went to extensive lengths to safeguard it from exploitation by others, namely the Klingons. The Tholians just wanted everyone to leave well enough alone, which was understandable after the revelation that they shared a link to the Shedai.

To this end, Starfleet established a formal presence in the Taurus Reach, ostensibly as part of its ongoing exploration mandate but in actuality a cover for the more clandestine activities involving learning about the Shedai. Starbase 47, informally named "Vanguard Station," was the waypoint connecting the area to Federation space and interests. The *Endeavour*, initially under the command of Captain Zhao Sheng and later Khatami after Zhao was killed, was one of three ships assigned to the station to assist in carrying out surveys of the Reach. Starfleet's activities were more than enough to set off the Tholians, and their anger over Starfleet's continued forays into the region and their discoveries about the Shedai eventually triggered a massive offensive against the station. Known among those who survived the fight—including Kirk, Khatami, and a number of their respective crews—as "the Battle of Vanguard," the incident and indeed the entire Vanguard project had been classified by none other than Admiral Heihachiro Nogura. For at least the next century, only those individuals with the highest security clearances and the absolute need to know would have access to the details of the operation. As far as the rest of Starfleet was concerned, the project never happened.

The first rule of Vanguard, thought Kirk, recalling what Nogura had once said, *is that you don't talk about Vanguard.*

"How are your guests holding up?" he asked. "None the worse for wear, I hope."

Khatami blew out her breath, an obvious sign exhaustion was beginning to take its toll on her. "As well as might be expected, I suppose. Have you ever retrieved a deep-cover operative after something like what they've been through?"

"No. I know agents for these sorts of missions are screened and tested and trained to within an inch of their lives, but they can't possibly prepare you for everything. There's no way to anticipate all the variables that come with operating behind enemy lines without support."

"It takes a special kind of person to even volunteer for something like that in the first place," said Khatami. "And who knows how many candidates wash out of training for whatever reason." She shook her head. "It's not something I'd ever want to do."

Kirk replied, "Agreed. I've had a small taste of undercover work. Can't say I liked it all that much."

"I heard about that." Khatami chuckled. "They surgically altered you to look like a Romulan, so you could steal a cloaking device from a Romulan ship?"

"I thought the ears looked pretty good on me, but my first officer disagreed with me. The whole thing makes for a pretty long story."

Khatami said, "Get us out of this, and you can tell it to me over dinner. I'm buying."

"Deal."

They rounded a final bend in the corridor and Kirk recognized the reinforced hatch of a cargo bay. A pair of security officers, a Vulcan male and a human female, stood guard outside the door.

"Just protocol," said Khatami, indicating the guards with a wave. "According to my orders, our guests are to remain quarantined until they're debriefed by Admiral Nogura. I've been honoring the spirit of that directive as best I can, but circumstances have forced me to get creative." She explained how the agents had assisted her crew with repairs as well as deploying the sensor buoys before returning to their "special accommodations."

Kirk said, "Nogura's given me provisional authority to talk with them, just in case . . ." He let the sentence trail off as they arrived at the cargo hold's entrance.

"In case something happens to them, or us," said Khatami.

"Right." Kirk frowned. He had no love for this aspect of covert Starfleet operations. "How's that old saying go? Plan for the best, expect the worst?"

Khatami gestured to the guards, and the female ensign tapped an entry code into the door's keypad. The heavy hatch slid aside to reveal a cargo bay virtually identical to those on the *Enterprise*. The main difference was the temporary housing facility installed here to care for the three Starfleet operatives. Living space, common area, and a field medical clinic were all located in the center of the hold, and inside the clinic space Kirk saw a young woman in a blue Starfleet uniform tending to something at a desk. She was petite in build, her brown hair was styled in a bob not too dissimilar to Khatami's, and her uniform insignia indicated she was a nurse.

"Captain," she said as she approached, then nodded to Kirk. "I'm Lieutenant Holly Amos, one of Doctor Leone's assistants. Welcome to the *Endeavour*, sir."

Kirk replied, "Thank you, Lieutenant. Anything new to report about our friends?"

"All of Doctor Leone's tests show they're all physically and psychologically sound, which is pretty impressive considering the strain they've been under for such an extended period. It'll take a while for them to completely acclimate back to life away from Klingons, but so far the early signs are all very positive. The crew took a bit getting used to having them working with repair teams and other tasks, so we've opted to have them stay here when there's nothing specifically requiring their assistance. Still, they didn't waste any time before pitching in. I guess it was good therapy, in a way." Gesturing around the cargo bay, she added, "I just wish we could've offered more than this. We're not exactly the posh resort they likely wanted to visit for shore leave after a long, grueling mission."

Nodding in understanding, Kirk said, "All in good time, Lieutenant."

"Speaking of Doctor Leone and all of his tests," said Khatami, "where *is* he? I figured he'd be down here."

"He was until just a few minutes ago, Captain," replied Amos. "He ran to the mess hall for coffee." She nodded toward the food synthesizer set into the wall of the temporary facility's common area. "Apparently, this one isn't programmed properly. He said even the packets in the field rations tasted better. You know how he can get without his special blend."

Offering a knowing smirk, Khatami said, "Indeed I do."

As they spoke, the door to one of the facility's sleeping areas opened and a woman stepped through. She wore a red jumpsuit like those used by the engineering staff but without the accompanying boots, opting instead for simple slippers to cover her feet. Even with the surgical alterations that made her appear Klingon instead of human, Kirk had no trouble recognizing Morgan Binnix, the leader of the three deep-cover agents, from the personnel file he had reviewed at the beginning of this mission.

"Commander Binnix," he said in greeting. "I'm Captain James Kirk of the *Starship Enterprise*."

She blinked a few times before a small smile crept onto her lips. "My apologies, Captain. I'm afraid I'm still getting used to being called by my real name." She extended her hand and they exchanged pleasantries. "It's a pleasure to meet you, sir. Your reputation precedes you."

"It's not all true," replied Kirk. Then, with a grin, he added, "Well, just the good parts."

The doors to first one, then the other of the two remaining sleeping areas opened to reveal their occupants. As with their companion, Kirk recognized Phillip Watson and David Horst despite their disguises as Binnix made introductions. After granting Lieutenant Amos permission to return to her work, Khatami directed everyone else to the chairs and sofas in the common area set up for the agents.

For the next several moments, Kirk listened with rapt attention while Binnix and her colleagues recounted their past three years on the Klingon homeworld. While the operatives tried to keep things brief and to the point, they could not help adding detail to certain subjects, observations, or anecdotes. Content to let them lay out their informal report at their own pace, Kirk still found himself asking questions, especially when it came to topics of the military. The agents' information about the new models of warship under construction at facilities throughout the Empire were of particular interest. So far as he could surmise, Binnix and her team had done remarkable work, collecting a veritable treasure trove of data that would provide months if not years of research fodder for Starfleet Command as well as associated intelligence agencies along with research and development groups. That they had accomplished so much over such a short period of time at great risk to themselves and seemed to have come through it all relatively unscathed emotionally or psychologically was amazing.

"And everything you've told me is documented, or supported by information you collected and brought with you?" Kirk asked, still processing what he had heard.

Watson replied, "All of that and a whole lot more. Every last bit of the data we pulled together from multiple sources over the course of three years is in that storage module."

"About the only thing we didn't do was put a big bow on it for Admiral Nogura," said Horst.

Shifting her position on the sofa where she sat to Kirk's left, Binnix asked, "Captain, do you know if the Klingons were able to track us this far?"

Kirk said, "We had no such indication, at least up until the point we left the *Enterprise.*" He used that opening to describe the details of the cover mission under which he, Sulu, and Uhura were working while carrying out the search for the *Endeavour.*

"You can be sure they'll use every available resource to find us," said Watson. "It's bad enough we got away with operating undetected for so long. Once they realize just how much information we collected, they'll be out of their minds to find us."

Horst added, "On the other hand, they'll also want to avoid attracting unwanted attention, and their worst fear is that we are traitors who've taken up working for the Federation or another enemy power. If they manage to piece together who we really are?" He shook his head. "I honestly have no idea what they'll do."

"They won't make any direct accusations," said Khatami. "All that does is give us the opening we need to reveal what we know about Klingon espionage efforts within Starfleet and the Federation." She scowled. "This is the problem with spying. Each side knows the other sides do it, but nobody can admit it because we all have to pretend nobody knows what anyone's talking about."

Kirk realized he was already growing accustomed to listening to Binnix and her colleagues discuss such sensitive topics despite their appearance. He had almost forgotten they still looked like Klingons. Their disguises had served them well during their mission, just as Klingon agents had unfortunately thrived while conducting espionage after being surgically altered to appear human. How easy was it for the individual to conform to their new identity? How hard would it be for that person to shed their manufactured persona and resume a normal life? His own brief stint masquerading as a Romulan was more than enough such subterfuge for him. He could not begin to imagine the challenge these three agents had faced for so long.

The sound of the ship's intercom filtered through the cargo

bay, followed by a high-pitched, almost nasal voice. *"Yataro to Captain Khatami."*

"My chief engineer," said Khatami for Kirk's benefit. Rising from the chair in which she had been sitting opposite him, she crossed to a nearby communications panel and thumbed its activation switch. "Khatami here."

Yataro replied, *"Captain, you asked me to review our sensor data pertaining to the disruption field we encountered during our skirmish with the Klingon ship. I apologize for not seeing to this task sooner."*

"You've had your hands full, Commander," Khatami said. "I take it you've found something in the logs?"

"I will of course require time to conduct a more thorough review to corroborate my findings, but at the moment I am reasonably certain the technology employed against us is Klingon in origin."

That was enough to get Kirk and the agents out of their seats, with Kirk leading the way across the cargo bay to join Khatami at the comm panel.

"Klingon technology?" he asked, glancing to Binnix and her companions.

Watson's features were a mask of confusion. "We didn't come across any information about anything like this."

"If this is an Imperial Intelligence project," said Binnix, "that group is so compartmentalized it's ridiculous. Different groups can be running dozens of projects for which there's no cross communication between departments."

Kirk said, "It's not as outrageous as it sounds. We've encountered similar technology before, but it was far less powerful than what you've described. This could be an updated version of that." He frowned. "But this isn't Klingon space. It's not Federation space, either, but that doesn't mean our diplomats won't yell at their diplomats once this gets out."

"What about the Orions you mentioned?" Watson asked.

"Is it possible they're involved somehow? Working with the Klingons?"

"It's absolutely possible." Kirk knew the Orions or even just individual Orion ships and captains were not above aligning themselves with anyone who promised a profitable venture. Starfleet Intelligence reports occasionally detailed instances of Orion merchants flouting their people's supposed "neutrality" while engaging in all manner of questionable behavior.

"And if there were Klingons already here in the asteroid field," said Khatami, "then they certainly contacted someone to report on the *Endeavour* and their own lost warship. They might even be sending additional ships to make sure there are no loose ends."

"We need to contact the *Enterprise*," said Kirk. He had to inform Admiral Nogura about this, but he also needed to warn Spock in the event the technology was used against his ship. "We can use the *Dreamline* to get away from this location before transmitting a message, but my people need to know about this."

To the comm panel, Khatami said, "Yataro, download all the information you have on this technology so Captain Kirk can take it back to his ship. Get it here as quickly as you can."

"*Understood, Captain,*" replied the engineer. "*Yataro out.*"

With the connection severed, Khatami turned to Kirk. "If the Klingons find us, they'll finish what they started. We're sitting ducks down here." She gestured to Binnix and the others. "You need to take them and their data cache along with whatever we recorded in our sensor logs, get back to the *Enterprise*, and get them the hell out of here."

Binnix held up a hand. "Hold on a minute."

"You know it's the proper course," Khatami said. "You and your information are the priorities, but this other thing is something we can't overlook either. Somebody has to get all of this back to Starfleet." She looked to Kirk. "My ship's busted, so that leaves yours."

"After everything you went through to bring us in?" Horst

asked. "Due respect, Captain, but there's no way in hell I'm getting a ride home without you."

The idea of leaving Khatami and her crew at the potential mercy of the Klingons, the Orions, or whoever else might chance across the crippled *Endeavour* was anathema to Kirk. There was no chance of him choosing that course of action while even a hint of another option could be found.

"The Klingons haven't found us yet," he said. "It's still a big asteroid field, and they have no idea where to look. We've got time to figure this out, but one way or another, we're all getting out of here."

Khatami eyed him. "Nogura's going to have your ass."

The comment was enough to make Kirk offer a low, humorless chuckle.

"Only if he comes and gets it."

Twenty

The red alert klaxon sounded mere seconds before everything else on the *Enterprise* bridge seemed to go haywire.

"Deflector shields are fluctuating," reported Ensign Chekov from the science station. "It's like a power drain."

Sitting in the captain's chair, Spock noted how the rest of the bridge crew was already going through their assigned checklists in order to assess the impact of this apparent attack on the ship's critical systems. After canceling the alarm, he asked, "Are the shields holding?"

"For the moment, sir," Chekov replied. "But the drain is consistent."

From where he stood behind Spock, Admiral Nogura said, "This can't just be background radiation from the asteroid field. We've been here for hours."

"Agreed," Spock replied. "Something has changed since our arrival in the area. Mister Chekov, the modifications Engineer Scott made to our sensor array should prove useful in this regard."

Turning from the science station, the ensign said, "Aye, sir. Scans are being disrupted along with the shields, but the new configuration seems to be helping mitigate that. I've requested additional power from engineering to the sensors."

"This is definitely a power drain, sir," reported Lieutenant Ryan Leslie, the venerable *Enterprise* crew member who had taken over the navigator's station while Chekov worked at the science console. "Shields are down to eighty-four percent and dropping. Navigational deflectors are being disrupted as well."

Nogura said, "Something definitely doesn't like us being here."

An alert tone from the science station made Spock and the admiral turn to where Chekov was looking up from the console's hooded viewer. "I think I've got something, Mister Spock. Sensors show an object of artificial construction positioned on one of the nearby asteroids. From what I can tell, it's the source of the disruption, but its power signature is so small I almost missed it."

"I find it unlikely that is an accident." Rising from the command chair, Spock positioned himself between Leslie and Lieutenant Rahda at the helm. "Mister Chekov, relay those coordinates to navigation. Mister Leslie, plot us a course to that asteroid that allows us to avoid any other nearby asteroids. Lieutenant Rahda, proceed on that heading at one-quarter impulse power."

The image on the bridge's main viewscreen shifted as the *Enterprise* banked to port and a particularly large asteroid shifted past the screen's right edge. It took only seconds before the ship's course brought another, much smaller chunk of dull rock drifting into view. Centered on the screen, it quickly filled the image.

"Asteroid's diameter is just under five kilometers, sir," reported Chekov. "Its mineral composition is consistent with those of the larger bodies we know are contributing to the field's natural background disruption effects." He paused, adjusting several controls on the science console while keeping his attention on the station's sensor viewer. "I've pinpointed the source of the artificial readings, Mister Spock. Locking onto it with sensors."

When the alarm siren wailed this time, it came with a

noticeable fluctuation in the overhead lighting as well as every screen and console on the bridge. Spock was certain he even felt a minor yet still distinct variation in the artificial gravity field. There was a momentary sensation in his stomach, gone almost as he became aware of it.

Lieutenant Leslie called out, "Shields are down to sixty-two percent, and the rate of drop-off is accelerating, Mister Spock."

"Somebody definitely doesn't like us snooping around," said Nogura. From his expression, the admiral also had experienced the fleeting waver of gravity. Stepping down into the command well, he reached for the arm of the captain's chair to steady himself.

"Route emergency power to the deflectors," Spock ordered. He knew if the *Enterprise* lost its defensive shields, whatever was attacking the ship would have free rein over the rest of the ship's sensitive onboard systems, and there was no way to predict what that might mean. Communications, transporters, and tractor beams were obvious first casualties, but could it hamper computer access? What about life-support? Was it possible for it to interfere with the warp engine's antimatter containment systems? None of these were desirable scenarios.

"Mister Chekov," he prompted, "have you pinpointed the source of the disruption?"

Still hovering over the science station, the ensign gestured toward the viewscreen. "Aye, sir. It's just under one thousand kilometers directly ahead of us, on the surface of that asteroid."

Nogura moved to stand next to Spock. "Let's see it."

On the viewscreen, the image zoomed toward the asteroid until it focused on a small section of the rock's surface. Now visible was an obviously metallic shape resembling an octagon with a cap generating a soft blue light from within.

"It measures about three meters in diameter, sir," said Chekov. "Scans show it's embedded approximately two meters into the rock, and beneath that is a larger rectangular object that appears to be its primary power source. I'm also seeing indications of sensor and communications equipment."

Leslie said, "Mister Spock, routing emergency power to the shields is helping, but we're still experiencing a drop-off. We're at fifty-seven percent and falling."

Pointing toward the viewscreen, Spock said, "Mister Leslie, target phasers on that object. One-quarter strength. I would prefer it neutralized but not destroyed."

"Good thinking, Commander," said Nogura.

"Aye, sir." The navigator made the necessary configurations via his console and seconds later a pair of blue-white energy beams streaked across the viewscreen, converging on the asteroid. They were gone almost as quickly as they had appeared, followed by a brief flash illuminating a small section of the asteroid's surface.

Chekov said, "No change in readings, Mister Spock."

At Spock's prompting, Leslie fired a second time and the results were repeated on the viewscreen. Even as they were rewarded with another flash from the asteroid, lighting around the bridge returned to its normal levels and any static or other interference on various display screens disappeared.

"We got it, sir," Chekov reported. "Whatever it is, I'm detecting no power readings."

On the viewscreen, Spock saw that the image had returned to a close-up of the object. The cap sitting atop its octagonal surface was dark, offering no hints to the energy it had been generating minutes earlier.

"Notify Mister Scott to transport that object to cargo bay one," he said. "Perhaps more direct scrutiny will yield some answers."

"Someone put it there," said Nogura. "The big questions are who and why."

"There is something else to consider," Spock replied. "Just based on its location, this object could not have disrupted the

Endeavour or the Klingon warship. There must be more of them scattered throughout the asteroid field. As such, they pose a continued danger to the *Enterprise*, to say nothing of Captain Kirk and his team."

Not for the first time, he wondered how the captain, along with Uhura and Sulu, was faring. The mission parameters called for strict communications silence, so he had no way to know if they had been successful in locating the *Endeavour* or had perhaps fallen prey to a device like the one on the bridge viewscreen.

Such thinking was inappropriate, Spock decided. Instead, a better use of his time awaited him in the ship's cargo bay.

"This is a Klingon contraption."

Montgomery Scott stood next to the squat metallic device. It still bore traces of soil and rock fragments brought along with it after the engineer transported it from the asteroid it called home. After arriving in the cargo bay and upon getting his first look at the device, Spock observed the noticeable lack of identifying symbols. As Ensign Chekov had estimated, it stood just over two meters tall and was nearly three meters wide. Scott had gained access to the device's innards through a panel in its side, behind which was a dense collection of relays, optical cabling, and a few things Spock could not identify. Pulling his arm from the opening, Scott held up a dark, featureless block.

"See this?" He offered the object to Spock, who took it and began turning it over in his hands. "A Klingon power-flow regulator. Pretty generic design. It's mostly for military equipment not intended for use aboard ship. Force field generators, mobile weapons platforms, that sort of thing. Like any good bit of Klingon technology, it's built to last under less than optimal conditions."

Standing next to Spock, Nogura said, "He's right. I've seen them before."

Spock turned the object over in his hands. Its surface was smooth but it had heft, suggesting a component tightly packed with internal mechanisms of the sort needed to carry out the task for which it was designed. There also could be no mistaking familiar Klingon text engraved into the module's outer covering.

"Would regulators of this type be available to other parties? Perhaps via a black market or other unauthorized means?" he asked.

"It's not just the regulators, sir," Scott replied. "Other parts as well as the internal configuration are all consistent with Klingon design. The power cell? It's the same kind used in all sorts of portable equipment along with signal buoys, torpedoes, and other automated devices intended to be launched from a Klingon ship. Everything is marked in their language too."

Nogura said, "So, it's either the Klingons, or someone using their apparently experimental technology?"

"It looks that way, Admiral," Scott replied. "I wasn't able to retrieve the primary power cell from where it's still jammed into that asteroid, but Mister Chekov was able to get a better look at it with sensors. It's a compact fusion reactor, the sort you'd find in small shuttles or other limited-range transports. Very reliable, and they can operate for months without maintenance or replacement. It also puts out some major power, Mister Spock. It'd have to in order to do what it did to us."

"How did it manage to hide from our sensors?" Nogura asked. "I know the asteroid field's background radiation provides some cover, but I'd think with the modifications you made to the *Enterprise* sensors, you would have detected it earlier than we did."

By way of reply, Scott reached back into the object's access panel and withdrew another, much larger component. It was a long cylinder, heavy enough the engineer needed both hands to get it through the opening before holding it out for Nogura and Spock to examine.

"I found this installed among the relays routing power from the energy cell to what I think has to be the disruption-field generator itself as well as its onboard sensor array. I ran a tricorder scan on it and it's a form of power-management circuit. It controls how much energy the entire thing needs to operate, including forcing it into a sort of 'stealth mode' where it reduces power usage to the bare minimum. Combined with the fits the asteroid field is already giving us, that makes this beastie all but undetectable."

Having retrieved the engineer's tricorder from a nearby worktable, Spock aimed it at the device and studied its scan readings. A thought had begun forming as he listened to Scott's report, and the tricorder was now confirming his hypothesis.

"Mister Scott, do you recall our encounter with Captain Koloth and his ship, the *Devisor*?"

Scott smiled. "Indeed I do, sir, and I was wondering if you might make the same connection." For Nogura's benefit, he gestured to the device. "The Klingons used something very similar to this little devil about a year ago, Admiral. It was installed aboard Koloth's ship and did a nasty number when he used it on us. Pushed right through our deflector shields and knocked out our warp engines with its first shot."

"The power drain on the *Devisor* was significant," Spock added, recalling details of the encounter. "This ended up being Koloth's undoing."

Scott said, "From the looks of things, this is very similar to that weapon, but it trades its overall impact on a targeted ship in favor of more efficient and sustained energy usage. The ultimate effect is the same, with the target being disabled and vulnerable to attack or boarding."

"Stationing these on asteroids or any other relatively static position seems shortsighted," Nogura replied. "Maybe this is just a test-bed location while they refine the technology."

Nodding, Spock said, "A logical conclusion. The device in its present form is small enough to be installed aboard a vessel. As effective as it is with its comparatively limited power supply, solving the power utilization issues while tying into a ship's warp engines would greatly extend its capabilities."

The whistle of the ship's intercom echoed through the expansive cargo bay. It was followed by the voice of Lieutenant Leslie, whom Spock had left in command of the bridge in his absence.

"Bridge to Mister Spock. Sir, Ensign Chekov reports our sensors have detected another of the disruption-field generators, located on an asteroid not too far from our present position."

Crossing to a comm panel set into the wall behind the Klingon device, Spock pressed its activation control. "Mister Chekov, I take it from the lack of alarms the generator has not activated?"

"That's correct, sir," replied the ensign. *"So far as I can tell from this distance, it's in some sort of standby mode. It may be waiting for a ship to close to a predetermined range before powering up and activating its disruption beam . . . or whatever it activates."*

Scott said, "With the onboard communications package, these things could talk to each other, Mister Spock. Maybe they coordinate their efforts depending on how a targeted ship tries to escape?"

"Quite possible," Spock replied. "Mister Chekov, continue your scans, and see if there are any more of the devices within the immediate vicinity. Mister Leslie, maintain our present position until further notice." After receiving acknowledgment from both officers, Spock severed the connection before returning his attention to Nogura and Scott. "It would seem our 'simple' search-and-rescue operation has taken a most unexpected turn."

Nogura replied, "If the Klingons are operating out here in nonaligned space, we need to find out a lot more than we know right now. If the Orions are involved, then you can be sure they're profiting off whatever ships this energy field or whatever you want to call it has caught. Right now, it's a threat to civilian and Starfleet traffic, but there's no way the Klingons are going to all this trouble to hijack a few civilian transports or freighters." He pointed to the disruption-field generator. "That's a new weapon for use against the Empire's enemies. Namely, us."

"Based on the available evidence and information," Spock said, "I agree with your assessment, Admiral. Further, I submit the danger to Captain Kirk and his party is more severe than it is to us. It would be advisable to ascertain their current status."

His gaze still fixed on the Klingon device, Nogura shook his head. "At the moment, we don't even know where they are or if they've found the *Endeavour*. Attempting to contact them here in the field would likely endanger them if the Klingons, Orions, or someone else is out there listening. If they've found the *Endeavour* and its crew and the agents are still alive, then we risk them being captured before we can get to them. Meanwhile, finding out the truth behind this new weapon just became a mission priority."

"But what about the agents and their information?" Scott asked. "Isn't that the whole reason we're here in the first place, sir?"

"This obviously isn't as critical as securing the agents and their information, at least not as things currently stand, but we can't just let it go. We have no idea how big this threat is, or when it might be ready for deployment against us." Nogura paused, releasing a long, slow breath. "Kirk and his team can handle themselves at least long enough for us to investigate this a bit further. If they can't, they'll contact us in accordance with their mission protocol. For now, I choose to believe our not hearing from them means they're okay."

Spock replied, "Or, they are unable to request our assistance for any of several reasons."

"I know, Commander. Believe me." Closing his eyes, Nogura pinched the bridge of his nose as though attempting to ward off a sudden headache. "But your captain has a reputation for being pretty resourceful. Hopefully he's living up to it right about now."

Twenty-one

Despite the research outpost's remote location in one of the Ivratis asteroid field's densest areas, Le'tal insisted that all reasonable precautions be taken to avoid announcing its presence. This included masking its power output and restricting outbound communications. Even inbound transmissions were received or even acknowledged only if they conformed to the tightly controlled schedule. The outpost's garrison commander, Karamaq, also ensured the patrols he sent into the field at irregular intervals came and went using randomly selected circuitous routes designed to reveal whether the ships were being followed. As for other vessels that might call on them, such occurrences were only supposed to happen as a result of specific circumstances falling under the category of "emergency." All of these protocols and so many others were designed to protect not only the outpost and its occupants but also the secret and important nature of the work taking place here.

It was therefore to Le'tal's great surprise that she received notice of an inbound communication, from a vessel making an unannounced visit.

"Perhaps someone might explain this rather glaring irregularity," she said as she walked into the outpost's control center.

Turning from where he stood next to a Klingon soldier sitting at the center's communications station, No'Khal offered a disapproving grunt. "A Klingon ship is on an approach course.

Outer boundary sensors detected it and we have been tracking its progress as it makes its way deeper into the asteroid field. This is not a random occurrence, my friend. This ship knows we are here, and they are hailing us. We have not yet responded."

Le'tal frowned, considering this revelation. Looking around the control center, she noted that even with the unusual situation now developing, the outpost's command hub continued to operate as though it were any other evening. Located at the facility's top level, the compartment was hexagonal in shape and capped with a high, domed roof. Five of the room's six walls hosted their own set of four oversized display screens, with the exit set into the wall behind her. Beneath each set of screens were rows of controls and indicators arrayed in a variety of colors and configurations. Most of the stations were devoted to the outpost and its internal systems, while two at the room's far end were detailed to overseeing the numerous tests conducted by the experimental disruption-field equipment. Additional workstations were positioned in three pairs at the room's center, though at this time of night only those devoted to sensors and communications were staffed with watch personnel. In accordance with Karamaq's wishes, these posts were always monitored by members of his security force, the only soldiers working in an environment otherwise dominated by civilian scientists and engineers.

And just where is Karamaq?

The thought taunted Le'tal as she considered possibilities. Was he still caught in the cocoon of drink-induced slumber? It would not be an unusual occurrence, she reminded herself.

To the soldier sitting at the communications console, she asked, "Where is your commander?"

A large, muscled specimen with long dark hair flowing over the shoulders of his uniform tunic, the Klingon shifted in his seat. "I have summoned him, Doctor Le'tal. He is en route as we speak."

Le'tal nodded. If nothing else, the soldiers under Karamaq's command always conducted themselves as professionals, rather than falling into the tired stereotype of military members disrespecting civilian workers. It was a refreshing change, and one Le'tal was convinced was the product of Karamaq wanting to curry favor with Imperial Intelligence. It was they, after all, who placed a great deal of importance on this project, and this meant the uncommon practice of extending courtesies to those not in uniform.

"They are repeating their hail, Doctor," reported the soldier, whose name Le'tal could not remember. "Now they are requesting immediate clearance to dock, and they are transmitting a proper clearance code. I have verified its authenticity."

His companion, seated at the sensor station, added, "They continue their approach. Scans identify the craft as a standard Klingon Defense Force personnel transport normally used by ranking officers."

No'Khal said, "Verified encryption key for their communications, and a correct clearance code for landing. Whoever they are, they are well aware of our security protocols. Someone from Imperial Intelligence, perhaps?"

"That is the most likely explanation," Le'tal replied. She waved to the communications officer. "Direct them to the hangar bay, and inform your Commander Karamaq to meet us there."

With No'Khal following her, she made her way from the control center. Her instincts were telling her she was not going to like whatever this ship was bringing to her.

The hangar bay was the largest single facility within the outpost. Built into the asteroid's bedrock, it was well protected from bombardment and concealed for the most part from the prying eyes of sensor scans. A double set of reinforced blast doors offered protection from the harsh vacuum of open space, though the entire chamber was constructed from the same material.

In an emergency, the outpost's entire contingent of personnel could be relocated here, as it was by far the safest location in the facility.

Possessing no true warships, the outpost's military contingent instead utilized a squadron of four well-armed scout craft. As the research conducted here was not general knowledge to the rest of the Klingon Defense Force or even the High Council, operations of this sort tended to rely on whatever limited resources could be made available by Imperial Intelligence without raising too many unwanted questions.

The four ships assigned to Commander Karamaq and his security force along with the single civilian personnel transport for use by the outpost's science and support contingent took up less than half of the cavernous hangar bay's deck space. This left plenty of room for the outpost's newest arrival. Unlike the scout ships that bore scratches, dents, chipped paint, dulled metal, and even dirt as evidence of extended duty here in the Ivratis asteroid field, the mysterious transport looked as if it had only just launched from a construction facility's orbital docking bay. Undersized and cylindrical, it possessed a pair of warp nacelles, which also served as landing gear, tucked along the primary hull's underside. A pair of impulse engine ports flared outward from its back end, and its forward section angled to resemble a spear tip. Its cockpit interior was visible through a transparent canopy, and Le'tal saw a pair of Klingons sitting at the ship's controls. Neither of them seemed interested in leaving their seats. At the craft's midpoint a hatch was embedded into the thick reinforced hull, and as it slid aside, a narrow ramp extended from its base until it reached the hangar bay's deck.

"Remind me," Le'tal said, whispering to No'Khal. "Are we supposed to take a single knee, or prostrate ourselves in total supplication?"

Her friend eyed her with subdued amusement. Standing to his other side, Commander Karamaq, dressed in his most formal uniform and doing his level best to hide the fact he might still be at least somewhat intoxicated, also heard the remark and glared in her direction with obvious disdain. Neither of her companions could say anything before the sound of footsteps on the transport's metal ramp caught their attention. Descending from the ship was a Klingon male Le'tal did not recognize. Though he wore a variation of uniform similar to Commander Karamaq's soldiers, she could see at a glance it was too clean and well tailored to make this an officer with any real military experience aboard a ship or ground station. Instinct told her this was a bureaucrat, someone interested in status reports and allocation budgets and other administrative minutiae for which Le'tal had little patience. She imagined him as the sort who pondered the reports she sent and disapproved of how she and her team spent their time and the Empire's resources.

"I am D'khad," he said, which Le'tal supposed was his version of a greeting.

"And I am Karamaq," replied the commander, stepping forward. If he was still suffering the effects of too much drink earlier in the evening, he did not show it. "I am charged with the security of this facility."

D'khad conducted a rapid and obvious head-to-toe inspection of Karamaq. While his expression did not change, his tone was more than sufficient to convey his disinterest. "Yes. I have reviewed the personnel roster." Moving his gaze to Le'tal, he said, "I presume you are Doctor Le'tal, leader of this facility's primary research initiative."

"That is correct," she said. "We were not expecting guests, or else we would have made proper arrangements to receive you. Regardless, we bid you welcome." It took every iota of self-discipline she possessed to school her features and her voice. She already disliked this Klingon.

"I am not here to engage in useless pleasantries," D'khad replied. "I carry with me information and special instructions from Imperial Intelligence. Most of what I have to say affects Commander Karamaq and his security detail, but it also impacts this facility and everyone in it. You are aware of the Federation starship currently conducting a search of the asteroid field, yes?"

"The *Enterprise*," Le'tal said. "We are aware it is seeking answers about the loss of another vessel." She quickly recounted the incident between the first Starfleet ship and the Klingon battle cruiser and how their encountering the disruption-field generators was an accident.

D'khad said, "I am not concerned with any of that. Of course losing one of our own warships is unfortunate, but the Empire has lost far more vessels for less noble reasons. Indeed, my superiors—and yours—view what happened as a successful test of your technology."

"We would have preferred a test that did not cost Klingon lives," No'Khal replied.

"Duty is sacrifice." D'khad glanced to Karamaq before adding, "The warriors aboard that vessel swore their lives to the Empire. They died defending it, even if they were not aware of the circumstances responsible for their demise. Their loss will be remembered with honor."

For the first time since emerging from his shuttle, he began pacing a slow circuit around the cargo bay on a course that took him in the general direction of the parked scout ships. Looking to her companions for guidance or perhaps reassurance, Le'tal walked after him, with No'Khal and Karamaq following suit. Judging by his body language, Le'tal decided D'khad seemed as unimpressed with the ships as he was with their commander.

"The information I am authorized to share with you is highly classified." Pausing his laconic walking, D'khad turned to once more face them. "Several days ago, three spies escaped from Qo'noS. We do not yet know for certain who they are working for, but we suspect they have committed treason against the Empire by allying themselves with the Federation."

"Surely not." Karamaq's expression was one of unfettered disbelief after the courier recounted the unpleasant details of the spies' operation on the homeworld and the extent of their activities.

To Le'tal's surprise, D'khad did not use that opportunity to offer a snide reply. Instead, he said, "It came as quite the shock throughout the intelligence branch, and the impacts and potential damage go all the way to the High Council itself. One of the spies had been posing as aide to Councilor Maroq. Needless to say, his future services to the Empire were deemed . . . unnecessary."

"And we are sure these spies were working for the Federation?" No'Khal asked.

"Our suspicion is only strengthened by the knowledge that the spacecraft they stole to make their escape made its way here." D'khad paused, eyeing Le'tal and the others with a smug expression. "So, a stolen vessel traveled here at the same time a Federation starship was in the same area, outside the normal limits of a Starfleet border-security patrol."

Karamaq said, "Starfleet ships have occasionally been detected in the region." Then, under D'khad's withering gaze, he added, "Though it is unusual, and I agree the timing is concerning."

"What of the battle cruiser that engaged the Starfleet vessel?" asked Le'tal. "Was its captain aware of this situation?"

Shaking his head, D'khad replied, "No, just as he had no knowledge of your activities. So far as we are able to determine, he simply exercised his own initiative and reacted to detecting the Starfleet ship in the area. That was unfortunate. Had he acted differently, he might have contained this debacle before it could spiral out of control." As he spoke, Le'tal once again noted the total lack of remorse about the loss of an imperial vessel, its captain and crew, but said nothing.

"The Starfleet ship," said No'Khal. "It was believed destroyed. Our sensors detected its warp engine overload."

Scowling, D'khad replied, "We must remove all doubt, one way or the other. If there were survivors, then we must determine whether the spies are among them. Apprehending them is of vital importance to the Empire."

"Then why is the Klingon Defense Force not sending ships better equipped to handle a situation such as this?" She gestured to her companions. "No insult intended to Commander Karamaq or his soldiers, but they are a security detail."

"My warriors are more than up to the task," said Karamaq. "The honor is to serve."

D'khad replied, "That is good, Commander, as for the moment this responsibility lies with you. As one might imagine, this is a delicate situation for the Empire. We cannot have public disclosure of this embarrassment, and neither can we have just anyone from the military converging on this region and possibly learning of your operation here. This is, after all, still a classified Imperial Intelligence project. Ships with captains and crews who can be trusted with this information are being selected as we speak, but until they arrive, it falls to those of us already here."

"Assuming there are survivors and they did not retreat from the area," Le'tal said, "where do we begin our search? They could be anywhere within the asteroid field."

"Long-range sensors detected nothing moving away from the region in the aftermath of the skirmish between the *Endeavour* and our ship. Then there is the *Enterprise*, here searching for anything that might explain the other vessel's destruction. No, Doctor. If there *are* survivors, they are still here, somewhere. We must find them before the *Enterprise* does."

"And what of the *Enterprise*?" Karamaq asked. "Our escalated level of activity will surely draw their attention. It is unlikely we will be able to avoid further confrontation."

D'khad's expression fell flat. "You are correct, Commander. It may be in our best interest to seize the initiative in this regard." He turned to Le'tal. "I imagine the technology you are testing here should prove most helpful with this. Would you agree, Doctor?"

"I would," Le'tal replied, though she was unhappy about drawing unwanted scrutiny from the *Enterprise* or anyone else.

Drawing himself to his full height, Karamaq said, "I will begin preparations for the search to begin immediately." Without waiting for acknowledgment, the commander pivoted on his heel and walked at a brisk pace across the hangar bay. Le'tal knew it would take only moments for him to summon his security force and put them to work readying the scout ships for departure.

"What about me and my people?" she asked. "What are we supposed to do?"

D'khad replied, "For now, your work remains your foremost priority. My superiors are pleased with your work, but these spies and their treachery carry the potential to impact our military effectiveness in the face of our enemies. We may find ourselves seeking any available advantage in order to maintain our readiness to defend the Empire."

It was the answer Le'tal expected, of course. She and her people were not military officers. They possessed few if any of the skills necessary to be of use during the coming search, to say nothing of whatever action might be required should survivors from the *Endeavour* be found. What concerned her was the potential for her team's work to be interrupted, disrupted, or even terminated as a consequence of whatever was about to happen beyond her facility's boundaries. There was precious little she or her people could do about that, and she could already feel her frustration rising in the face of her apparent powerlessness. What if this search operation resulted in an escalation of the already tense relations between the Empire and the Federation? She knew the answer. In the face of strained or collapsing diplomatic efforts between the two powers, the High Council would direct imperial priorities and resources to military action as it always did when it felt there was no other viable course. Those like her and her team would be forgotten as the Klingon people became embroiled in yet another conflict.

Le'tal could only hope the coming search was as quick as it was fruitful.

Otherwise, she concluded, *none of this will matter anyway.*

Twenty-two

Under normal circumstances, lights flickering on a starship was sufficient cause for everyone aboard to take notice. Such an occurrence was almost always attributed to some form of interruption in power flow to an appropriate system. Was one or more of the thousands of components that went into the construction and operation of such a complex craft in need of attention, repair, or replacement? Determining whether the cause was innocuous or the result of something more worthy of concern was for the ship's engineering personnel, with their captain, first officer, and other interested parties wasting no time making it known they were aware of the situation and would be wanting updates.

When it happened now, there was an immediate and visceral reaction in Atish Khatami and the handful of officers on duty in the ship's improvised auxiliary control center. Just the lighting alone was enough to prompt such a response, but an audible pitch drop in the low, omnipresent drone of the ship's impulse engines only served to make everyone move that much faster. Standing to one side so as not to impede any of Khatami's people from their work, Kirk exchanged glances with Uhura before they both lunged for different workstations to see what was going on.

"Mister Klisiewicz?" prompted Commander Katherine Stano, rising from where she and Captain Khatami were sitting at a small field table and crossing the room to the science officer.

Standing at the console configured for his use, the young lieutenant replied, "Fluctuations in the impulse engines, Commander." He frowned as he continued to study the readings. "It's like it came out of nowhere. We've had constant monitoring of all onboard systems all along, and there was no hint of any sort of problem before now. I don't understand it."

"How can we help?" Kirk asked.

Klisiewicz said, "I appreciate that offer, sir, but I don't even know what's wrong yet."

Reaching for the console's intercom control, Khatami slapped it to open an internal frequency. "Khatami to Yataro. Please tell me you're seeing this impulse power issue and you already have a solution."

The *Endeavour's* chief engineer replied, "*We are attempting to diagnose the impulse fluctuations, but this may take some time.*"

As if to emphasize his statement, lighting in the control center faded completely, replaced within seconds by dimmer, more limited emergency lighting. Kirk noted that more than half of the room's consoles had also deactivated.

"*I have switched us to emergency battery power,*" said Yataro over the open connection. "*This requires disabling all but the most critical systems. I am afraid that also means intraship communications, Captain.*"

Stano said, "No problem. I'll get runners started distributing communicators." She moved back to the small desk and grabbed a data slate before motioning to where Lieutenant Hector Estrada stood near what until moments ago had been his substitute communications station. "Come on, Hector. You need a job for the time being anyway."

"Aye, Commander," replied the communications officer. "Just a little more of that adventure and excitement they promised me at the Academy."

Once they were through the control center's open door and gone, Khatami said to Klisiewicz, "Stay here, Lieutenant. You're in charge of whatever Yataro left us." She turned and headed for the door, motioning for Kirk and Uhura to follow her. It was a short jog to the impulse deck's engineering space, which was far less roomy than the main engineering space to be found in a *Constitution*-class starship's secondary hull. Only upon entering the room did Kirk realize he no longer heard the *Endeavour's* impulse engines. Yataro had wasted no time taking the system offline.

That can't be good, Kirk decided.

The room was utilitarian by design, intended for work by engineers and technicians with a need to crawl in, over, under, or around access conduits, ladders, and catwalks surrounding the starship's massive impulse engines. Already a cramped compartment, it appeared stuffed close to overflowing with personnel and equipment. Whether it was relocated from the *Endeavour's* primary engineering decks before the warp drive section was jettisoned or had been scrounged from elsewhere in the saucer section and repurposed for use by Yataro and his team, Kirk did not know. Portable computer interfaces sat atop tool boxes or equipment crates, connected by optical cabling to power relays or open access panels wherever Yataro or one of his people could find or create an interface. They were working without benefit of the starship's primary and secondary oversight systems and were making do however they could and with whatever was available. Kirk decided Scotty himself would be proud of the *Endeavour* crew's ingenuity.

"Mister Yataro," Khatami said as she entered the compartment. "Talk to me."

A pair of legs was all that was visible of the engineer. The rest of him was inside an open access panel set into a large, squat gray cylinder lying on its side and extending into the bulkhead behind it. The *Endeavour's* port impulse engine manifold was currently the focus of attention for a half dozen of the ship's engineering staff, each hovering at another open port or panel while wielding tools or scanning equipment. Extracting himself from the panel in which he worked, Yataro pulled himself to his full height. His lavender skin and red jumpsuit were covered in dirt and grime, and there was a hole in the garment just below his left knee. There were other minor tears and rends in the fabric, each bearing mute testimony to the effort Yataro had been expending for a sustained period.

The slender Lirin raised his right hand, which held a large rectangular component with connections on each end as well as two of its four sides.

"This power coupling is burned out," he said. "Along with three others. All are beyond repair and will have to be replaced."

Standing next to Kirk, Uhura asked, "Four? Out of eight? Was there some kind of power surge?" When Kirk cast a quizzical look in her direction, she said, "Cross-training, sir. Mister Scott has been helping me broaden my horizons."

Yataro replied, "We are carrying out diagnostics on the entire power-relay system, but we have so far detected no indications of a power surge."

"One failed coupling by itself, I could buy," Kirk said. "Under the current conditions, I'm surprised more circuits and relays haven't blown or burned out, but four?"

"In an emergency, the system could've continued to operate with up to three couplings out of commission," Khatami said. "Just our luck it'd be four." She turned to Yataro. "We have replacements, right?"

Nodding, the engineer replied, "We have a full set of replacement couplings, Captain: eight for each engine. However, I am hesitant to install any of them until we find the root cause of the issue. We need to determine whether our power systems are faulty or are plagued by an even greater problem."

"And how long will that take?" Khatami asked.

Yataro paused as though to consider his answer before replying, "At least two hours to make even a preliminary diagnostic on the entire system. A more thorough check will of course take longer."

"Start with the preliminary look. We'll go from there based on what you find."

Before Khatami could say anything else, the group was joined by another of the engineers. Kirk could not help giving the young man a quick visual inspection, noting the dirt on his jumpsuit, hands, and face. His hair was disheveled but the lack of dark circles under his eyes indicated he was having a better time dealing with fatigue than many of his shipmates.

"Yes, Lieutenant?" Khatami asked, but before he could answer she gestured to him for Kirk and Uhura's benefit. "This is Lieutenant Ivan Tomkins. It was his idea to deploy the sensor buoys to boost our communications and sensor abilities. If not for him, we might never have known you were coming until you knocked on the hull."

Tomkins, appearing uncomfortable with the praise, cleared his throat. "I apologize for interrupting, Captain, but I couldn't help overhearing Commander Yataro's report." To Yataro, he said, "I'm sorry, Commander, but I have an updated estimate based on the initial checks you asked me to carry out. It could be closer to four hours before we complete a check of the entire system."

"Four hours," Yataro said. His oversized blue eyes widening, he shook his head. "How could I have been so inaccurate with my first estimate?"

Tomkins replied, "I don't think you were, sir, just like I don't think you missed anything." Looking to Kirk and the others, he added, "We're not finding anything that could account for whatever took out the couplings. No overloaded circuits, no defective cabling or junctions, nothing. It's as though they just decided to self-destruct on their own, and we know that's impossible."

"Quite right," Yataro said. "This is most concerning."

Kirk recalled what he knew of the power systems governing

starship impulse engines. It had been a long time since he studied the finer points with any detail, but he still prided himself on knowing how and why things worked aboard a ship, in particular the one to which he was assigned as captain. While he could never hope to match Montgomery Scott's technical proficiency, he was no slouch, either.

"Those couplings are designed to compensate for power surges," he said, recalling whatever journal or blueprint from which he had memorized that information. "In fact, they're supposed to disperse those very surges and protect against overloads to other, more sensitive systems. If anything, they should be among the last components to fail in the face of such a surge."

Yataro replied, "You are correct, Captain. Indeed, when you put it in such stark terms, I am forced to consider a rather unpleasant explanation for our current predicament."

"Sabotage," Uhura said. When Kirk again glanced in her direction, she shrugged. "Somebody had to say it."

"Are you kidding me?" Khatami closed her eyes before reaching up to rub the bridge of her nose. "Of course you're not. This day is just getting better and better."

"We have to consider every possibility, no matter how much we might not like it." Kirk suddenly felt exposed, standing here in the confined engineering space. "The question is who would have the sort of expertise to inflict that sort of damage without making it look immediately obvious."

Tomkins said, "You mean besides our entire engineering staff?" He looked to Yataro. "Any one of us has that skill set, sir."

"But perhaps not opportunity," Yataro replied. Before saying anything else, the Lirin glanced around the room and Kirk instantly knew what the engineer had to be thinking. If indeed a saboteur lurked among them, they might very well be present at this very moment, within earshot and able to hear everything being said.

As though picking up on Yataro's unspoken cue, Khatami said in a low voice, "Look, it's not like the entire crew has access to this part of the ship. With a little time, we should be able to narrow down a list of suspects." She sighed. "The agents. They've helped us with various repair efforts since we set down here."

Kirk had already been thinking in that direction. "We can't rule it out."

"One of them could be a double agent?" Uhura asked. "Or all of them, for that matter."

"It is worth considering they also assisted in our deployment of the sensor buoys," Yataro said. "One of them developed a malfunction not long after they were placed." The chief engineer then provided for Kirk and Uhura's benefit a brief rundown of that incident and his and Tomkins's effort to maneuver a replacement buoy into position.

"So, left unchecked, that buoy could've alerted someone to the *Endeavour*'s presence here," Kirk said. "By itself, it doesn't sound like much, but now?"

Khatami said, "If it is one of the agents, and they are attempting to attract attention, then the supposed malfunction makes sense." She looked to Yataro. "They won't be helping you anymore, Commander. I don't want to confine them because that'll just arouse their suspicions. I'd prefer to try luring them out and see what else they're up to."

"That could be dangerous, Captain," Kirk replied. Under normal conditions, the threat of a spy or saboteur aboard a starship was a matter of grave importance. The *Endeavour*'s current predicament only made things worse.

Nodding, Khatami blew out her breath. "Agreed. The problem is we don't really have the time to be wasting on this, and there are a lot of ways to screw up and alert the saboteur we're onto them." She shook her head. "We'll have to take it slow until we can figure it all out, but first things first. Mister Yataro, how long will our reserve battery power last?"

Without hesitation, the engineer replied, "At our present rate of usage, approximately thirty-six hours. We can extend that, of course, but only marginally, as we are already operating on a restricted power protocol." He gestured to the room's far side. "The starboard impulse engine remains operational. I only took it offline in order to complete our diagnostics, but there is nothing else preventing us from returning it to service."

Tomkins added, "We should still restrict power usage to just the critical systems, but at least we'll have some breathing room."

"Do it," Khatami said, "and proceed with your repair of the port engine." She frowned. "I want you to take care of it all personally, Mister Yataro. Keep your eye on whoever you get to help you with it."

"You are concerned about another member of the crew?" asked the engineer.

"At the moment, I'm concerned about everyone," Khatami replied, "but I can't go around not trusting anyone for however long we end up stuck down here. You're my chief, Mister Yataro, so I'm counting on you to get it done."

Yataro nodded. "You may rely on me, Captain."

"Good, because if you end up being the saboteur, I'm going to drop-kick you through the nearest airlock."

Though he appeared ready to counter that declaration, the Lirin instead shifted on his feet before exchanging glances with Tomkins. "Let us take the steps necessary to avoid that."

After the two engineers moved farther into the compartment to resume their work, Khatami grunted something Kirk could not understand before slumping against a nearby bulkhead. She was not in distress, he knew. Instead, she simply looked tired.

"I need a long, hot bath and about a month's sleep," she said. "Preferably somewhere with a beach."

Uhura replied, "I like the sound of that."

"Same here," said Kirk. "In the meantime, if you think it will help things move faster, where can we pitch in?"

It was then that Commander Stano entered the room. Her face was flushed and she was slightly out of breath. Kirk suspected it was the result of her using ladders and Jefferies tubes to move about the ship, but she looked as though she had been scrambling through them as fast as possible to get herself here.

"You all right?" Khatami asked, studying her first officer. "Why didn't you use your communicator?"

Waving away the question, Stano said, "I dropped the damned thing down a maintenance shaft. Remind me to carry a spare, I'm a klutz." She paused to catch her breath before continuing, "We've got a new problem. Klisiewicz found something on sensors. A ship's just entered the buoys' extended scanning range, and its propulsion signature pings it as being Orion."

Khatami regarded Kirk. "Friends of yours?"

"Could be. I had a feeling they didn't buy our cover story, and that was before we led them on a chase through the asteroid field." Kirk grimaced, realizing his likely triggering of the Orion captain's suspicions had caused her to start snooping around.

With Khatami in the lead, the group made its way back to the temporary control room to find Lieutenants Klisiewicz and Estrada standing at their respective workstations. Noticing their arrival, the science officer turned from his console.

"According to our recognition database, it's officially listed as an Orion merchant ship," he said, anticipating Khatami's request for a status report.

Uhura said, "That's their euphemism for a pirate vessel." Frowning, she looked to Kirk. "I guess we should be thankful they're not Klingons. Small favors, or whatever you want to call it, but remember, Orions usually aren't interested in destroying a ship. They'd rather disable and plunder it."

Kirk replied, "Unless they're working with the Klingons. Then all bets are off."

"What are they doing, Lieutenant?" Khatami asked Klisiewicz.

Consulting his instruments, the younger man said, "Judging by their speed and course, I'd say they're looking for something."

"Any guesses on what that might be?" Estrada asked. He tapped his own console. "I can't pick up any sign of incoming or outgoing communication. They're pretty much running quiet."

Klisiewicz, back to examining his sensor readings, looked up from the console. Dread clouded his features.

"They're changing course and heading directly toward us."

Twenty-three

"I hate these things."

Kirk sighed as he fastened the closures on the Starfleet-issue environmental suit he now wore. Molded from a synthetic polymer designed to form around its occupant's body, the silver suits were but the latest iteration of a technology introduced three centuries earlier. The first garments designed to shield humans from the harsh environment of space were oversized and cumbersome, with the wearer required to carry bulky equipment on their back just to provide limited life-support. As humanity ventured outward from its homeworld to the other planets of Earth's solar system, the technology to carry those early explorers and protect them upon arrival continued to advance. Suits of this type became more robust and efficient at protecting the fragile bodies they encased, becoming lighter and more comfortable to the point such garments were little more than another variation of uniform to be worn.

Kirk still hated them.

"For whatever it's worth, I never liked them, either," said Morgan Binnix from where she stood near an adjacent equipment locker in one of the *Endeavour*'s extravehicular activity preparation rooms, closing the front of her own suit. "I flunked basic EVA training the first time." She shook her head. "Damned embarrassing, let me tell you."

Standing to Kirk's other side, Sulu was also donning a suit. "I prefer these to the civilian ones we had earlier." He was attaching the garment's life-support system and verifying its connections. "At least with these, I know where everything's supposed to go."

"Always a silver lining with you, isn't there?" Kirk punctuated the comment with a knowing smile. "That's one of the things I've always liked about you, Mister Sulu."

Sulu offered his own grin. "Now if I could only convince Doctor McCoy."

"I wouldn't hold my breath, if I were you."

Given what they were about to do, Kirk knew the momentary humor was a good way to alleviate tension. Anything that took someone outside the relative safety of a spacecraft was to be taken seriously. While each of them might be experienced with this type of activity, there was always a danger and therefore justifiable anxiety if not outright fear, none of which was helped by knowing this was shaping up to be anything but a normal excursion outside the ship.

"Captain Kirk."

Turning from his locker, Kirk saw Binnix staring at him. With the exception of the helmet she held in her hands, she had completed the process of donning her EV suit. She regarded him with an uncertain expression.

"Yes?" he asked.

"Thank you for this. I can appreciate the position you're in, and it'd be easy to just toss us into a brig until it's all over. If I were in your shoes, I might already have done just that."

Despite his and Khatami's best efforts not to alert Binnix and her companions about the sabotage and the suspicions of their involvement, it became obvious to the agents something was amiss when they were at first cut out of assisting with preparations to face the Orions. It had not taken Binnix long to surmise the reasons for that, and confront head-on the unspoken accusations.

"You have to admit," Kirk said as he reached for his own helmet, "it doesn't look good to the casual observer."

"I'm not worried about casual observers," Binnix replied. "But I need *you* to trust me, and my people. We spent too long doing what we were doing, sacrificing anything resembling a normal life, to throw it all away."

Without prompting, she had handed over to Kirk and Captain Khatami the pair of portable, encrypted data-storage crystals she and her colleagues brought with them from Qo'noS. To Khatami's surprise, Binnix also gave them a decryption chip that she had programmed from memory so the captains could access the protected data the crystals contained. The measure circumvented the original intention of Admiral Nogura being the only person with the authority to open the crystals. While the data could not be transmitted over a communications link or transferred to another computer system without the admiral's authorization, which included a retinal scan, Kirk or Khatami could still access it directly if the need arose.

"Always have a backup plan," Binnix said at the time. Her original contingency was to give such a chip to Khatami in the event circumstances warranted it. Facing accusations of treason, she decided this was one way to quickly demonstrate her trustworthiness and that of her team. The act was enough to warrant court-martial and possible incarceration, assuming she or anyone else aboard the *Endeavour* made it out alive.

Like Khatami, Kirk was not completely convinced Binnix and her fellow agents were not responsible for the sabotage of the ship's impulse power systems, or even the mysterious malfunction that plagued one of the sensor buoys. On the other hand, Binnix's companions were as quick to denounce the accusation as she had been, and Kirk admitted his gut instinct was to believe them. Far more troubling was the notion that someone else—a member of the *Endeavour* crew—might well be responsible. If true, that opened up a host of new problems for Khatami and her people, to say nothing of Kirk, Uhura, and Sulu. He had already discussed this possibility with Khatami, and while it was a matter of concern, there simply was no time right now to deal with it.

"Jim."

The voice belonged to Captain Khatami. She entered the prep room at a rapid pace, making her way past other rows of lockers to join him, Sulu, and Binnix. Her body language and expression were more than enough to tell Kirk she was not bringing good news.

"Orions?" he prompted.

Khatami nodded. "We thought they'd passed us by. I should've known we couldn't be that lucky. Sensors have picked up a pair of smaller ships. Probably personnel transports. The other ship seems to have retreated almost to the limits of our scanning range."

After Lieutenant Klisiewicz's initial detection of the Orion ship, everyone on the *Endeavour* had braced for the moment when the pirates realized they had found the crashed starship. When the ship did not approach close enough to all but guarantee a positive sensor return, Kirk wanted to breathe a bit easier. Still, nothing about the situation felt right. Despite apparently being in the clear, he pressed Khatami to put people out on the *Endeavour*'s hull, manning the phaser cannons placed along the saucer section. His argument was simple: Even with the buoys providing enhancement for the ship's scanning abilities, sensors could be fooled, or otherwise rendered useless. It would be better to have people outside, ready to employ the weapons without first relying on sensor scans to identify a threat. He had even volunteered to go outside and oversee the placement of the phaser cannons and arrange people into a defensive perimeter, for no other reason than to spare Khatami from adding one more item to her ever growing list of things demanding her attention.

His fears were confirmed less than an hour after the *Endeavour* captain deployed the first teams onto the hull and the sensor buoys positioned around the canyon's perimeter ceased functioning. The result was to render the grounded ship all but blind and deaf for little beyond the canyon itself.

"Where are they?" Sulu asked.

"Somewhere at the far end of the canyon." Khatami closed her eyes long enough to rub her temples. "They set down just a few minutes ago, but our sensors can't penetrate the surrounding background radiation down here without help. I suspect they know this."

Sulu asked, "So what's their plan?"

"They're pirates," Binnix replied. "Your ship represents a sizable payday if they can salvage anything of worth, Captain."

"They can't be thinking of boarding us?" Kirk asked. Even in its present condition, the *Endeavour* still boasted a crew of over four hundred people, with an arsenal large enough to arm most of them.

Khatami said, "They wouldn't have to. All that's needed is to disable the power systems and wait us out. There aren't enough functional escape pods to accommodate everyone. Besides, where would we go? We'd never be able to clear the asteroid field before they were on us." She gestured to the EV suits Kirk and the others wore. "There aren't enough of those to go around, either. So, what do they do? Even if we could generate deflector shields sitting on the ground, we can't spare the power for them. If I'm the Orions, I cut our power, force us to take every desperate action to stay alive for a few minutes longer, and then I've got the run of the place." Her features hardened. "I don't much like the idea of standing around waiting to die."

"And that's before we factor in our information cache," Binnix said. "We can't let the Orions have that either. I'll destroy it before I let that happen."

"I'll destroy what's left of my ship before that." Khatami

frowned. "Of course, without the warp drive that's a bit harder than it would normally be, but I'm betting Yataro and his engineering team could figure out something."

Kirk shook his head. "We're not there yet, Captain. If they wanted, they could've taken out the ship's impulse engines by strafing us. They didn't do that, which probably means they're trying to avoid damaging us as much as possible." It seemed so obvious now. "They're coming to us over land."

"You mean outside?" Sulu asked, making no effort to hide his disbelief. "A ground assault?"

Kirk replied, "It's what I'd do. They can't take us all on at once, but they won't have to. Launch a multipronged offensive and do what Captain Khatami said. They find a way to take out our power or cause enough other damage that it places us at immediate risk. Then they just wait for us to react."

"But a frontal assault?" Khatami said. "That's insane."

Sighing, Kirk nodded. "Right. Just insane enough to work."

Twenty-four

Spock almost missed it.

"Thank you, sir," said Ensign Chekov as he exited the turbo-lift and made his way to the *Enterprise* bridge's science station. "I can take over now."

His attention still on the console's sensor viewer, Spock replied, "Very well, Mister Chekov."

The younger man, assigned to the station and freeing Spock to tend to other duties while in temporary command, had remained at his post well past his normal duty shift. Spock had almost instructed him to take a rest period, but the ensign's natural talents for interfacing with the ship's sensors were matched by his tenacity and devotion to, as he described it, "picking up the slack" while Kirk, Uhura, and Sulu were off the ship. As there had been no noticeable degradation in the man's effectiveness or attention, Spock opted to let Chekov continue working, relieving him just long enough to eat a quick meal and tend to other personal matters before returning to the bridge.

Only as he began pulling away from the viewer did Spock catch the merest flicker of . . . something emerging from the constant stream of incoming sensor data; something that was not there before.

"Just a moment," he said, his attention still focused on the readings. With practiced ease, Spock moved his right hand across an adjacent row of controls, entering commands to manipulate the steady influx of information and tighten their focus on this new object of interest.

No, he realized. *Not just* one *object*.

"Two Klingon vessels on an intercept course," he called out, leaving the science station to Chekov. "Go to red alert. Shields up, place weapons on standby."

His command came an instant before the alarm sirens sounded across the bridge. Stepping around the red railing and moving to stand next to the captain's chair, Spock silenced the alarm with a touch of the proper control. Looking to the communications station, he said, "Notify Admiral Nogura."

Lieutenant Elizabeth Palmer turned in her seat. "Aye, sir."

"Tracking them now, Mister Spock," said Lieutenant Rahda from the helm station. She had activated the tactical scanner, which extended up from the console, and was peering into it. "They were moving in a close formation but now they've separated." She glanced over her shoulder. "They look to be scout-class vessels rather than warships, but I think they're trying to flank us, sir."

It was not an outlandish tactic, Spock decided. By approaching the *Enterprise* from open space rather than within the field, the ships and their commanders forced him to consider using the field as cover. Complicating matters was his desire to remain close by rather than retreating from the area, in the event Captain Kirk or his team attempted to make contact.

Chekov reported, "They've powered up their weapons, Mister Spock, but I'm picking up no indications they're attempting to target us."

"Sound general quarters, Lieutenant Palmer," Spock said. "All hands to battle stations." Settling into the command chair, he added, "Helm, stand by for evasive maneuvers."

Consulting the astrogator situated just in front of him and between Rahda and Lieutenant Leslie at navigation, he noted its readings were being updated with the positions of the approaching ships relative to the *Enterprise*. Also depicted were those asteroids in closest proximity to the ship and individual trajectories as they drifted through the field. The readings were enough to tell Spock that avenues of escape from the approaching ships were few. Almost all of them involved venturing farther into the asteroid field itself.

From the science station, Chekov reported, "Both ships are accelerating, Mister Spock. They're definitely maneuvering to pin us between them."

Glancing once more at the astrogator, Spock ordered, "Evasive action. Course one four six mark nine. Speed at your discretion, helm."

On the bridge's main viewscreen, the image shifted as the *Enterprise* banked upward and to port, effecting the turn necessary for the course into the field. Under Lieutenant Rahda's skilled guidance, the ship glided past two immense asteroids.

"The Klingons are changing course to follow," Chekov said. "Sensors are detecting targeting scans from both ships."

Without waiting for an order, Rahda maneuvered the *Enterprise* into a steep bank to port, using the move to place another of the large asteroids between it and the starship's pursuers. Using the moon-sized body for cover, she then executed a climb toward another asteroid. She repeated the move twice more, each time varying direction and angle through the field while working to place obstacle after obstacle in the Klingons' path.

Behind him, Spock heard the turbolift doors open and shifted just enough to see Admiral Nogura stepping onto the bridge. He did not ask for a status report, but instead simply moved to stand next to the command chair and take his own look at the astrogator.

"Company," he said.

Spock raised an eyebrow. "Indeed."

"One of the ships has a target lock," Chekov said. "They're firing!"

Rahda chose that moment to push the *Enterprise* to port and it arced close enough to yet another asteroid that it triggered a proximity alarm. The move was just fast enough to make the Klingons' attack miss the ship, but Spock and everyone else were treated to a pair of brilliant crimson disruptor bolts slamming into the massive chunk of rock.

"Well done, Lieutenant," Spock said. "Bring us about. Mister Leslie, prepare to target the Klingon ships."

Before Rahda could respond to the order, there was another round of disruptor fire, this time from the other Klingon ship pursuing them from their opposite side. The attack came too fast even for her skill and reflexes, with the ship shuddering around Spock and everyone else as the *Enterprise*'s deflector shields absorbed the strike. Nogura, still standing next to the command chair, leaned against the nearby bridge railing for support.

Still bent over the science console's sensor viewer, Chekov said, "Only a glancing blow, sir. Lieutenant Rahda avoided the worst of it, and our shields handled it well enough."

"I suppose it's too much to hope we might have a chat with the Klingons and convince them of the error of their ways," Nogura said.

His tone along with his expression were enough to communicate the sarcasm behind the comment. Nevertheless, Spock had considered the possibility of attempting contact with the Klingon ships, if only to determine whether they might provide a reason for their attack. There had to be some justification for the provocative action, which if reported to higher authorities would only serve to spark a heated exchange between Federation and Klingon diplomats.

"They're continuing with their pursuit, Mister Spock," Rahda called out. "Definitely trying to outflank us."

"Alter course to engage the closer ship, Lieutenant," Spock said. As Rahda carried out the order, he looked to Nogura.

"Doctor McCoy refers to this type of action as giving someone a taste of their own medicine."

The admiral snorted. "I may end up liking that man after all."

"Closing on Klingon ship," Rahda said.

Next to her, Leslie added, "Phasers ready, Mister Spock."

The order to fire died in Spock's throat as the ship trembled and every light and screen and indicator on the bridge blinked, flickered, or simply died out. When the primary illumination failed, it took an extra second for emergency lighting to kick in. Even before he felt the minor yet distinct fluctuation in the ship's artificial gravity, he knew what was happening.

"Another of the disruption-field emitters," Nogura said, echoing his thoughts.

Holding on to her console to avoid being thrown from her chair, Rahda was consulting her tactical scanner. "The Klingon ships have broken off their attack, sir. They're keeping station fifty thousand kilometers off our stern."

A trap?

Spock had only seconds to consider that thought before a noticeable change in the pitch of the *Enterprise*'s engines reverberated across the bridge. He gripped the command chair's arms to remain seated as inertial damping systems struggled under this new onslaught. After verifying neither Nogura nor anyone else had been knocked off their feet, he looked to the science station. "Mister Chekov, can you pinpoint the source?"

"Working on it, sir." Dividing his attention between the sensor readings and various other controls at the console, Chekov worked with frantic purpose. "I think I've got it. Bearing two five seven mark four. Distance, nine thousand kilometers." When Chekov turned away from the station, Spock noted the perspiration on the younger man's face.

"Transfer those coordinates to navigation," said Spock. "Mister Leslie, target that location and fire at will."

Lieutenant Rahda's maneuvering of the ship into position

brought the asteroid to the center of the main viewscreen. It took Leslie only seconds to make the necessary adjustments before he unleashed a phaser barrage at the drifting rock. Twin beams of blue-white energy joined at a single spot on the asteroid's surface. A fleeting, intense flash of light erupted from the point of impact. Seconds later the bridge illumination returned to normal and the hum of the *Enterprise*'s engines settled into its more familiar drone.

"Emitter destroyed, sir," Chekov said, looking up from his console.

Rahda added, "The Klingons are altering course to intercept us again." She was already tapping controls, getting the ship underway and preparing to resume evasive maneuvers.

"They know we're onto them," Nogura said. "Which means they're not going to want us leaving so we can get clear and notify Starfleet of what they're doing out here."

It was a logical assessment, Spock decided. To further the admiral's theory, there was also the distinct possibility the Klingons were aware they were missing the emitter that now resided in the *Enterprise*'s cargo hold. They would waste little time arriving at the conclusion that their presence and their activities here were compromised. What remained in question was how far they were willing to go now that their secrecy was endangered. Based on his past experience dealing with Klingons, Spock was confident he already had his answer.

And that is most unfortunate, he admitted to himself. While he preferred to avoid casualties if at all possible, the Klingons certainly harbored no such reservations.

"They're close enough for us to get a phaser lock, sir," Leslie said.

Using the astrogator to verify the enemy ships' approach vectors, Spock said, "Target to disable weapons and propulsion, Lieutenant."

The navigator keyed the appropriate controls and Spock

watched the viewscreen as multiple phaser barrages lanced across space to strike the closer Klingon ship's deflector shields. Though smaller than the battle cruisers with which Spock was familiar, it still harbored similar design features. A bulbous forward hull extended outward from a short, cylindrical neck to a larger, more angular drive section. Two nacelles were nestled almost against the hull's underside, giving the ship an illusion of freefalling through atmosphere toward a planet's surface.

Banking away, the smaller, sleeker enemy vessel fired as it withdrew. The *Enterprise* shuddered from the force of the impact against its own shields but Leslie followed with another strike of his own. This time his aim was true and he was rewarded with a flash along the Klingon scout's aft shields. Spock saw its starboard impulse engine sputter before failing altogether.

Chekov said, "They're moving off, Mister Spock. Sensors show they're running on half power, and their maneuvering ability has also been compromised. It looks like they're retreating."

"The other ship's coming around," Rahda warned.

Dividing her attention between her instruments and the helm console's tactical scanner, she made a series of rapid course adjustments to bring the *Enterprise* around to face the new threat. On the viewscreen, the second Klingon scout ship was coming into view, arcing around another of the asteroids. The instant it was clear its forward disruptors flared red, each launching a double dose of energy bolts.

"Evasive," Spock ordered, but Rahda was already reacting. Her rapid action was enough to avoid two of the disruptor bolts but the remaining pair still found the *Enterprise*'s shields. The impact this time was enough to rattle everyone on the bridge, and for the first time an alert sounded in response to inflicted damage.

"Starboard shields down to sixty-eight percent," Chekov called out.

On the viewscreen, the Klingon ship was maneuvering for another shot but Leslie was ready, unleashing a full spread of phaser fire against the other vessel's shields. Spock saw the barrage push through to reach the ship's hull.

Rahda, peering once more into her tactical scanner, said, "You hit their forward disruptors."

"They're altering course and accelerating away," added Chekov. "Nice shooting, Mister Leslie."

Spock said, "Agreed. Well done, everyone."

Behind him at the communications station, Lieutenant Palmer said, "Mister Spock, engineering reports only light damage. Our shields absorbed the worst of it, and repairs are already underway."

"Excellent." Rising from the command chair, Spock turned to Nogura. "Admiral, with respect to your earlier point, it is obvious the Klingons are unhappy about our presence in this area. If they did not previously believe we possessed knowledge of their disruption-field technology, they surely do now. We have to prepare for the possibility they may return with greater force. With this in mind, I submit we need to clear the asteroid field at least long enough to transmit to Starfleet the information we have collected to this point."

Crossing his arms, Nogura cast his gaze toward the deck as he considered the suggestion. "I appreciate what you're saying, Mister Spock, but I have another perspective. If we go with our theory that this is all some sort of experiment being conducted in secret, then chances are good the facility supporting this testing is small and with limited resources. The asteroid field provides perfect cover for this sort of thing. Remember, we had no prior knowledge of anything like this, even with the reports we were getting from agents like Morgan Binnix and her team. That's usually a good indication it's an effort being carried out from within a cell of Imperial Intelligence. Information would be highly compartmentalized to a point where even the High Council might not be aware of the project's existence. This means they would have to operate without attracting attention. You can't do that and deploy a heavy military presence to what's supposed to be a top-secret outpost in the middle of nowhere."

Before Spock could reply, he was interrupted by the sound of the turbolift doors opening. He looked up to see Leonard McCoy walking onto the bridge, wearing a blue short-sleeved medical smock in lieu of a standard duty uniform tunic.

"Spock, you'll be happy to know there were no serious casualties during that last ruckus," said McCoy, forgoing any sort of formal greeting. "One broken ankle and a couple of minor lacerations. My staff's patching everyone up and they should be cleared for duty in the next few hours."

"Thank you, Doctor," Spock replied. Certain he already knew the answer to his next question, he asked it anyway. "I presume you opted against sending this report over the intercom for some other reason?"

As always, McCoy got right to the point. "Yeah. Now that we know Klingons are crawling all over this asteroid field, when are we going after Jim and the others?"

"We were just discussing that, Doctor," Nogura said. "In a manner of speaking, anyway." He returned his attention to Spock. "Commander, if I'm right, then whatever facility is here overseeing this project will be lightly defended. We may not have a better opportunity to investigate and—if necessary—neutralize it."

McCoy asked, "Did I miss a meeting? Do we think the Klingons captured Jim?"

"No," Spock replied. "We have not yet heard from Captain Kirk or his party. For the moment, we continue to abide by this mission's communications protocols." Even as he spoke the words, he saw the doctor's expression turning to one of disapproval.

"Protocols?" McCoy glanced to Nogura before adding, "I think we can all agree this mission's nothing like we thought it was going to be when we started. We can't just leave Jim and the others out there with everything else that's going on. Everybody knows we're poking around out here anyway, so let's get our people before the Klingons do."

"Doctor," Nogura said, his tone turning hard. "Are you always this insolent?"

"When it comes to the safety of this crew, you're damned right I am." After two full seconds of silence, McCoy cleared his throat. "Sir." It was enough, Spock noted, to garner from the admiral the faintest hint of a smile.

Attempting to defuse the growing tension, the first officer said, "Doctor, for now the Klingons seem focused on us. We have no indications the captain and his team have been compromised, and neither do we know if they have found the *Endeavour*. Until we have such confirmation, the logical course is to avoid doing anything that might expose their activities or our connection to them." In a concession to Nogura's observations, he added, "Indeed, by increasing the intensity of our own investigation, we may well draw all of the Klingons' attention away from anything that might endanger the rest of our people."

"Let's also not forget," Nogura said, "if we're right, then the Klingons are conducting secret military operations in nonaligned space. It's likely the Empire will disavow any knowledge of the project, as it's definitely a treaty violation. Meanwhile, we can't give them a chance to relocate this technology and continue perfecting it to a point it can be more aggressively deployed against us."

McCoy frowned. "So you're saying it's now or never."

"That is exactly what I'm saying, Doctor." Nogura placed a hand on McCoy's arm. "I know you're worried about your captain and shipmates. Believe me when I tell you I am as well. But even with the unexpected developments this mission has taken, it's still the one we all accepted. We'll find them, Doctor. I promise."

"I'm holding you to that, Admiral."

"I would expect nothing less." Nogura turned to Spock. "Commander?"

In response to the prompt, Spock said, "Mister Chekov, do you have sensor readings for the retreat course taken by the Klingon ships?"

Turning from the science station, the ensign nodded. "Yes, Mister Spock. At least, until the asteroid field's background radiation disrupted our sensors."

"Utilize all available information to formulate a search pattern," Spock said. "We will begin immediately."

It was not much, he knew. Still, it was a start.

Twenty-five

Darkness. Total, all-encompassing darkness.

Holding up his hand, Kirk was only able to see the material of his suit thanks to the soft glow of his EVA helmet's internal lighting along with the feeble illumination of the life-support controls on his chest. Looking down, he could just make out the hard, unyielding surface of the asteroid's canyon floor. The gravity here was just under one-sixth of what he was used to feeling aboard ship. Beyond the rock outcropping he had chosen for cover and concealment, visibility dropped off beyond just a dozen meters, succumbing to unrelenting blackness. Behind him, the *Endeavour*'s saucer section loomed in the near darkness. What illumination there was came courtesy of the ship's running lights and whatever escaped through those few ports that had not been lost during its rough landing. Kirk at first had considered asking for the external lights to be shut off, but in the end he preferred to see at least something of the terrain in front of him.

Looking out from his hiding place, he could not help the sense of déjà vu washing over him. The darkness reminded him of the seeming eternity he had spent adrift in an interspatial void, caught in the doorway between universes that had claimed the *Enterprise*'s ill-fated sister starship, the *U.S.S. Defiant*. He had been utterly alone, his only companion the sound of his own increasingly labored breathing as his suit's oxygen supply inexorably dwindled.

At least now, Kirk could take some comfort from knowing he was not alone, either in this universe or even out here at the bottom of this canyon.

"The tour guide promised us spectacular sights," said Morgan Binnix, her voice filtering through the speakers inside Kirk's helmet. *"I'm starting to feel cheated."*

Shifting his position allowed him to look to his left, where Binnix stood just beyond an arm's length from him. Her silhouette already visible thanks to the *Endeavour*'s lights, her own helmet's interior illumination highlighted her face. The telltale indicators of her suit's life-support system marked her location. She was his partner out here. Other members of the *Endeavour*'s crew along with Lieutenant Sulu as well as agents Phillip Watson and David Horst were out here, positioned in similar fashion at different points around the saucer's rear half, supplementing the four teams tasked with operating the phaser cannons already deployed atop the ship's hull. In the meantime, Captain Khatami and additional *Endeavour* personnel were in the process of donning whatever EV suits remained and preparing to augment the group already deployed outside.

"This isn't exactly what I signed up for," Kirk said. "When you're training for starship command, defending a fixed position isn't something they typically spend a lot of time teaching at the Academy."

Studying such things was a component of his history courses as a cadet. Everything from the Spartans at Thermopylae to the Western Front during the First World War had captivated his attention. While his instructors had little to say so far as referencing these battles to modern starship combat tactics, Kirk enjoyed the challenge of translating the ancient strategies into something useful. The more unconventional, the better, so far as he was concerned. Such thinking served him well during his tenure at the Academy in everything from training simulations to exercises pitting classes against one another in ground combat drills designed to emphasize teamwork and ingenuity. Though it was many years ago, Kirk still took a bit of shameless and admittedly immature pride at having never lost any of his class's Capture the Flag exercises. A few of those were even conducted on moons or planets with atmospheric conditions requiring the use of EV suits, something Kirk had not enjoyed but to which he adapted because that was what victory required. As it happened, those same bits of unorthodox strategy and wayward thinking he learned in school came in handy during the ensuing years.

And here's hoping they don't fail me now, he thought.

A tone sounded from the speakers in Kirk's helmet, signifying the activation of a new communications frequency, and was followed by the voice of Captain Khatami.

"Endeavour *to Captain Kirk. Are you all ready?*"

Consulting the tricorder he brought with him, Kirk checked the diagram he had programmed into the device. It now displayed a technical schematic of the *Endeavour*'s saucer along with icons representing twenty-four people distributed in twos along the hull. Four of the pairs were assigned to the phaser cannons already deployed by the ship's security contingent, while the others were arranged in a pattern designed to provide a unified front along with overlapping fields of fire for the phaser rifles every person carried. Kirk had already directed the phaser cannon crews to maneuver the larger weapons into a formation designed to provide maximum protection for the *Endeavour*'s aft section that housed the precious impulse engines. They also would offer covering fire for everyone else if they ended up retreating to secondary fire positions along the ship's hull.

"As ready as we're going to be," he said. "What about our visitors?" He knew that the *Endeavour*'s captain had ordered the reactivation of the starship's starboard impulse engine. Though only operating at one-third its normal capacity, that was still enough to allow use of the sensors, communications, and other shipboard systems they needed.

Khatami replied, *"Sensors show at least fifty life-forms on the surface, all Orion. They're spreading into a skirmishers line, but so far there's no indication of their point of attack. We're jamming their communications and their ships' sensors, which also means their personal scanners or tricorders or whatever the people on the ground are carrying. That'll confuse them for a while, but it won't matter when they get close enough to start shooting."*

"They have to get here first," Kirk said.

"We're not going to have to wait long," said Commander Katherine Stano. Kirk knew the *Endeavour's* first officer had taken up a position opposite his on the defensive perimeter's far side, coordinating her actions with his so they could divide the task of overseeing the effort. *"According to scans, the first of them have closed to within a hundred meters."*

Adjusting the settings on his tricorder, Kirk reduced the size of the device's *Endeavour* schematic, allowing him to study a graphic representation of the canyon floor. Fifty green icons now were visible, arranged in a curved line and moving toward the crippled starship across the vast swath of broken ground he had taken to calling "No-Man's-Land." It took him only a moment to see the formation for what it was, taking advantage of the terrain to cover the entire open area to the vessel's rear. Their line was shrinking as it advanced, indicating some level of communication between them.

"Captain, are you sure their comms are jammed?" he asked.

"So far as we can tell while basically working with one arm tied behind our back down here," Khatami replied. *"It's also possible they're using a frequency outside the normal scanning range."*

Binnix said, *"Sounds sneaky enough for a bunch of pirates."*

"We can reconfigure our systems," the *Endeavour* captain continued, *"but it'll take a minute or so. By then, the first of them might already be on you."*

Kirk said, "Do it anyway. Jamming their personal comms will add to the confusion once we engage them, and we'll need every advantage we can get."

"Copy that," Khatami replied.

Not content to rely solely on his tricorder, Kirk looked across the canyon floor and tried to see past the maze of jagged rock jutting up from the asteroid's uneven surface. Left unchecked, the darkness along with the topography of No-Man's-Land would do an excellent job of masking the Orions' advance until they were almost on them. Sound certainly wouldn't be of use out here in vacuum. He strained, searching for even the barest hint of light or movement, anything that might give away the position of someone approaching.

"Captain Kirk," said Commander Stano through the open frequency. *"They're getting close. Everybody stand fast."*

Next to him, Binnix held up her own tricorder, which like his had been programmed to provide a tactical overview of the area. Glancing at his own scan, he noted the canyon floor's broken terrain was providing their attackers with the same sort of cover he and his fellow defenders now enjoyed.

He adjusted his suit's communications frequency to the channel set aside for every member of the hastily assembled *Endeavour* defense force. "This is Captain Kirk. Those of you with tricorders already know the first line of Orions is almost on us. Final check for all weapons on heavy stun. Don't wait for my signal. If you have a target, neutralize it. Phaser cannon crews, the moment you see an opportunity, take it. Wide beam."

"I have no idea what kind of tactical training your typical Orion gets," said Binnix. *"But if they have any brains at all, they'll go after the cannons the instant the first of them fires."*

Kirk agreed. While he hoped the cannons were his ace in the hole, perhaps successfully stunning the majority of the Orions before they got too close, experience and harsh lessons learned long ago had taught him differently.

"Plan for the best. Expect the worst," he said.

Binnix replied, *"I prefer something I came across years ago, while reading about twentieth-century warfare. Something called Murphy's Laws of Close Combat. One of them was, 'No battle plan survives first contact with the enemy.' It's actually pretty adaptable to all sorts of situations."*

"Sounds about right," Kirk conceded.

He was once more studying the schematic on his tricorder when the first hint of movement caught his attention from somewhere to his left. It was fleeting and when he tried to focus on the source it seemed to disappear.

"Get ready."

That was all Kirk had time to say before the darkness was pierced by a brilliant shaft of green-yellow light aimed in his general direction. The beam went far enough to his left that he was in no danger, but that was enough for other members of the *Endeavour* crew to take action. More than a half-dozen streaks of blue-white phaser energy erupted from the defensive perimeter, searching for the source of that initial shot. This, of course, provoked more fire from various points out in No-Man's-Land. Within seconds the area was being blanketed with streaks of crisscrossing weapons fire. Despite the visual cacophony erupting all around him, Kirk heard nothing inside his suit helmet.

"Kirk to *Endeavour*! Hit the lights!"

Now the darkness was beaten back as the lights scattered across the starship's hull flared to life. Seeing his own arms and Binnix hunkering beside him behind the jagged outcropping made Kirk push himself even closer to the rock, doing his best to present as small a target as possible. To his right and left, members of the defensive team were taking advantage of the illumination to find targets, unleashing new volleys from their phaser rifles. Just at the edge of the lights' reach, Kirk saw more than a dozen figures scrambling for cover, each of them clad in

EV suits that were nearly as black as the darkness they used to conceal their movements. They ducked behind outcroppings or jumped into depressions, craters, or whatever else presented itself.

All through this the weapons fire continued from both sides, with neither—so far as Kirk could tell—gaining anything that might resemble an early advantage. The combination of terrain and low visibility was the biggest hampering factor, only somewhat mitigated by tricorder scans tracking enemy positions. Some of the Orions were feeling bold, as he saw several of them maneuvering between places of concealment. They were probing, looking for avenues of approach and better places to fire from cover.

A single blue phaser beam shot across the dim landscape, catching one of the dark-suited attackers in the chest and causing its body to jerk and flail before falling to the ground. The lower gravity here ensured it was not a violent fall, with the now stunned Orion collapsing in a gentle heap to the canyon floor.

"Captain Kirk," said Lieutenant Brax, the *Endeavour's* security chief. *"A somewhat larger concentration of attackers is attempting an aggressive approach from our right. They may be trying to get around our positions to attack the ship directly."*

"Phaser cannons," Binnix said, punctuating her statement with a double shot from her own phaser rifle toward a target Kirk could not see around the rock protecting him.

"Right." Into his helmet mic, he said, "Rotate two of the phaser cannons to cover that area. They don't have to hit anything, but maybe it'll be enough to make the Orions rethink their strategy."

Brax replied, *"My thinking as well, sir. I believe the remaining cannons should be ready to act in similar fashion to our other side."*

Already ahead of him, Kirk was consulting his tricorder. The schematic now showed the dozens of green dots arrayed in small clusters of five or six moving away from one another, as though the Orions were separating into teams assigned to tackle individual objectives. Another group of eight figures were gathering where Kirk expected to see it based on Brax's observations.

Yes, he decided. *Something's up.*

"*This is Stano*," said the *Endeavour*'s first officer over the open link. "*All teams, pay attention to their dispersal pattern. They're gearing up to hit us from multiple directions. Phaser cannons, lay down a spread. Let's see if we can't get them to back up a little.*"

No sooner did she issue the command than a bright crimson energy beam slammed into the rock that was Kirk's temporary shelter, chewing away a large hunk of the stone and reducing it to fragments. Though the shot went high, he still felt the salvo's impact and flinched at the sound of small rock fragments striking the back of his helmet.

Then, despite being unable to hear it, the abrupt flash of light from somewhere to his right was enough to make him glance over his shoulder in time to see one of the phaser cannons, still sitting atop the *Endeavour*'s hull as it moved to track possible targets, explode.

Twenty-six

Knowing it was futile, Netal cast another disdainful look at his portable scanner and once again was frustrated by the unit's inability to provide him information.

"Use the terrain," he hissed into his excursion suit helmet's audio pickup. "Stay with your team. Cover one another's advance. We still have the advantage of movement."

Despite its impaired condition, the Starfleet vessel was disrupting at least some of the frequencies used by the equipment Netal and his people carried. This included the communications channels available to him via his excursion suit's helmet. He was able to talk with the other members of the advance party from the *Vekal Piltari*. Contacting the ship itself or even the pilots of the two transports used to ferry his people to the asteroid's surface was proving impossible. Netal suspected the *Endeavour* was able to jam certain frequencies while others, including the one being used by him and his people, remained unaffected. This was a good thing, for however long it lasted.

The sudden illumination of the ground ahead of him thanks to exterior lighting on the wrecked ship made Netal and his team scurry for somewhere to hide, and he only just made it behind an area of rock protruding from the canyon floor before phaser fire began streaking back and forth. A quick glance told him the other five members of his team had made it to cover. He had no immediate idea how the remaining members of his hastily assembled team were faring. Weapons fire from the *Endeavour* as well as multiple points along the ground behind the ship's aft section told him that at least the majority of them were still mobile.

The starship's lights were welcome enough. Even though they complicated matters as he and his people pressed forward, it was not unexpected. Upon their arrival, he had directed his people to keep their suit lights at the lowest possible setting— just enough to see the ground ahead of them—to hopefully avoid detection. It was a risky proposition, and Netal worried his team's approach might be detected by the Starfleet people now arrayed outside the wrecked ship. Natural rock formations and other terrain had provided sufficient concealment that allowed him to utilize his scanner as they advanced. The broken, even chaotic topography here favored his people if they could use it to cover their movements. At the same time, the vessel's lights helped to chase away at least a small portion of the oppressive darkness choking everything down in the bottom of this immense cavern. This exposed his people's movements, even with the obstacles guarding their approach.

What remained a mystery was how the Starfleet crew had deployed whatever response force awaited him. The crashed ship's location near an area of the canyon where towering rock walls sheltered it on three sides limited avenues from which to strike, and likewise reduced any defensive perimeter's requirements for providing covering fire along those approach angles. It did not help that the primary objective, the impulse engines, were directly in the line of defense and attack. Netal was acutely aware he and his people were challenging Starfleet officers well trained in weapons and combat tactics. Further, based on what he knew about this class of starship and assuming everyone had survived whatever event brought them to rest here, the *Endeavour* crew outnumbered his advance party eight to one. The real number was likely somewhat lower, if for no other reason than there probably were too few excursion suits to outfit the entire complement. Still, Netal was confident there would still be many more Starfleet people than Orions if this fight went on for any appreciable length of time. He and his people needed to accomplish their goal and get clear of this mess before it consumed them.

"Group two," he said into his helmet pickup. "Are you able to advance?"

Through the helmet's speaker, Avron replied, *"There is much shooting, but we have sufficient concealment. I believe we can get close enough to the objective."*

Thankfully, the Starfleet crew had not yet found a way to jam this low-power frequency. For the moment, at least, Netal and his people could communicate with one another. Even if that measure failed, he had already instructed his people how to proceed. He considered the Klingon frequencies programmed into his suit's communications system, either to contact the *Vekal Piltari* or even the Klingon base he knew was hidden somewhere in the asteroid field. However, D'zinn had warned him such a measure was one of last resort, to avoid if at all possible exposing the Orions' partnership with the Klingons.

Options remain, Netal thought.

As for Avron, despite the pilot being out of her natural element, she sounded remarkably calm and confident. It was one of the reasons Netal chose her for this task. She had participated in previous boarding parties when the *Vekal Piltari* had seized a wayward freighter or other civilian vessel, and her conduct during such encounters had earned her D'zinn's notice. Based on such prior performances, the captain had agreed without hesitation to Netal's request to add her to his team.

Adjusting his crouching stance behind the outcropping, Netal shifted the oversized pack on his back as he studied the scene before him. The ground between his present location and the *Endeavour* was significant, though much of it provided plenty of natural protection thanks to the broken, uneven terrain. Weapons fire helped him identify in general terms where his people and the Starfleet ship's crew had taken up positions using whatever natural cover they could find.

Netal also spied first two and then another pair of larger weapons, farther in the distance and sitting atop the wrecked ship's hull. Phaser cannons. He had seen such armaments before, but only on rare occasions when dealing with black marketers looking to unload surplus Starfleet equipment without attracting too much attention. Unlike those, the authenticity and reliability of which he tended to question when interacting with less than savory brokers, these looked quite functional. How would their Starfleet operators employ them?

Consulting his scanner, he noted each of the attack teams had positioned themselves according to his plan. While most of his people would serve as distraction and diversion, one group had a single mission: get close enough to utilize the devices they carried against the starship's impulse engines. Even if the engines could not be destroyed, Netal was confident of inflicting damage sufficient to further cripple the already wounded vessel.

For the first time, Netal gave serious consideration to the possibility of capture—or worse—at the hands of the *Endeavour* crew. He knew Starfleet regulations discouraged the use of deadly force even in tactical situations unless no other option remained. However, given the current situation's chaotic nature, one could not rule out unfortunate consequences. Then there were the political ramifications of this action. Except in rare instances, the Orion Syndicate took every measure to present a stance of neutrality when it came to the Federation as well as its enemies and allies. If he or other members of his group were captured, that alone would be enough to cast unwelcome light on other Syndicate activities. Exposing the Orions' involvement with the Klingons and their covert experiments here would cause even more strife for D'zinn and the *Vekal Piltari* as well as her superiors. Were the rewards they hoped to gain from this partnership worth the risk they carried?

Those are matters for the attention of others, Netal conceded, although being relieved of such responsibility did little to ease his concerns.

The flash of weapons fire caught his attention, and he noted his people's movements were not going unnoticed. Already members from the *Endeavour*'s defense force were adjusting their fire as his own people pressed forward. Even with the cover and concealment provided by the canyon's broken terrain, there would still be a point when there was nothing left to provide shelter. At that point, it would come down to whoever maneuvered faster and fired their weapons with greater accuracy.

"*Netal*," said Avron. "*They are bringing their larger weapons to bear.*"

With no sound to provide hints or other warnings, Netal was forced to shift his position behind the outcropping to get a better look at the phaser cannons. Indeed, two of the weapons were rotating on their platforms, controlled by the two-person teams overseeing their operation. Were they tracking his people's movements? He knew the capabilities of their targeting scanners, but the terrain would still help to mitigate their effectiveness.

Then, one of the weapons disappeared in a brief, violent burst of energy. Ducking for cover behind the broken rock, Netal still sensed the shockwave from the abrupt explosion reverberating in the ground beneath his feet. The force of the detonation consumed the entire phaser cannon along with the two suited figures operating it as well as a section of the starship's hull plating. He noted the puff of escaping, freezing atmosphere as it vented through the breach.

"*What happened? Did we do that?*" It took him an extra moment to realize it was Ralanna speaking, the young Orion who served as one of the *Vekal Piltari*'s sensor technicians, drafted into this action by Netal, who needed everyone capable of carrying a weapon.

"I have no idea." Despite the damage to the ship's exterior, Netal suspected the vessel's construction was strong enough to absorb the worst of the blast, but the people inside would still be scrambling to assess and repair damage. That might draw attention and resources from other, more vulnerable areas. This might well be the best chance for him and his people to press their attack.

Peering out once more from his hiding place, he saw members of the starship's defense contingent reacting to the explosion. At the edge of the circle of light cast off by the *Endeavour*'s external illumination, he caught sight of his own people scrambling among the shadows, searching for a means to capitalize on this unexpected development. Netal felt his own muscles tensing in anticipation as he hoisted his disruptor rifle. To his left and hunkered down behind another piece of exposed rock, Vodat mimicked his actions.

"*Should we move?*" Vodat asked. "*We may not have a better chance.*" The junior engineer was here over the protests of Tath, who claimed he needed every available technician to assist with the *Vekal Piltari*'s repairs. Tath's concerns were overridden by D'zinn, which resulted in Vodat being placed as Netal's immediate companion for the assault team. To Netal's surprise, the young Orion's voice held no hint of fear or uncertainty.

Before he could answer, Netal flinched at another abrupt flash of light, and looked to his left to see a second Starfleet phaser cannon consumed by a brief, powerful explosion. Like its predecessor, the blast's effect was brief thanks to vacuum out here on the surface of the asteroid, but it still was powerful enough to punch its own hole through the crashed starship's outer hull.

What is causing this?

The thought screamed in Netal's mind, but he had no answer.

He had seen no weapons fire tracking toward either of the phaser cannons. They had exploded as though of their own volition, which made no sense. Was it a malfunction, perhaps caused by damage sustained during what would have had to have been a violent landing for the *Endeavour*? There was no way to know. All Netal could see at this moment in time was that fate and good fortune had apparently chosen to smile upon him for reasons he did not understand.

"Netal! Look!"

Vodat's shout over the open communications frequency was loud enough that Netal could not help wincing inside his helmet. The younger man's hand on his arm made him look to where his companion pointed, and he realized that this second bizarre explosion was doing more to shake up the Starfleet personnel deployed outside the *Endeavour*. In pairs or even trios, people were turning from their defensive positions to investigate the new damage. Netal was sure he sensed their anxiety and insecurity as they struggled to discern what had happened.

Now, he admonished himself. *We must move in. Now!*

"Avron," he said into his helmet's audio pickup. "Advance on the target."

————————

Kirk had no idea what the hell was going on.

The loss of the second phaser cannon was as inexplicable as the first. What happened? There had been no incoming fire, at least not enough to account for the total destruction of either weapon. For the briefest of moments, he felt for the four *Endeavour* personnel lost in the pair of explosions. They never stood a chance, and what about the ship itself? From his vantage point, Kirk could see the large wound in the crippled starship's upper hull. There had been a brief escape of atmosphere, but so far as he knew, no one inside the ship had been in that area. The bulk of the crew was confined to interior spaces, away from compartments near the outer hull. He knew Captain Khatami and her people would already be scrambling to assess the resulting damage and take any necessary corrective action. Khatami and her crew did not need him or anyone else calling for updates or offering other unwanted distractions. There was still plenty with which to be concerned out here on the surface.

Do your job, Captain, Kirk scolded himself. *Let Khatami do hers.*

"Nothing hit those things," said Morgan Binnix, her voice low and tight as it filtered through his helmet's speakers. *"They just exploded on their own."*

An accident? Perhaps once, Kirk conceded. Twice? Unlikely.

"Sabotage," he said. "It has to be. Damn it." Switching to the communications frequency shared by the small force he had assembled, he snapped, "Phaser cannon crews, do not activate those weapons. Repeat, do not fire those weapons. They may have been rigged to explode. All teams, watch your fields of fire. The Orions may take advantage of this to move on us."

Binnix said, *"It's what I'd do."* To emphasize her point, she shifted her position next to the large piece of jagged rock extending upward from the canyon floor and raised her phaser rifle. *"Movement out there, Captain."*

"I see them." And indeed he did. Shadowy figures lurching and leaping from one place of concealment to the next. Several of the attackers were tracked by phaser fire from somewhere along the defensive line. He thought he saw one of the Orions fall, but the pirate was too far away and lost in the gloom for him to be sure.

"They're shifting their positions," Binnix said, and when Kirk looked in her direction he saw she was consulting her own tricorder. *"Some of them, anyway."*

Studying the unit's readout was enough to confirm Kirk's initial suspicion about the assault force's deployment. Most of the incoming Orions were likely intended as distraction or harassment. He guessed their primary goal, aside from clearing out as many defenders as possible, was to shield the movements of two smaller, faster-moving groups from within their ranks. It was these units that required the most attention, as they almost certainly were the ones tasked with inflicting some form of serious harm on the *Endeavour*.

We'll just see about that.

The defiant thought barely had time to register with him before Kirk was adjusting the settings on his tricorder and attempting to tighten and refine its scanning capabilities. Not nearly so powerful as a space vessel's onboard sensors, this smaller unit only had so much range while being hampered by the asteroid field's background interference. Becoming frustrated with the tricorder's lack of cooperation, he was almost ready to chuck the thing altogether when one of its indicator lights abruptly flashed green.

"Some kind of device," he said, glancing toward Binnix. "Each of those two groups has one, in backpacks or satchels. I'm not picking up any sign of explosive material, but their outer casings look to be shielded. They're not very big, but if they're bombs, then they don't have to be." He held the tricorder so she could see it.

She replied, *"If they* are *bombs, then just one positioned in the right spot could be enough to cripple one of the* Endeavour's *impulse engines. Maybe both, if they have time to place it correctly."*

"We're not going to let that happen." Kirk shook his head. "We can't. It's that simple. Kirk to Stano, are you watching the Orions' deployment?"

There was a brief pause before *Endeavour*'s first officer replied, *"Yes, Captain."*

"Bring one person from your section and head for the rear of the ship. Mister Sulu, that goes for you and Lieutenant Uhura too. We're on our way now. Everyone else, maintain your positions and your fields of fire."

"Aye, sir," Sulu said. *"We'll meet you there."*

As he prepared to move from his place of concealment, Kirk heard Binnix say, *"You know I'm coming with you, right?"*

"Wouldn't have it any other way."

No sooner did he take his first step away from the protective outcropping than a streak of disruptor fire drove into the other side of the rock. Kirk flinched at the blast's proximity, his instinctive jump backward sending him momentarily off balance in the asteroid's lighter gravity.

"Kirk!" Binnix grabbed his left arm, helping to steady him. *"You all right?"*

Before he could answer, something moved to his right, obscuring part of the illumination from the *Endeavour*'s external lighting. Binnix's immediate reaction was to pull the stock of her phaser rifle to her shoulder and fire the weapon at an unseen target. She fired again as Kirk raised his own rifle, ready to provide cover fire. He was in time to see two dark figures repelled by the force of Binnix's weapon strike. Set to heavy stun, the rifle would of course cause no permanent damage. In the distance behind him, Kirk caught sight of two more attackers maneuvering between rocky obstacles and aimed his weapon in their direction. They disappeared from view before he could fire, prompting a grunt of frustration.

"Come on," he snapped.

With Binnix on his heels, Kirk lunged from their defensive position and aimed himself at the *Endeavour*. Around them, sporadic exchanges of weapons fire streaked through the near gloom that was not totally pushed back by the starship's lights. The low gravity here made movement easy enough, provided one possessed the training and skill necessary to maneuver in such an environment. Without the sound of energy discharges from the different weapons, it was an almost surreal sensation. Sudden movements and especially abrupt changes in direction carried risks. Still, it had taken little time to reacquaint himself with the process of operating in his EV suit over ground in a tactical setting.

Then he bounded around a particularly large piece of rock rising up from the canyon floor and found himself face-to-face with seven Orions.

Well, he thought. *Damn.*

Twenty-seven

They were close.

They were so close, and yet to Netal the objective still seemed so very distant. Not out of reach; not yet, at least, but any thoughts of his task being easy were vanishing with each passing moment.

"This way," Netal said to his companion, Vodat. The words came out more as a barked command than simple guidance. Perhaps that in itself was a testament to how frustrating the situation was becoming. He pushed away the unwelcome, distracting thought and concentrated his attention on the scanner in his left hand. "We are getting closer to their defenses. Be ready to fire." Shifting his disruptor rifle so its barrel rested across his left forearm, he felt the fingers of his right hand tighten around the weapon's pistol grip.

Using the scanner to guide him, along with Vodat and the rest of his team, over the canyon's broken terrain, Netal saw they were approaching a point where the ground cover would no longer protect them. Before him was the massive hull of the crashed starship, many times larger than the *Vekal Piltari* while looking far more fragile. Its impulse engine ports faced outward from the resting place the ship had found in this corner of the canyon. From this distance, he now could see the heads and even upper torsos of a few of the *Endeavour*'s crew. Most took refuge behind rock formations or in holes undoubtedly cut by their weapons into the canyon floor. Others were scrambling from one position to another. Fighters from both groups were visible, maneuvering in and around the various natural impediments provided by the asteroid. Punctuating all of this action were irregular exchanges of weapons fire as each side sought an advantage over the other. At such proximity, one did not need a scan of the area to determine an enemy's location. This was battle at its most primitive, with two opposing forces facing off on largely open ground.

"Some of the Starfleet people are shifting their positions," he told Vodat. "They may be realizing our intentions, or at least they suspect as much."

"*Netal,*" said Avron over the assault team's communications frequency. "*More Starfleet personnel are coming out of the ship. They may suspect what we are attempting.*"

She indicated where to look and Netal noted more than a dozen figures, each clad in the distinctive silver Starfleet excursion suits, emerging from an airlock set into the side of the *Endeavour*'s enormous, saucer-shaped hull. Others, he saw, were appearing from access points along the hull's upper portion. Most carried phaser rifles, moving quickly in the reduced gravity. Already outnumbered, at least so far as he was able to determine with his scanner, the fight now was shifting even further in favor of the Starfleet crew.

It was now, he knew, or never.

"Will you be ready to deploy your device?" he asked.

Avron replied, "*Yes. We are almost in position.*"

In fairness, it was not a logical leap to make. Surely the starship's captain knew—absent extreme circumstances—its crew would likely outnumber any group attempting to make an unauthorized boarding. Orion vessels did not carry a complement of a size at all sufficient for such a bold action, hence this secondary plan put into motion by D'zinn. As for the tactic itself, damaging or disabling the crashed vessel's primary power source was the most effective means of mitigating its greater numbers. The crew's priorities would shift to survival, their attention drawn to immediate needs, and leave them vulnerable to exploitation. If Netal and his people were successful, it would place them in a powerful position over the *Endeavour*'s captain. This had been enough to convince D'zinn to go forward with the plan. Netal could only hope the *Vekal Piltari* commander's faith in his proposal was well founded.

"Avron," he said, "be ready to move. Everyone else, increase your rate of fire. We need to continue distracting as many of their people as we can, for as long as possible."

After receiving acknowledgments from other group leaders, he tapped Vodat on the shoulder before gesturing for his team to follow him. A quick look across the expanse of open terrain separating him from the starship showed more weapons fire as his people heeded his instructions. The reactions from the Starfleet personnel were what he expected, but whereas their shots continued to originate from largely static positions, the reports from his group's weapons appeared more chaotic. His people were firing on the move, probing and hunting for openings in the defensive perimeter that could be exploited.

It did not take long for Netal to find his own opportunity. A small yet still discernible gap had appeared in the defensive line, possibly a consequence of only two or perhaps four of the *Endeavour* crew moving from their positions to redeploy elsewhere. He spied at least two figures maneuvering toward the ship, where the massive impulse engine ports remained visible. Two others moved in a similar direction as though intending to meet up with their colleagues.

"*Netal,*" said Avron over the comm link. "*Now is our time.*"

Raising his disruptor rifle, Netal replied, "Agreed. Advance on the target."

He stepped from behind the rock cropping, shifting the bulky pack across his back again and allowing his weapon's muzzle to lead the way as he pressed forward. Without really aiming, he fired as he lunged first left, then back to his right, using the lower gravity to his advantage while bounding from rock formation to jagged outcropping. Lacking sound to warn him of incoming fire or the possible approach of *Endeavour* personnel, he had no choice but to divide his attention between the ground at his feet and possible threats from ahead of him or to either side.

Then there was no more cover.

A stretch of open ground lay before him and the crashed ship. It took Netal a moment to realize that he had somehow breached the defensive line. This was confirmed when movement to his right made him turn in that direction in time to see a pair of silver-suited figures scrambling to shift their weapons toward him. Vodat, following behind him, was faster and her aim sure as she leveled her disruptor rifle on the new threats. Two pairs of rapid-fire disruptor bolts crossed the intervening space, striking their targets with surprising precision. Both Starfleet defenders were pushed against the rocks behind them before they slumped to the ground.

"We must keep moving," Netal said, gesturing for Vodat and the other five members of his team to follow him. "Now that we have breached their lines, they will rally their forces with even greater ferocity."

Two more targets presented themselves as he led the way forward, this time emerging from a ditch or depression behind a low stone formation. The transparent faceplates of their helmets reflected the *Endeavour*'s lights, drawing attention to themselves as if they had activated a homing beacon. Netal gave them no chance, firing his weapon and catching both Starfleet officers before they could bring their phaser rifles to bear. Once they fell, there appeared to be no one else in the immediate vicinity. His approach to the vessel had brought them to its aft starboard quarter, not far from the impulse engines. He was close enough to see that only one of the two engines was active, and that at an obviously reduced level. Were they damaged or simply preserving resources? Also visible were members of *Endeavour's* crew redeploying to defend that area.

"Almost there, Vodat," he said.

The younger man replied, *"Others are having success, as well."*

Glancing to his left and right, Netal saw the other members of his assault force engaging *Endeavour* personnel at close quarters. From what he could discern, the engagements appeared somewhat balanced, with each side claiming small victories either in advancing on the target or defending against that action. A quick study of his scanner told him his people had broken through the line at several points. Avron's group in particular looked to be making good progress toward their target, though he noted additional icons representing Starfleet personnel converging on their location. The symbols depicting *Vekal Piltari's* crew members also were maneuvering in response to these developments. Other *Endeavour* crew members maintained their positions, sticking to whatever scheme their commander had put into motion to protect the ship. They were being augmented by still more people emerging from three different airlocks around the hull. Left unchecked, their number would quickly grow to dwarf his team.

"The airlocks," Netal said into the open comm frequency. "Fire on the airlocks. Try to keep them from getting more people outside."

Kneeling as he unlimbered the pack from his back, he watched his instructions heeded in seconds with new salvos of disruptor fire concentrating on the three portals. The effects were just as immediate. Anyone still inside the airlocks backtracked to the safety of the ship's interior. Those who had made it to the surface scrambled for cover. The suppressive fire supplied by his assault force was having the intended effect, keeping most of the Starfleet people at bay.

With practiced ease and with Vodat helping him, Netal extracted an oversized rectangular container from the pack. Opening it revealed the compact, multibarreled launcher and accompanying portable control console. Not a weapon in the conventional sense, each of the device's six barrels carried a portable magnetic field inhibitor. Of Andorian design, the inhibitors were intended for use by covert operatives charged with such distasteful activities as sabotaging ships, ground vehicles, and other electronics in such a manner as to make the disruption appear accidental. D'zinn and the *Vekal Piltari* crew had acquired several of the devices thanks to a mutually beneficial black-market transaction with a Tellarite arms dealer. With the targeting scanner and activation controls built into the remote control, deploying the package of inhibitors was a simple matter. Activating the portable console, which featured controls that were accessible even through his excursion suit's padded gloves, Netal needed only seconds to home in on his desired placement: the *Endeavour*'s starboard impulse engine. If everything was going to plan, the starship's port engine would be the target of Avron's team.

"Deploying now," he said, pressing the appropriate control. That simple act was answered as six projectiles ejected from the launcher, each of the inhibitors powered by its own limited-range flight system. Following the course Netal had given them, they arced up and away from him and toward the *Endeavour*. It took only moments for the devices to cross the gap before affixing themselves at irregular intervals along the outer frame of the starship's starboard impulse engine.

All that remained was to activate them.

"*Netal!*"

The warning from Vodat was sharp and high pitched, causing Netal to look up in time to see a lone figure in a Starfleet excursion suit and carrying a phaser rifle, staring directly at him.

———————

For what seemed like an eternity, Kirk stood all but frozen in place, staring at the seven Orions who appeared equally startled to see him. His mind screamed a simple statement.

This is not *a good day.*

All but one of the pirates carried short, ugly disruptor rifles. The remaining Orion was kneeling beside some kind of packing container, next to which sat an odd, squat device perhaps a meter tall. Its most prominent feature was the set of six tubes packed in a tight circle. He had no idea what it was, only that it looked decidedly unfriendly.

"Captain." The voice of Lieutenant Sulu echoed in Kirk's helmet. *"Whatever they launched at the* Endeavour *came from somewhere near your position."*

"So I'm learning, Mister Sulu."

The kneeling Orion locked eyes with Kirk, who in that one brief moment understood that his adversary was quickly realizing his plan—whatever it might be—had reached critical mass. Perhaps he was beginning to comprehend his own fate was no longer in his own hands; the situation was spiraling so far out of control there was no longer any hope of escape. Regardless, there was a mission to complete, and no choice left to him but to finish what he had started.

The Orion's right hand moved for the strange construct. In that moment Kirk saw the control panel. Realization dawned at the same instant his phaser rifle raised as though of its own volition. He felt his finger tightening on the weapon's firing stud. Everything to this point had happened in the space of mere heartbeats.

He was still too slow.

Kirk did not deliver his first phaser volley in time to stop the Orion from pressing some control on the compact panel. He was only vaguely aware of something flashing in the distance behind him even as the phaser beam struck the Orion's chest. The pirate's hand was still on the controls when his body seized in response to the stun beam before he slumped forward and collapsed to the ground. This was enough to shake his companions from their hesitation and they reacted by bringing their disruptors to bear. Backpedaling in search of cover, Kirk continued firing his rifle. Several of his shots missed while others found targets, sending those Orions falling to the canyon floor. He flinched as a streak of red energy passed a bit too close in front of his helmet's faceplate. Intense light overloaded his vision and he instinctively dropped to one knee, firing his weapon blind.

By then, Kirk had company. He felt a hand on his shoulder just as his vision began to clear, and he was able to make out blue streaks of phaser energy lancing past him to strike the few remaining Orions. Each staggered, falling to the ground. The entire group was down in seconds, leaving him alone.

Almost alone.

"*You okay?*" Morgan Binnix said, and he again felt her hand on his shoulder.

Kirk grunted, pushing himself to his feet. "I've been better." Blinking away the last of his compromised sight, he raised his phaser rifle and checked the immediate vicinity. He pivoted from right to left, his weapon's muzzle guiding the way as he searched for threats.

"*I think we've managed to stop them, sir,*" reported Sulu after Kirk requested status reports from those officers he had designated as section leaders, tasked with overseeing a specific area of the *Endeavour's* defensive perimeter.

"*We're doing a head count now,*" added Ensign Kerry Zane, a member of the starship's security detail. His deep voice boomed through Kirk's helmet speakers. "*We lost four when the phaser cannons blew, but no other fatalities. We've got between forty-five and fifty Orions accounted for. We're doing another sweep to be sure, but what are we supposed to do with them all?*"

Kirk grimaced. "That's a good question." He continued his survey of the area, now seeing members of the *Endeavour* crew moving about and collecting unconscious Orions wherever they lay upon the canyon's barren terrain. Most were being moved to a point perhaps twenty meters away from the crashed ship. As the wreck itself moved into his field of vision, he noted several figures in silver Starfleet environment suits clambering on or near the ship's hull and in particular the massive impulse engines.

"*Captain Kirk,*" said Lieutenant Brax over the still active communications frequency. The *Endeavour* security chief's voice seemed more anxious than usual, even accounting for the present circumstances. "*The Orions have succeeded in deploying something against the ship's power systems. It appears to have drained all power from the starboard impulse engine.*"

Moving to stand next to him, Binnix said, "*Uh-oh.*"

Over the link, Commander Katherine Stano added, "*I can't make contact with Captain Khatami or anyone else on the ship, but they may have their hands full right now.*"

Kirk felt his jaw clenching as he considered the possibilities as well as the ramifications. It was not as though the *Endeavour* had many contingency plans left to which they could turn if their current situation continued to deteriorate. If the new damage was extensive, this was more than a simple setback. It could very well place the crippled ship in mortal danger; even more so than they already faced, and perhaps more than could be overcome with the time and resources available to them.

Work the problem, he thought, forcing himself to focus. *Figure it out.*

"Commander Stano," he said. "I suggest having Lieutenant Brax detail some of his security people to erect a few emergency shelters out here. We can use them as a temporary brig. We'll have to organize a security detail to look after them, but it's probably better than bringing them inside."

The first officer replied, "*Good idea, sir. No sense letting fifty more sets of lungs suck on whatever life-support we've got left in there.*"

"*So I'm guessing a hot shower and a nice meal after a tough day at the office isn't in my near future,*" said Binnix.

Shifting his position, Kirk turned to look back at the group of fallen Orions she had helped him neutralize. "Doesn't sound that way. How about emergency rations and an interrogation?" He gestured to the Orion who had manned the device apparently responsible for inflicting further damage on the *Endeavour*. When he glanced to Binnix, he noted the woman with her artificial Klingon features was smiling.

"Sounds like fun."

Kirk was unable to suppress a small chuckle before he said into his helmet pickup, "Mister Sulu, find Lieutenant McCormack, then ask Mister Brax to let you borrow a few of his security officers. I've got a job uniquely suited to your talents."

"Aye, aye, sir," replied the *Enterprise* helm officer. *"On our way."*

Binnix regarded him with obvious curiosity. "What are you thinking?"

Kirk turned his attention away from the *Endeavour*, instead staring past the illuminated ground that surrounded the crashed starship's hull and into the curtain of total darkness beyond. He tried to imagine what awaited them out there.

"I'm thinking it's past time we took control of this situation, rather than simply reacting."

Twenty-eight

Stalking the *Vekal Piltari*'s command center, it was all D'zinn could do to keep her rising ire in check. Why did the dimly lit room feel even more cramped than normal? It made no sense, particularly given that most of her crew was off the ship. Several of the stations were unattended, leaving her alone with her pilot and two crew members at sensors and communications. Everyone else who had not already been detailed to Netal's raiding party was in the engineering spaces, assisting with the ship's final repairs.

And yet, the command center was stifling.

"Make another attempt to reestablish contact," she snapped, forcing herself to will away the unproductive feelings her imagination conjured while she was forced to wait here while others acted on her behalf.

Gonet, the young Orion male who at this moment in time had the misfortune of overseeing the merchant vessel's communications systems, turned from the console with an expression of dread. "I am sorry, D'zinn. I have made five such attempts, with no success. The Federation ship appears to still be jamming our signals."

"Do not cease your efforts until you *are* successful, or I relieve you of that task. Find a way around that disruption."

His eyes widening in obvious fear, Gonet mustered a simple nod. "Yes, D'zinn." He returned his attention to his instruments, leaving her alone to battle with her own thoughts.

The Federation starship, despite its impaired condition, was still able to interfere with the communications between the *Vekal Piltari* and her second-in-command. Netal had not made contact since he and the team he assembled had departed for the asteroid and arrived on its surface. While she had no delusions of her crew being able to overcome the complement of a Starfleet vessel—even one in such dire straits as the *Endeavour*—she had been hopeful Netal and his team might find a way to exploit the situation for Orion benefit.

That the vessel had survived its encounter with the Klingon warship was amazing. It was also something of a mystery. Her own ship's comm systems had detected the starship's distress buoy adrift near the Ivratis asteroid field's outer boundary. Gonet along with her senior communications technician, Pimujin, were able to decipher its message thanks to decryption keys obtained from what D'zinn preferred to describe as an "unconventional supplier." The narrative provided by the buoy painted a rather different picture from what she now knew to be true. The message logged by the *Endeavour*'s captain indicated she was aware her ship was facing imminent destruction, and indeed the device's own sensors had recorded the detonation of the vessel's warp engines. Not present in that data was the survival of the ship's saucer-like main hull section and its crew. So far as D'zinn could surmise, this was a deliberate attempt at misdirection on the captain's part. Why had she lied about her fate and that of the people she commanded? Perhaps the Starfleet ship had been participating in some type of secret mission that required official deniability in the event it suffered unfortunate circumstances?

That they had found the ship at all was also another noteworthy feat. For that, she credited Melac, the eager, young, and recent addition to her crew. It was he who caught a fluctuation in the *Vekal Piltari*'s sensor data that was so slight even those with far greater experience with such equipment might have

missed it. Thanks to his diligence, they discovered the four automated Starfleet buoys deployed around the rim of the massive
canyon on the asteroid that turned out to be the *Endeavour*'s
hiding place. Despite the best efforts of the Starfleet crew to
conceal their presence, Melac found them. Perhaps it was luck
or just good timing, but D'zinn could not argue with the results.
Neither could she ignore the questions his find raised.

Something here was amiss, hence her decision to allow Netal
the chance to reconnoiter the situation and investigate opportunities to exploit for her benefit. After all, working with the
Klingons was a temporary arrangement. There was also the distinct possibility their "partners of convenience" could choose
to abrogate their agreement. D'zinn always preferred to plan
for worst-case scenarios, so if this was such a case, she wanted
to be ready. The Federation starship and whatever mystery it
harbored might well result in an even more profitable venture,
provided she was in a position to take maximum advantage
of it.

For that to happen, she had to talk to Netal.

"What about our scans?" she asked, continuing to circle the
command center's outer periphery. "Are we still unable to penetrate the interference?"

Turning from the main sensor station on the room's left side,
the muscled Melac replied, "Still nothing, D'zinn. Even with our
modifications, the disruption here is very strong. In order to
obtain clearer readings, we will have to move closer."

Maneuvering the *Vekal Piltari* closer to the asteroid where
the *Endeavour* sought refuge, to say nothing of guiding the ship
into the canyon, carried no small measure of risk. At last report,
Tath informed her that while repairs were completed, there remained additional diagnostic tests before he could certify all of
the restored systems as operational. The engineer and his team
had been working nonstop in the wake of her ship's encounter
with the civilian transport she was certain was not at all what

it purported to be. Where had that troublesome vessel gone? There had been no sign of its departure from the asteroid field, at least so far as her ship's scanners were able to determine. Was it still here, hiding somewhere? Experience and instinct told D'zinn that the ship was much closer than anyone else might suspect. Going to the canyon and confirming her suspicions would be most satisfying, she decided, especially when she ordered the *Vekal Piltari*'s weapons to destroy the *Dreamline*.

"D'zinn."

Shaken from her reverie, she looked up to see Melac regarding her with new excitement as he motioned toward the sensor control station.

"The interference blocking our scans," he said. "It has vanished."

Uncertain how to interpret this news, D'zinn looked to Gonet. "The disruption of our communications has ceased?"

"It appears so," replied the harried young Orion. "All frequencies are clear. At least, the ones we've modified to function here in the asteroid field."

Moving around the command center to join him at the communications station, D'zinn gestured to the console. "Well? Attempt to reestablish contact."

Was he trembling? D'zinn watched the young male shift his position so that he once more faced the console. She noted how he flustered when she drew close, and had to remind herself that his youth and inexperience when coupled with her proximity might well be interfering with his ability to concentrate on his duties. Under any other circumstances she would have found the insecurity amusing, but this was neither the time nor the place for such nonsense.

"Channel open," Gonet said after several moments spent hovering over his controls. "I have made a connection to Netal's dedicated frequency, but he does not respond to our calls."

Was he alive? D'zinn suspected that was the case. Barring

accident or the belief that no other option remained with respect to personal survival, Starfleet officers were not in the habit of indiscriminate killing, in battle or even a skirmish such as the one she had sanctioned.

Gonet held up a hand. "Wait. I am receiving an acknowledgment of our hail." Pressing several controls in rapid succession, he looked to D'zinn. "It appears to be coming from Netal's excursion suit communications link, but I do not believe it is him."

"What?" D'zinn glared at the younger male. "How is that possible?" Even as she spoke the words, she had her answer.

"Put it through," D'zinn said, frustrated that the suit systems did not allow for visual communications.

Recessed speakers around the command center crackled before static cleared and a new voice pushed through the communications system.

"Orion vessel, this is Captain Atish Khatami of the Starship Endeavour. We have captured your entire assault force that carried out an illegal attack on a Federation vessel. There were no fatalities among your people, and you have my word they'll be treated well. However, rest assured this action will not go unanswered. The smart play for you right now is to withdraw from this area and take no further action against my ship. Do that, and I'll see to it your people are returned to you as soon as possible. You've already caused one interstellar incident. Let's not compound that mistake with another. There might even be a way to mitigate the damage already done here. Make the right decision."

"It is a recorded message, D'zinn," said Gonet. "It begins again as soon as it ends."

Gesturing to the console, she released an irritated grunt. "Turn it off."

What was she supposed to do now? The bulk of her crew had participated in the raid, and if the Starfleet captain was to be believed, then all now were prisoners. She certainly did not have the resources to launch anything resembling a rescue mission, and attacking the *Endeavour* while Netal and the others remained in custody was out of the question.

"You appear troubled, my old friend."

So lost was D'zinn in her thoughts that, until hearing his voice, she had failed to notice Tath had at some point arrived in the command center. Where had he come from? Turning toward him, she saw the engineer seemed even more weathered and tired than normal. The dark brown coverall garment he wore while tending to the *Vekal Piltari*'s engines and other systems was dirty and torn. His disheveled appearance was a testament to his efforts to repair the ship's damage even while most of his technicians had been conscripted for Netal's assault on the *Endeavour*.

"As always, your gift for understatement remains unequaled. How long have you been standing there?"

Tath maintained his usual composed demeanor as he nodded toward Gonet and the communications station. "Long enough to hear the message. Our options at the moment remain limited. While our repairs are completed, I would advise against taking this vessel into any sort of confrontation in its current state. Our reduced crew complement is but one more factor."

"I know." D'zinn nodded. This was the sort of counsel she would normally seek from Netal, and in his absence she welcomed it from her longtime friend. The difference in age and life experience compared to hers often gave Tath a perspective she not only lacked but needed, depending on the situation. "There are larger issues demanding our attention. We attacked a Federation ship. Even if I could make a convincing argument that we believed it to be an abandoned derelict, the act itself brings with it the potential for serious consequences." The Orion Syndicate's efforts to present the appearance of neutrality were its utmost priorities. Ship captains who strayed from that mandate often found themselves disavowed, sacrificed as rogue agents operating without authorization. It was this deniability—fragile though it might be—that kept the Federation from dispatching the might of its Starfleet against Orion interests.

Tath replied, "I am aware of the possible ramifications, but I do not believe we have yet reached that point. Tell me, has the Federation vessel made any attempt to call attention to potential rescuers?"

The question gave her pause, and D'zinn realized her failure to consider that detail until brought to her attention.

You fool!

She grimaced as her own thoughts chastised her, but there was no excusing such a simple oversight. In the rush to survey the crashed ship, and with Netal's plan to force its crew into a state of capitulation, she had missed a key aspect of the entire situation. Thanks to Tath, she now was able to consider things from a new, better perspective.

"They were not simply hiding from the Klingons after that encounter," she said, smiling at her friend. "The faked message. Using the warp-engine overload as cover to mask their movements. They could not afford to be found by anyone except whoever Starfleet sent to rescue them, which means they carry something of great value; something more important than even the ship's technology, much of which already commands high prices among the different illicit markets."

Weapons and other systems to be found aboard Starfleet's most advanced vessels were among the most sought-after items when it came to the numerous merchants with whom D'zinn did business. That by itself was enough to make her want to investigate the *Endeavour* and determine whether anything might be salvaged from the wreck. Even after finding the crash site, she knew at least some of the crew was still liable to be aboard, but none of its personnel had used the escape pods or shuttlecraft transports.

"There is also the matter of the *Enterprise*," she said. "So far as we have been able to determine, neither ship has made any attempt to contact the other. That alone is odd."

The asteroid field made it all but impossible to track the movements of the other Starfleet ship as it ostensibly carried out its search mission for the *Endeavour*. Still, there had been no indication it had sent out even general hailing messages in a bid to reach the other ship. Had Starfleet dispatched it to this region to confirm the vessel's fate, or was there something more at work here? A hidden agenda—trying to find and rescue the *Endeavour*'s crew and whatever else of value it carried—might also explain the still suspicious activity of the civilian transport responsible for causing her so much grief. D'zinn remained unconvinced that ship was what it claimed to be. The longer she pondered this, the more she believed its pilot and perhaps even its passengers were working in concert with the *Enterprise* to find the other starship while avoiding unwanted attention.

"There is definitely more to this situation than we know," Tath said. "For that reason alone, I recommend caution." He paused, his gaze wavering for a moment to the deck plating at his feet before returning his attention to her. "We have already committed—and perhaps lost—far too much."

"Starfleet is not like dealing with the Klingons," D'zinn replied. "We can at least be thankful for that." She was confident Captain Khatami would hold to her word and see to it no harm came to Netal and the rest of her crew. This did not mean they would be returned to her, despite the *Endeavour* captain's assurances. Such decisions would likely come from her superiors, who doubtless would take a great interest in this matter, but before that, the recriminations would come. There would be consequences for what she had allowed to happen here, of that she was certain. The Syndicate was rarely forgiving about such things.

Compounding her problem was the inescapable fact that she could do nothing to salvage the situation. All she could hope was that the Federation might cast its ire on someone other than her own superiors; someone with an even greater incentive to avoid Federation and Starfleet scrutiny.

The Klingons, she thought. *This is their problem now.*

"Set a course out of the asteroid field," she ordered. "We are leaving."

"D'zinn?" Tath's tone was obvious. He could not believe what he was hearing. "Are you certain this is the wisest course?"

"I am certain of nothing anymore," she replied. "But I know we are now caught between two adversaries who likely will make our lives very difficult in the near future."

Of course, D'zinn doubted she would be alive to see any of that.

Twenty-nine

"Well done, you two."

Kirk could not help a satisfied smile as he along with Atish Khatami greeted Lieutenants McCormack and Sulu when they emerged from the airlock and into the EVA preparation room. With the chamber behind them once again sealed and pressurized to match the *Endeavour*'s interior environment, both helm officers had removed their suit helmets. Both looked sweaty and tired but also more than a bit pleased with themselves.

Nodding to Kirk, Sulu replied, "Thank you, sir. It's nice to catch a win once in a while."

"More than just a win, if you ask me," Khatami said, reaching out to tap McCormack on the shoulder. "Is there anything in the quadrant you two can't fly?"

McCormack exchanged knowing glances with Sulu. "Haven't found it yet, Captain."

"Same here," Sulu added. Moving to a nearby bench, he deposited his helmet on an adjacent storage rack before beginning the process of extricating himself from his suit.

"We're going to have to recycle the air in here if this keeps up," Khatami said. Looking to Kirk, she asked, "Is he as bad as she is?"

"At least."

Khatami smiled. "Having them retrieve those transports was

a sharp idea. Lieutenant Klisiewicz tells me the sensor buoys are once again operating normally. We've got our eyes and ears back."

Nodding in approval at the report, Kirk gestured to Sulu and McCormack. "They're the ones who made it happen. No complications, right?"

"No, sir," McCormack replied as she worked the closures on her EV suit. "There were two Orions aboard each transport, and they offered no resistance when we arrived. We had them pretty well outgunned. They've been transferred to Lieutenant Brax for safekeeping with our other guests."

At Kirk's direction and using the *Dreamline*, both helm officers along with teams from the *Endeavour*'s security section made their way to where the Orions had left their small personnel transports before embarking on their ground assault. The primary objective was to deny the pirates any ability to use the craft against the crashed, vulnerable starship. Whether they might be of any other use remained to be seen, but Kirk preferred to have several options available. He lamented the fact the ships, even working with the *Dreamline*, were nowhere near a size needed to facilitate an evacuation of the *Endeavour*'s crew, but he decided they might come in handy at some point. This situation was still a long way from being over.

Removing her EV suit left McCormack wearing the standard black single-piece coverall responsible for maintaining her body temperature while encased in the heavier protective garment. It bore no name or rank designation. She crossed to a storage locker and removed from it an olive-drab jumpsuit. This variant featured a patch where a Starfleet insignia might normally reside, embossed with her name and rank.

"Our scans showed the port impulse engine's back up and running," she said as she pulled on the jumpsuit.

"Yataro and his people came through again," Khatami replied.

"The starboard engine's hopeless, but they were able to salvage components from it to help with the other one." She glanced around the corridor. "Of course, we're now officially out of spare impulse engines, so if we get hit again with those things, it's going to be a bad day for all of us."

Kirk said, "According to Lieutenant Klisiewicz, the Orions used a portable electromagnetic-pulse emitter system. It's an Andorian design, for use as a nonlethal weapon by their Imperial Guard units. They're not supposed to be available anywhere except the Andorian homeworld, but like anything else, you can probably find them on one black market or another."

"Based on what we know from the tech specs we pulled from the library computer, it shouldn't have been able to do what it did," Khatami added. "Not to a ship our size. I guess they made some modifications. Brax was able to capture the other before it could be used. Lucky for us they didn't launch it against the port engine. Even deactivated for repairs, there's no telling how much of the pulse it generated might still have ruptured conduits, circuits, or relays." She released a tired sigh. "We're really starting to push our luck out here."

Pulling on the jumpsuit provided to him by Commander Stano shortly after his arrival with Kirk and Uhura, Sulu said, "I think it might be time to call in the cavalry, sir."

Kirk nodded. "I agree."

His mission parameters as defined by Admiral Nogura specified making contact with the *Enterprise* if he, Sulu, and Uhura were the first to find the *Endeavour*. At the time, doing so carried the risk of leaving Khatami and her people at the mercy of anyone who might wander down here with less than noble intentions. However, the situation had changed. There was no longer any secret hiding place to protect. At least one Orion ship was still out there with the knowledge of the *Endeavour*'s location. Whether that vessel was in league with the Klingons or someone else remained to be seen, but that did not matter. The priority now was evacuating the crippled ship's crew to safety, along with Binnix and her fellow agents and their storehouse of intelligence data. Kirk suspected Nogura would give him grief for the interpretation of his orders, but he also believed he had adhered to the spirit if not every letter of those instructions. On the bright side, he would face Nogura's wrath only if the admiral and the *Enterprise* succeeded in rescuing them all.

The metallic chirp made Khatami pull a communicator from under the back of her uniform tunic, and she flipped open the device's antenna cover. "Khatami here."

"*XO here, Captain,*" replied Commander Katherine Stano. "*Something's happened. We just transmitted a high-power burst communications signal.*"

"What?" Khatami made no attempt to hide her surprise. "Who transmitted this signal?"

"*No idea. Whoever it was certainly didn't have authorization.*"

Kirk asked, "Any idea who it was intended for?"

"*It wasn't a very powerful transmission, sir,*" replied Lieutenant Uhura. "*But it was configured to punch through the local interference from the asteroid field. There wasn't much range to it, but I'm guessing anyone in the immediate vicinity could have picked it up. Lieutenant Estrada and I are still going over the whole thing, looking for clues. The message wasn't even encrypted. It doesn't appear to be directed to anyone specifically, but it provides our approximate coordinates and mentions 'three undesirables' who are threats to the Klingon Empire. The coordinates are close enough they can lead anybody who might be listening right to our front door.*"

Reaching up to rub the bridge of her nose, Khatami blew out her breath. "Wonderful. Orions or Klingons? I guess we take our pick. Meanwhile, who the hell just gave away our position?"

"The same person who crippled your impulse engine," Kirk replied. "I think we've removed any doubt we have a saboteur on board."

His hands clasped behind his back as he stood before the briefing room's viewscreen, Spock studied the computer-generated schematic of the Ivratis asteroid field. The rendering—presented in a vector graphics format similar to those used in a tactical diagram—was as complete a picture of the region as could be assembled. Navigation maps from the *Enterprise*'s library computer were augmented with information from the ship's recent sensor scans of the area as well as data pulled from the *Endeavour*'s original distress buoy. With their knowledge increasing as the search continued for any sign of a permanent Klingon presence within the asteroid field, the resulting computer model was comprehensive. Even still, far too much of the region remained a mystery.

Thanks to his Vulcan hearing, Spock heard footsteps from the corridor outside the briefing room before the doors parted. He turned at the sound to see Doctor McCoy enter, pausing at one of the chairs arrayed around the conference table. At some point since their last encounter, the *Enterprise*'s chief medical officer had exchanged his short-sleeved medical smock for his regulation blue uniform tunic. Spock offered a single formal nod in greeting.

"Doctor."

McCoy said, "Chekov told me I'd find you down here." His eyes shifted to look past Spock to the viewscreen and its schematic. "Doing a little homework?"

His right eyebrow cocking as he pondered the question, Spock replied, "Indeed, and there is still much work to be done."

"It's not like you to be off the bridge when Jim's not aboard." McCoy crossed his arms. "Everything all right? You're not hiding from Nogura, are you?"

Spock shook his head. "The admiral is resting."

It was well beyond even the extended duty shift to which the first officer had assigned himself while Captain Kirk was off the ship. Despite his best intentions, Nogura had finally conceded the need for at least some sleep after the many long hours spent monitoring the search efforts. Spock knew that in addition to himself, Doctor McCoy, Mister Scott, and other senior members of the crew were continuing with their duties. The chief engineer was still working with the *Enterprise*'s sensor and communications systems, searching for ways to extend their effectiveness despite the asteroid field's continued interference. That effort kept him contained within the depths of the starship's engineering spaces.

For his part, McCoy operated under a longstanding rule of his own imposition, in which he directed himself to remain on duty during anything other than normal circumstances. The doctor used that time to monitor the crew's well-being and stepped in to suggest or order rest or meals when he felt individual crew members were pushing themselves beyond their limits. This included keeping watch over the captain, or in this case whoever the captain left in command. While Spock had rebuffed such practices during the early years of their time together aboard the *Enterprise*, he had come to value McCoy's counsel.

Spock saw no reason to admit this to the doctor, of course.

"I simply preferred to work in quiet for a time," he said. His review of the information being collected by the *Enterprise*'s sensors as it traversed the asteroid field had proven insufficient. With that in mind and after leaving the bridge in Ensign Chekov's capable hands, he directed the ship's main computer to transfer all available information on the region to the briefing room's interface. Here, in relative solitude while still being only moments away in the event of a change in the situation, he had set to work.

"There was a time," McCoy said, "not all that long ago, you know, where I'd have to order you off the bridge to get some rest when you were hell-bent on carrying out . . . well, whatever you thought needed carrying out."

"And I recall both you and the captain encouraging me to have more confidence in our junior officers to manage various situations," Spock replied, "thereby freeing me for more pressing duties." He gestured to the viewscreen. "Would this not constitute 'character growth' in your eyes, Doctor?"

With a single, quiet snort, McCoy smiled. "I wish Jim could hear you say that."

"I am working on that as well." Turning his attention back to the screen, Spock waited until McCoy moved to stand beside him. After a moment of shared silence, the doctor grunted.

"It's probably too much to hope the Klingons are just hiding right in the middle of these asteroids, isn't it?"

Spock replied, "If you mean the center of the field, I did consider that possibility, if for no other reason than logic suggests placing the maximum distance between one and one's potential hunter. However, nothing in any of our scans of the Klingon vessels traversing the region indicates a trajectory in that direction."

He stepped to a control pad set into the bulkhead at the right of the viewscreen and entered a command sequence. The screen responded by filling in the silhouettes of asteroids represented by the simple line drawings, to a point where several areas of the image had little or no space visible between them.

Spock said, "Asteroid fields, particularly ones spread across a large area, are generally not so dense, and in truth the Ivratis field for the most part is no exception. That said, there *are* numerous sections where the debris drifts in much closer proximity. This of course presents navigational hazards for ships attempting to traverse the region."

"And damned tempting if you're an Orion pirate or someone else up to no good," McCoy replied. "Even with knowledge of the area, it'd take a hell of a pilot to fly through something like that."

Studying the viewscreen's enhanced image, Spock said, "Agreed, and while I do not believe the Orions or the Klingons possess a pilot of Lieutenant Sulu's skill, I submit they do have a broad working knowledge of the asteroid field. Even with constant drift, experienced pilots using navigational computer systems and course projection models can still plot routes of safe passage. Unfortunately, our present knowledge is lacking in that regard."

McCoy folded his arms across his chest before proceeding to rub his chin. From past experience, Spock knew it was a habit the doctor tended to display when he was lost in thought.

After a moment, McCoy asked, "Is any of this helping us get a line on where Jim and the others are?"

"While that is also a goal of this exercise, I have not yet compiled sufficient information to answer your question."

McCoy cast a doubtful expression. "Come on, Spock. I've seen you figure out where aliens took Jim when he was dozens of light-years away. This should be easy. We had a general idea where they were going when they left the ship, didn't we? Captain Khatami gave us at least that much. How hard can it be to figure out a probable course for that deathtrap Nogura made Jim use and follow it?"

"The issue with the captain and his team is not quite so simple," Spock replied. "Assuming they found the *Endeavour* and given the lack of communication from the *Dreamline*, we can surmise the captain felt compelled to maintain operations security until such time as circumstances were favorable enough to risk making contact."

"Or, they didn't find the *Endeavour* and they're just in trouble."

"That is a distinct possibility, Doctor."

"Hell of a way to boost my morale, Spock."

The whistle of the ship's intercom filtered through the briefing room, interrupting Spock's reply.

"Bridge to Mister Spock," said Lieutenant Elizabeth Palmer, the communications officer currently on bridge duty.

Crossing to the conference table, Spock reached for the communications panel set into its polished surface and keyed its activation control. "Spock here."

"Sir, we've just detected a high-powered burst transmission originating from somewhere in the asteroid field. Based on the attached identification protocols, I can confirm it's from the Endeavour *but not Captain Khatami or Captain Kirk. Based on its content, it's a general distress call to anyone within range. It provides coordinates to the* Endeavour's *location, but it also mentions three individuals I think are meant to be the intelligence agents, sir."*

McCoy scowled. "Who in blazes would send a signal like that?" Then his expression turned to one of horror. "They've got a spy on board the *Endeavour*?"

"It is a logical conclusion," Spock replied.

"There's more, sir."

Rolling his eyes, McCoy blew out his breath. "Of course there is."

"Just moments after we detected the original message, we picked up a much more powerful signal sent via high-energy tight-beam transmission. This one is Klingon, sir. It was encrypted, but using an older code already deciphered by Starfleet Command and the protocols were in our computer banks. The message relayed the same information, but emphasized what it refers to as 'three individuals of particular interest.' We're still working to determine the intended recipient, sir."

"Probably the entire Klingon fleet," McCoy said.

Ignoring the doctor's comments, Spock replied to Palmer, "Lieutenant, do you have sufficient information to calculate the second message's point of origin?"

"Yes, sir."

"Notify Admiral Nogura of this development and request he meet us on the bridge. Transfer both sets of coordinates to the helm and have them plot rendezvous courses for each. Spock out." As he severed the connection, Spock sensed McCoy staring at him.

"What are you thinking, Spock?"

The first officer drew himself up to his full height, "To further answer your earlier question, Doctor, it appears the time for homework has passed. Now we must prepare for the test."

Thirty

His tricorder leading the way, Yataro maneuvered through the cramped confines of the Jefferies tube. Designed for functionality rather than aesthetics, these access conduits were intended for use by the engineering team and other technicians tasked with maintaining the ship in peak operating condition. The restricted space could be problematic for those with larger physiques, but Yataro's slim build offered him some advantage with maneuverability. Only his head, far larger and elongated compared to many humanoid species, offered a challenge in navigating certain junctions or other narrow crawlways, but he managed well enough.

Access panels, control modules, power distribution hubs and their associated components, optical cabling, and the odd tool or supply locker were stuffed into every parcel of available space along the bulkheads or beneath duranium grilles serving as deck plating.

Even with his rigorous standards for cleanliness when it came to tools and equipment as well as the areas in which his people worked, it was impossible to keep every centimeter of a starship's innards as pristine looking as sections where the majority of the crew spent their time. There was no avoiding the odd spot of lubricant on a bulkhead or deck plate. The sleeves and padded knees of Yataro's jumpsuit bore witness to that.

Letting his tricorder hang from the strap across his chest,

Yataro used both hands to pull himself out of a horizontal shaft and onto the landing of a maintenance ladder well. A bright orange, tri-sided ladder ran through the center of the vertical conduit, and he reached for it to steady himself. Behind him, the slightly labored breathing of David Horst preceded the Starfleet Intelligence agent's arrival into the shaft. He had done a commendable job keeping the pace Yataro set, but his human physiology made the transit a bit more difficult.

"I think I'm starting to get a little old for this kind of thing," Horst said as he pulled himself to his feet. He wiped his forehead with his right sleeve, and as during their initial meeting, Yataro was struck by the man's Klingon appearance. His surgically altered features remained at odds with his Starfleet jumpsuit, but by themselves the engineer decided it was an impressive feat of alteration.

"Something wrong?" Horst asked.

His wide eyes blinking several times in rapid succession, Yataro replied, "No. I apologize, Mister Horst. I admit I was . . . intrigued by your Klingon countenance. I also admit to more than a small measure of admiration for the training and preparation you and your colleagues must have undertaken to ready yourselves for your assignment. Then you spent three years working with and among an entire civilization not your own, unable to reveal your true identities for fear of prosecution."

Horst held up a finger. "And death. Don't forget that part."

"Indeed." Yataro shook his head. "It really is quite remarkable. I do not know that I would be capable of carrying out such a demanding task."

The agent smiled, revealing that even his teeth had been subtly manipulated to appear more Klingon than human. "No offense, Commander, you're not really the ideal body type for this kind of thing."

Though he understood humor and in particular the propensity for many of his shipmates to engage in it, such things were not his strong suit. Still, he recognized the agent's remark for the harmless quip it was intended to be, and nodded in agreement. "Quite right." Gesturing with his tricorder, he said, "We are almost there."

It took several minutes of crawling and climbing through the network of maintenance conduits linking decks and turbolift shafts to reach their present location. Starting from an access point near the transporter room on deck seven, they worked their way down and across to a cargo bay two levels below. According to his tricorder they were now on the correct deck. Yataro pointed to another Jefferies tube leading from his left.

"Cargo bay one is in that direction," he said, using his tricorder to indicate their path.

Horst asked, "And you're sure this is where the signal came from?"

"According to the system logs, the transmission originated from a communications router located on this level." Yataro led the way into the next Jefferies tube, crawling once again on hands and knees. "What the logs do not show is how the router was accessed or by whom."

His quick review of the automatic archives, which recorded all interfaces with any of the *Endeavour*'s onboard systems, told him a second block of entries had been deleted from the database. He had already discovered one section removed in the wake of the trouble visited upon the ship's port impulse engine. The entries corresponding to one hour before the incident were missing. It was an obvious maneuver designed to mask someone's activities and identity. In response, the chief engineer took small comfort from the knowledge that only a small percentage of the ship's crew possessed the technical expertise and authorization to access computer logs in this fashion, but that still left a pool of more than forty potential suspects. After discovering the first log-entry deletion, Yataro placed a trace in the system in hopes of identifying the culprit. He was only somewhat surprised to discover that same measure countered as easily as the access logs themselves. Might this actually help him to narrow his list of persons who might be responsible for this sabotage? Yataro did not know yet.

After crawling through the conduit for nearly a minute, Yataro heard a telltale signal from the tricorder still hanging from his shoulder. A glance told him they had arrived at a gray rectangular box mounted to the bulkhead to his left. Relay hubs like this one were scattered throughout the bowels of the ship, assisting the main computer's communications subsystems without routing recorded and real-time data through an extensive network. Ahead of him, he observed the sealed, reinforced hatch where he knew it would be. Having memorized the *Endeavour*'s interior schematics and after spending a fair amount of time traversing the ship's network of maintenance crawlways, he knew precisely where he was.

"Cargo bay one is on the other side of this wall," he said, tapping the bulkhead next to the hub. Maneuvering himself into a sitting position, he shifted to his right so that Horst had room to join him. "According to the access logs, this is the junction used to send the message."

Horst gestured to the hub. "Want me to open it?" He reached for the unit's front panel, then stopped himself before casting an embarrassed look in Yataro's direction. "Sorry. You should be the one to do that. You want to make sure there's no inadvertent evidence tampering."

"You believe I suspect you of this act?" Yataro asked.

"Don't you?"

Regarding him for a moment, Yataro replied, "If I did, you would not be here."

Indeed, he had discussed the matter with Captain Khatami even before the Orion raid. Morgan Binnix's decision to surrender the sensitive information cache collected by her and her fellow agents during their assignment on Qo'noS, Horst's and

Phillip Watson's continued assistance with the *Endeavour* engineering team despite working under a cloud of suspicion, and Binnix's actions out on the asteroid surface during the raid had done much to engender trust from the starship's crew. Further, Yataro considered the notion of one of the agents being a saboteur or spy to be simply too convenient.

This belief was only strengthened when considering the predicament in which the agents and the rest of the crew found themselves. Trapped here with no means of escape? It would be sheer lunacy to act in such a compulsive and ultimately futile manner. For seasoned operatives trained to think and act without any support, committing such clumsy acts of sabotage that could be so easily traced back to them seemed unlikely. Finally, there was the simple matter that neither Horst nor his companions had been left unsupervised long enough for any of them to get this far into the maintenance crawlways and transmit the message from this location.

Which meant someone else was responsible. Barring the unlikely scenario of a stowaway hiding somewhere aboard the wrecked ship, that left only one alternative: a member of the crew.

"So far as I am concerned, Mister Horst, you and your fellow agents have demonstrated your trustworthiness. Further, I brought you with me as I thought I might require your particular talents. You have advanced experience in communications systems and subsystems, do you not?"

Horst nodded. "I do."

"Very well, then." Yataro gestured to the junction box. "Open the relay and let us see what we can learn."

Releasing the catches holding the box's access panel to the bulkhead, Horst asked, "I was going to ask you about that. What *are* we hoping to learn? You said whoever did this wiped their activity from the access logs."

"That is correct." With the panel cover removed, Yataro leaned closer and examined the junction box's compact control pad, which consisted of a small display and two rows of multi-colored buttons. While communications typically were routed through devoted subsystems within the ship's main computer, one could still access the system directly from entry points like this one in cases of emergency or malfunction elsewhere in the internal network.

"Now I see where you're going," Horst said after a moment spent studying the panel. "Each of these direct interfaces has its own memory storage."

Yataro nodded, pleased at the man's astuteness. "The contents of their onboard memory banks are transmitted every hour to the main computer for inclusion in the primary system access logs. However, the buffer itself is not usually cleared. It is simply overwritten with new information as needed. Most of the time, these direct interfaces are not utilized because we can access the primary systems more easily via computer terminals and workstations." He pointed to the control box. "Without additional data to overwrite the buffer, its last entry should still be in there."

"And you think our saboteur may have forgotten that little detail?" Horst shrugged. "Maybe they were in a hurry and didn't have time to wipe the buffer before they had to get back to wherever they wouldn't be missed."

"That is my theory."

Raising his tricorder from where it rested in his lap, Yataro activated the unit and set its scan function to receive external data. He reached for the junction box's control pad to complete the connection, but paused at the sound of movement to Horst's left. A figure lay on the Jefferies tube deck plating, cloaked in shadow but holding what Yataro immediately recognized as a small, palm-sized type-1 phaser.

"Mister—"

The weapon's whine drowned out the rest of his warning, and harsh blue-white energy washed through the conduit as the phaser beam lanced across the empty space and struck Horst as he turned to face the new arrival. It expanded, engulfing his body, and he vanished, disintegrating in an instant without a sound.

Dumbstruck by the attack's speed and brutality, Yataro fell back from his sitting position, scrambling away from the control box but finding no cover or other safe harbor in the cramped passageway. His mind raced with an endless stream of panicked thoughts in what he knew with utter certainty would be his final seconds of life, until settling on one frantic realization: he had seen his killer's face in the flash of the phaser beam that had killed Horst.

"You!"

Then everything disappeared, consumed by unrelenting white light.

Thirty-one

Mi'zhan watched the last vestiges of Commander Yataro disappear, leaving behind only the faint odor of his phaser's energy discharge along with disintegrated flesh. Under normal circumstances he knew the automatic atmosphere scrubbers that were components of the ship's life-support system would remove the last remnants of such aromas from the air. With power to noncritical systems reduced or eliminated while the *Endeavour* operated on only one impulse engine, such luxuries were not currently available. Not that it mattered. He suspected no one would venture this far into the maze of access crawlways while whatever lingering evidence of Yataro's and Horst's deaths remained. For the moment, he was safe.

Rotating the compact phaser in his hand, Mi'zhan grunted as he examined the weapon. Its size was deceptive, not nearly as large or robust as the disruptors with which he had become proficient so long ago. He still had to admit it was a useful tool. Before undertaking this assignment, he believed Starfleet phasers were small and weak, possessing no real power and certainly not on par with traditional Klingon energy weapons. His training under the unwavering gaze of his instructors soon disabused him of that uninformed opinion, and those lessons were now cemented by the action he had just been forced to take.

"Damn it," Mi'zhan said, aloud even though there was no one to hear.

Shaking his head, he slid the phaser into a pocket on the right leg of his green, Starfleet-issue maintenance jumpsuit. He had not wanted to kill the engineer or even the intelligence agent. The former was too valuable a member of the *Endeavour*'s crew and his absence would be noticed in short order. As for the agent, instinct made Mi'zhan want to neutralize him as penalty for the uncounted crimes he must have committed against the Empire. However, he knew Horst and his fellow spies would be of great value if they could be returned to Qo'noS. That was of no matter now, given what Mi'zhan had been forced to do here. He would not miss the spy, whose altered features were an insult to all Klingons. Even if it became necessary to kill the other two agents, whatever information they had collected during their time slinking about the shadows of the homeworld would still be of immense interest.

"Who's slinking about the shadows now?" he asked, though of course no one answered.

Out of habit, Mi'zhan had long ago taught himself not to speak aloud in native *tlhIngan Hol* even when he was alone. It was another harsh lesson instilled without mercy by his instructors. Candidates were forced to wear bracelets that could not be removed and transmitted everything they said to computers used by the faculty of the school where he received his training. Any breach in the language rules—speaking in his own tongue rather than Federation Standard, even in private or alone—resulted in an electric shock channeled by those same computers through the bracelet. The effects were painful to an almost incapacitating degree and only increased in intensity if multiple infractions occurred within a prescribed time frame.

At the beginning of his instruction, Mi'zhan had experienced unconsciousness from the force of the shocks he received. That punishment occurred only once, after which he took steps to conform. He stopped reading or accessing any information offered in *tlhIngan Hol*. He forced himself even to think in Standard, penalizing himself for failure in this regard by speaking aloud in his own language until he received the obligatory bracelet shock. By the time he graduated from the indoctrination program and received the surgery to transform him from a Klingon into a human, he had all but subsumed his real identity far beneath a detestable Earther facade. The only thread to his true heritage he allowed was to refer to himself in the privacy of his own thoughts by his given name. This small act reminded him of his parents and his family house, and that he was acting to bring honor to them as well as glory for the Empire.

Deploying on his first assignment had been far easier than he anticipated. He was told during his training that agents like himself—far more experienced, of course—had been operating in secret from a time just before the outbreak of the Klingon-Federation War more than a decade earlier. While he was skeptical, it soon became apparent his instructors were truthful. How else could he have been inserted into Starfleet personnel records and maneuvered into an assignment aboard one of the Earthers' most advanced, even prestigious battle cruisers? His entire existence to that point was nothing more than a fabrication, an elaborate lie forged as part of his cover identity. The Empire, over the course of years spent grooming agents like himself for such duty, had learned the risks of attempting to replace an actual person with someone altered to resemble them. It was better to create a person without ties, someone whose past could be configured to meet the requirements of a specific assignment, and incorporate the necessary skills into that individual's preparation and training.

His routing to the *Endeavour* was just one of several personnel assignments earlier in the year with the purpose of restoring the ship's complement to its full strength. Along with the other starships of its design, the ship represented the greatest threat to Klingon interests. Serving aboard one and learning all its secrets was an assignment carrying with it much honor, provided Mi'zhan successfully completed his mission and returned to Qo'noS to relay all he had learned.

Such a task was not always easy to accomplish, as he had already discovered. One such example was his attempt to learn just why the *Endeavour* was recently required to replace so many members of its crew. A pitched battle involving the cruiser with another of its class, the *Enterprise*, had resulted in numerous casualties. The details of the incident were classified far above the station of someone such as the human Mi'zhan had been groomed to portray. Despite his best efforts, he was unable to learn anything prior to arriving aboard the *Endeavour*. Even his attempts to glean information from the ship's crew after he began his assignment here proved fruitless. It was as though everyone involved and who survived the battle had either erased all traces of memory from their consciousness, or else they operated under an agreement that commanded their secrecy. Surreptitious investigation of the vessel's library computer failed to uncover anything, but expunging computer files was easy to accomplish.

As I well know.

Moving to the communications hub, he examined the open access port, trying to determine how much progress Yataro and Horst had made before he interrupted them. A press of the appropriate control on the module's keypad told him the component's onboard memory still retained a record of its last activity. As the chief engineer surmised, Mi'zhan had indeed left incriminating evidence of transmitting the unauthorized signal from the ship. Along with the sabotage of the ship's impulse engine, it was the first deviation from his normal routine since joining the *Endeavour*'s crew.

"What is life without the occasional risk?" he murmured. He glanced to his left and right, ensuring he was alone in the Jefferies tube. So far, no one had seen fit to encroach on his solitude, but he knew he could not remain here for long without his absence from his regular duties being noticed. Further, there was precious little time before someone, perhaps even the captain herself, asked after Yataro or Horst. He needed to finish his work here and return to his station as quickly as possible.

In the months since his arrival aboard the vessel and its subsequent assignment to explore the Taurus Reach, he carried out his assigned shipboard duties, acting just like the officer he pretended to be. He did nothing that might draw unwanted attention upon himself. The goals of his being placed here were long-term, many if not most of them unknown to him. During his training, he came to understand that he might operate in his undercover capacity for great stretches of time, doing nothing beyond the normal tasks of a Starfleet officer. Contact from his superiors might come only after months passed, at which time he would be given specific mission parameters and instructions. As was the case with other agents he knew to be inserted deep inside Federation territory and the Starfleet hierarchy, everything about his assignment was designed to safeguard his identity and mask his presence as a Klingon asset. Unless otherwise directed, his instructions were to observe and understand what was taking place around him. At some suitable point, he would be contacted, debriefed, and given further direction.

Since beginning his assignment, Mi'zhan had received no such contact. Things might well have continued in that fashion until his alter ego's tour of duty with the *Endeavour* ended and he was sent to another ship or station. Then Captain Khatami received her mysterious orders taking them well away from the Taurus Reach to this odd region of space near the Klingon border. The captain and the rest of the ship's senior staff had remained silent on the issue, offering only the barest of insights into their new mission. This was enough to pique Mi'zhan's interest, but his efforts to learn more faced many obstacles, if he was to avoid drawing attention.

Once he learned of the surgically altered spies and their escape from the homeworld, he realized the magnitude of what Starfleet had accomplished against the Empire. The agents could not be allowed to return to Federation space, and the information stolen from Qo'noS must be prevented from being used against the Empire's interests. He had no idea how to go about doing any of that, and then the *Endeavour* had its ill-fated encounter with the Klingon battle cruiser followed by their landing on this cursed asteroid. What was he supposed to do in the wake of that? His attempt to neutralize the ship's impulse engines had only been half successful, placing the crew on guard at the thought of a saboteur in their midst. There would likely be no second chances in that arena, and he had varying success with smaller acts of disruption. Setting one of the sensor buoys to attract attention had not worked, but disabling the phaser cannons deployed outside the ship had reaped some minor benefits. Of course, now the *Endeavour*'s crew was fully aware of the enemy lurking among them who had killed four of their shipmates.

Irritated at the simple thought of reliving the events of the past days, Mi'zhan wiped the communications hub's onboard memory. Now there would be no record of any direct access to this interface. That completed, he paused, reviewing the steps he had taken to conceal his activities. So far as he could remember, he had taken care of everything.

Had his effort been of worth? The signal was a play of desperation in the wake of his partial successes and failures that threatened to expose him. However, if the Federation was using surgically altered agents to infiltrate the Empire, this was something that needed immediate exposure. He was now angry with himself that his message had not included more information about the spies themselves and their true identities. Given the burst transmission's limited parameters, Mi'zhan was forced to economize the information he sent. He could only hope the matter would be given its due attention once the proper people were informed and could take action.

Assuming they received his message, of course. Mi'zhan did not even know whom he might be summoning with the message. It was believed Klingon ships might be operating in the area, for reasons as yet unknown. Were they working in league with the Orions responsible for the ground assault on *Endeavour*? There was no way to know such things. Not yet, at least.

Making his way back through the network of conduits and crawlways, Mi'zhan was sure to check the immediate surroundings before emerging from the Jefferies tube. After verifying he had not been observed, he moved at an unhurried pace down the dimly lit corridor.

At his approach, the doors to the impulse control room parted to reveal the cramped workspace buzzing with activity. The engineering staff, faced with keeping a crippled starship functional until rescue arrived, had received little time for rest since the crash. Their situation was only compounded by the setbacks Mi'zhan gave them. For a brief moment, he wondered how they might react if they were to learn the truth about him.

He stood to one side of the room, considering his next course of action and how he might best deal with the lingering threat of the two remaining agents. What else could he do here? Given the crew's heightened state of alert and even paranoia, further acts of sabotage were likely not an option. He would need to be more creative, and he was deciding just how to go about doing that when he was interrupted by someone walking toward him.

Maintain your bearing, he thought.

Mi'zhan recognized the new arrival as Master Chief Petty Officer Christine Rideout, a human female and one of the ship's engineers. She was not an officer but instead an enlisted Starfleet specialist. Like him she wore a green jumpsuit, and her dark hair was cut short enough that the back of her neck was exposed.

"Have you seen Commander Yataro?" she asked as she walked closer to him. "We're not yet done with the final diagnostics on the port impulse engine and want to review what we've got so far."

"No," replied Mi'zhan, known to the *Endeavour*'s crew as Lieutenant Ivan Tomkins, "I haven't seen him."

Thirty-two

Entering the hangar bay at a run, Le'tal saw it had turned into a swarm of activity. She winced at the level of noise permeating the vast chamber. How could such an immense room be so loud? Shouted orders, calls for assistance, or warnings about things she did not understand filtered through a cacophony of sounds produced by moving heavy equipment she could not identify across the deck to the pair of scout ships that now sat at the room's center. Klingons wearing uniforms or maintenance coveralls, all of them members of the outpost's security garrison, moved between the ships and various adjacent rooms as well as supply, equipment, or weapons lockers. While her lack of military experience saw to it she could not identify all of the tasks currently underway, she still knew enough to recognize battle preparations when she saw them.

She paused at the bay's open entryway, its heavy pressurized hatch open as work continued, searching among the numerous faces. It took her a moment to find Mak'dav, the military garrison's second-in-command, standing near one of the scout ships, talking to four other officers. Like most Klingons, the lieutenant was tall and muscular, with a gold sash hanging across his broad chest. He seemed ready to burst from his uniform at the slightest provocation, and Le'tal harbored no doubts he would be a fierce opponent in a fight.

Each of the subordinates nodded in utter solemnity in

response to Mak'dav's instructions, which she could not hear. When they turned and headed toward different destinations around the hangar bay, Le'tal noted the Klingon courier, D'khad, standing to one side in his impeccable uniform as Mak'dav issued his orders and set his people to their tasks.

"Lieutenant!"

She had to shout if she hoped to be heard over the din, and her voice carried enough for both Mak'dav and D'khad to turn in her direction. While the courier's face was impassive, the lieutenant's features were more than enough to communicate he was less than interested in talking to her just now.

"Where is Commander Karamaq?" she asked.

"Doctor." His one-word greeting was low and terse. "The commander is out with one of the scout ships currently on patrol. He chose to investigate the reports of the crashed Federation ship for himself, and he left me in charge to continue with our preparations." He emphasized his reply by gesturing at the hangar bay around them. "As you can see, we are quite busy just now."

"Busy doing what?" Le'tal glanced to D'khad, who said nothing, before refocusing her attention on Mak'dav. "Are you preparing to attack that Starfleet ship?"

The lieutenant grunted, exchanging knowing looks with D'khad. "Of course. You heard the message we received. That vessel carries aboard it a threat to the Empire. It is our duty to do everything in our power to see that threat neutralized. Commander Karamaq's orders were to prepare for such action."

"I understand your perspective, Lieutenant, but there are other concerns at stake here. This installation, for example. Its security and secrecy are my responsibility."

Mak'dav glowered at her. "The security of this facility has always been Commander Karamaq's purview, Doctor. When he is not here, that responsibility falls to me. It is the only reason our garrison is here in the first place. We provide the blanket under which you sleep, content in the knowledge that you are protected from those who might wish to see your efforts exposed and thwarted for the advantage of our enemies. The actions we are preparing to take will see to that continued secrecy *and* security."

Not even bothering to hide her contempt, Le'tal leveled an accusatory finger at the commander. "This is not the time for a battle of egos, Lieutenant. You know of what I speak. If you launch an attack against the Starfleet ship—a vessel incapable of defending itself to any reasonable degree—you risk leaving us vulnerable to attack from other parties. I remind you the *Enterprise* is still out there. It stands to reason they detected the same message we did." She turned to her right so her finger now pointed at D'khad. "Just as it is very likely they are aware of the message you sent. You violated every security protocol we have. Indeed, you have not given consideration to any of our procedures since your arrival."

"My foremost priority is the apprehension of the spies," D'khad replied. "I have made no secret of this, and the simple fact is my priorities outweigh yours, Doctor. As for the *Enterprise*, it will be dealt with in due course."

Now Le'tal simply laughed. "Dealt with?" She pointed toward the center of the hangar bay before turning her attention back to Mak'dav. "Did we not already try that? Was the result not two vessels in need of repair? No insult intended to you or your garrison, Lieutenant, but the *Enterprise* is far too formidable for your scout ships to challenge it. I understand and respect you feel an obligation to act, but it is senseless to waste personnel and resources on a battle you know you cannot win. The life of a single soldier pledged to serve the Empire no matter the cost is too valuable to waste on such folly."

"You know nothing of service to the Empire." A growl of contempt punctuated Mak'dav's reply. "And I have neither the time nor the desire to explain it to one such as yourself. Mind your research and your experiments, Doctor. *That* is where your value lies, but always remember your value is determined by what glory it brings to *all* Klingon people. Your work here is a kindness granted by those you disdain."

Le'tal glared at him. "Feel free to use that reasoning when we are all held to account for whatever security breach compromises this facility and allows all of our work to fall into enemy hands." She redirected her ire to D'khad. "Or is preventing that not a foremost priority? Have the spies acquired such damaging information that we have no other recourse but to take leave of our senses? You sent a message to your superiors, did you not? Are reinforcements better suited to confronting the *Enterprise* not on the way?"

"I have not yet received a response to my message," D'khad replied. "However, I know from the briefing I received prior to my traveling here that the nearest Klingon base is more than a day distant at maximum speeds. This does not account for other vessels that may be operating in the area, but I do not have access to that information. In the absence of other orders or direction, I am empowered to act." He gestured to Mak'dav. "So we act. The garrison's four scout vessels should at least be able to serve as a distraction and a nuisance to the *Enterprise*, providing more time for reinforcements to arrive."

"Commander Karamaq is likely already en route to the coordinates provided by our mysterious benefactor," Mak'dav said, before pointing to the ships parked on the hangar deck. "These two will join him presently. The time to strike is now. Perhaps one of the spies reconsidered the idiocy of betraying the Empire and is attempting to make amends." He scowled. "We are happy to use their information before seeing to it they pay for their crimes against the Klingon people."

"Or the Empire has a spy of its own aboard the Starfleet ship," Le'tal replied. "That would make sense, would it not? We spy on the Federation and have for many years, so it stands to reason they would do the same to us. I would wager leaders from both sides are keenly aware of such activities, and they justify it as the price of vigilance. If we all know we spy on one another, then what is now so urgent that we throw aside all caution?"

Mak'dav replied, "As you say, Doctor: the price of vigilance."

To her, it all sounded just so useless. "Why such haste? If what you seek is so important, can it not wait for a proper attack force in order to ensure victory? Your recklessness invites danger. What could be worth such a price?"

His expression now one of unmasked scorn, D'khad shook his head. "My dear Doctor, you simply have no idea."

While the First City held many charms, there were none greater to Kesh than the courtyard of his own home. He occupied the lone chair positioned on the small veranda, a tankard of bloodwine nestled between clasped hands resting in his lap. His boots rested on the parapet of the fire pit set just below ground at the center of the stone terrace. The fire was little more than glowing embers at this point, presenting no impediment to his night vision and affording him his favorite view.

Situated on the outskirts of the Old Quarter, his house did not look inward toward the city with all of its lights and distractions. Instead, the Kannaga Mountains to the north dominated his view. It was in those mountains that he had come of age, hunting *mIl'oDmey* with his father and grandfather. One of those formidable saber bears was his first kill, and its hide still adorned one wall of his study inside the house. That room like the rest of his home was filled with all manner of similar trophies and other mementos, but as he grew older Kesh found he held increasingly less need to collect such things. Family heirlooms and gifts from his children or close friends were to be treasured. On the other hand, reminders of past accomplishments, first as a soldier of the Empire and later a representative of its government, held less sway with him as the years marched ever onward.

Instead, something as simple as the opportunity for quiet, reflective moments was what now brought him satisfaction.

After purchasing the property years earlier in the wake of his wife's death, he had overseen every detail of the house's construction, ensuring that trees or terrain obscured his view of the city or even other nearby homes in all directions save one. It was his desire when he returned here to separate himself from the demands of his office to the maximum possible extent. He naturally was not completely insulated from those stresses. Technology and a cadre of assistants saw to it the work of the Klingon people was never far from his thoughts, but this was still his refuge, a sanctuary to which he could retreat and—for a time, at least—put aside the stresses of duty to which he had committed his life.

The sounds of footsteps behind him told Kesh that time was over.

"Chancellor, I apologize for the intrusion. You have a visitor."

Shifting in his chair, Kesh looked over his shoulder to see one of his aides, Duvoq, standing at the edge of the terrace, just outside of the entrance to the house. Next to him was Novek. The grizzled older Klingon regarded him with a somber expression. Meanwhile, Duvoq looked anxious at being forced to interrupt his chancellor even for what must surely be something of importance for his closest friend to come calling at this late hour.

"It is all right, Duvoq," Kesh said, rising from the chair. "You know Novek needs no invitation to enter my home." He held up his tankard. "Bring more bloodwine."

Despite the seriousness of whatever had brought him here, Novek still managed a wry grin. "But no chair?"

The remark prompted a small laugh from Kesh, who in turn gestured again to his aide. "And a chair for my feeble old friend."

Novek waited for Duvoq to disappear into the house before

turning his full attention to Kesh. "I bring most unpleasant news, Chancellor. Imperial Intelligence has discovered disturbing new information about the spies."

Eyeing his tankard, Kesh drained its remaining contents before releasing an exasperated sigh. "Do we yet know the extent of the information they stole?"

"No. That is still being determined, and I fear the process of knowing all details will be quite time-consuming." Novek paused, looking back toward the house as if to confirm his next words could not be overheard. When he spoke again, it was in an even more hushed tone.

"They were not Klingons, Chancellor. The spies were in fact humans. Agents of Starfleet Intelligence surgically altered to appear Klingon."

Kesh felt his muscles tighten in involuntary anger as he processed this revelation.

"Are you certain?"

"This information comes from the Intelligence director himself." Novek began pacing the terrace's perimeter. "He stresses he came to know this thanks to a resource he has within the Starfleet hierarchy. My attempts to gain more information about that resource were rebuffed, citing 'security concerns,' but he assures me the report is genuine and accurate."

That Imperial Intelligence had been using covert operatives of its own within the Federation and Starfleet was not a secret. The existence of such tactics, in use for years, had already been exposed on at least two occasions of which Kesh was aware. He also understood that, for obvious reasons, the identities of such agents remained closely guarded secrets for all but those few individuals with direct need for such information. Not even he knew the names of those working clandestinely behind enemy lines, and the Intelligence director was duty bound to safeguard—even from him—their identities at all costs. That Starfleet might employ similar stratagems made perfect sense.

Knowing this did little to assuage his irritation at how easily these three agents had infiltrated so many sensitive elements of the Klingon government and military. That they had been here for years, working undetected, only further fueled his anger.

What else had they done? Acts of sabotage? One of the agents was in a position to influence military policy and even resource procurement. Had they used that access to somehow undermine something critical like weapons development or ship construction? Each of the Empire's technological advancements for the past decade, many of them still experimental and not yet ready to deploy, could be exposed. While he did not expect the Federation to launch any kind of offensive against the Empire, any tactical advantage imperial forces hoped to enjoy with the new generation of warships might still be irrevocably affected. Plans for expansion and conquest would all have to be reexamined in the face of this mess. Some might be scuttled altogether, and even as the Empire drew up new strategies, fear that the Federation was already in a position to counter them would always be present. No matter what else the spies might have accomplished, that overarching specter of uncertainty would likely be their lasting impact.

Was there nothing that could be saved from this debacle?

"So," Kesh said after a moment, "what the Intelligence director meant to tell you is that all of the information these agents acquired during their time here is in danger of falling into Starfleet's hands."

Novek replied, "Assuming they or their information makes it back to their superiors. That is not yet a certainty, Chancellor."

They fell silent as Duvoq arrived with a chair for Novek, which Kesh directed be positioned near the fire pit, then waited until he returned with refreshments. The younger Klingon offered a tankard to Novek before placing a larger stone decanter of bloodwine near the pit's edge. Only after the aide once more took his leave and they settled into their seats did Kesh resume their conversation.

"You have word about the hunt for these spies?"

Novek drank deeply from his tankard before replying, "From an unexpected source. It appears the Federation starship we hoped was destroyed in the Ivratis asteroid field has survived, at least after a fashion."

Listening as his friend relayed information from the mysterious agent embedded with the crew of the *U.S.S. Endeavour*, Kesh could only shake his head in disbelief. His surprise deepened as Novek recounted the starship's crash landing and the attack by Orion pirates, and the agent's efforts to sow doubt and fear while attempting to learn details about the operatives the *Endeavour* hoped to return to Starfleet.

"This is confirmed?" he asked.

Novek nodded. "It corroborates information provided by the Intelligence director. He also verified there is an agent operating aboard the *Endeavour*. That operative had no specific assignment other than observation, but it is fortunate he was there at all."

"That Intelligence was able to place a spy aboard one of Starfleet's most revered vessels." Kesh could not help but laugh. "That is a remarkable achievement."

"It is normally a difficult proposition," Novek replied. "However, the *Endeavour* was in unexpected need of a great many crew replacements, and we were able to seize the opportunity. According to this agent, his actions may have attracted sufficient attention that his discovery was inevitable. Given how much time has elapsed since the message was sent, this may have already occurred. If that is the case, then I suspect inserting an agent anywhere in Starfleet will be much more difficult after this incident."

That was almost certainly true, Kesh conceded. "But we do not yet know for certain this has happened?"

"No, Chancellor." Finishing his bloodwine, Novek helped himself to the decanter near the fire pit. "There is something else. It appears Imperial Intelligence has not been forthcoming about some of their recent activities."

It required another refill of his own tankard as Kesh listened to his friend explain the research and development taking place in the Ivratis asteroid field. While it was not unusual for the Defense Force or the intelligence branch to carry out clandestine weapons development programs, that this one was occurring beyond the Empire's borders was troublesome. That this secret research effort also involved Orions only made things worse. The Orion Syndicate, for all its prattling about remaining "neutral" with respect to its interactions with the quadrant's major interstellar powers, could and did take advantage of any situation that stood to make them a profit. Their involvement in any imperial action that placed them at odds with Starfleet would not be received kindly by the Federation.

"The asteroid field is in unclaimed space," Novek said. "But that will not matter if Starfleet can point to it as a cause for the loss of their vessel."

Despite his role as chancellor of the High Council, Kesh never fancied himself a diplomat. He appreciated the idea that politics was its own battleground, but he preferred to leave it to those better suited to waging that kind of war. If what Novek said was true, then this situation had taken on an added dimension that only promised more trouble.

"And the *Enterprise* is still operating in that region?" Kesh asked.

Novek grimaced. "Yes, Chancellor."

Pushing himself to his feet, Kesh took his own turn pacing the length of the veranda. He paused at the edge of the stone platform, looking first to the trees surrounding his house and finally beyond them to the distant mountains. Under the sunlight reflecting off the surface of the Praxis moon, he could see snow covering the tallest peaks. In another month the snowline would descend to cover the top third of the mountains. That would make for good *mIl'oD* hunting, he knew, but the thought offered him little solace, for he also was sure he would not be able to partake of the time-honored ritual. Such were the realities of the office he held.

"Contemplating a military action against Starfleet was not how I envisioned spending this evening," he said, drinking the last of the bloodwine in his tankard. He considered refilling the vessel, then decided against it. "But this situation now threatens to spiral out of control, and must therefore be contained."

He turned his back on the mountains, facing Novek. "Do we have any ships in position to be of use to this situation?"

"Two battle cruisers, Chancellor," his friend replied. "They can be there within hours at maximum speed, but what is their mission?"

"This unsanctioned research effort. See that it's no longer a concern. Make sure the same is true of the *Endeavour*, and whatever spies it might harbor."

"And what of the agent aboard the *Endeavour*?"

Kesh sighed. "He is a soldier of the Empire. He will understand."

Thirty-three

The *Endeavour*'s main briefing room was different from that of its *Enterprise* counterpart. While its dimensions were the same, the polished wood conference table was different, shaped like an oval with its lateral ends chopped away. A three-sided viewer sat at the table's center, and there was a viewscreen set into the room's far wall. The room also featured a circular dropped ceiling, with translucent panels set into a metal frame and the entire construct resting on four angled metal stanchions. Reduced lighting cast the room's corners into shadow, while softer illumination in the dropped ceiling provided an almost gothic atmosphere.

Eight chairs were arranged around the table, and a computer terminal sat at the end of the table opposite Kirk's seat. To his right was Captain Khatami and to her right sat Commander Katherine Stano. Also present and sitting opposite Khatami and Kirk was Lieutenant Brax. Morgan Binnix occupied the chair next to him, while Phil Watson leaned with crossed arms against the stanchion just behind his fellow agent.

"We have completed a phase-one search of the ship," said Brax. Two of the Edoan security chief's three hands rested in his lap, while the one attached to the arm at the center of his torso held a tricorder. "We found no sign of Commander Yataro or Agent Horst. So far as we are able to determine, Captain, they are not aboard the ship."

Khatami, leaning forward in her seat so her forearms rested atop the conference table, tapped its surface with the nail of her right forefinger. "That's impossible, Lieutenant. Neither of them had any reason to leave the ship. They have to be somewhere."

"I have already ordered the search teams to begin another sweep," Brax replied. "We will continue to observe all phase-one search protocols during the effort."

"Excuse me," Watson said. "Phase one?"

Stano replied, "A phase-one search is basically checking the entire ship from top to bottom. Every nook and cranny, every Jefferies tube, storage locker, ladder well, turboshaft; anywhere on the ship a normal humanoid crew member might be able to fit. Phase-one protocols assume the person we're searching for is incapacitated or unable to call out for help, or they can't respond to attempts to locate them."

"You mean dead," Binnix said.

"Not necessarily," Kirk replied. "Until located or the search is called off, the assumption is the sought-after party is injured or otherwise unresponsive."

Khatami added, "It also assumes the person or persons in question aren't deliberately working to avoid such a search. I can't imagine Yataro ever wanting to play hide-and-seek, but if he did I'm willing to bet he'd wait for a more appropriate time." She paused before looking to Binnix and Watson. "I can't speak for your fellow agent."

"You've got to be kidding." Watson pushed himself from the stanchion. "Are you seriously accusing Horst of something? You think he hurt or killed your engineer? He was *helping* Yataro, remember? Hell, we've *all* been helping you since we got here." Stepping closer to the conference table, he looked at Brax as he gestured toward the bulkhead. "Did you already forget I just came in from helping put together your little bunkhouses for our big pirate sleepover party you've got going? And that was after the help we gave you during the repairs, to say nothing of

Binnix volunteering for that firefight we just had outside the ship. You're welcome for all of that, by the way."

Turning in her seat, Binnix eyed her companion. "Phil." She spoke in a soft voice, but the warning in her tone was unmistakable.

"We appreciate your assistance throughout this situation, Mister Watson," Khatami said. "But I'm sure you can understand the position I'm in. Sabotage aboard my ship, four of my people dead, with two more unaccounted for. Tell me if our roles weren't reversed you wouldn't have the same concerns."

Watson closed his eyes, drawing a deep breath as he held out one hand. "Okay. Fair enough. I'm sorry, but accusations of being a traitor after everything we've been through tend to irritate me."

"If I honestly believed you were behind any of this, we wouldn't be having this conversation and I'd have drop-kicked you through an airlock." Khatami held the other man's gaze for an additional moment before adding, "You're *welcome*." To his credit, Watson decided against pushing the point any further, but he remained standing with crossed arms behind Binnix.

"For whatever the hell my opinion's worth," Stano said, "the timing just doesn't work out for either of you or Horst to be involved. Not for the impulse engine or the phaser cannon malfunctions. None of you were on the impulse deck when the damage occurred, for one thing."

Brax added, "And Captain Khatami instructed me to ensure none of you were given unsupervised access to any of our weapons."

"It's what I would've done," Binnix said. "It stings to hear it said about you, but I get it."

Kirk shifted in his seat. "Agent Binnix saved my life out on the surface. One might argue it was an obvious move to counter suspicion, but I like to think I read people better than that." He shook his head. "No, I don't think any of you is responsible for our problems, but that means we have an even bigger one. A member of the crew has to be our saboteur."

Silence hung over the room for several seconds, long enough for Kirk to realize only then the palpable absence of warp engines providing power to the *Endeavour*. The low, omnipresent drone was something he long ago grew accustomed to hearing. Years of service in space made the sound such an ingrained part of life aboard a starship. To not hear it now only hammered home the point that the *Endeavour* was but a shadow of her former self. Having it compounded by the stark realization someone among them might be a traitor only served to deepen the sense of dread Kirk was trying with great difficulty to keep at bay.

"Do you believe we are only dealing with one person?" Brax asked.

Everyone at the table exchanged looks of uncertainty before Khatami replied, "To be honest, that was my assumption, but you're right, Lieutenant. And now I have a new nightmare, assuming I actually get to sleep any time soon."

Stano said, "I don't know that it's more than a single person." When Kirk and the others turned to her, she gestured toward the briefing room doors. "Let's face it. With the secondary hull gone and several decks of the saucer unusable, we're pretty crammed together in here. Someone working alone would have a hard enough time doing what's been done to this point without being noticed. Two or more, trying to work together?" She shook her head. "I'm not buying it."

Before anyone could respond, the communicator next to Khatami's right hand beeped for attention. When she activated the device, she and everyone else at the table were greeted by the voice of Lieutenant Hector Estrada.

"*Sorry to disturb you, Captain, but I figured you all would want to hear this. We're being hailed by the* Enterprise *on a secure coded frequency.*"

That was enough to evoke smiles from everyone in the room. At Kirk's suggestion, the communications officer had been working with Lieutenant Uhura and one of the *Endeavour* engineers once the sensor buoys deployed to the asteroid's surface were back online. Since everyone in the region now seemed to know the crashed starship's location, there was no reason not to call for help. To that end, Estrada and Uhura, with the assistance of Master Chief Petty Officer Christine Rideout, amplified the ship's transceiver array and pumped an outgoing signal through the buoys in the hopes of catching the *Enterprise's* attention. It was still a tall order given the background interference permeating the field, but Kirk reasoned they had nothing to lose at this point.

Kirk and Khatami were the first to their feet, and Kirk was already moving toward the viewscreen in the room's far wall.

"Excellent work, Lieutenant. Pass on my thanks to the master chief as well. Pipe that communication down here." Looking to Kirk, Khatami added, "I figure we can spare the power for something like this."

Gathering near the screen as it activated, the group watched as it coalesced into a grainy, static-littered image that was still clear enough for Kirk to make out Spock's visage over the encrypted channel. Just the sight of his first officer was enough to make him feel more at ease. He sat in the command chair on the *Enterprise* bridge, flanked by Doctor McCoy and Admiral Nogura.

"Spock, you have no idea how good it is to see you."

"Likewise, Captain."

McCoy asked, *"Everybody okay over there?"*

A brief exchange ensued, with each side updating the other on the condition of both ships, including the status of Binnix and her agents, the Orions' attempted raid as well as the potential saboteur still running loose aboard the *Endeavour*. Kirk and everyone else, but Khatami and Stano in particular, listened with fascination as Spock described what the *Enterprise* crew had learned about Klingon activities in the area. This included their encounter with Klingon scout ships and the strange disruption technology that everyone now believed was the cause for the *Endeavour's* misfortune. No one in the room was happy to hear about the signal sent from the asteroid field and presumably intended to summon Klingon reinforcements to the area.

"We don't know how or even if the Orions are in bed with the Klingons on this one," Nogura said, *"but I'm not ruling it out. Why else would they be hanging around here once they knew the Klingons were in the area? They're smart enough to know nothing can come from that, unless there's a way for them to get something out of the deal."*

Binnix said, "The Klingons won't care about being called out for weapons testing. Their top priority is us and our data module. They know we haven't had a chance to transfer it to anyone. Even if we had the time to send it to you over this shaky connection, the data crystals are programmed to prohibit any attempt at data transfer until they're in your possession, Admiral."

Standing next to her, Watson added, "It'll destroy the entire archive if we try to circumvent it, sir. Seems like a pretty good reason for you to come get us."

Khatami eyed the agent before returning her gaze to the screen. "Admiral, I'd love to hear you say you're on your way right now to get me and my people out of here, but I think we both understand that's not the right play here. This disruption technology they're working on isn't even the real problem. If they know we're here and we've got the agents and their information, they won't sit idle while we hustle them home. They've already called for help, but you know they're going to throw whatever they've got at us well before then."

Nogura nodded. *"My exact assessment, Captain."*

"We believe we have pinpointed the location of a Klingon outpost within the asteroid field," Spock said. *"We are en route to investiga—"*

Static exploded across the image, washing away Spock and the others before the screen deactivated.

"Captain Khatami," said Estrada over the intercom. *"We just lost the transmission. I'm not yet sure how it happened."*

Kirk exchanged knowing looks with Khatami. Like him, she already knew what had caused the abrupt interruption.

"Our friend's back at it," Stano said, giving voice to their suspicions.

Estrada replied, *"Lieutenant Uhura and I are trying a couple of tricks to backtrack what happened, Captain. I'll keep you updated."*

A new voice filtered through the open comm channel. *"Klisiewicz cutting in, Captain. Sensors are still working, and we're picking up a pair of signals at the outer limit of our scanning range. They're Klingon."*

"Scout ships?" Stano asked.

"Looks that way, Commander." There was a pause before Klisiewicz added, *"Probably the same type as the ones Commander Spock described from the* Enterprise's *earlier run-in. They don't seem to be heading in our direction yet, but their sensors are active like they're looking for something. If we can see them I'm pretty sure they can see us."*

Kirk said, "The Klingons aren't the Orions. If they've been told about the agents, then when they come, it won't be because they're hoping to score whatever they can sell on the black market."

"They'll do whatever it takes to destroy the ship," Khatami replied.

Stano added, "It's not just us. The Orions are sitting ducks outside."

As part of the containment protocols Kirk suggested and put in place by Lieutenant Brax, all of the Orions taken into custody following their assault had been placed into one of five emergency shelters, erected outside the *Endeavour* on the asteroid's surface. A pair of security officers was posted outside each of the shelters. To ensure none of the Orions entertained any foolhardy notions of escape, Brax had ordered all of them to surrender their environmental suits. All of that equipment was placed outside the shelters in case it was needed while remaining effectively out of reach for any of the prisoners.

"We can't risk bringing them inside," Khatami said. "There's too much going on without having to guard fifty loose cannons. We could disable their transports and transfer the Orions to them." She gritted her teeth in obvious frustration. "They'd still be vulnerable out there."

"What about the deflector shields?" Kirk asked. "Any chance we can use them? Extend them to protect the Orions, too?"

"On the ground?" Watson grimaced. "Has that even been tried before?"

Stano said, "Not with a starship. At least, not that I can remember. Then again, most starships aren't supposed to be on the ground in the first place. Even if it worked, one impulse engine's not enough to hold off any kind of prolonged attack."

"Maybe it doesn't have to be that long," Kirk said. "We just need to buy time. Spock and Nogura know from the severed communication something must be wrong here. They'll come for us. We only need to hang on long enough for them to find us." Not for the first time since his arrival aboard the stricken *Endeavour*, he longed for the technical prowess of Montgomery Scott. If anyone could conjure a means of putting his unconventional plan into action, it was the *Enterprise*'s chief engineer. Kirk suspected Commander Yataro possessed similar skill, but his gut told him the Lirin, along with David Horst, was dead.

And we still have to deal with that, on top of everything else, he reminded himself.

Binnix eyed him with open skepticism. "I've only known you a short time, Captain, but I think that look on your face tells me you're about to suggest something crazy. I feel like I should start praying."

"It wouldn't be the worst idea," Kirk replied.

Right now, he would take all the help they could find.

Thirty-four

This was his chance.

Mi'zhan knew these were precious moments, not to be wasted. The impulse deck was awash with activity as the *Endeavour*'s engineering staff carried out frantic preparations for the approaching Klingon vessels. Most of the personnel were focused on their duties. It should be easy for him to add a little chaos to what was already a recipe for uncertainty and fear. Better still, it appeared he might well be able to carry out his hastily formulated plan in plain sight, with no one being the wiser. If everything went according to his intentions, by the time anyone suspected something was wrong and Lieutenant Ivan Tomkins was the saboteur in their midst, it would be too late and the approaching Klingons would take care of the rest.

"Lieutenant Tomkins, all readings show the port impulse engine is operating at one hundred percent capacity."

The report came from Master Chief Petty Officer Christine Rideout, the *Endeavour*'s senior enlisted engineer, who was working at a console to his right. Like most human females, she was of slender, athletic build. Unlike several of her engineering counterparts aboard the ship, she preferred a green jumpsuit garment similar to his, rather than the red Starfleet tunic and black trousers normally worn by those assigned to a starship's operations division. Mi'zhan could not recall ever seeing her wear the skirt variant of the uniform, which he had always found impractical for those in the engineering department.

"Thank you, Master Chief," he said, remembering to use the informal mode of addressing her by her rank.

"We'll have to keep an eye on these power levels," Rideout replied. "Especially when we kick in the shields."

"Agreed."

Like Mi'zhan, Rideout was one of the more recent additions to the *Endeavour* crew, coming aboard during that period when Starfleet assigned several replacements for crew members killed during that still-classified mission in the Taurus Reach earlier in the year. A review of her personnel record informed Mi'zhan she had previously served as the chief engineer of the *U.S.S. Huang Zhong*, a smaller *Archer*-class scout ship with a crew of fourteen. That ship had suffered its own bout of misfortune but Rideout along with most of its crew survived. Rather than seek a comparable billet on a similar vessel, she instead opted to serve as a subordinate to Commander Yataro aboard the *Endeavour*. The chief engineer and his staff had taken an early liking to her, impressed with her skills as well as her mastery of the easy, often inane human banter Mi'zhan loathed.

Her attention still focused on the streams of diagnostic data scrolling across all four of her console's status monitors, Rideout said, "Hold on. Two of the shield generators are showing temperature spikes in their flow regulators." She muttered something Mi'zhan could not hear but assumed was a form of human obscenity, for which the master chief had repeatedly demonstrated unusual proficiency.

There could also be no denying Rideout's technical acumen. Together, she and Mi'zhan had determined the best possible configuration for bringing what remained of the *Endeavour*'s deflector shield generators back online. Without its warp engines for power, the wounded starship's only hope resided in its single remaining impulse engine, which had been repaired thanks to the ingenuity of Commander Yataro, Rideout, and even Mi'zhan. He was not sure the hasty repairs and reconfigurations of the compromised systems would work. Yataro would be the one to make such assessments, and he was most decidedly unavailable. While Captain Khatami dispatched members of the ship's crew to search for the missing engineer, it fell to the rest of Yataro's department to finalize preparations for what everyone believed was the coming skirmish with Klingons.

Let it be so. The thought warmed Mi'zhan's heart.

Rideout said, "We're going to have to make manual adjustments all through this." She released an audible sigh that clearly signaled her growing frustration. "We are way past whatever cushion the original engineers laid in when they wrote the specs for this stuff."

Her stress along with those of her crewmates was palpable as they hurried through their various tasks. They could not know Mi'zhan had only contributed to their growing anxiety with his second burst message to whoever might be out there listening. Another transmission so soon after the first, coupled with the crew's inability to find Yataro and Horst, only heightened their fear and uncertainty. There was a risk to repeating this action, especially now that Captain Khatami and her people were suspicious of anything that might smack of the turncoat taking action against them. Further, finding a communications hub that could avoid scrutiny even in the short term was its own challenge.

Mi'zhan realized there were areas of the ship now cordoned off for use by the crew, but which he could access via Jefferies tubes or other crawlways. It had taken some effort, but he made his way to a maintenance shaft near deck two, just beneath the ship's main bridge. After sending his signal, he had programmed a personal communicator to establish a remote link with that hub, bypassing the access-control logs that had complicated his earlier attempt to make outside contact. If necessary, he could use the communicator to send another message. It was a ploy that would not evade discovery for very long, but that was not necessary. If Klingon ships were on the way, then his job would be simple.

All he had to do was make sure the *Endeavour* could not raise whatever remained of her deflector shields.

"We've patched this thing together with spare parts and no small amount of luck," Mi'zhan said, playing up his Ivan Tomkins persona. "I'm amazed it hasn't blown already."

It was but the latest issue they had tackled just in the past several minutes. The precarious state of many of the *Endeavour*'s onboard systems continued to provide challenges, which only worsened as the ship's power reserves were taxed to their limit. It was difficult enough to keep more than four hundred people alive inside the hulk of what had once been a powerful space vessel. Making that same wreck sturdy enough to withstand a possible attack was something else entirely. Mi'zhan's anxiety was amplified by the fact that by simply doing nothing, he might well achieve his end goal. However, the lack of action could be enough to expose him before his simple yet effective strategy came to fruition.

Unfortunately, his first attempt to sow fear among the *Endeavour* failed. He had hoped sabotaging the ship's port impulse engine would create enough confusion to allow him an opportunity to inflict further damage to a critical system such as life-support. The suspicious nature of the incident was detected far sooner than he anticipated, as was Captain Khatami's predictable tightening of security around such vulnerable areas. This forced Mi'zhan to become more creative.

It pained him, having to work alongside his fellow crew members and pretend to be one of them. While he had accepted that as an integral part of his mission while undergoing training, his intended role was that of observer. His instructions on this were quite clear: take no action that might risk exposing his identity or activities. What could not have been anticipated was the situation in which he now found himself. Here he was, alone and in a position to contain or neutralize a very real threat to the Empire. The stakes were significant. Only he now possessed the opportunity to take direct action.

"Hang on." Mi'zhan offered a bit of manufactured irritation, releasing a long sigh. "Something's wrong with this console." Playing up his exasperation at this new problem, which in reality was entirely fabricated, he dropped to one knee and removed an access panel from underneath the console. Now he was able to access the circuitry and rows of transtators that controlled the flow of energy within the distribution network. This particular bank was dedicated to the impulse engine's control systems as well as its array of vital oversight processes and charged with routing power from the engines to systems across the ship—or what remained of the ship. Each transtator was the size of a thumbnail, sequenced in varying numbers depending on the level of energy being regulated. They were designed to work in tandem while balancing power-flow requirements, and the loss of even a single transtator from a series was enough to introduce performance issues in the affected system.

Rideout moved to kneel beside him, trying to get a look under the console. "What's up?"

"One of the transtators looks to be burned out." Mi'zhan reached into a pocket of his jumpsuit and retrieved a multipurpose macrotool. "Can you get a replacement?"

"On it." Rideout pushed herself to her feet and crossed to a nearby equipment locker.

Her attention was away from him, and it would take her but a moment to pull a replacement transtator. Mi'zhan had to act now if he was going to do what needed to be done. A quick glance around the room told him none of the other engineers were looking in his direction. They were too engrossed in their own duties to notice one more technician with his hands full of innards from one more console. Reaching into the access panel, he positioned the macrotool not over one of the transtators but instead before one of the power flow regulators. He thumbed the tool's activation switch and the device's tip pulsed with energy.

The communicator nestled within one of his jumpsuit's other pockets chose that moment to beep. Someone was attempting to contact it. Now?

"Here you go, Lieutenant." It was Rideout, coming back from the equipment locker and carrying a new transtator. She held out her hand, offering him the component.

Ignoring her and the communicator, Mi'zhan kept his attention focused on the flow regulator. He needed just two seconds.

"Lieutenant Tomkins!"

The voice echoed across the impulse deck, and despite himself he flinched in response. Jerking his head toward the source he saw Captain Khatami standing at the entrance, flanked by Lieutenant Brax and the human woman from the *Enterprise*, Uhura. The security chief was holding a phaser, while Uhura wielded a tricorder pointed at him. All around the room, the other engineers halted in their tracks, turning to see what was going on.

They know.

"Step away from the console, Lieutenant," Khatami said. "Do it now." Her voice was firm and her expression was cold and hard. Anger burned in her eyes.

A sudden jolt of panic coursed through Mi'zhan. They knew! Somehow they had discovered him. What had he done wrong?

It doesn't matter, you fool. Act! Now!

His thumb moved over the macrotool's power setting, increasing it to maximum at the same time he swept it across the inside of the workstation's access panel. The results were immediate as the tool's energy beam sliced through the flow regulator. Feedback from the stressed component washed across the bank of transtators, overloading them and causing the entire console to go dark. Alarms rang all around the impulse deck and engineers reacted as their training had taught them. Near the door, Khatami and Brax sidestepped to avoid being caught in the rush as crew members moved to consoles and emergency stations.

It was all Mi'zhan needed.

Dropping the macrotool, he pulled the compact type-1 phaser from the pocket along his right thigh. It was up and aiming at Khatami just as another of the *Endeavour* engineers moved past her. She looked back in his direction and her eyes widened in shock just as he pressed the weapon's firing stud.

Khatami lurched out of the line of fire, pulled to her right by Brax as the phaser beam passed through the space she had occupied heartbeats earlier. The security chief dragged her with him, his Edoan physiology allowing him to use his three legs to scramble past the row of consoles in search of cover. Uhura and everyone else in the vicinity clambered away, offering Mi'zhan an avenue of escape through the open doorway, but there was no point to that anymore. With nowhere to go and no place to hide, he knew his mission was over. Though he had already partially succeeded in his plan to leave the wrecked starship, there was still one more thing he could do.

Pivoting on his heel, he turned to see the access conduit leading to the capacitance cell for the *Endeavour*'s port impulse engine was open. The energy storage component had just recently been tested as part of the overall repair of the engine. His earlier sabotage efforts had failed to destroy it, but Mi'zhan had one more opportunity. Destroying the cell now would cause a feedback pulse with sufficient power to cripple the engine, forcing Khatami and her crew to survive on battery power before the approaching Klingon ships finished destroying the *Endeavour*.

He raised his phaser and aimed it at the open conduit before he felt cool energy wash over him. His vision was blinded by bright blue light as every muscle in his body tensed. Then light and color fell away to darkness.

Thirty-five

"Mister Spock. We've got them."

Ensign Chekov's voice seemed to raise an octave as he turned from the science station, and there was no mistaking his satisfied expression. There was a time when Spock might have sought to instruct the young officer on how to better hold his emotions in check, especially while serving on the bridge. On the other hand, Chekov's exuberance was an indelible aspect of his character. This was something Spock first noted upon the ensign's arrival aboard the *Enterprise*. The observation continued while guiding him through a broad range of training aimed at expanding his knowledge and skills beyond what he already possessed as a navigator. Chekov had demonstrated an early aptitude and initiative toward learning the duties of a science officer as well as showing an interest in the functions of starship security. While junior officers were expected to master a host of skills in various areas, Pavel Chekov strove to exceed even those demanding requirements.

Therefore, Spock was inclined to allow him an occasional well-earned lapse of decorum.

Swiveling the command chair to face the science station, he nodded in approval. "Excellent work, Mister Chekov. Route those coordinates to the helm. Mister Scott, have you detected any sign of disruption-field generators?"

Seated at the engineering station next to the turbolift, the chief engineer turned in his chair. "Not yet, sir. On the other hand, if any are deployed near the outpost itself, I'd expect it to be positioned in such a manner that it could be used without interfering with the base itself."

The combined efforts of Scott and Lieutenant Palmer had taken away much of the difficulty in finding the facility the Klingons had to be using from within the Ivratis asteroid field to control their experimental technology. Using the disruption-field generator retrieved earlier, and after studying its onboard communications system, Scott was able to access its logs and the frequencies used by the device to receive commands from the Klingon outpost, which included coordinates and time stamps from the point of origin. While Spock knew the location would not be exact owing to the movement of asteroids within the field, it was enough to extrapolate probable intersection points for the *Enterprise* to follow.

From where he stood near the bridge's main viewscreen, Admiral Nogura asked, "Can we see it, Ensign?"

Chekov nodded. "Yes, Admiral."

The main screen shifted so that a single immense asteroid was now centered in the image. Oblong in shape, the rock was a collection of deep crevasses and jagged peaks, as though it was but a piece broken away from something far larger.

Nogura stepped closer to the screen. "What's our current distance?"

Seated at the helm station, Lieutenant Naomi Rahda replied, "Seventy thousand kilometers and closing, Admiral." The Indian woman tapped out a sequence on her console. "The debris field is a little denser here, Mister Spock."

"Slow to one-quarter impulse power," the first officer replied. "Increase image to magnification factor six."

At the navigator's station next to Rahda, Lieutenant Ryan Leslie made the necessary adjustments and the image on the main viewscreen jumped to bring the asteroid into sharp relief.

Studying the asteroid, Spock noted its topographical details as well as the obvious signs of habitation. Even from this distance, the magnified image as generated by the sensor telemetry provided a host of details. A half-dozen dull-gray modules of varying size sat atop a larger platform affixed to the asteroid's surface. Conduits, scaffolding, and support frames surrounded everything, and on the construct's lowest level light escaped from a massive opening. The entire facility was coated in brownish dust indicating it had been subjected to the asteroid field's unwelcoming environs for some time.

"Sensor interference is clearing, Mister Spock." Chekov had returned his attention to the science station's hooded viewer. "It appears the largest portion of the outpost is partially buried within the asteroid's bedrock. I'm picking up eighty-seven individual life signs." A moment later he added, "Also picking up the energy signatures from two scout-class vessels departing the outpost."

Spock said, "Red alert. All hands to battle stations. Lieutenant Palmer, hail those vessels." He ordered the audible alarm muted even before it could begin wailing across the bridge, by which time everyone had reported ready status from their various stations.

"No response to our hails, Mister Spock," Palmer reported from the communications console.

Chekov added, "Their shields are up and weapons active. They're on an intercept course."

Making his way around the bridge railing, Nogura moved down just behind Spock's left shoulder. "Someone's not happy to see us."

"Maintain heading," Spock said. "Full power to forward deflectors. Mister Leslie, target firing solutions on both vessels. Lieutenant Palmer, open a channel." Once the communications officer indicated she had established a connection, he offered in a louder voice, "Klingon vessels. This is Commander Spock of the Federation *Starship Enterprise*. I remind you that this is free space. We have no desire for hostilities, but we will be forced to respond to your provocative actions if you do not alter your course. Please respond."

Palmer reported, "Nothing, sir."

At the helm, Lieutenant Rahda was staring into her station's tactical scanner. "They're breaking off from each other, sir. Definitely maneuvering to catch us in a crossfire."

"On-screen," Spock ordered.

The image on the viewscreen shifted to depict a pair of small, agile vessels banking in opposite directions. Glancing at the astrogator between Rahda and Leslie, Spock noted the positions of both enemy ships as they maneuvered to put the *Enterprise* between them.

"Target whichever vessel comes in range first," Spock said. "Fire to disable if at all possible, but the safety of the *Enterprise* comes first, Mister Leslie."

Rahda said, "The ship to our starboard is coming around and trying to lock disruptors."

Without waiting for further orders, the helm officer guided the ship in that direction, bringing the scout ship into view just as Leslie punched his console's firing controls. Twin beams of energy streaked across space and impacted against the Klingon vessel's shields. Leslie followed with a second salvo as the other ship fired its own weapons. The disruptor strike missed, passing down and out of the viewscreen's frame, but Leslie had better luck. His second round of fire also hit the ship's shields before the vessel moved out of view.

"Photon torpedoes, Mister Leslie," Spock said. He wanted to end this engagement before it dragged on too long or spun too far away from his ability to control.

As Rahda's piloting brought the *Enterprise* face-to-face with the second Klingon ship, Leslie acquired the new target and fired. Two photon torpedoes, pulsing red with barely restrained energy, arced across space and slammed into the other vessel's shields. The navigator followed with additional phaser strikes timed to hit just as the torpedoes detonated, and Spock watched the energy beams drill into the other ship's hull.

"Direct hit, Mister Spock," Chekov reported. "Their shields are overloaded and I'm scanning a breach in their secondary hull near the engine compartment."

Her attention once more on her tactical scanner, Rahda said, "The other ship is coming around, sir. Angling for another shot."

"Do not give it to them, Lieutenant." To Spock, the other vessel's commander was acting in a most illogical fashion. Surely they knew at this point they were hopelessly outmatched? Even working with another ship, they still lacked the firepower to withstand any prolonged engagement against the *Enterprise*. The entire exercise was a waste of time, resources, and possibly life if things deteriorated that far.

Nevertheless, the Klingons pressed the attack, using one of the nearby smaller asteroids for cover long enough to maneuver for another run. By that time Rahda had guided the *Enterprise* into position to defend. Seconds later the scout vessel appeared on the viewscreen, working its way out from behind the asteroid.

"Fire," Spock said.

As before, Leslie unleashed a coordinated strike using both photon torpedoes and phasers. Two torpedoes collided with the Klingon vessel's shields, which held until a third torpedo hit at the same point of impact.

"Their shields are down!" Chekov called out.

Leslie was already following with phasers. The two beams of blue-white energy pierced the scout ship's hull just forward of its impulse engine ports, and the orange glow from their power plants dimmed but did not die out.

"Scans show their impulse power is down sixty-three percent." Chekov looked up from the sensor viewer. "They're changing course and maneuvering away, sir."

With nothing left to stand in their way, it took only moments for the *Enterprise* to navigate the asteroid field back to the large body of rock that was home to the outpost. Once again the facility occupied the center of the bridge's viewscreen. At which point Spock turned to Nogura.

"Admiral, I believe whatever happens next falls under your purview."

Pursing his lips, Nogura drew a deep breath and let it out in slow, deliberate fashion. "We can't let them leave here with their technology intact."

Scott rose from his chair. "With Lieutenant Palmer's help, I may be able to access their computer and download the relevant information."

"That would require considerable time," Spock replied. "And there is still the captain and the *Endeavour* to consider." While they had been making their way here, Captain Kirk and his team along with the crew of the *Endeavour* were preparing to deal with their own attack. How were they faring? With communications disrupted, there was no way to know.

Nogura looked to Scott. "Commander, with the specimen of technology you recovered, do you think you could extrapolate its control processes, and give us some insight into how the Klingons might plan to deploy it?"

"I believe so, Admiral." The chief engineer nodded toward the viewscreen. "It'd be nice to have the whole package, but I'll take what I can get, sir."

For Spock, this was sufficient.

"Mister Chekov, scan that facility for all uninhabited areas and identify its primary power and life-support systems. Feed that information to Mister Leslie." After asking Lieutenant Palmer to establish a hailing frequency, Spock rose from the captain's chair. "Klingon outpost. This is Commander Spock of the *Starship Enterprise*. Your presence in this area of space for the conduct of weapons research is a violation of treaties between our respective governments, and your actions against this vessel and the *U.S.S. Endeavour* could be considered acts of aggression. We have scanned your facility and know you are largely defenseless. We also are aware that a transport capable of carrying your entire complement is present in your landing bay. You have five minutes to evacuate your base, at which time it will be destroyed."

To Spock's surprise, the hail was answered.

It was not a Klingon warrior who appeared on the viewscreen. Spock determined she was not a soldier owing to her distinct lack of military uniform. Instead she wore a dark, drab utility coverall, and her black hair was pulled back from her face to reveal her dark-olive complexion.

"*I am Doctor Le'tal.*" There was a slight faltering in her voice, but she managed to affect an otherwise composed bearing. "*This is a research facility. You are correct that we do not possess defenses aside from our military garrison, which you have already encountered. I am told both of those vessels are incapacitated.*"

Spock said, "Upon your evacuation, you will be permitted to transfer the crews of both vessels to your ship."

"*And if we refuse to evacuate?*"

"Your facility represents a threat to Federation security," Nogura said. "We will destroy it whether you evacuate or not. The choice is yours."

It was not a threat Spock wanted to make, and while he would not admit as much—at least not here on the bridge—he was grateful to the admiral for recognizing the ethical dilemma such an ultimatum forced on him.

Le'tal looked to something beyond the viewscreen's frame before turning to face Spock once more. "*We will evacuate, Commander Spock.*"

"Our sensors are monitoring your communications and main computer," Spock said. "We will know if you attempt any sort of data transfer or emergency sanitation procedure. Take nothing with you and leave. Your five minutes begins now."

Defeated, Le'tal nodded. "*Very well,* Enterprise. *Your mercy in this regard is . . . appreciated.*" Her imaged faded, replaced by that of the outpost perched on its asteroid.

"I doubt that," Nogura said. "Klingons don't tend to look kindly upon those who surrender or otherwise capitulate to an enemy."

While Spock agreed with the admiral's observations, his focus was already moving to other concerns. His gaze drifted to the chronometer set into the console just above the astrogator before him. Rahda had set it for a five-minute countdown, and it was already dropping toward four minutes and thirty seconds.

Spock knew he would spend every single one of those seconds wondering about Captain Kirk and the *Endeavour*.

All that remained for Le'tal was to accept defeat.

She had chosen a seat next to a window in the transport's passenger cabin. Unable to look any of her colleagues in the eye, she instead focused her attention on the oval-shaped portal as the craft lifted away from the landing bay. As the transport banked toward the bay's entrance, she caught sight of the now deserted deck. D'khad, conniving *petaQ* that he was, had departed aboard his own ship within moments of the *Enterprise*'s ultimatum to evacuate the outpost. He had not even offered to carry anyone else with him. Thankfully, the transport already assigned to the facility was more than capable of carrying the entire staff.

"*We will rendezvous with Lieutenant Mak'dav,*" said the transport's pilot over the communications system. The *Enterprise* commander had graciously allowed for the retrieval of crews from both of the damaged scout ships, after which Le'tal and her people were to continue with their exit of the asteroid field.

But first, she was to watch the obliteration of her work.

Not just yours. You are not the only one being wronged here today.

It had taken the efforts of a great many people over a long

period of time to do what she and her team had accomplished here. To act as though she was the only one affected was not just wrong on a factual level, but also unacceptable given her role as the project's director. Le'tal had never been one to deny due credit to deserving individuals, and had always made a point of recognizing noteworthy achievements in front of the entire staff. It was a simple yet effective means of building and maintaining morale, a time-honored tradition observed by all successful leaders. Even Karamaq understood and agreed with her on this, regardless of their lack of shared experiences or how else he might feel about her personally.

And just where is Karamaq?

The thought occurred out of nowhere. In the rush to evacuate the outpost she had somehow neglected to even consider the commander or the two ships he had taken out on patrol. Had they found the *Endeavour*? Le'tal hoped that was not the case. The political situation between the Empire and the Federation was precarious enough without Karamaq escalating the issue with something like this. Indeed, she wondered how much good faith she and her people might have engendered if they had instead acted to assist the Starfleet crew during their time of need. She found it discomforting to realize that she had not even considered this possibility before now. Had her interactions with Karamaq—and D'khad, for that matter—and the stress caused by those encounters blinded her to such an obvious solution?

It was, Le'tal decided, a weak excuse.

A shadow passed over the bulkhead before her and she turned to see No'Khal settling into an adjacent seat. He said nothing, but instead regarded her with that composed, almost paternal expression in which she often sought comfort. This time, however, it served only to heighten her shame.

"And so ends a promising career," she said, pushing herself back into her seat. Even from this angle she was still able to see the outpost as it receded in the distance, now looking so much more like a fragile shell perched atop the asteroid than she had ever seen it. "All of our work, about to be annihilated as though it never existed."

No'Khal eyed her with his usual unwavering patience. "You know that is not entirely true. The original research and design plans are still safe, archived at an Imperial Intelligence records facility. Someone will one day be able to access that information and perhaps begin our work anew."

"Someone," Le'tal said. "But not me."

Despite being forced to leave behind almost all of her personal possessions, Le'tal still had been able to grab the backup data storage cache of her personal computer files. All of her reports, logs, journals, and other documents important to the research and experiments conducted at the outpost were safe in a pocket of the small bag containing those few precious items she was able to pack before No'Khal all but dragged her from her quarters to the landing bay.

"There's something you have not yet needed to learn about our chosen line of work, my friend," he said. "Scientists within the Empire are a commodity. Skilled scientists, even more so. Our glorious leaders are not in the habit of wasting valuable resources. That mentality comes from running a civilization that is always dealing with ongoing problems of resource availability. The Empire finds itself surrounded on almost all sides by adversaries. Our ability to expand and locate resource-rich worlds is limited. This presents a challenge to our leadership, who have learned to be prudent when it comes to conserving valuable assets of every flavor. That includes bright young scientists who hold in their minds ideas and solutions for dealing with our enemies as well as securing our borders."

Le'tal shifted in her seat. "Does that include bright young scientists who fail to accomplish their goals?"

"What failure?" No'Khal gestured toward the porthole. "You succeeded in your mission. You proved a workable concept.

Demonstrated it in theory and practice. The physical manifestation of the work we did here may be lost, but the essence of its value remains. There will be another day for you. Trust me."

Le'tal regarded her dear friend, realizing his words and manner were having their intended effect. "You speak as though setbacks of this type are not unknown to you."

"The stories I could tell you." No'Khal paused, his expression shifting ever so slightly, as though he was recalling a pleasant memory. "Stories I should not tell you, but perhaps I will anyway. What better way to pass the time?"

Before she could answer, flickering light filtered through the porthole and Le'tal turned in her seat to see the first moments of the outpost's destruction. The transport's pilots had angled the craft so the scene was visible to anyone caring to look through their ports on the ship's starboard side. She could not look away as the *Enterprise*, now hovering over the facility, rained several volleys of orange bursts of energy at different points all across the outpost.

"Torpedoes," No'Khal said. He had moved so that he could observe the action through another nearby port. "Most effective."

Le'tal said nothing, her attention riveted on the outpost's quite thorough eradication. The *Enterprise* dispatched another salvo of torpedoes, which turned out to be all that was needed. Whatever remained of the base disappeared in a rapid succession of blasts, which were snuffed out by the vacuum of space, leaving behind only debris scattered to drift in the asteroid field along with a new crater where the outpost once sat.

"So much for that." Settling back into her seat, she returned her attention to No'Khal.

"Not so much an ending as you might think." No'Khal smiled. "Perhaps instead a new beginning."

One can hope, Le'tal decided. *One can only hope.*

Thirty-six

Karamaq was certain he felt his blood coursing through his veins, warming in anticipation.

It had been too long since he last faced an enemy in battle. Not since the previous war with the Federation had he even set foot on a true warship. His career in the time following that ignominious chapter in Klingon history saw to it he was assigned a succession of posts and assignments he often felt were beneath him. Was it punishment for some perceived lapse of honor or duty? The ship on which Karamaq served during the war, the *I.K.S. Tong Vey*, was one of the first vessels to fall to Starfleet adversaries during a battle near the Ophiucus system. While protecting a supply caravan, the *Tong Vey* and other vessels were targeted by the sudden arrival of a single, powerful Starfleet vessel. Though other warships were destroyed, his survived to fight another day. That day never came. The *Tong Vey*'s repairs took longer than anticipated, by which time the war was over as suddenly and inexplicably as it had begun.

Then Karamaq's life fell to disgrace.

His appointment as garrison commander providing security for a band of annoying scientists was but the least objectionable of the assignments he received after the war. At this point, dying with honor in battle was a distant, fanciful dream. Even the scout ships he commanded did not warrant names but merely numbers. Nevertheless, his own personal and family pride

demanded he conduct himself as a proper soldier of the Empire
no matter the task asked of him. It was the only existence he had
ever known, following in the footsteps of his father and generations before him to serve. Others might view his career trajectory as penance, but Karamaq refused to give such judgmental
detractors the satisfaction of seeing him react to their derision.
So long as he wore the uniform of a Klingon warrior, he would
give it the respect that was its due.

And now, perhaps, he might well see his perseverance rewarded on this day.

The bridge of the *wa'* was barely large enough to deserve
such a description. Two seats for the craft's pilots took up most
of the compartment's available space, positioned as they were
before a wide, curved console separating them from the oversized viewscreen. The compartment featured no other stations
and there was no room for another seat or even for Karamaq
to pace. This did nothing to assuage his growing impatience
while he waited for the ship and its companion to reach their
destination.

"How much longer?" He was growing bored with the image
on the viewscreen, which thanks to the sensor data it received
was showing nothing but jagged, unforgiving rock face as the
wa' descended deeper into the canyon.

Seated in the left position, Soriq turned from his controls
and regarded Karamaq. He was more slender than the average
Klingon male soldier, with a bald scalp and a thin mustache that
drooped down along the edges of his mouth.

"We have descended nearly halfway to the bottom of the canyon, Commander."

In the other chair, Bar'not sat hunched over a sensor monitor.
The interface viewer cast a dim orange glow across the young
Klingon's face. Unlike Soriq he had hair, long enough it required
a band to keep it pulled back from his face. The leather tie rested
at the base of his skull and the resulting ponytail fell between his

shoulder blades. When he looked away from his instruments, Karamaq saw the uncertainty in his eyes, and when the younger Klingon spoke, it seemed out of reluctance.

"Our scans are registering the Starfleet cruiser's hull, Commander. There is a power source, and more than four hundred life signs, though from this distance I am unable to distinguish between different species. Some of the life-forms appear to be outside the ship, either on the asteroid surface or in some kind of structure. I am also detecting indications of their own sensors, but they are operating at a reduced level." He looked up from his controls. "The ship has no defenses, Commander."

"Excellent." Karamaq nodded in satisfaction. Destroying the four sensor drones Bar'not detected during their approach was a prudent decision, he decided. Eliminating the *Endeavour's* ability to summon help was useful, of course, but to find it was a helpless target at the bottom of this canyon? The thought made Karamaq smile. The crevasse would serve well enough as the wounded starship's grave.

"Notify the *cha'* we are continuing our descent," Karamaq said, referring to the other scout ship.

Bar'not said, "Commander, I'm registering three ships ascending from the canyon floor." The younger Klingon scowled as he studied his instruments. "They are small personnel transports. Two are Orion, and the other one is a transport of Alpha Centaurian design." Looking up from the console, he cast a confused look at Karamaq. "The Orions are towing the other ship with a tractor beam."

"Orions." Karamaq knew of the aborted raid against the *Endeavour* orchestrated by D'zinn, the foolish captain of that Orion scow assisting Doctor Le'tal with her testing of the disruption-field technology. At least, so far as he knew, that attack had failed, so what was this? Though his combat instincts may have been dulled by being away from battle, he was still suspicious. "Are they armed?"

"Their weapons and shields are not active, Commander," Bar'not replied.

Karamaq grunted, unsure what to make of this. "Raise our shields and place weapons on standby."

"One of the Orion vessels is hailing us," Soriq said.

This should be interesting, Karamaq thought. "On-screen."

The image on the viewscreen changed to that of a burly Orion male. Karamaq recognized him as Netal, D'zinn's second-in-command aboard the *Vekal Piltari*.

"Commander. It is good to see you. We have effected an escape from the Federation ship, but most of my people are still being held hostage. Your arrival is most fortunate, and we would be grateful for your assistance."

Something about the Orion's demeanor bothered Karamaq, but he could not identify the source of his discomfort. He was stiff, and the tone and delivery of his speech seemed somehow forced. Nevertheless, the worries of a troubled Orion did not concern him.

"This is not a rescue mission, Orion. I act on behalf of the Klingon Empire, to which that ship represents a threat. I see you've claimed a prize. Take it and consider it compensation for your loss."

Now Netal's manner seemed genuine. He leaned closer to the screen's visual pickup, his expression turning irate. *"You would kill my people? After what we have done to help you?"*

"You and your people were useful for a time," Karamaq replied. "No longer."

Netal drew in a long, deep breath. *"D'zinn knew you would betray us at the first opportunity. She never trusted you, Klingon."*

"D'zinn should have come to that realization sooner. She might have avoided paying such a price for her ineptitude. Instead she is soon to find herself answering to her own superiors for her failures." Karamaq stepped closer to the screen. "You, on the other hand, have an opportunity of your own. Break off your approach and leave immediately. Take your salvage with you, and consider yourself fortunate."

"*No, I do not believe I will do any of that, Klingon.*" Netal's angered visage lingered for an extra beat before the connection was severed, restoring the image of the two Orion transports and their captured vessel.

Bar'not jerked in his seat, turning from his console. "Commander! One of the ships has launched something. It is too small to be a missile or torpedo."

"Show me." Karamaq looked back to the viewscreen in time to see six diminutive objects arcing away from one of the Orion ships. They seemed inconsequential. Was this a ploy of some kind?

Then they struck the *wa*'s shields.

"Some kind of energy surge!" Soriq called out. His fingers moved across his controls in response to the sudden change. "It is feeding off the shields themselves. Registering a massive feedback through the shield generators." His warning was accompanied by alarms sounding in the cramped bridge and a series of alert indicators flaring to life across the helm console. "Our shields are down!"

Sitting in the *Dreamline*'s pilot seat, Kirk smiled as the electromagnetic-pulse emitters wreaked havoc on the Klingon ship. On one of the helm console's sensor monitors, he watched as the second set of emitters, launched by Lieutenant Sulu from one of the captured Orion transports, unleashed similar chaos on the second Klingon vessel.

"Remind me to thank the Andorian Guard the next time I see them." Kirk reached for the console, keying a communications frequency. "Kirk to Sulu and McCormack. It's showtime."

In response to his command, the tractor beams holding the *Dreamline* in position between and behind the Orion ships deactivated, leaving the transport free to navigate. Kirk raced through the process of bringing the craft's engines online. On the console's targeting scanner he noted the Orion ships breaking away, their own shields and weapons activating. With Sulu and McCormack each flying one of the transports, they along with the *Dreamline* now formed a hasty trio of ships poised to defend the *Endeavour*. He also watched as the two Klingon scouts, already recovering from the unexpected attack, split away from each other.

"Just like we talked about, pilots," Kirk said. "Take it to them and keep them off the *Endeavour*." Looking over his shoulder, he added, "Commander Stano, I could use your assistance."

In the seat next to him, Netal muttered something unintelligible. His mood likely was not helped by the phaser pointed at his head courtesy of Commander Katherine Stano. The *Endeavour*'s first officer stood just to the left of the doorway of the *Dreamline*'s cockpit, out of frame for the communication system's visual pickup.

"Up and out of there, big boy," Stano said, gesturing with her phaser for the Orion to stand up. "For what it's worth, I'm sorry the Klingons screwed you over."

Netal glowered first at Kirk before turning his attention to Stano. Behind the first officer, a pair of *Endeavour* security officers stood with phasers at the ready. "And you? What are your intentions?"

Holstering her phaser as the security guards took custody of the Orion, Stano slid into the copilot's seat. "Captain Khatami gave her word. You and your people won't be harmed. Of course, her word won't matter if we can't keep the Klingons off our backs." She pointed a thumb toward the cockpit doorway. "Guards, secure our guest." Once Netal and his escorts were gone and she was able to study the helm console's status readouts, she looked to Kirk. "Captain, you have to know your reputation precedes you. So, with that in mind and on a scale of one to Kirk, how crazy is this plan?"

Though his attention remained on his controls, Kirk could not hold back a small grin. "I'll admit it's up there."

The idea to use the pulse emitters had been Lieutenant Uhura's, once the *Endeavour*'s engineers recovered and studied the devices following the Orion assault on the ship. Realizing the nonlethal weapons could be used again seemed to have no constructive purpose at the time, but with the crippled starship's deflector shields inoperative and a Klingon attack on the way, necessity and desperation had joined forces to prompt this unorthodox action. Mounting the launchers captured during the Orion raid was a simple matter, with deployment of the emitters routed from each launcher's control pad to the helm console of their respective ships. Kirk's plan was that the tactic might distract the Klingons long enough to buy time for the *Endeavour*'s engineering team to restore the shields. That the insane scheme had worked even better than he hoped was a bonus. The question now was whether he and the team he had assembled for this task could seize the advantage given to them.

We're about to find out, aren't we?

With the power-up process complete, Kirk guided the *Dreamline* on a course away from the canyon wall. He divided his attention between the helm controls and the targeting scanner, trying to track the Orion and Klingon ships. Everyone, it seemed, had made the smart decision to pull up and out of the canyon, preferring to risk the asteroid field rather than the canyon and its much tighter quarters. Of course, this now meant everyone would have to be aware of the asteroids as well as their respective adversaries.

Never a dull moment.

"I can keep tabs on them," Stano said. Despite getting a very brief tutorial from Sulu and McCormack on the transport's operation, the *Endeavour*'s first officer was an accomplished pilot in her own right. This made the learning curve easier but Kirk could tell from her voice she remained somewhat apprehensive. "And I've got sensors and weapons, too."

Though he was not Sulu, Kirk still considered himself a fair pilot. The unfamiliar controls took some getting used to but skill, experience, and even instinct helped him settle into handling the transport. He had worried about not being able to get the *Dreamline*'s engines up and running in the event the ploy with the emitters failed to disrupt the Klingons, but so far the transport was behaving itself.

"Weapons at ready status," Stano said. "We're still not a fighter ship, but at least we've got shields. That puts us one up on the Klingons."

"*Sulu to Captain Kirk,*" said the *Enterprise* helm officer over the intercom. "*They're starting to get a little cranky out here, sir.*"

Kirk exchanged glances with Stano. "Time to get in the game."

Coordinating his effort with Sulu's, he guided the transport into a low banking turn, bringing the craft's nose around so that one of the Klingon ships came into view. The Orion ship piloted by Sulu was giving chase, attempting to maneuver in behind the other vessel. Meanwhile, the Klingon ship was barreling toward one of the larger asteroids in the distance.

"*McCormack here,*" said the *Endeavour* helm officer. "*I think we made them mad with that little trick of ours. Our bogey is trying to get a lock on us. I don't know how long I can keep them off our tails.*"

Ahead of the *Dreamline*, Kirk watched as Sulu's ship unleashed a pair of salvos toward the Klingon scout. One of the disruptor beams impacted against the unprotected vessel's hull even as the enemy ship arced up and to port in a bid to escape. A quick look to the targeting scanner told him Sulu was doing a decent job keeping his quarry on the run. McCormack, on the other hand, was on the receiving end of similar harassment.

"Hang in there, McCormack," he said, punching controls and breaking off his pursuit. "We're coming."

Stano said, "Shields or no, these ships weren't designed to go up against Klingons. At least not for very long."

"I know." Kirk felt his jaw clench. "But they just need to do it long enough."

Thirty-seven

"He's a Klingon."

Atish Khatami watched Anthony Leone frown at his tricorder as he waved its portable scanner over the head of Lieutenant Ivan Tompkins. The *Endeavour*'s chief medical officer was rarely a happy person, but it was obvious the readings he was getting from his scans of the engineer were doing nothing to improve his mood.

"Surgically altered," Leone continued. "Pretty damned good job of it too." He gestured past Khatami to where Morgan Binnix and Phil Watson stood just outside the brig cell. "Even better than the job done on them, and that wasn't shabby at all. I'm still not sure how he was able to fool my medical scanners in sickbay." He regarded Tomkins. "Anything you want to offer?"

The prisoner said nothing, though his gaze shifted for the briefest of moments to Binnix and Watson. Khatami saw the corner of his mouth twitch, as though he was suppressing a sneer at the sight of the two agents who still sported their Klingon features.

For his part, Tomkins—more accurately, the Klingon transformed to look like someone named Ivan Tomkins—glowered at Khatami. He had said nothing since being revived from the effects of Lieutenant Brax's phaser. Now he sat, restrained at the wrists and ankles to a chair and seemingly content not to utter another word for all eternity.

"How long have you been aboard my ship?" Khatami asked. With her arms folded across her chest, she paced around the room in a circle with Tomkins at its center. "Did you replace the real Lieutenant Tomkins? Hell, was Lieutenant Tomkins even a real person, or just a fabricated identity?"

Tomkins remained silent. He no longer even looked at her, but instead fixed his stare at the wall in front of him.

Only through the efforts of Lieutenants Estrada and Uhura had they even been able to expose him. After discovering his latest transmission intended for anyone who might be listening, the communications officers were able to determine the signal's point of origin, and send a hail to that location. Tracking that signal to its recipient led them to the impulse deck and the communicator in Tomkins' pocket. Despite their ingenuity, it had not been in time to prevent the damage the spy inflicted on the *Endeavour*'s already beleaguered deflector-shield system.

Standing in a corner of the brig behind Khatami, Lieutenant Brax said, "This is most unfortunate, but perhaps the situation is contained. We know Klingon agents have been operating within the Federation and Starfleet for many years. Based on what Starfleet Intelligence has been able to learn, operatives of this sort are deployed as individuals rather than teams. In theory, this reduces the likelihood of their activities being detected." The Edoan paused, shifting his stance on his trio of feet. "Regrettably, I am not well versed in such matters."

"None of us are." Khatami paused her pacing as she came to stand in front of Tomkins. "I don't have time for this nonsense right now. What else have you done to sabotage my ship? Another bomb? Something else rigged to overload?" She stepped closer, and when she spoke this time she allowed menace to creep into her voice. "Have you killed any more of my people?"

Once more, Tomkins offered no reply.

"Tell me what I need to know to keep my people safe," she said, her eyes still fixed on his. "If I lose one more person because of something you've done, there won't be anything of you left for Starfleet Intelligence to interrogate."

As expected, Tomkins stared straight ahead. He did not move; did not blink. He barely breathed. If Khatami did not know better, she would swear he had lapsed into a coma with his eyes open.

It took every ounce of her willpower for Khatami not to place her boot in the center of the man's chest and kick him over. She briefly considered what it might feel like to beat him to a pulp and then order Brax to jettison him to the asteroid's surface. None of that would happen, of course, but she could not help the ugly thoughts. Guilt quickly replaced fury and shame beset sorrow as she stared at the spy who wore the face of someone she had once trusted.

Exasperated, Khatami stepped back from him; she held her arms at her sides, forcing herself to deny Tomkins the satisfaction of seeing her clench her fists. "What the hell are we supposed to do with him?"

"Starfleet Intelligence will want him," Binnix replied. "It's not often we capture one of these bastards, let alone get to hold them long enough to get anything useful out of them."

Brax said, "Agent Binnix is correct. The last time Starfleet discovered such a spy, he was extradited back to the Klingon Empire. Of course, he was exposed in front of many witnesses on a Federation space station with an abundance of civilian traffic. That is not the case with Lieutenant Tomkins here."

"What he's trying to tell you," Watson said, "is there's no one around to know you're about to be delivered to a deep, dark hole from which there's probably no escape, and sooner or later you'll tell everything you know to anyone you can get to listen." He leaned forward, his expression turning sinister. "And believe me when I tell you the journey will be a lot more memorable for you than the destination."

Khatami did not even want to consider the implications of

what Watson described. Was it bravado? A bluff with the aim of unsettling their prisoner? Perhaps it really was the truth, a brutal, unwelcome truth that for reasons she did not want to fathom constituted the reality behind the mission of Starfleet Intelligence and other covert agencies. She did not want to believe such things were possible in this day and age; they did not have a place in the enlightened society she had sworn to protect.

She knew better. In this moment, she almost did not care.

Almost.

Doing her best to rein in her volatile emotions, Khatami turned for the door. "Keep him here." She looked first to Brax before giving one last glare to Tomkins. "Give my people any reason at all and you'll take a walk outside to join the Orions. I hope you can hold your breath."

Her communicator beeped before she could say anything else, and she pulled it from her waist and flipped it open. "Khatami here."

"Klisiewicz, Captain. We're getting updated reports from Commander Stano. They've engaged the Klingon ships. The trick to sabotage their shields worked, but it's still a dogfight. Stano's worried they can't hold the line long enough."

If the lieutenant was experiencing any tension at the prospect of sitting down here with the rest of the crew, wholly vulnerable to a possible Klingon attack, Khatami decided he was doing a fine job hiding such feelings. She almost envied him.

Along with Leone, Binnix, and Watson, Khatami stepped out of the room, waiting for its doors to close before continuing the conversation.

"What's the word on the shields?"

The *Endeavour*'s science officer replied, *"Still nothing from the impulse deck, Captain."*

Behind her, Phil Watson said, "Maybe I can help." When Khatami turned toward him, she saw that he along with Binnix and Leone were regarding her. Watson held out his hands. "At this point it can't hurt, right?"

Frowning, Binnix shrugged. "Same here, Captain. We'd like to try."

Khatami used a thumb to point down the corridor. "Go."

Nodding in thanks, the agents took off at a run down the passageway, heading for the nearest access ladder and leaving Khatami alone with Leone. The doctor looked at her with his usual expression of resting discomfort.

"If you ask me to try and fix that thing, you may as well set the self-destruct right now."

"Lucky for you that's not even an option anymore." Raising her communicator closer to her mouth, Khatami said, "Klisie-wicz, you and Estrada get on whatever's left of our comm systems. Find me a way to contact the *Enterprise*. We've still got at least one of those buoys left, right?" She knew the sensor buoys were gone, destroyed either by the Orions or the Klingons. "Let's get that damned thing flying."

The science officer replied, *"We can launch it and reprogram it in flight. Let's just hope the Klingons don't shoot it down. We're on it, Captain."*

"I'll be on the impulse deck. Keep me posted." Snapping shut her communicator, Khatami turned to Leone. The doctor stared at her with obvious empathy. Then he offered one of his trademark sardonic smiles.

"Just another fun day at the office, am I right?"

"Right."

Leaving a pair of security guards to guard the entrance to the brig and Leone to return to sickbay or wherever he felt he might be needed, Khatami jogged down the corridor until she reached an access ladder. From there it was an easy climb up two levels to reach the impulse deck. She charged into the compartment to find it an even greater scene of chaos than during her last visit. All around the room, members of the *Endeavour*'s engineering team had pulled open consoles, junction boxes, equipment lockers, and even parts of the impulse engine manifolds and other components of the propulsion system. Tools and cabling littered the floor. Legs disappeared into access panels, attached to engineers working on something within the beleaguered ship's innards that Khatami could not see.

She was just in time to see sparks erupt from one of the consoles that had been reconfigured to oversee the deflector shield controls. Standing in front of the console, Master Chief Petty Officer Christine Rideout ducked and rolled away from the workstation to avoid being caught by sparks or debris. She landed heavily on one knee before allowing herself to collapse to a sitting position on the deck.

"Son of a *bitch*!"

Khatami lurched forward to help, but Morgan Binnix and Phil Watson, working together at an adjacent console, got there first. They each extended hands to Rideout and the engineer took them, allowing the agents to pull her to her feet.

"You all right, Master Chief?" Khatami asked as she stepped closer.

"Only hurt my pride and my ass, Captain." Rideout swiped her left arm across her forehead, using her sleeve to wipe away perspiration. Her damp black hair was matted to her head and streaks of dirt ran down the sides of her face. With her right hand she pointed with the macrotool she still held toward the damaged console. "You can kiss that relay goodbye. We just overloaded the entire bank of transtators and the flow regulator."

"We don't have any replacements?" Binnix asked.

Rideout grimaced. "I think we've got another couple of regulators. What I don't know is if we've got enough spare transtators." Looking to Binnix and Watson, she said, "Find me thirty of those damned things. Pull them from any system that's not keeping us alive right now."

"They might not all match," Watson said.

Waving away the observation, Rideout said, "At this point, I'll take anything that can carry current. We'll figure out how to configure whatever you find me." As the agents moved to carry out their new task, the engineer looked to Khatami. "Get anything useful out of Tomkins?"

"He's a Klingon," Khatami replied.

"That just makes a perfect day even better." Rideout stepped closer to where two junior engineers were assessing the damage from inside the monitoring station. "Without a way to control the power flow from the impulse engines to the shield generators—which is what this hunk of crap is supposed to be doing—we can't risk bringing them online. They'll blow apart and take nice chunks of neighboring hull with them, and anybody in the vicinity is a goner."

Khatami rubbed her forehead. "We're running out of time to play it safe, Master Chief. I don't know how long Stano and Kirk can keep the Klingons off our backs. Whatever you're going to do, do it fast. Otherwise, the only thing that'll be left to do is die."

"On the bright side," Rideout said, "that'll likely be fast too."

"I knew you were an optimist, Master Chief."

Rideout chuckled. "Captain, I've survived two ships crashing with me along for the ride. This is nothing."

Thirty-eight

Kirk was getting tired of this game.

"To port!"

Katherine Stano's warning came an instant before the helm console's proximity alarm sounded, alerting him to the danger of colliding with an asteroid. He saw it in his peripheral vision, looming to his right as he guided the *Dreamline* into a sudden turn. The maneuver required an almost instant compensation in some other direction as he found himself steering the ship toward still another hunk of drifting rock.

After assisting Lieutenant McCormack against the Klingon scout ship pursuing her, exchanging the roles of hunter and prey with their adversaries was beginning to take its toll. This part of the asteroid field was much denser than the area closer to the *Endeavour*'s crash site. If it was foolhardy to draw the Klingon scout ship here in a bid to keep it from any attempt at attacking the helpless starship, it was all but insane to do so at the transport's present speed. Kirk had accelerated the *Dreamline* to one-quarter impulse power, counting on instrumentation and his own reflexes to avoid catastrophe. He had given brief thought to allowing the ship's computer to handle navigating the flurry of obstacles, but could not bring himself to fully trust the automated systems in a situation such as the one he and Stano now faced.

"They had to slow down," she said, before tapping a sequence of controls on her station. The targeting scanner now showed

Kirk the Klingon scout ship decelerating in order to avoid plowing into the asteroid the *Dreamline* avoided by a narrow margin. Indeed, he was certain he could have reached through the cockpit canopy and brushed his fingers across the rock's surface as they passed.

Using the momentary break in the constant pursuit, Kirk pushed the transport into a course around the asteroid before kicking away and accelerating. The ship's engines groaned in protest at the abuse they were receiving, but Kirk ignored the accompanying warning status lights. He had seen the Orion transport piloted by Lieutenant McCormack enter the targeting scanner's rangefinder, noting how the *Endeavour* helm officer was using the asteroid for cover even as it closed the distance with the Klingon scout.

"Oh, Marielise, you sneaky devil," said Stano. "You see what she's doing, right?"

Kirk nodded. "I think so." At this range, there was no way the enemy ship did not see the Orion vessel coming at it, but each vessel's respective course through the asteroid field saw to it there were only limited navigation options. Using this to her advantage, McCormack treated the field like a maze, choosing the correct path that led to her goal. There were few places for the Klingon ship to go that did not expose it to almost immediate danger from nearby asteroids. Its captain would have to choose which adversary to go after, with either option leaving the scout vulnerable to attack.

"She's good," Kirk said.

Stano grunted. "Damned right, she is. Just don't tell her."

Using the targeting scanner to plan his next move as the *Dreamline* broke into a far less dense area of the asteroid field, Kirk applied greater acceleration. He knew he would only have a few seconds before the Klingon ship matched his move and began closing in for an attack. Adjusting the transport's course, he aimed it for a much smaller asteroid near the edge of another grouping.

"If you're doing what I think you're doing," Stano said, "that looks like a pretty tight fit."

Kirk kept his eyes on his instruments and the scanner. "That's what I'm counting on."

He waited until the proximity alarm cried out for attention once again before cutting speed as the *Dreamline* closed to less than two hundred kilometers, and then he directed the ship on a curving dive that took it under the asteroid. According to the scans, the drifting rock was a few dozen kilometers across at its widest point. It took only seconds to navigate that distance before Kirk accelerated again, arcing the transport up and over the top of the asteroid. Had he correctly timed his maneuver?

More adjustments rolled the transport over, bringing the Klingon scout into view just as it was attempting to mimic Kirk's tactic. Stano did not wait, firing the *Dreamline*'s phasers at the oncoming ship. The salvo caught the other ship with a direct strike against its primary hull. Evidence of the damage was immediate, with sliced hull plating just below where Kirk knew the ship's bridge was situated.

"Nice shooting, Commander," Kirk said.

Stano replied, "He's taking evasive action."

The enemy ship veered away in what the *Dreamline*'s targeting scanner told Kirk had to be an attempt to reach cover back in the asteroid field. It was the scout pilot's bad luck that his quick maneuvering brought him into the weapon sights of Lieutenant McCormack's ship. The *Endeavour* pilot unleashed full disruptors on the other vessel, with multiple strikes tearing into the scout's hull. Kirk watched its impulse engines flicker and die and the ship's nose drop as its pilot lost maneuvering ability.

"Damn it."

Kirk watched the Klingon vessel plunge toward an asteroid, inertia guiding it into a collision course from which it could not escape. It took only seconds for the vessel to close the distance before it impacted on the asteroid's surface.

Stano released a long, slow breath. "It was him or us, sir."

"Doesn't mean I have to be happy about it."

As Kirk took to the helm console once more, the cockpit's communications system crackled to life.

"Sulu to Captain Kirk. We could use some help here! I can't shake this Klingon ship."

Redirecting the *Dreamline* on a course back to the *Endeavour* crash site, Kirk replied, "We're on our way, Sulu." The flight through the asteroid field had taken them some distance from the ship.

"I can plot us a speed course back," Stano said. "The way you fly, it won't take us long at all to get there."

Kirk nodded as he reset the targeting scanner for a wider range. It took a moment for the system to recalculate based on the *Dreamline*'s position relative to the *Endeavour*, and when the image coalesced he could see the remaining Klingon scout on its relentless pursuit course of Sulu's ship. Somehow, the *Enterprise* helm officer had managed to stay fairly close to the crash site while continuing to evade his adversary.

"We're hit!" Sulu's cry of alarm barked from the intercom. *"We've lost impulse power. I'm trying to use maneuvering thrusters to bring us back under control."*

Stano pointed to the targeting scanner. "Captain, look."

The compact readout showed an icon representing Sulu's ship slowing almost to a stop while another symbol, this one depicting the Klingon scout, seemed to increase its speed as it pulled away from its quarry.

"They're going after the *Endeavour*," Kirk said. "And they're still a sitting duck."

Atish Khatami had certainly considered her own death by various means on various occasions over the course of her career. Such a possibility was an unfortunate reality one simply accepted as part of life in Starfleet. She had imagined dying on the bridge of her ship during a fierce battle or falling to an enemy attack on a planet's surface, or even just a simple accident while exploring a newly discovered world. Unpleasant images of hull breaches, alien contagions, and illnesses of the sort that still plagued her species haunted her thoughts every now and then.

Never, in all her years of service, did Khatami ever imagine dying in an engine room while holding a power cable attached to what for all intents and purposes was a live bomb.

"All right, everybody," said Master Chief Rideout, who was holding on to another section of the same cable with which Khatami had agreed to help. "We're almost there." The engineer had her other hand inside the access panel to the damaged console overseeing the deflector shield controls. All around her were pieces of burned, broken, or simply discarded components. The cable in Khatami's hands led into the access panel, before which stood Rideout and Phil Watson. Standing next to the agent was his colleague, Binnix, who held a macrotool in one hand and a fistful of transtators in the other.

"What about these?" Binnix asked, holding up the transtators.

Without looking, Rideout replied, "Forget them."

Binnix cast a glance in Khatami's direction before looking at the components in her hand. "You don't even know what—"

"Doesn't matter," Rideout snapped. "No points for cuteness now."

Watson asked, "We're all going to die, aren't we?"

"Could be." Rideout pulled herself from the access panel. "But I really am hoping to avoid that."

"Master Chief?" Khatami prompted. "What's going on?"

Stepping over to the nearby workstation, Rideout began keying several of the multicolored buttons. "There's no time to configure the replacement transtators to work with this setup. There's too much damage to the flow-regulation subsystems, and half of the damned things would likely blow with the power demand anyway. So I reconfigured the distribution nodes on a second impulse capacitance cell and tied it directly to the shield generator's flow regulator, bypassing all that other junk."

Peering inside the conduit, Khatami eyed the squat, gray hexagonal cylinder. The cable she held was attached to one end, while another length of cabling ran from its other end deeper into the innards of the shield control system.

"That sounds like a lot of things that add up to something I'm really not going to like," she said. "Sound about right?"

"Sounds exactly right." Rideout glanced over her shoulder and gestured to the cable in Khatami's hands. "You can let go of that now."

The captain did as she was asked, and the cable dropped to the deck. Connected as it was from the access panel to another conduit on the opposite wall, there was no way for Khatami to know what Rideout had just joined together.

"It bleeds off the excess energy that will come through the cell," Rideout said. "Instead of just letting it go, I'm channeling it to another power relay feeding the shield generators." She looked at Khatami again. "Beats letting it loose in here and cooking all of us."

"Do we want to be somewhere else when you turn this on?" Binnix asked.

Rideout nodded. "I would. I like the Bahamas myself. Or Pacifica. That's a nice tropical planet. Maybe I'll go there if I live through this."

"Take me with you," Watson said.

"It's a date."

"*Auxiliary control to engineering,*" said Lieutenant Klisiewicz over the intercom, which Rideout had ordered restored so she and her people would not have to fumble with personal communicators. "*Sensors are picking up a Klingon ship descending into the canyon. Two of our ships are in pursuit but it looks like the Klingons will get here first. We need those shields!*"

Watson groaned in irritation. "We haven't even had time to run a diagnostic to make sure we got all the connections right."

Eyeing the ramshackle setup that was the culmination of frantic effort on the part of Rideout with the assistance of Binnix and Watson, Khatami felt her mouth go dry. "Master Chief, we're out of time."

Rideout offered a small, humorless smile as she reached for the topmost row of controls on her console. "Sometimes you just have to say 'what the hell,' am I right?" She tapped one button that blinked a steady red.

Nothing happened.

Thirty-nine

"I'm still not picking up any sign of shields from the *Endeavour*," Stano said. "What the hell are they doing down there?"

Pushing the *Dreamline* into an angled descent, Kirk could see a small circle of light all alone in the darkness outside the cockpit canopy. He knew it was the *Endeavour*, at the far end of the canyon but growing larger with every passing second as the transport dropped ever lower. Below them, and effecting its own dive into the valley, was a much smaller light plunging toward the helpless starship. The Klingon scout's pilot was exceptional, he decided, employing a series of evasive maneuvers that within the canyon's confines were as impressive as they were audacious.

"*Enterprise*," he said into the newly established comm frequency. "Spock, where are you? We're running out of time down here."

Over the open channel, his first officer replied, "*Estimated time of arrival is one minute, forty-three seconds, Captain.*"

"This will be over before that," Stano said.

Nobody needed to say aloud what everyone knew was at stake. A single strafing run against the unprotected *Endeavour*'s already stressed and weakened hull would be devastating.

Ignoring Stano's comment, Kirk said into the pickup, "McCormack, did you reach Sulu and the others?"

The *Endeavour*'s helm officer replied, "*We're maneuvering into position now, sir. There doesn't look to be any hull damage, but the ship's on emergency power. We're in an area of pretty high background radiation, so I'm getting in as close as possible before engaging transporters."*

The lieutenant did not need to say anything else for Kirk to know this meant McCormack and her ship were too far out of position to be of any assistance. Given the damage to the Orion transport piloted by Sulu, there had been no choice but for McCormack or Kirk to break off and attempt a rescue. McCormack suggested her own commandeered Orion vessel was better suited to that effort and Kirk had agreed, so now he and Stano were making a run for the *Endeavour* crash site in an attempt to head off the remaining Klingon ship.

It was a sound plan except for one problem. Even with the refinements given to it by Montgomery Scott, the *Dreamline* was not a combat vessel. This was a definite drawback when confronting a Klingon craft built for that very purpose. Back in the asteroid field, Kirk could use its hordes of obstacles to counteract the enemy ship's greater speed and maneuverability. In open space or even something like a dive toward the bottom of an asteroid canyon, the scout had all the advantages.

"Kirk!"

Stano's warning came just as he saw the scout make an abrupt change of direction, peeling up and away from its mad descent into the canyon and away from the *Endeavour*. Now it was climbing, and the helm console's targeting scanner showed the ship beginning to climb and angle back toward them.

"Somebody doesn't like being chased," Kirk said. This far into the canyon, there were few options available so far as evasive action. He therefore decided aggressive action was preferable to retreat, and increased the *Dreamline*'s speed. Even though they were only traveling at a bare fraction of available impulse power, the slight acceleration was enough to make him nervous. The feeling only worsened as he adjusted the transport's heading to place it on a collision course with the Klingon ship.

Stano pushed herself back into her seat. "Okay, this plan just went all the way to Kirk, didn't it?"

"Afraid so."

The targeting scanner indicated a phaser lock and Stano unleashed another barrage of phaser fire. The twin beams of blue-white energy passed just beneath the scout as Kirk cut the *Dreamline* to port. His fast maneuvering was still too slow to avoid a volley of disruptor bolts slamming into the transport's aft shields. The salvo was followed by a second round, and with the third attack, alarms erupted across the cockpit. Kirk almost flinched as the enemy ship passed close enough to the cockpit's canopy he was sure he could see seams between individual hull plates. All the while, caution alerts were sounding from different indicators on the helm console and the surrounding status monitors. Then all of the lights went out as the power of the *Dreamline*'s impulse engine faded. There was a pause before the ship's backup generator activated, bringing with it emergency lighting and power back to the cockpit.

"Main power's out," Stano said.

Kirk said nothing. He was too busy using the transport's maneuvering thrusters to regain control of its descent into the canyon. "We've got bigger problems. I can't get a diagnostic on the impulse engine. Shield generators are out too."

After a futile attempt to glean more information out of her own console's array of status readings, Stano said, "If they come back to take another swing, we're screwed."

"They're not interested in us." Kirk pointed to the targeting scanner, which only now was coming back online after the shift to emergency power. The tactical diagram showed the Klingon scout returning to its dive toward the canyon floor.

"Kirk to *Endeavour*," he said after activating a communications frequency. "You need to get those damned shields up right now."

Khatami could only watch as Rideout, assisted by Binnix and Watson, tore even more components out of the deflector shield power-flow regulation system. She had no idea how much of the housing's internal structure was even intact anymore.

"Have you figured out what went wrong?" she asked.

Buried past her shoulders inside the open panel giving her access to the system's innards, Rideout said, "That was the easy part. The power flow to the shield generators was high enough to trip a fault-protection circuit. Actually, it tripped four of them." Pushing herself out of the conduit, Rideout reached for a spanner before sticking her head back through the open port. "I guess that'll happen."

"We didn't think of this before?" Binnix asked.

"In my defense, I was busy bypassing a bunch of stuff we can't fix or replace just now. I'm trying to save all our asses. You want it now or you want it pretty?"

Khatami moved closer. "Okay, Master Chief. What do we do?"

"We bypass everything."

"What?" said Watson, who at Rideout's direction had returned with a second impulse capacitance cell from storage. "What does 'everything' mean?"

Once again extracting herself from the conduit, Rideout grabbed the short gray cylinder from the agent. "I mean everything. These cells have their own flow regulators. I can connect them in sequence and bypass their safeties a lot easier than I can reconfigure the shield generator system." She paused, as though for the first time considering the idea to which she had just given voice. "On the other hand, there won't be anything to keep them from blowing up in our faces." Then the engineer shrugged. "Kind of late to be worrying about that now."

With Binnix's help, Rideout maneuvered the capacitance cell through the access panel and into position next to its companion inside the conduit. Together, they connected the cells and routed cabling to power connections and transfer relays, and Khatami saw control panels on each of the cells flare to life.

"Auxiliary control to Captain Khatami," said Lieutenant Klisiewicz over the intercom. *"Incoming Klingon ship. Its weapons are active and locked on us!"*

Using the *Dreamline's* maneuvering thrusters, Kirk managed to put the transport into something approximating a controlled freefall toward the bottom of the canyon. With almost total darkness all around the cockpit canopy, the only visible light sources outside the ship were the *Endeavour's* saucer section and the Klingon scout. The enemy vessel had returned to its descent, now angling for what could only be a strafing run against the defenseless starship.

"The impulse engine's completely offline," Stano said as she returned to the cockpit and hauled herself back into the copilot's seat. "I can't even get a diagnostic to run." Looking through the canopy, she asked, "Can you land this thing?"

Kirk applied more power to the maneuvering thrusters in response to the ship's sensors and the information they provided about the ground below them. "Landing isn't the issue. *Crash*-landing might be a bit of a problem." It had been a long time since he had flown anything larger than a Starfleet shuttlecraft, and as the transport made its descent he could feel its weight fighting him. "Kirk to *Enterprise*. Where the hell are you?"

Spock replied, *"Estimated arrival in thirty-five seconds, Captain."*

Still not good enough! The infuriating thought was almost enough to make him slam his fists against the helm console, for all the good that would do. To be so close and yet so helpless was a maddening feeling. It was not one for which Kirk had any patience. There had to be some option left to him. *Any* kind of option. Whatever it might be, he could not see it. They could not even spare the power needed to fire the *Dreamline*'s phasers in one last futile attempt to stop the Klingon ship.

Consulting her instruments, Stano said, "They're lining up for an attack and locking disruptors." Unlike Kirk, she did not restrain herself from hitting her console and instead slapped it with the heels of both her hands.

Neither said anything as the Klingon ship unleashed a volley of disruptor fire. Four shots, pulsing bright crimson, rained down toward the *Endeavour* and Kirk braced himself for the devastation he was already imagining.

All four disruptor bolts didn't detonate against the starship's hull; instead, a violent surge of yellow-white energy spread outward from the point of impact, revealing the protective blanket of the *Endeavour*'s deflector shields.

"Hot damn!" Stano smacked her console again, this time in triumph. "They did it!"

It was evident the pilot of the Klingon ship was not expecting that turn of events, having already adjusted the scout's course to take it up and away from whatever destruction its gunner must have anticipated. Kirk, still unable to do anything but control the *Dreamline*'s descent, grunted in mounting frustration as he watched the enemy vessel arc back toward the crash site, already setting up for a second attack.

Then it shuddered under the onslaught of what Kirk immediately recognized as Starfleet phasers.

"Spock!" he shouted into the comm link. "Welcome to the party, *Enterprise*!"

Looking up through the cockpit canopy, Kirk and Stano saw the starship—his ship—dropping into the canyon. Phaser banks mounted on the saucer section's underside flashed again, catching the Klingon ship amidships. The other ship broke off its attack and Kirk saw it was struggling to retain its altitude.

"Their main power's offline," Stano reported, her attention focused on her sensor screen. "I'm showing a hull breach in the aft section. Their life-support system's fluctuating as well and I'm seeing outages in their navigation and guidance systems. They're in big trouble, sir."

Having arrested the *Dreamline*'s descent, Kirk now was reasonably certain the transport would not plow into the canyon floor. After asking Stano to find them a decent landing site, he tapped the communications controls.

"Klingon vessel, this is Captain James Kirk of the *Starship Enterprise*. There's no reason to keep up this fight. We stand ready to assist you if you'll accept our help."

Stano eyed him. "I don't think I could be as nice, sir. They *did* just try to kill my crew right in front of me."

"Fair enough," Kirk said.

One of the smaller display monitors set into the bulkhead to his left and near the edge of the canopy activated, its image coalescing into that of a Klingon male. His appearance was disheveled and Kirk saw small fires burning at two of the consoles behind him.

"*I am Commander Karamaq of the Klingon Defense Force.*" When he spoke it was with clipped tones, and the anxiety was evident in his voice. "*Do you truly expect me to believe you would help us after your ship just crippled mine?*" He turned from the screen, barking orders Kirk could not understand.

"They're losing attitude control," Stano said.

Through the canopy, Kirk saw the Klingon ship tumbling away, its arc and speed taking it away from the *Endeavour* crash site. Instrumentation told him the vessel was no more than a few hundred meters above the canyon surface, but its spin was increasing as it fell.

"Spock, tractor beam. Lock on and bring them to a safe—"

The rest of the order died in Kirk's throat as the Klingon ship, now several kilometers from the *Endeavour*, plummeted the remaining distance to the canyon floor. Its aft section struck first, hitting near the edge of yet another crevasse. The rest of the vessel collapsed in on itself and the entire hull rolled over the ravine's edge. A brief fireball consumed the ship, gone as quickly as it had come, as the scout vessel disappeared with the resulting wreckage out of sight.

"Enterprise *to Captain Kirk. We were unable to lock on in time, sir. I am sorry.*"

Now guiding the *Dreamline* toward a landing near the *Endeavour* crash site, Kirk exchanged looks with Stano, who shrugged.

"They made their choices," she said.

Kirk nodded in reluctant agreement. "No apologies, Spock. I know you did the best you could. The important thing is you saved the *Endeavour* and its crew, and us. As always, I can't thank you enough."

"*Orders, Captain?*"

"We've got a lot of work to do and a lot of people down here who are anxious to go home, Mister Spock. We should probably get started."

Forty

It made for a tight fit, but every member of the *Endeavour*'s crew was able to assemble on the *Enterprise*'s shuttlecraft hangar deck, accompanied by a sizable contingent from the host vessel. Just for this occasion, large viewscreens had been mounted at regular intervals along the port and starboard bulkheads as well as before the immense clamshell doors separating the bay from the vacuum of space. Displayed on each of the screens was an image of the *Endeavour*'s saucer section as rendered through data collected by the *Enterprise*'s sensors.

Standing at the back of a dais positioned before the forward screen, Kirk studied the formation with satisfaction. It was only while donning his dress uniform in preparation for this occasion that he realized this was the first time he had called such an assembly since taking command of the *Enterprise*. It was a rarity for a starship's crew to gather in this fashion while underway. He could simply have transmitted a broadcast for everyone to watch anywhere on the ship. That was still happening for those members of his crew tasked with overseeing their duty stations, but Kirk felt the proceedings deserved something more formal and respectful.

Turning to look down the line of officers standing to his left at the back of the dais, Kirk observed his senior staff—Spock, McCoy, Scott, Sulu, and Uhura—standing alongside their *Endeavour* counterparts. As with their respective captains, everyone on the dais sported their dress uniforms, with Scott standing out from the assemblage due to the kilt and matching shoulder plaid in lieu of trousers. A silver, ornamental sporran hung at the front of his waist below a wide black belt. Cradled in the engineer's arms was a set of traditional Scottish bagpipes.

At the platform's forward edge, Captain Atish Khatami stood at a thin black podium. She took a moment to smooth the sides of her dress uniform tunic. The *Enterprise*'s quartermaster had been hard-pressed to meet the demand, but she and the rest of her department had come through providing new uniforms for the *Endeavour*'s crew. That included dress uniforms for its senior staff. Khatami's green tunic was a match for Kirk's, though with its own array of medals and decorations reflecting her decades of service to Starfleet.

On the podium rested a standard-issue Starfleet data slate. She pressed a control set into its top and a boatswain's whistle echoed across the hangar deck. Any lingering, hushed conversations fell silent as more than six hundred sets of eyes turned to focus on her.

"Crew of the *Endeavour*," she began, her voice carried and amplified by the intercom system to the very back of the hangar. "You and I have been through much together. It's been my honor to serve as your captain. A starship and its legacy are defined by the actions of its crew, and your actions over the course of our service together have been exemplary. You've enjoyed sweet victories, endured bitter tragedies, and risen to the call of duty and sacrifice in the most noble and honorable of fashions and in the finest Starfleet tradition.

"Many of you are recent additions to the *Endeavour* crew. Many more of you have been with me for a long time, even before I was named your captain. You served under Zhao Sheng, as demanding and inspiring a leader as I've ever known. It is his example I've always strived to follow. If he were here today, I believe Captain Zhao would tell you how proud he is of each of you, that you continue to live up to his expectations. I don't know what the future holds for us, whether we will be assigned to another ship or if this marks the end of our service together. Even if we are no longer a crew, we will always be a family."

She paused for the unexpected rush of thunderous applause that began rolling across the hangar. Despite the solemn nature of the gathering, Kirk could not help a small smile. When the applause faded and silence fell once more over the deck, Khatami called an end to the proceedings. A chorus of low murmurs reached Kirk's ears as the formation broke and members of the *Endeavour* and *Enterprise* crews began separating into smaller groups. Others, presumably *Enterprise* personnel but Kirk could not readily tell from this distance, made their way to the exits, returning to duty stations or bound for some other pursuit. Along the hangar's bulkheads, men and women in utility coveralls were already setting to work disassembling the equipment brought in for the ceremony. Kirk knew that within an hour, the entire space would be converted into temporary billeting for a good number of the *Endeavour*'s crew during the trip back to Starbase 24.

After observing her crew for an extra moment, Khatami turned from the podium and crossed the dais to Kirk, extending her hand to him.

"Thank you for this, Captain," she said. "And for everything."

Kirk smiled. "It seemed the least we could do."

It had taken a monumental effort on the part of the *Enterprise* crew to evacuate and find billeting space for *Endeavour*'s complement. Every available bed was called into service, with other areas like recreation rooms and other noncritical ship's areas converted to temporary billeting. By far the largest portion of the displaced crew would reside here, with every attempt being made to ensure their stay was as comfortable as possible.

As for what remained of the *Endeavour* itself, a detachment from the Starfleet Corps of Engineers was already en route to assess the situation. The team of specialists would conduct a thorough examination of the primary hull section and determine whether salvage was possible. According to Khatami's own engineering staff, the saucer had weathered its rough landing and subsequent damage well enough that recovering and repairing the hull before returning it to service was not out of the question. Despite protests from Starfleet Command about the difficulty of the task and that simply scuttling it might be a more effective option, Admiral Nogura had convinced his peers to undertake the effort.

As he looked around the hangar deck, a sudden wave of melancholy gripped Kirk. "I can't imagine what it must be like to lose a ship."

"Here's hoping you never have to experience it for yourself." Khatami drew a breath. "I know, it's just a ship, and ships can be replaced, but you can't help how it gets inside you. Even if they give me another one and it ends up being better, it still won't be the same."

"You're absolutely right about that," Kirk said. After all he had been through with it and them, he simply could not imagine a life that did not include the *Enterprise* and his crew.

As though forcing herself not to wallow in sadness, Khatami asked, "What about the Orions?"

"They've been quartered in two of our cargo bays," Kirk replied. "Once we get to Starbase 24, they'll be taken into custody and questioned. I have no idea what might happen after that. There's a lot they and the Orion Syndicate need to answer for."

"You're damned right about that." Khatami's expression darkened for a moment before she took a deep breath, regaining her composure. "What about Tomkins, or whatever the hell his name is?"

"He will be my problem, Captain," said a new voice.

Kirk turned to see Admiral Nogura in his own dress uniform approaching the podium. Walking with him were intelligence agents Morgan Binnix and Phil Watson. Thanks to the skilled collaboration of Leonard McCoy and Anthony Leone, the two intelligence agents had been given back their human features. It was only his second time seeing them following their operation and Kirk was still getting used to their new looks.

Shouldn't that be old looks? He almost smiled at the thought, but held himself in check.

Looking to Khatami, Nogura said, "Rest assured, Captain, the Orions and Lieutenant Tomkins will not escape justice for their crimes. I honestly do not know what form that justice will take. As you might imagine, the situation is anything but simple, but it will be my top priority upon our return to Starbase 24. The deaths of Commander Yataro and your other officers will not be for nothing, I promise you." He turned to Binnix and Watson. "The same is true for Agent Horst. You have my word."

Kirk knew Nogura had already received several encrypted burst transmissions from Starbase 24 and Starfleet Command. According to the reports the admiral shared, both the Klingon High Council and the Orion Syndicate were already disavowing all knowledge of the activities within the Ivratis asteroid field. Nobody believed any of it, of course. Kirk suspected the Syndicate would do anything to avoid feeling Starfleet's wrath, and despite their bravado even the Klingon Empire would not want to go to war over something like this. Experience told Kirk diplomats on all sides of the table would work overtime to find some mutually agreeable solution to this dilemma.

Yet another reminder to avoid anything to do with politics.

"What about this technology the Klingons developed?" Khatami asked. "I know the base was destroyed, but you know they'll rebuild or refine the system itself. It might take time, but I can't see the Klingons letting go of something they've proved works."

Nogura replied, "That's true, of course. The Empire relies on the expertise and vision of a great number of very influential Klingon scientists. Any advantage those individuals can provide for the military will always be welcome. Though they would never admit it, their scientists in many ways are far more influential in setting the course for Klingon prosperity than their High Council or their generals. This is but a momentary obstacle the Empire will soon overcome. It is nothing compared to the problems they will soon face while attempting to determine the extent of the damage done by Agent Binnix and her team."

"I'm guessing those same leaders and diplomats are losing their minds about all of that right about now," said Binnix.

"You have no idea, my dear." Nogura smiled. "And you have no idea how much I'm enjoying it."

Watson replied, "Happy to be of service, Admiral."

His expression turning serious, Nogura said, "The simple truth is that the work carried out by you two and Agent Horst was extraordinary. I've only had time to make the most cursory review of the information you brought back, but the potential disruption it represents to the Empire's long-term planning in any number of areas is incalculable." He paused, sighing. "On the other hand, the Klingons are nothing if not adept at finding ways to navigate adversity. They will undoubtedly succeed in mitigating at least some of the damage of your actions. Hell, they may find a way to lessen all of it, but the time needed to do any of that will be significant. It means resources taken away from other efforts, so even if there's no direct impact, there are still intangible benefits."

"Such is the way of spycraft, Admiral," Binnix said. "We knew the deal when we took the assignment."

"So did David," added Watson.

Nogura said, "Nevertheless, it's my mission to see to it your efforts are not wasted, and Agent Horst's death was not in vain. For one thing, his sacrifice gave us insight into just how far the Empire's efforts go in infiltrating the Federation and Starfleet." His gaze shifted to Khatami. "We owe a debt of gratitude for that to Commander Yataro, as well."

"Thank you, Admiral," Khatami said.

Kirk asked, "Do we have any idea how extensive their network of operatives might be?"

"We can guess," Nogura replied. "At the height of the war with the Klingons, there was a comprehensive sweep for such agents. Only a handful were found, but we suspected there were many more. Then, priorities shifted and the Klingons did not seem to be the problem they once were. After we narrowly avoided a new war thanks to the Organians, and with the exposure of the agent you found after the Klingons attacked Starbase 42, as well as that mess at the K-7 space station, Starfleet quietly resumed that hunt. So far, we've had no success, but we'd be foolish to think there aren't more operatives lurking out there."

"Agreed," Kirk said. He suspected the revelation of Lieutenant Ivan Tomkins—or whatever his Klingon name was—would refuel a new initiative to root out other such agents. The influence they could wield and the damage they might inflict was simply too great to ignore.

Khatami said, "You know the Klingons will be doing the same thing." She gestured to Binnix and Watson. "Considering how deep into their power structure they were able to penetrate, the Empire won't rest until they've scrutinized every living soul within their borders."

Nodding, Nogura replied, "Again, an intangible benefit of our agents' efforts."

"Paranoia can be as useful a weapon as a phaser," said Binnix.

Watson chuckled. "Amen to that."

"It won't be easy for any of our agents still working inside Klingon territory." Kirk tried to fathom such an existence, with the ever-present danger of discovery compounded by the rampant fear and anger fueling such searches now that the Klingons were sure spies and potential saboteurs walked among them.

Already certain how Nogura might answer his next question, Kirk asked it anyway. "How you do propose handling that, sir?"

"Handling what? Starfleet agents working behind enemy lines?" Nogura regarded Kirk with a wry, knowing grin. "My dear captain, I have absolutely no idea what you're talking about."

ACKNOWLEDGMENTS

As always, I extend heartfelt appreciation to my editors, Ed Schlesinger and Margaret Clark. *Agents of Influence* is the twenty-second *Star Trek* novel I've written or co-written, and the eighteenth while working under guidance from either or both of these individuals going back fifteen years. They've put up with a lot of my shenanigans over that period of time, and yet they keep calling me. Maybe they're confusing me with someone else. Nobody tell them, okay?

Thanks also to John Van Citters at CBS. A fierce protector of the *Star Trek* "brand," he's also a lifelong fan and a champion of Simon & Schuster's *Star Trek* publishing efforts. He extends to us a great deal of latitude and trust that we'll do right by this franchise we all love so much.

My hetero life mate, occasional writing partner, and frequent sounding board, Kevin Dilmore: Even when we're not collaborating on a project, you're still helping me, whether you know it or not. Here's to more than twenty years of never-ending boneless wings, spirited brainstorming, and unmatched friendship.

Doug Drexler, the steely-eyed missile man himself: many *MANY* thanks for your invaluable insights into the inner workings of *Star Trek* ships and technology.

Last but not least, there's you: the reader. Many of you have been along for the ride throughout most if not all of those afore-mentioned novels and a bunch of other novellas, short stories, and other mischief. Thanks again to you for the continued sup-port. You're the reason we're doing this, after all.

See you in another book or so!

ABOUT THE AUTHOR

Dayton Ward: Author. Trekkie. Writing his goofy little stories and searching for a way to tap into the hidden nerdity that all humans have. Then, an accidental overdose of Mountain Dew altered his body chemistry. Now, when Dayton Ward grows excited or just downright geeky, a startling metamorphosis occurs.

Driven by outlandish ideas and a pronounced lack of sleep, he is pursued by fans and editors as well as funny men in bright uniforms wielding Tasers, straightjackets, and medication.

Dayton is believed to be working on his next novel, and he must let the world (and his editors) think he *is* working on it, until he can find a way to earn back the advance check he blew on strippers and booze during that one wild weekend in Las Vegas.

Though he currently lives in Kansas City with his wife and two daughters, Dayton is a Florida native and maintains a torrid long-distance romance with his beloved Tampa Bay Buccaneers.

Visit Dayton on the web at **www.daytonward.com**.